PRAISE FOR FINDERS

Space travel and faster-than-light drives blend with world mythology…
//…a fun story with convincing worldbuilding and a delightful triad
romance at its heart.

— *Publishers Weekly*

Space Opera with a fine, wide sweep of time behind it, intriguing
"Clarkean" magical science, and an engaging, edgy threesome of central
characters. Fun to read, and best of all, the promise of more to come.

— Gwyneth Jones, author of the Aleutian trilogy, winner
of the World Fantasy, Clarke, Dick, and Tiptree awards

An action-packed space adventure with so much heart. // This
thought-provoking, crunchy science fiction novel comes with deep
conversations, technological wonders…

— Tansy Rayner Roberts, author of the Creature Court trilogy,
winner of multiple Ditmar and WSFA Small Press awards

Scott's science fiction has always been remarkable for its worldbuilding and *Finders* is no exception. Once you read this thrilling
new science fiction saga with its unforgettable characters, you'll be
wanting more.

— Catherine Lundoff, award-winning SFF author

Also by Melissa Scott (selected works):

Dreamships
Trouble and Her Friends
Dreaming Metal
Shadow Man
Night Sky Mine

Note: the crew of the *Carabosse* made its first appearance in "Finders" (*The Other Half of the Sky*, Athena Andreadis editor, Kay Holt co-editor; Candlemark & Gleam 2013), and *Finders* readers will hear echoes of two important mythic presences encountered in "Firstborn, Lastborn" (*To Shape the Dark*, Athena Andreadis editor; Candlemark and Gleam 2016).

FINDERS

Melissa Scott

Candlemark & Gleam

For information, address
Athena Andreadis
Candlemark & Gleam LLC,
38 Rice Street #2, Cambridge, MA 02140
eloi@candlemarkandgleam.com

Library of Congress Cataloguing-in-Publication Data
In Progress

ISBN: 978-1-936460-88-5
eISBN: 978-1-936460-87-8

Cover art by Eleni Tsami

Editor: Athena Andreadis

Proofreader: Patti Exster

www.candlemarkandgleam.com

CHAPTER ONE

A SALVOR'S GUIDE TO THE ANCESTRAL ELEMENTS:
Display mode: pocket, long form

BLUE (Standard Palette 15th ed. VS 1-199): the most common element. Can be found alone, as part of an Ancestral device, or in conjunction with other elements. Made up of interlocking hexagonal units. Carries instructions and programming.

GOLD (SP 15th ed. VS 400-599): appears in about the same frequency as RED, usually found in Ancestral devices, rarely as "depot nodes" unconnected to any other element. Base units are spherical, dodecahedral, or icosahedral, and are generally twice the size of a BLUE hexagon. Absorbs and responds to input from BLUE instruction sets.

RED (SP 15th ed. VS 600-799): appears in about the same frequency as GOLD, usually found in Ancestral devices, almost always found in conjunction with both GOLD and BLUE. (Claims of depot nodes and RED/GOLD hybrid nodules remain unproven.) Base units are tetrahedral, octahedral, or, rarely, deltohedral, and are generally twice the size of a BLUE hexagon. Responds to GOLD input with action/output.

GREEN (SP 15th ed. VS 200-399): the rarest of the elements. Can be found alone or as part of an Ancestral device. Base units are cylindrical and half the size of a BLUE hexagon. Provides "life" to the other elements, which remain inert unless activated by GREEN.

WARNINGS:

ALWAYS OBTAIN ACCURATE SPECTRA USING CERTIFIED DEVICES.

DO NOT COLLECT materials that do not match the listed spectra. Elements which do not match the listed spectra on standard devices are damaged, drained, or not elemental material, and have caused death, injury, and catastrophic illness.

The publisher of this guide is not responsible for damages resulting from failure to follow this guideline.

𝄄 ⺟ 𝆏 ⁊

A thousand years ago the sky cities fell, fire and debris blasting the Burntover Plain. Most of the field was played out now, that handful of towns that had sprung up along the less damaged southern edge grown into three thriving and even elegant cities, dependent on trade for their technology now rather than salvage. Cassilde Sam had been born on the eastern fringe of the easternmost city, in a Glasstown crèche above the Empty Bridge, and even after two decades of hunting better salvage in the skies beyond this and a dozen other worlds, the Burntover still drew her. It was the largest terrestrial salvage bed ever found; it still had secrets, depths not yet plumbed.

But not today, not by her. Never by her, unless something changed.... She closed the shutters in the window above the workbench, cutting off the seductive view, the raw land of the Burntover rusty beyond the black-tiled roofs of Maripas. There was snow in the air, the thin hard flakes that came across the Blight and carried the sting of that passage. Two hundred years ago, that snow would have been a threat to everyone in the city, carrying poison enough to burn and even kill, if the circumstances were right; even fifty years ago, people had taken the snow seriously enough to stay indoors while it fell. And even in her own childhood.

She remembered those days with sudden, startling clarity, running for home through emptying streets while the sirens wailed and the red-and-black banners blossomed on every screen and from every city flagpole. The crèche doubled as an official shelter, and almost always there had been strangers trapped with them, travelers, teachers, neighbors, the occasional visiting parent, share and share alike of whatever supplies they had to hand. After a couple of days, tough young men hooded and goggled and gauntleted would brave the searing wind to sell overlooked necessities at three times their normal prices. But now that Racklin had unlocked the Aparu-5 command set, and the GOLD based satellites could reliably measure the drifting toxins, it was only the compromised that avoided the incoming snow. People like her.

She looked down at her hands, the skin paper-thin over her knuckles, a few darker sunspots showing against the brown. She'd always carried a healthy weight—solid curves that made her lovers grin—and muscle maintained by the work at hand, but over the last year she'd grown gaunt, the flesh melting away from her bones. She killed that thought, and turned her attention to her workbench, frowning at the scrap of BLUE floating in the matrix. It showed the familiar halo that indicated dissolution had begun, and she switched on the power, feeding gentle current through the conductive gel. The BLUE shimmered and split, breaking into dozens of tiny hexagons, the building blocks of a command chain. She slid the matrix into the reader, peering down through the magnifying lens, reading the patterns backlit against the pale jelly. All of them were familiar, disappointing: plain scrap, part of a bag she'd picked up in the high-market beyond Barratin. It was a useful source of spare parts, not the sort of thing that contained new code.

And that was a reminder of repairs she needed to make, something to take her mind off her own problems. She hauled out the sensor core from *Carabosse's* ventral array, ran the sonic probe around the faint line that marked the hemisphere, and split it open. The BLUE inside was badly faded—the instruction sets wore out over time, though no one had ever been able to isolate the exact cause. Luckily, it was a simple set, and she pulled out another matrix, touching keys to set the gel to incubate. She had a full supply of blocks in her kit, and began hooking them out of their storage cells, building the instructions block by block against the pale gel. *Go seek hold go*, the delicate hexagons slotting neatly against each other to create a larger ring. *Fix track find go....*

When she reached the second clause she hesitated—she'd had an idea about that, a different, perhaps more efficient way of defining the search—but this was not the time to experiment. Even with all the documentation in the world, Dai wouldn't be able to figure out what she'd done, and there was an ever-increasing chance that she wouldn't last to explain it to him herself. She finished the pattern, the rings joining to create the familiar snowflake of a BLUE control string, and set the matrix to cure overnight.

That was the end of the chores she'd brought with her from the ship. She shut down the workbench and drifted back to the narrow kitchen, where the clock read four minutes past the sixteenth hour. She filled the iron kettle that came with the rented room and set it to boil on the island's largest eye while she dug out a packet of tea. The Ancestors had to have been fond of tea: there wasn't a single Settled World, Core to Edge, that didn't boast some decoction of boiled leaves and berries. Ashe had laughed at the idea, in the days before the war, before she'd gotten sick—but she wouldn't think of that now, either. Ashe was gone, and that was the end of it.

A chime sounded, and she glanced at the cooktop, but instead the door slid open. She reached for the narrow-beam welder she kept handy in lieu of a blaster when she was on a civilized world, but relaxed as she saw Dai Winter in the doorway.

She slipped the welder beneath the counter as he let the door close behind him. He had done his best to brush away the snow from the shoulders of his coat, but the smell of it came with him, dank and bitter. It caught in her throat, and Dai hastily shed the offending garment, hung it in the bathroom and turned the vent to high.

"Sorry," he said, still keeping his distance, and his pale eyes were filled with concern.

Cassilde swallowed her cough, tightening the muscles along her ribs to hold it in. She took a careful breath, mouth pressed tight, nostrils flaring; she choked again, swallowed bile, but the second breath came more easily. "I'm all right."

She sounded breathless, she knew, but blessedly Dai took her at her word and set the stacked tins that held their dinner on the counter beside the now-singing kettle. The food came with the room, at a surcharge, from the *bilai* on the ground floor: another small luxury they pretended they could afford.

"Bad day?" he asked, carefully casual, and began unlatching the tins. The waiter-boy would come along after midnight and retrieve them from outside the door.

"So-so. Though I put together fresh BLUE for the ventral core, so that's a win." Cassilde set the tea to steep. "And you?"

Dai avoided her eyes. "All right. The snow's supposed to end tonight, you'll be clear in the morning."

"To do what?" She controlled the urge to clash the enameled iron cups that matched the kettle, set them gently on the counter instead. "We're not credentialed to bid on any of the jobs at hand." And if they couldn't bid, there would be no money, and they were already at the end of the savings.... It was not something she needed to say, but Dai grimaced as though he'd heard the words.

"I shouldn't have fired Lanton," he said. "I know that. But he was impossible."

"And he was skimming from the take," Cassilde said. "And you're right, that would have gotten us in trouble sooner or later. But we should have had the replacement in line first."

Dai dipped his head. He was a big man, taller than she by more than the breadth of his hand, and she was by no means small. A dangerous man, one might have said, looking at him, with his knotted muscles earned in high salvage, hauling significant mass in varying gravity, sandy hair cropped short, the evening's stubble coming in pale on his lantern jaw. She'd taken his measure long ago.

"We've had an inquiry," he said. It was something of a peace offering. "An answer to your notice."

"Oh?" She was intrigued in spite of herself. With new permits up for bid, on a new section of an Ancestor's wrecked sky palace, lost in long orbit for at least a hundred years, scholars with a class-one license could name their price. And the ones they might afford, the ones with a class-two license and a supervising master, were already hired. Even Lanton had a new job, with someone who should have known better. "What's the catch?"

"I think it's Ashe," Dai said.

Cassilde froze just for an instant, then very deliberately poured them each a cup of tea. Summerlad Ashe had been their first scholar, partner and lover and friend, brilliant and unscrupulous as you have to be in salvage. But when the Trouble broke, he'd chosen the Entente over the Verge, and put those same talents to use against them. She'd be damned if she trusted him again.

"He wouldn't dare," she said firmly, as though she could make it true, and Dai nodded, turning his attention to the *bilai* tins.

They didn't speak of it again over dinner, or after, focusing instead on the routine of weather and ship maintenance and the list of permits still up for bid. They couldn't do anything without a scholar, though Dai poked at his board for a while in an attempt to find something.

"Nothing in the class-threes. What about the class-fours?" he said, and turned the board so she could see the screen. "If we got a couple of them, we could work under remote supervision, and still make a decent profit."

Cassilde took the board, running her fingers over the screen to follow the math. Class-four salvage was the least demanding, wreckage that was presumed to contain only standard materials, none of the Ancestral elements that brought in the real money. "These are all high mass. *Carabosse* can't handle them."

"I marked three that are within tolerance."

"Right." Cassilde skimmed through the first survey reports, hoping to be convinced. Yes, they were all three within the limits, but with the fuel they'd have to spend to get them in, and the ordinary metals indicated in the survey.... She shook her head. "I don't see it. I'm sorry."

"We have to do something."

"I know." Cassilde held out the board and Dai took it from her. "We have to talk to this person. It would be stupid not to."

"I know," Dai said, and tuned the board to entertainment.

She thought she was tired enough to sleep early, but the Lightman's cheated her, shortening her breath every time she lay down, and by the time Dai came to join her, she was wide awake again. She sat up, reaching for her wrap, and Dai gave her a wary look.

"All right?"

She shrugged. "Can't seem to get comfortable."

"Take the rest of the pillows."

"Thanks." Dai shoved them to her side of the bed, and she stacked them into a rough pyramid, but didn't lean back.

"I'm awake," she said. "I'm going to brew a cup of sleep-eze and try again."

"All right," he said, and settled on his single pillow, but she felt his eyes on her as she left the room.

She set the kettle to boil again, found the box of foil packets, and emptied first one and then a second into the empty cup. Two was supposed to be the maximum dose for someone half again her size, but she'd developed a tolerance over the years. While the water heated, she reached for her own board, called up the answer to her advertisement. It had been deliberately low-key, intended to discourage treasure-hunters and novices, and the response was just as bland, anonymized credentials and an offer to meet at one of the teashops in the Saranam. All perfectly normal, all what you'd expect at a time when scholars were in high demand. There was nothing at all that reminded her of Ashe. She touched the screen, confirming the appointment before she could change her mind.

The water was boiling, and she mixed the sleep-eze without really paying attention, the cherry-sweet scent rising as she stirred. When it was cool enough, she drank it off, and turned back to the bedroom. Dai's eyes opened, but he said nothing, waited as she settled herself carefully against the pillows. This time, her breath didn't catch, and she reached across to squeeze his shoulder. She saw the flash of teeth as he smiled, and then closed her eyes, letting the drug take hold.

𝔸 𝕎s 𝕏 𝟋

She was late for breakfast, rose heavy-eyed and paid for a double-long shower before she could bring herself to face tea and biscuits and the inevitable pork-product slices. Dai didn't say anything, however, his attention instead on his board, tuned to news mode, and she managed to eat enough to forestall any further comment.

"They've put up a couple more lots for bid," he said, after a moment.

In spite of knowing better, she felt a surge of hope. "Anything we could go for?"

"Not without a scholar."

Cassilde swallowed a curse. Of course not, and of course she should have known. "I agreed to the appointment."

Dai looked up sharply. "And what do we do if it's Ashe?"

"It won't be," she said.

But of course it was. Dai checked in the doorway of Brass-an-Saranam, the teashop where the high-class salvors did business, and Cassilde put her hand in the small of his back and pushed him on. Ashe gave them both his usual sardonic smile, and waved a hand toward one of the sunken booths.

Three steps down, it was quiet and warm, the winter light diffused and colored by the amber skylight and the translucent window. She had wondered how Ashe could show himself here, where he and his desertion were known, but in the dim entry there had been a shadow disfiguring his cheek, and in the light of the booth it resolved to a data mote the size of his thumb clinging to the skin beneath his left eye, drawing attention from his prominent nose and well-shaped mouth. There had been a fad for motes in the last year or so, at least for deactivated ones, worn like bright jewels on skin and hair, but this one was active, his skin pink around the spots where the fine wires had burrowed into the nerves.

"Clever," she said, and he bowed.

"Thank you."

"Looks painful," Dai said.

For a moment, she thought Ashe would deny it, but then he shrugged. "Uncomfortable, sometimes. You get used to it."

Cassilde lifted an eyebrow at that, and stepped past him to take her place at the head of the low table. Both the cushions and the footwell were heated, and she wriggled her toes where the others couldn't see. The Lightman's that was slowly killing her left her sensitive to cold.

"You think damn well of yourself," Dai said, to Ashe, who shrugged again.

"I'm good, and you know it."

"You're as good as you say you are," Cassilde said. "And so are we. Our skills are not at issue." She stopped, seeing a waiter-girl approaching with a filled tray. "Bribery, too."

The color rose in Ashe's sallow face, but he made no answer. And that was odd: he disliked being caught in one of his schemes almost as much as he disliked the given name he never used.

Cassilde let the girl serve them, a pot of floral tea for herself and Dai, coffee for Ashe, thick and ropy in its copper pot. Verge versus Entente again, the teas of the far-flung Edge systems poised against the coffee popular in the Core, where the stars lay close enough to each other that the Ancestors had knit them into retimonds, worlds and systems linked by a single communications web. There were plates of biscuits as well, pale circles decorated with sugared flowers or stamped with a star and crescent moon: definitely bribery, she thought, not provocation, and settled to enjoy it while it lasted.

She watched the men eye each other as they all took ritual tastes of the food. She was not so naive as to think Dai was the only one who had been hurt, for all that his face showed his pain more clearly. Ashe might cultivate a brittle disdain, but he had felt the break perhaps more keenly. Of course, he had chosen to leave, and not long before she'd been diagnosed with Lightman's, when they were still wondering what the odd symptoms might mean—but that was unfair. The Trouble was well begun, and his obligations had been complex. Still, the old suspicion sharpened her voice.

"What do you want, Ashe? Exactly and in detail, please."

"I'm offering to go in with you on a bid for some section of this latest discovery," Ashe said. Only the flicker of his gaze, one quick glance from Dai to her, betrayed that he was not as utterly confident as he sounded.

"Offering," Dai said.

Cassilde ignored him. "Why?"

Ashe shrugged. "You need a scholar, and I need work—"

Cassilde slammed her hand hard on the table, rattling the teacups. "Don't give me that! What do you want, Ashe? Tell me now and tell me straight, or walk away."

Even then, he hesitated for an instant. "I want to bid on a specific piece of the contract—it's not an obvious choice, but I have reason to think it may be more profitable than it looks at first sight." He touched the data mote in his cheek. "But it will take a really good team to pull it off. You're the best I know. Still."

Cassilde poured herself another cup of tea. That was Ashe for you, the lure of the exotic larded with compliments, *no one can do it but you*, and yet…. She looked at Dai, saw him already half willing to believe. "What does that thing tell you?"

"My mote?" Ashe touched it again, the almond-shaped body

glowing pale green behind a blackened filigree. The golden wires glittered where they pierced his skin.

"What else?"

Ashe smiled, ruefully. "You're right, that's how I got my information. It's a Palace piece, I'm sure you can see that. It was inert when I got it, but I had a speck of GREEN left, and I—revived it. And when I compared its records to the first scout reports, I saw that the Claim-court had undervalued one segment—well, not undervalued, precisely, it's a fair value for the obvious salvage, but there's more there."

"How's it classed?" Cassilde asked.

"It's a class-two site," Ashe answered. "No direct supervision required, unless you find something outside spec. Otherwise it's just the share-out at the end."

Dai shook his head. "If we bid on something like that, everyone will know we've got a lead."

"Not really," Ashe said. "You've just lost your scholar, you've got a new one on short notice, untried, an unknown quantity—you've never worked with me under this license, no one needs to know you worked with me before. Why wouldn't you bid on a class-two, and take the sure thing?"

"Because we don't do sure things," Cassilde said.

"No," Dai said slowly. "It could work."

It could. It probably would, like all Ashe's schemes, though like all Ashe's schemes there would be a dozen things he hadn't mentioned, and trouble to spare. And it was tempting—there was the possible payout, certainly, and they desperately needed one good run. The chance that they would find something truly unique, some as-yet-unknown artifact, the secret of the Ancestors—well, that was the dream of everyone who went into salvage, no secret and no surprise. Somehow she'd find the money for the bid.

"Is the license real?"

For a moment, she thought he'd turn it into a joke, but he read her better than that. "Yes."

"All right. I'm willing. If Dai agrees."

Dai nodded. "Yes. I'm in."

"Right." Cassilde looked back at Ashe. "You'll show us this segment, and if it's what you say—we'll take you on. Standard contract, quarter shares with one for the ship, and everything in writing. Is that clear?"

"Clear," he said, and she pretended not to have seen the flicker of hurt in his dark eyes.

"So show me."

"I'd rather not do it here," Ashe said, and she thought it took an effort not to look over his shoulder. "Perhaps somewhere more private?"

Cassilde's mouth tightened, and Dai gave a heavy sigh. "There's always the ship," he said.

They took the public tramway across the city, the express line that ran high enough that they wove in and out of the bands of mist that were indistinguishable from the lowering clouds. The line terminated at the port, and from the station she could see the vast expanse of the landing field stretching empty into the fog. A few lights cut through the murk—the field beacon, of course, and the band of red and gold that was the tower, fainter lights that marked the hangars and machine shops and support buildings. A long way off, a siren sounded, and a moment later light flared, a ship lifting from one of the middle tables. The color of the light marked it as an in-system ship, burning chemical fuel at least for the lift: a shuttle staging out to the jump-out station and the big intersystems ships.

The ship was parked outside rather than docked in the security of a hangar: it was a reasonable enough savings here on Cambyse, far enough from the Entente's core to be spared the pilfering endemic in those ports, and close enough to the Verge that most people recognized what ships were worth robbing. They took the auto-taxi to the field edge, and walked from the gate, where the Port Security kiosk glowed golden in the fog.

Carabosse had never been impressive, just another pre-war Fairy-class scout bought surplus and converted for salvage. They had added a second pair of cannon after the war, when the weapons were cheap and things were still unsettled enough that demobbed crews were raiding the more distant salvage fields, and the welds still showed raw against the fading paint. The outboard grapples were folded neatly against the ship's belly between the landing struts, and they and the bulk of the oversized engines at the stern coupled with the dropped sensor bulb forward gave the ship a hunched, insectoid look. Cassilde glanced over her shoulder, waiting for Ashe to complain again about having to carry cargo outboard, but he dropped his gaze and followed her meekly up the ramp.

The planet-side environmentals spun up as she came through the hatch, lights flashing to life as she led the way to the main midships compartment. Central lit up at her approach, screens flaring to standby, heat seeping from the floors, and she dropped into her usual chair at the head of the narrow table. "Dai, why don't you start some tea? Ashe, let's see what you've got."

Dai turned to the galley console, and Ashe produced his board from beneath his coat, unrolling the spare screen to show the clustered documents. Cassilde took it, the images rotating to find a convenient position, and began to page methodically through the records. It was a fairly typical find, the kind that was becoming increasingly rare in the Cambyse system, chunks of loosely associated wreckage drifting in long orbit that had only just come into range of a salvage ship. The scout that had spotted the first of the chain had been a small-time operator, their ship even smaller than *Carabosse*; they'd had neither the manpower to exploit the find themselves, nor, probably more to the point, the firepower to keep it. Wisely, they'd taken it to the Cambyse Claim-court, accepted the finders' fee, and left to it to the Court to establish the patrols that currently kept off looters while the recovery bids were still in process.

It definitely hadn't been a ship; that was obvious just from the general description, for all that the Claim-court had been scrupulously noncommittal. The individual units were too large, too specialized—too complex in places, too simple in others, though obviously they'd once been part of some coherent whole. It couldn't be anything but the ruins of one of the Ancestors' orbital palaces. Before the Fall, the First Dark, there had been dozens of them in the Cambyse system, weaving a bright artificial ring around Cambyse itself. Most of them had been salvaged long ago, but others occasionally appeared, either returning on long orbits or possibly abandoned in transit between systems, and there was always a bidders' war over what were likely to be the richest sections.

"Which one did you want to bid on?" she asked, and Ashe leaned over her shoulder to touch keys.

"Here—this big trailing section. It masses low, and the quick scan confirmed it's hollow. The Court survey has it pegged as possible support or storage volume, based primarily on its position in the train, but I don't think that's right."

Cassilde scanned the numbers. "Not tech-rich."

"No. The mass is too low, and there aren't enough exotics."

Dai set two cups on the table, keeping a third for himself as he looked over Cassilde's other shoulder. "Yeah, but would they show on a quick scan like that?"

"If it was engineering or control space, it would," Cassilde said. Not much tech meant not much of the Ancestral elements. Maybe a decent amount of BLUE, the most common of the bunch, but everyone needed BLUE. Between that and the non-exotic salvage, they might be able to clear enough to replenish the GREEN she'd had to use on herself lately.

"Absolutely," Ashe said. "But I think it's living space—passenger volume—and you know that's where the most interesting goods are always found."

That was at least partly true, Cassilde thought. In the past, the most valuable finds had come from what seemed to have been the habitable volumes of the palaces. They weren't necessarily the most useful things—those had been the drive and navigation units from what were deemed tenders and runabouts, simple enough that the humans known as the Successors could not only borrow but mostly reproduce. They had gone down to the Second Dark, but enough of that knowledge had been saved, and the revived civilization of Entente and Verge had built on it to develop re-engineered FTL, the REFTL drive that carried trade throughout human-settled space. But the finds that made salvors' fortunes these days weren't the technical innovations; it seemed as though everything that human science could reproduce had already been found. These days, the money was in elementals, and the weird. And if there was enough of either—at worst, she might live long enough to make another strike, leave Dai with at least enough money to keep the ship.

She damped that sudden hope. "What do you think we're looking for? What does that bug tell you?"

"Toys," Ashe said promptly. "I'm not pretending it's anything important, but you know the kind of money they bring. Enough to earn all of us a new stake." He shrugged. "And at the very least, there will be raw materials to take."

"You'd be willing to go for that?" Dai asked. He sounded skeptical, and Cassilde couldn't blame him. Ashe had always fought to preserve their finds intact.

"I think there are toys there," Ashe said. "Good ones, maybe even unique and fabulous things. From everything I've been able to work out, this was the owners' living space, not the crew's. The things that could be there—it's almost unimaginable."

Dai stared at him, and Ashe said, "And, yes, if we don't find anything else worthwhile, we can recoup costs on salvage value alone. I'm good with that."

"I don't believe him," Dai said, to Cassilde, and she nodded.

"Neither do I."

"I need the work," Ashe said. "And for this I need a team. It's not that complicated."

That could be true, Cassilde thought. Ashe was, as she had said, every bit as good as he claimed, but he wasn't an easy man to work with. "All right," she said. "Put together a bid, and if I approve it, we'll put it in."

"May I stay on the ship?" Ashe asked. "Your find-files are here anyway, and it would just be easier—"

"No," Dai said, and Cassilde lifted her hand.

"Why can't you work at wherever it is you're staying?"

"I'm not really staying anywhere." Ashe gave her a look that mingled annoyance and embarrassment. "I told you, I needed the work."

"That badly?" Cassilde cocked her head in disbelief.

"That badly." Ashe shrugged. "Not everyone loves me since the Trouble."

And that was certainly true. Cassilde glanced at Dai, saw the same uncertainty written in the big man's face. She lifted her eyebrows, and received the faintest of nods in return. "You can stay," she said. "In fact, it might be just as well for us to move back aboard, too—it'll save us money we can use for the bid. Dai, why don't you go back to the hostel and make arrangements? I'll stay here and work with Ashe."

Something flickered across Ashe's face, but was gone before Cassilde could be sure what she'd seen. "Thanks."

"Do you have baggage somewhere?" Dai asked, with only a little reluctance. "I can fetch it."

Ashe shook his head. "I've been traveling light."

He prodded the bag he'd brought with him from the teashop. He meant to imply he'd been working passage, she thought—he held, or used to hold, a tech-2's license, and there was always work on the intersystems ships for technicians—but she'd never known him to manage with fewer than two bags before. And if that single carryall was all he currently owned, then either he was in serious trouble or he was in truth poorer than she'd ever known him to be. With her luck, it would be both. "Then we'd better put together a good bid," she said, and nodded for Dai to leave.

𝌀 𝌆 𝌤 𝌏

She spent the rest of the day watching over Ashe's shoulder as he roughed out the bid and filled in the details at her direction, then sealed the final version and submitted it before she could change her mind. She would be emptying every account they had to make this work, but even if they found nothing more than what the original survey said was there, they should make a small profit. If things broke badly, of course—she put that thought aside with the ease of long practice. They would make their own breaks; they always had.

Dai returned at sunset, and he and Ashe hauled the baggage cart up the ramp in the day's last watery light. There was no place to put Ashe but in his old cabin—they had always each kept space of their own, though she and Dai still shared the big bed in the master's cabin and even Ashe seemed to feel the awkwardness, retreating to its privacy as soon as they had finished a quick dinner. Dai waited until his door was solidly closed to take her arm.

"I want to make a round of the port bars," he said, not quite whispering.

"Problems?"

He shook his head. "I want to get a feel for the job. There's bound to be gossip." She waited, and he gave a reluctant smile. "And, yes, I'm curious about Ashe."

Cassilde nodded. "So am I. But the job comes first."

"Understood." Dai shrugged himself back into his heavy coat, and Cassilde closed and latched the hatch against the night wind.

She was in bed by the time Dai returned, the ship powered down for the night. Ashe was presumably asleep, or at least hiding in his new/old cabin, and she saw Dai hesitate as he slid the door open. He saw she was awake, and relaxed slightly, stripping off his vest and pullover and subsiding onto the edge of the bed to unlace his boots. She sat up, propping the pillows behind her, and waved a hand across the nearest sensor to bring up the lights. He smelled of cold and the snow, of beer and frying and other people's mists, only the bitter tang of the snow to tell her this was Cambyse and not any of a dozen other ports.

"Any news?"

Dai shrugged. "Lots of gossip about the find, but nothing I hadn't heard. People are really confident, though."

Cassilde considered that. It was the first floating palace found in the system in at least five years, and the orbit almost certainly ensured it hadn't been stripped yet. A certain confidence was warranted, and had driven the bids higher than usual. "No surprise. Any talk of claim jumpers yet?"

"Only the usual. If there are any, they'll go for the obvious pieces first."

"What about Ashe?"

"Nothing." Dai stood up again to finish undressing, slid between the sheets beside her, cold radiating from his skin. "No interest, no talk, nothing."

"It's been eight years." Eight years since the Trouble ended, settled by mutiny and a coup that Ashe had somehow briefly been involved in, eight years since there had been any reason to notice him. Maybe it was enough. Cassilde waved her hand across the sensor to dim the light again. She wound herself companionably around Dai, his skin still cool to the touch. He shifted to make them fit, and she felt him sigh.

"What do you want to do about him?"

Cassilde froze. She knew exactly what he was asking, but she would be damned if she'd admit it. "What do you mean?"

Dai sighed again. "I'd take him back."

"I wouldn't." She paused, considering. She had forgiven other lovers before this—even Lalie, and what she had done had been objectively worse—but somehow Ashe was different. "Not just now, anyway."

"If it would upset you—"

She shook her head. "No. Do what you want, it doesn't bother me. I just—I suppose I want an apology first."

"I think it's the only way I'll ever get one," Dai said.

And that was possibly true, and possibly involved a certain amount of coercion, and she turned her head away. "I mean it. Do what you want."

"I will," Dai said, and closed his eyes.

冄 屵 쓫 ⼦

She slept late the next morning, woke alone and emerged from the cabin washed and dressed to find Ashe at the library console in Central, files open across multiple screens. Dai was scowling at the galley station—checking supplies, she assumed, and Ashe spoke without looking away from the screens.

"Who's been keeping your find-files for you? They're an idiot."

"Ass." It was all she had, short of hitting him, and she turned on her heel and stalked away, half expecting to hear the sounds of a fist-fight behind her. She made her way down the full length of the ship until she reached the darkened control room. She keyed off the lights that came on as she came through the hatch, and settled into the co-pilot's seat, automatically assessing. She was cold, her fingers white and numb: that was the walk. It and the anger had left her short of breath as well. She could feel her lungs straining, each breath pinched close and tight, and for a moment she was tempted by the speck of GREEN she kept for the really bad days.

She drew her knees to her chin, forcing herself to breathe slowly, carefully, and the worst of the spasm passed. GREEN wasn't meant to be used as medicine, but, as with all the Ancestors' artifacts, over the centuries humans had figured out more ways to use the substance. It would clear her worst symptoms, buy her a week or two of normal breath and movement, but it would not cure her. And every pinhead dot of GREEN that she used to prolong her life was GREEN that could not be used to power the ship's Ancestral devices. And without GREEN, nothing would function. She'd had to make that choice too often lately, choosing between her own health and the ship's, and they had no money for more when their stockpile was exhausted. In fact, if they didn't find GREEN on this current job, they'd be in serious trouble.

If only the Ancestral elements didn't fade over time—if only someone, anyone, could find a way to restore their potency. But that was the Grail of the true scientists, the elemental physicists in their orbital labs, not a problem that could be solved by salvage. All salvage could do was find a few more pieces of the Ancestors' wreckage, and keep the systems going a little longer.

"Silde?" Dai loomed in the open hatch, taking stock with a single glance. "You good?"

She nodded, and saw him relax. "And you?"

Dai gave a crooked smile. "Ashe has some extra specs for you."

And that meant that whatever words might or might not have passed between them, they'd achieved enough of a truce that she wasn't allowed to challenge it. "Right," she said, and uncoiled from the chair. "How's it look?"

"Not bad," Dai answered. "You'll see."

Ashe had all the screens filled and a model projected above the table, one corner overlapping the teapot. Cassilde moved it, unreasonably annoyed, and Ashe gave her a half-smile that might have been meant as an apology.

"I've worked up a model from the original bid data. It's not perfect—gaps are red, guesses yellow—but it looks like living quarters to me."

Cassilde turned the model slowly, studying the details. The outer surfaces were taken directly from the original finder's observations: a truncated hemisphere, half stony asteroid, the other smooth metal. Ashe had marked an airlock or pressure door in yellow on the metal side, an obvious way in if he was right, and in spite of herself her spirits rose. She peeled back the surface to reveal an interior of five chambers, the airlock and a smaller space beneath it, then a larger room and two more chambers leading from airlock to hull. There was quite a bit of red, but the layout was familiar, and she looked back at Ashe.

"How confident are your guesses?"

"Sixty, sixty-five?" He reached for the model in turn, adjusted it to show only the darkest lines and the yellow ghosts. "I'm ninety percent sure on this, the big interior volume and two smaller ones." She nodded, and he turned it again, building back the earlier image.

"What's in it?" Dai asked, leaning on the back of a chair.

"That's the question," Ashe said. "Toys, like I said. If it's living space, I'd expect there to be RED and GOLD between interior skin and hull. But it could be almost anything."

Cassilde's eyes narrowed. That wasn't much to base a bid on, wasn't nearly enough to send Ashe back to them. "What are you really looking for? What does that thing tell you?"

"I don't know," Ashe said. He was wearing the mote at the base of his throat today, and he touched it nervously. "That's the trouble. I mean, yes, I have every reason to think there will be toys, but all this says is that this is, or was, a critical area, holding something vitally important. The implication is that it's lifesaving, maybe some sort of rescue device, or something medical, though I can't make that fit with the other things it's telling me about the section. Why would you put a lifesaving device in the middle of a residential area?"

This was why they'd taken on Ashe in the first place, Cassilde thought, caught up in spite of herself in the possibilities he was sketching. Even without the mote's help, he'd always had the gift for seeing the Ancestors' relics as they were meant to be.

"If the owner had a medical condition, maybe?" Dai said.

"The Ancestors were supposed to have been both incredibly long-lived and impossibly healthy," Cassilde said. "So say the records and that's confirmed by everything we've seen of their surviving ground settlements. No hospitals, no clinics, no medical facilities of any kind—"

"Except for the tower on Devona," Dai interjected.

"If you agree that's a medical facility," Ashe said. "Which I don't."

"So you're going to agree with Orobandi on that?" Cassilde lifted an eyebrow.

"Embarrassingly, yes," Ashe said. "I think the Ancestors were, if not actually immortal, possessed of such an immensely long lifespan and the ability to heal almost any injury that they might as well have been. Whatever human beings were to them, there was a fundamental physiological difference between us."

The words were more bitter than Cassilde had imagined, looking at her white, numbed fingers. "Which brings us back to the question. What do you think is there?"

"I don't know," Ashe said again. "I can't translate everything this thing tells me, and I can't guess, not from what I have. But if it's something the Ancestors thought was good for healing—imagine what it could do for us."

Cassilde flinched at Dai's stricken stare, heard her own breath sharp before she got herself under control. "Asshole. Get out. Our contract is cancelled."

"What?" Ashe looked genuinely bewildered. "You can't say this is a bad idea—"

Dai closed his fists, but his voice was frighteningly controlled. "You heard her, Ashe. Off the ship."

"But—"

"The Lightman's is now third stage," Cassilde said.

She heard Ashe's breath catch in turn, his eyes suddenly wide. There was nothing beyond the third stage, the point at which GREEN was required in ever-increasing doses just to maintain function. No one had ever been able to afford enough of it to know if it would preserve life indefinitely.

"If I'd known that," Ashe said, "I'd have put it to you right away. What I thought I had, I mean."

Cassilde studied him for a long moment, trying to read his true feelings. He looked contrite, appalled, shocked into silence—but this was Ashe, who'd always been the best liar of them all. And also the one most capable of casual, unanticipated kindness. She let out her anger with her breath. "Well. Now you know."

"Now I know," he echoed, and glanced at Dai. "I can't promise anything. You have to understand that. It's only hints and shadows."

"Better than nothing," Dai muttered.

Cassilde looked away. Hope was a luxury she couldn't afford, but she couldn't bring herself to deny it to Dai. "Right. We carry on."

Relief flickered across Ashe's face, and Dai sighed deeply. "You want me to price out supplies?"

Cassilde nodded. "Use the rainy day account. You'll need it."

"Right," Dai said, and reached for his board.

"In the meantime—" Cassilde pushed herself out of her chair, grateful that her legs didn't weaken. "In the meantime, I'm going to plot some preliminary courses. Buzz me when we get an answer from the Court."

"I'll do that," Dai said.

Cassilde nodded, and turned away. As she stepped over the hatch combing, she heard Ashe's voice, soft and aggrieved—*You could have told me*—but she did not look back.

CHAPTER TWO

Their bid was accepted without a second round—no real surprise there, Cassilde thought, as she sorted though the usual stack of minor changes and belated requirements. It was a big debris field, with enough class-two pieces to go around. The only reason anyone would have bid against them was their reputation. Dai spent the next forty-eight hours bargaining for supplies, while she fielded Claims-court questions and plotted out the least expensive courses, and Ashe brooded over his model, building and tearing down various versions. They lifted from the Maripas field a little after dawn on the third day, bank accounts empty but hull full of fuel and supplies, and she guided *Carabosse* through near-orbit traffic and settled onto the looping course that would bring them into the debris field in about five days. They would go silent then, as would the other salvors she could see on the mid- and long-range sensors, sneaking up on their claim for fear of attracting a pirate's attention.

The autopilot's screen glowed pale green, the projected course laid out both as a line and as a series of engine burns. She checked the fuel consumption again—they were traveling with a somewhat narrower margin than she liked—and was reassured to see the numbers solidly in the green. There was a tickle at the back of her throat, a dry, nagging tightness in her chest, and she tensed the muscles of her ribcage to keep it from erupting into a hacking cough. The Lightman's was back, growing slowly but steadily worse, and she fingered the little box of GREEN on the chain around her neck. She had taken to carrying it with her at all times, in case of an emergency that increasingly seemed inevitable, and she wondered again if it would be better to take it now. If she took a tiny dose, just the half of a pinhead, that might buy her enough freedom to get to the claim, and maybe even through the salvage—or she might crash anyway halfway through, and that would be a waste of the precious GREEN. You could never be sure how long any one dose would last; better to wait until she was sure she needed it. This was not too bad a day.

She checked the course again, and then the sensor nets, seeing four other salvage ships in range. She'd pinged each of them already, had felt them ping *Carabosse* in turn; she knew all of them at least by name, and had checked their bids against the master list. Nothing to worry about there. She closed down her board, working her shoulders as though that would ease the tightness in her chest, and left the control room.

There were lights on in the gunroom, coupled with the soft beeps of a simulation, and she paused in the open hatch to see Ashe frowning over the controls. He was halfway through a run, what looked like a three-pronged attack on the ship, and she waited until he leaned back, swearing under his breath, before she spoke.

"You think that's going to be necessary?"

He looked up sharply—a lesser man would have jumped—and controlled himself. "I hope not. But it's been a while since I've used a quad-mount cannon." He grinned. "Besides, your game library sucks."

She smiled back. "Sorry. Since you left, there weren't really players aboard."

"So you sold all my software?" Ashe disentangled himself from the controls and came to join her.

"Made a tidy profit, too."

"I'm so glad." He followed her back to Central, and waved her to a seat when she started for the tea maker. "I'll get it. Anything else you want?"

Cassilde shook her head, watching him perform the ritual, measuring dried leaves and drawing the water to steep them. There was no sign of Dai—probably he was in engineering or down in the holds going over the equipment—and she leaned back as Ashe set the cup in front of her. "Have you considered an apology?"

His hands stilled for a moment, and then he took his place opposite her—the same seat he'd always chosen, as though he'd never left. Her lips thinned, closing over an angry remark, and he met her eyes.

"I thought we'd been through this."

"You came back."

"Yes." He tipped his head back to stare at the ceiling, the long line of his throat bared, the mote clinging like a jewel to the notch of his collarbone. Cassilde waited, and after a moment he shrugged. "What else could I do? Salvage is what I know."

"And you made the Entente too hot for you," Cassilde said.

Ashe shook his head. "No one cares about me any more."

There was a note of bitterness in his voice that was more convincing than the words. The question trembled on her lips—*What exactly did you do in the war, Ashe? How were you involved in the mutiny?*—but she wasn't at all sure she was ready for that answer. "You could have found any dozen ships to hire you. Especially on Cambyse, especially now."

"We were good," Ashe said. "And I had this long shot, and I couldn't think of anyone else I'd trust, anyone else who would trust me…. But mostly—I'd missed you."

Cassilde sighed. She was not sure she believed him, or at least not entirely; he was just as capable of saying what he guessed would please her and making it sound like unvarnished truth. And yet a part of her yearned for everything to be just as it had been, for all she knew that was impossible. "Well, you found us."

Ashe nodded, wrapping his hands around his cup. Cassilde stared at them, seeing the familiar flaws, the crooked little finger that had set wrong while they worked their first big find and that he'd never bothered to have repaired, the ridged nail and the scar across his knuckle. And still she wasn't ready, not yet, and she dropped her eyes to her cup.

"What are the going rates for toys, back in the Entente?"

He seemed grateful for the change of subject. "Still about ten percent more than you're getting on the Verge. But there's been a run of broken and faked pieces lately, so most people want to buy through a known dealer. And that's a commission to pay."

"Right. Still, it's something to think about—if you're sure nobody's looking for you."

"Not that I know of," Ashe said, and pushed back his chair. "I'll work up a price list, if you'd like."

"Thanks." Cassilde watched the hatch close again behind him. The Trouble had nearly destroyed the Edge and the Core; the only thing that had saved them, in the end, was the fear of another Fall, another Long Dark. Humanity had survived two such periods, and the gap between the Ancestors' technology and their own showed exactly how much they had to lose. The people of the Entente had been willing to rise in rebellion behind the mutineers rather than see it happen. And yet... The Core worlds needed goods from the Edge, and the Edge needed things that could only be manufactured on the networked worlds of the Entente retimonds, and each side had always wanted full control of that trade. None of that had actually changed since the war; only the details of the contracts had been adjusted to make the trade seem fair again.

And Ashe had been on the wrong side of that, gone back to the Bodimandu Compact at the heart of the Entente for reasons she couldn't understand—obligations, he had said, looking hunted, but how he could owe his life to people he had never mentioned remained outside her comprehension. She had thought of him every time they came under fire, every time they dodged an ambush at a warpline entrance, wondering if he were on the other side of the guns.

They had been exempt at first—*Carabosse* was fast enough and small enough to be reasonably safe outside the convoys, and they'd made a decent living as a mailship, but then the attacks had increased, and it became clear that at least some of the ships causing the trouble were part of the Entente's fleet. In retaliation, a Medusan fleet had raided the Pardessos retimond, deliberately destroying sections of the trans-luminary network that bound those systems together—irreplaceable Ancestral technology—and the Entente fleets had retaliated against the Verge worlds that could not survive without interstellar trade.

Carabosse had been conscripted then, one more fast ship to run blockades and evade pursuit, and she and Dai had made six trips to the orbital mines of Lyabet, every square centimeter of the ship crammed with food-base that would barely last a day. They had taken off refugees, too, packed to the limits of their environmentals, and she still dreamed some nights of skeletal women and babies too weak even to cry. She had been sure they were poised at the edge of the Dark, ripe for another Fall, another age of chaos and destruction, but somehow they had pulled away. Part of the Entente fleet had mutinied, and the majority of the Entente had backed them. She still didn't know how, but if Ashe had been involved…

She was being morbid, and she knew perfectly well why. It was better than thinking about Ashe, better than remembering what it had been like to share bed and board with the two of them. These nights, her bed with only Dai in it felt treacherously incomplete. And that she would not tolerate. She shoved herself to her feet, collecting her cup and Ashe's and setting them into the cleaner. There was work she could do on the sensor net, improving its range with the last of their GOLD, and it was certainly better than this.

ᛕ ᜰ ᛉ ᚷ

Cassilde woke as the cabin door opened, Dai sliding in as quietly as he could manage. He let the hatch roll shut again, the thud as it sealed more felt that heard, and began to undress in the dark. He was already barefoot, shirt open over the thin undershirt, and she was not surprised to find, as he slipped between the sheets, that he smelled of sex and Ashe. She curled closer, both to make it clear she had meant what she said—how he dealt with Ashe was his business—and because it was treacherously pleasant. He shifted to settle them both more comfortably, and made a soft interrogative noise. She shook her head against his shoulder, and he relaxed with a sigh.

"You could have stayed," she murmured.

"The bunk's too small," he answered sleepily, and in spite of herself she smiled. She felt his laugh beneath her and closed her eyes. She missed Ashe with sudden pain, the wide bed empty where he should have lain, and she suppressed a sigh. She wanted him back, whether she forgave him or not. They had been good together, in bed and out, very nearly since the day they met.

She and Dai had met at the Technical Gymnasium and fallen instantly into partnership. They had been together ever since, paired when they could be in the same places, free to see others when they were apart. A lucky strike and an inheritance left to Dai's covey of schoolmates had let them pay off enough of the Gymnasium indenture to sign a share contract for *Carabosse*, and Ashe had been the gamble on top of that risk: he had a reputation for arrogance to go with his talent, and he was from the Entente, which all too often led to friction in small spaces. But he was long and lean and dark, just the physical type they both found irresistible; more than that, he was quicksilver, brilliant and clever and as quick to talk them out of trouble as he was to talk them into it.

By their third run, they'd gone to shares rather than salary, and Dai had admitted wanting to sleep with him. Cassilde had agreed it would be interesting, but it wasn't until after the fifth run—a big find, so big they'd sold the rights and bought out nearly a third of *Carabosse's* debt—that, drunk and celebratory, they'd all shared a bed. It had been good enough that Cassilde had caught herself finding excuses to do it again and again, and finally, after a night where they hadn't really found any excuse, just no reasons not to, she had dragged them to a late breakfast in the port.

That had been on Guelph, with its green skies and pinpoint suns and pale pink clouds that washed across the horizon. She'd deliberately chosen a nicer place than usual, and as they took their seats in the bower she saw Ashe give them both a worried look. She had waited until the waiter-girl brought tea and Ashe's inevitable coffee and the first round of little cakes, and then planted both elbows on the table.

"So. About last night." She saw Ashe wince, as she'd half hoped he would, and Dai laughed out loud.

"Don't tease."

Ashe looked warily from her to Dai and back again. "What about it?"

"I'm liking it," Cassilde said. "So's Dai, and so are you, by all evidence. I'd like to make it a more permanent arrangement."

Ashe drew a sharp breath, as though that was the last thing he'd expected. "What sort of permanent? And what sort of arrangement?"

"Share and share alike, same as we've been doing," Cassilde said. "Only you're welcome in our bed."

"For as long as we're all happy with it," Dai said. "And we part with no hard feelings."

Ashe nodded slowly. "All right. Yes."

They'd toasted the decision in tea and then in a bottle of Guelph's light, sweet wine, and things had been good for nearly ten years. Cassilde rolled over, careful not to wake Dai, automatically checking the ship's status line projected on the wall. Everything was in order, which was more than she could say for her own feelings: she wanted Ashe to apologize, to grovel for leaving them to worry through all the years of the war, and just as sharply she wanted him back again, and everything the way it was.

That was, of course, the one thing she couldn't have. Would second-best be to take him back, and the hell with apologies, or to make him beg for her forgiveness? She didn't know.

𝆮 𝇃 𝆺 𝆄

The memory and the question still nagged at her the next day as she settled into the cockpit to check the sensors' memory. Anything obviously important would have triggered alarms, of course, but she liked to run an eye over the routine matters as well, just in case something more dangerous was lurking in them. She folded out a keyboard to enter commands, compressing the data to a quick overview that showed her the last eighteen hours in a three-minute fast-time display. If anything stood out, she could slow things down, pull out the relevant section for closer examination, but she wasn't really expecting anything.

The image took shape on her display, a white triangle in the center for *Carabosse* and then the sensor net itself painted dull purple against the black. A collection of brighter purple objects faded into view, scattered along a shallow arc: the edge of the system's asteroid belt, mostly mined out now. The system marked all but a couple of them as known and mapped, and the two unknowns were flagged as having split from a larger object, probably one of the fragments already hollowed out by mining. She could still see the distant echo of *Doron*, their courses slowly diverging as *Doron* made its way toward its own section of the wreckage, and she ran the display forward, watching it slip out of the edges of the net. Just as it vanished, there was a flicker of something else, as though a second object—a second ship?—was momentarily moving in tandem with *Doron*.

She frowned, touching keys to isolate the moment and bring up a clearer image. The system considered, and then the image swam and refocused. There was *Doron*, easing out of the net, and there was the second blip, a ragged shadow that seemed to echo *Doron*'s shape. She typed in a command for the system analysis, and the answer box blinked thoughtfully for a moment before displaying its result.

Probable sensor ghost / echo.

She frowned. A ghost ought to have a source, something to have reflected the net's original catch, but there was nothing in the area that looked likely. She increased the magnification, but there was still nothing, not even debris, just *Doron* sliding out of range and the momentary flash of...something.

The hatch rolled back, and she glanced back to see Dai standing behind her. "Problem?" he asked, and she shrugged.

"The system says not, but—it's weird."

"Let me see."

She ran the images again, watching his face change as he saw it. "Weird, yes?"

"Weird," he agreed. "I don't see anything that would give us a ghost—"

"I don't, either." Cassilde drummed her fingers on the edge of the console. "And it's too late to ping, not without letting everyone know we think we saw something."

"If it's a pirate, that might not be a bad idea," Dai said. "If they think we're on alert, maybe they'll go bother someone else."

"Or maybe they jump us sooner," Cassilde said, and reached for the intercom controls. "Ashe. Come up to the cockpit, please."

There was a moment of dead air before the answer. "On my way."

Cassilde glanced up at Dai. "He's good at data."

"He is that," Dai answered, and still sounded skeptical.

Ashe watched the first presentation twice without commenting, then slid into the co-pilot's seat without waiting for permission. "And the system says it's an echo?"

"That's its best guess," Cassilde answered.

He folded out a keyboard of his own, called up the sensor net and began typing commands, the strings flashing across his screen almost too fast to read. He was digging deeper into the system, she saw, demanding that it list all its guesses and show the calculations behind them, his frown deepening as he worked.

"The system says it's just a ghost," he said, after a moment, "even if there's nothing to reflect—lensing from *Doron*'s internal gravity, it suggests."

"But?" Cassilde asked.

Ashe shrugged. "If it was a reflection, I'd expect it to last longer, not flash in and out like that. But it may well be nothing."

"You're thinking the lens is magnifying something outside strict range," Cassilde said. It had happened before, the effect of a REFTL ship's gravity fields briefly magnifying a sensor's effects.

"If that's it," Dai said, "what have we got?"

Ashe touched keys again, but shook his head. "There's just nothing there. A reflected mass, maybe about the same size as *Doron*? Which would argue the system's right and it's just a ghost."

"Or it's another ship," Dai said.

"There's no sign of one now," Cassilde said, shifting her own display to scan the ship's sensors. She was tempted to ping the system, put power into the active sensors, but didn't input the command. If there was another ship out there, running dark, it was better not to draw its attention.

"Raider?" Dai asked, and Ashe shrugged.

"Could be one of us."

That was most likely, of course, another salvage ship trying to reach its claim unobserved, and she shook her head. "Probably. But I'm going to adjust the system to yell if it sees anything like that again."

"Good idea," Ashe said, and Dai gave him a look.

"And does that mean you've heard something we ought to know?"

Ash shook his head again. "It's a big find. There are bound to be raiders."

That was true. Cassilde sighed, and began typing in the new commands, setting up a new section of the decision tree. Behind her, the hatch rolled back, and closed again, but she ignored it, concentrating on the work at hand.

Finished at last, she leaned back in her chair, staring at the darkened screens that displayed only the external star field. Her hands were cold, the skin pale from the reduced circulation, and she folded her arms across her chest, tucking her fingers into her armpits as though that would help. Her breathing was all right—a little shallow, just a little rasp at the end of each in-drawn breath. She shouldn't need GREEN today, and maybe not for a few days yet.

And if there was any reason to let Ashe back into her bed, that was it. If she was going to die, she might as well have what she wanted. Except, of course, that she wasn't sure she wanted to share the daily indignities of the Lightman's, minor as they were at the moment. Did she really want him to know that she could not lie flat without choking, or that there were the bad nights when she couldn't sleep at all? Did she want him to know how often she and Dai merely slept together, side by side in the too-big bed? Before the war, she might not have minded, but then she had thought they understood each other better.

Unbidden, Riese Two rose in her mind, smallest of the systems in the Collect retimond, its Orbital Transfer Station jammed with people bargaining for space on the next ship through. Ashe already had a space promised, traveling with a group from one of the Entente Universities, though he had yet to make that connection, and he kept scanning the crowd nervously for them. Cassilde herself had kept checking the occupancy telltales, sure that they were getting close to the station's limits, but to her relief all the lights stayed pale yellow. They had found a table at a tapasserie, paying three times the normal minimum just to have a place to sit, and they'd huddled together over their plates and the pitcher of wine, leaning close to hear each other over the roar of the crowd.

"Don't go," she blurted out at last, having nothing else that might stop him, and Ashe gave her a hunted look.

"We've been through this a hundred times—"

"Ashe." Dai reached across the table, put his hand over the other man's. "Please."

"I have to," Ashe said, as he'd said a hundred times before. "You know that."

"This is a war," Cassilde said, her voice hard. "But not your war."

"I can't stay here," Ashe said. "These districts may not be involved yet, but they're going to be."

"Not necessarily," Dai said.

"Use your brain for once," Ashe snapped. "This is a major Orbital Transfer Station, everyone's going to want to control it—"

"Which is a good reason to respect transfer station neutrality," Dai said stubbornly.

"It's a trans-luminary data repeater, too," Cassilde pointed out. "No one is going to touch those."

"Look around." Ashe waved at the crowd filling the concourse beyond the low barrier that enclosed the tapasserie. "Does it look to you like anyone else thinks this station is going to stay neutral?" Dai's eyes fell, and Ashe looked at Cassilde. "And before you say anything, my father asked. He's never asked anything of me before, gave me everything and never asked. I owe him this."

"Do you owe him your life?" Cassilde asked.

A smile tugged briefly at his mouth. "Well, literally speaking— yes."

"Be serious."

"I am." Ashe leaned forward. "Look. My family put me through University, let me go to salvage without a word of complaint, without even asking for a share of my profits. They're Bodi Claimant-kin, there are obligations that go with that."

Cassilde gave a soundless whistle. Obligations, yes, and a great deal of privilege, though if she understood the situation correctly, the privilege didn't seem to reach Ashe himself.

"And what about us?" Dai pulled his hand back, glaring.

Ashe gave him a frustrated look. "I am in your system, I am your comet, yes. I have been happy to orbit you these ten years. I don't want to go. But my family have a prior claim."

Cassilde stared at him, the gulf between Entente and Verge suddenly opening between them. "That was not—"

"That's not how I saw it," Dai said, in almost the same moment, but Ashe was looking past him toward the crowd.

"There's Tomas—I have to go." He was scrabbling for his carryall as he spoke, tossing station scrip onto the table. Dai reached for his sleeve, but he slipped away, disappearing into the crowd.

And that had been the last she'd seen of him, clapping a stranger on the shoulder and then gone, the gulf between them unbridgeable because there was no time left to talk. The Entente had words for what they had—dozens of them, patterns mostly built on planetary systems, from common to exotic, singleton and binary and everything else besides. The Verge had none, and needed none unless there was to be a contract; their contract had been for the ship and the shares, but she and Dai had meant it to cover everything else. Ashe had seen it as something different, them as the unchanging center, himself the third in orbit, and left them.

That was, she supposed, one more reason to take him back. That conversation was still unfinished, and it would be better to settle it before she died. There had never been anyone who fit them both so well. Even Soline Alysi, who had made a casual third for the two years after the Trouble—she had been good company, was still a good friend, but she had never filled the gap that Ashe had left. And she did still want him, far more than she had expected, which only left the doing of it. She gave a crooked smile and began shutting down her board, moving everything into auto-mode or standby. That might prove more complicated than she would like.

𝔸 ⺌ ⚔ ?

Dai did most of the cooking these days, though on this trip that consisted mostly of reheating pre-pack. He did his best to make the meals look more appetizing, turning them out of their containers onto reconstituted plates. Ashe had a model of the claim running, looking for the best place to set an exploratory lock, and he shrank it to pocket size rather than putting it away entirely. Cassilde eyed it over her beans and rice, and Ashe obligingly pushed it closer, waving a hand to rotate it.

"Looks like there's only one good place to put the lock," Dai said, joining them.

"Pretty much," Ashe said. He turned the model again, spinning it so that his arbitrary x-axis now lay parallel to the table-top. "I think that's storage space, or maybe support, but in any case the preliminary scan shows it as open volume. If that pans out, we can go in through there without the risk of anything else breaching, set up the generators, and get ourselves a decent atmosphere in about twelve hours."

"That's assuming the outer hull's intact," Cassilde said.

Ashe nodded. "It looks as though it is. The scan shows atmospheric residue, which would be a slow bleed at the worst. We could even work without a patch if we had to."

"I'd rather patch any gaps we find," Dai said, and Cassilde was hit by a sudden wave of déjà vu. They must have had this conversation a hundred times over the years, working their way out to a find site, poring over models that would almost certainly prove to be flawed.

"We've got enough cartridges to fill it twice over," Cassilde said. "Let's see what the hull looks like when we get there." If there was one obvious break, it would make sense to patch it, even if it would take extra time and a suited walk; a few small breaks, or the more usual pinpoint leaks—at that point, it would make more sense to generate a working atmosphere and top it up as needed. "Have you got a fallback for the lock?"

"A couple." Ashe spun the model again, two more ghostly locks flashing into view. "They're neither one ideal, but they should work. If we have to go in from the top, I'll want to establish an inner bubble before we try to open out."

Dai crooked his fingers at the model, calling out the numbers involved. "Yeah, I've got a Taunser that'll cover it."

"I'm really hoping the south pole will work," Ashe said.

"You want me to reheat that for you?" Dai asked, and Cassilde looked down at her plate, still mostly full.

"I'm not really hungry."

"I could fry it up with some cheese."

Cassilde shook her head. "No, thanks. Save it, I'll get to it later."

She saw Dai's mouth tighten, but he didn't say anything, just collected the plate and covered it for storage. Ashe gave her a wary look, and she gave him her best smile. "I have a better idea what we could do with the rest of the evening."

Ashe blinked, his eyes wary, and behind him Dai tilted his head to one side in silent question. She nodded, willing him to understand that she was sure, and Ashe cleared his throat.

"I—yes, if you're asking, but—"

"If you'd like to start with an apology, I'm listening," Cassilde said. "But it's not required."

"I—" Ashe stopped again, looked over his shoulder at Dai, then back at her. "Yes. Since you'll have me."

"Well, then." Dai turned away from the storage bins with a bottle and three small glasses. "Might as well drink to that."

The sweet sharp liquor caught at her throat, but a glass apiece eased the awkwardness. She ended up sprawled in the big bed in the master's cabin, her head comfortably pillowed on Dai's shoulder, Ashe's face against her hip. It felt astonishingly good, a missing limb restored, and she was drifting toward more comfortable sleep than she'd had in weeks when Ashe stirred.

"Don't go," she said, and Dai reached over to grab Ashe's arm.

"I'm not," Ashe said, and shifted into his familiar place at her back. In the dim light, she thought his smile was wry, as though he felt the same weird sense of homecoming, but then he'd settled himself and she closed her eyes, warmed through at last.

𝕒 𝕨 𝕩 ?

She slept better than she had expected, and woke more refreshed than she had felt in days. Both men were gone, and when she queried the internal sensors, they told her that Dai was in the hold, presumably going over their gear, and Ashe was running simulations in the gunroom. And that was fine, she told herself, and made her way to Central to stand staring at the ranks of pre-pack in the cupboard. Nothing looked appealing, and she couldn't say she was really hungry—and that was another sign that the Lightman's was getting worse. She slid her hand into her pocket, feeling for the little tube of GREEN, its touch comforting. If she could just hold off until after they'd done the first survey of the claim...

She killed that thought, and rummaged for a liquid meal. Sweet cream was the least offensive of the four flavors, and the insta-cool cap worked as advertised, chilling the thick liquid so that she didn't have to taste it. She drank it off and made her way down the long corridor to the control room.

There had been no alerts in the past eighteen hours, but she played back the record anyway, then searched it a second time at slower speed. Both came up empty, and she leaned back in her chair, steepling her fingers. *Carabosse* was running on autopilot, following the course she had programmed once they'd left Cambyse, the transponders silenced, sensor net extended to its maximum. It was still showing mostly debris, the first flicker of a Claim-court beacon just visible at the net's leading edge. It wasn't quite close enough to read the details, but she didn't risk pinging it. She would be able to get a passive read in a few more minutes, and that was soon enough. There was no need to draw attention, not when there were bound to be raiders lurking around a find this size. The Guard patrols couldn't be everywhere. Most of the other salvors would be making the same calculation, and she checked the proximity alerts for the third time. They were set to trigger at the ten-klick radius, and even as she watched, the screen lit with a warning: debris ahead.

She adjusted the net, reading the details. It showed as mostly stone and ice—an asteroid or maybe bits of a comet, not the find field itself. It was small, but there was enough of it that she folded out a keyboard, entered in the numbers to block out a change of course.

The sensor net chimed once, then a second time, and she sat up, shoving the keyboard aside to center the sensor display. Something was moving in the far edges of the net, running without transponders, without active sensors, just the whisper of its mass against the background gravity to give it away. She hit the kill switch, shutting down all primary power, everything but environmentals and the GOLD-based net, and held her breath, watching the shadow drift across the fringes of the ship's vision. It was too far away to get details, just a rough approximation of its velocity and a guess at its mass, and she pressed the intercom button.

"Dai. Ashe. We have a ghost."

Dai answered with reassuring promptness. "Same as before?"

"More solid. It's a real echo." Cassilde studied the screen. If she could see the stranger, they could see her—if they had a GOLD net, if they were looking, if she hadn't cut power in time. Too many imponderables, she thought. All they could do was wait it out. "Ashe, are you still in guns?"

"Yes. Want me to warm them up?"

"Not yet. I don't think we've been seen. No power except on my say-so."

"All right."

"I'm coming up," Dai said.

"Fine." Cassilde checked her read-outs again, confirming that they were as close to invisible as she could manage. In the main display, the stranger continued its slow progress across the screen, the image wavering a little as it tracked. Behind her, the hatch rolled back, and Dai took his place in the co-pilot's seat.

"Anything new?"

"No change." Cassilde frowned. "No, it looks like they're slowing."

"Damn." Dai started to reach for the sensor controls, stopped even before Cassilde shook her head.

"I don't think they've seen us," she said. "It's something else."

"They're maneuvering," Dai said.

"Can you read how big they are?"

He folded out his keyboard to query the system more closely. "Bigger than us."

Cassilde gave a sigh of relief. If it was a larger ship, and they were just barely picking up its mass, there was a good chance *Carabosse* was still invisible.

"Can you tell what they're doing?"

"Slowing," Dai said.

"Can I go to stand-by?" Ashe asked, and Cassilde realized she'd left the intercom open.

"Not yet," she said. "I don't think they've seen us."

"Still slowing," Dai said. "I'm getting a better look at them, Silde. Definitely a ship and definitely bigger than us, though not by much—it might be another salvor, we're in range of some of the other claims."

"I think we should go to stand-by," Ashe said. "At least let me warm up the guns."

"Not yet," Cassilde said. It wasn't like Ashe to be trigger-happy and she frowned again. "What do you know?"

"Nothing except that getting caught by a pirate would be bad," Ashe answered. "Before we even get a look at the claim…"

And that was the Ashe she remembered: nothing got between him and salvage. "It's too much of a risk they'll pick up the power use," she said. "You know that."

"Damn it," Dai said. "They've dropped off."

"Out of range or gone to ground?" Cassilde demanded. The screen was black again, just the faint lines that laid out the system gravity and the background scatter, debris dull purple against the void.

"I can't tell." Dai shook his head. "Let me ping her once, super-low power, GOLD frequencies only—"

"No," Cassilde said again. There was too much chance another ship would pick up active sensors.

"Any idea what it was?" Ashe asked.

"Not really." She looked at Dai. "What are the chances it's one of us?"

"Somebody running quiet out to their claim?" Dai shrugged. "It could be. Like I said, we're in sensor range of a couple of other sites."

"I don't think it's a salvor," Ashe said.

"If you know anything," Cassilde said, "say it now."

There was a little silence. "There were rumors before we left. Nothing solid."

"Damn it, Ashe," Dai said.

"It was talk," Ashe said. "The usual chitchat, somebody heard somebody say somebody else might have mentioned a smash-and-grab. Nothing we all haven't heard a thousand times. But, yes, it's possible that somebody else saw what I saw in that section. Not likely, I admit. But possible."

"There are always rumors," Cassilde said, as much to herself as to the others. She reached for her own keyboard and called up a second screen, overlaying it with the general find map provided by the Claim-court. As Dai had said, they were in range of two of the class-three sites, and as she zoomed out, she could see the rest of the field coming into focus, their own claim in the trailing end still thirty hours out. One of the class-ones was only fourteen hours away, and she glanced at Dai. "Any idea where they went?"

He reached across the screen to shape a cone of light, the wide end pointing away from their position. The left edge of the cone crossed the class-one. "That's what I make from the last readings."

Heading away, Cassilde thought, and plausibly toward the class-one, which would be an excellent reason to run silent. The claims that had already showed evidence of worthwhile salvage were always targets for claim-jumpers and pirates. And there were more claims, class-twos, at the far end of the cone, their contents not as certain as the class-ones, but highly probable: also worthwhile targets. Almost certainly another salvor, taking the same precautions they were. "All right. I'm bringing us back to low power. The sooner we're on our claim, the better."

CHAPTER THREE

As *Carabosse* entered the find field, they switched to working shifts, even Ashe taking his turn in the cockpit to back up the autopilot. Cassilde gave the other beacons a wide berth, not wanting to draw attention or to alarm anyone who might be well armed enough to shoot first, but at last they came up on the beacon that marked their claim. It transmitted a brief warning, and Cassilde responded with the code issued by the Claim-court. There was a pause, and the beacon went silent, lights flickering green across her comm screen. She heard Ashe sigh behind her, and Dai turned his attention to the short-range sensors.

"Starting the scan."

Cassilde held *Carabosse* steady as the system went to work, building up a picture first of the outer surface, and then, more tentatively, tracing the inner volumes. It looked very much like the models Ashe had built, and she allowed herself a relieved sigh of her own.

"South pole?"

"Looks good to me," Dai answered, and she touched keys to switch control entirely to manual.

The drive held the ship balanced against the local gravity, like a submarine trimmed to neutral buoyancy. In theory, she could use the drive fields to bring them in, but in practice it was much easier to use the maneuver jets, and she flipped the switches that brought them online. The gimbals unlocked as well, showing *Carabosse*'s position, and she reached for the control stick. "Going in."

She felt the hiss and rumble as the first thruster fired. The internal gravity damped any sense of motion, but she could see her position change on the screen. In her screen, the claim swung slowly, and she nudged the stick again, giving them just enough sideways thrust to tilt *Carabosse* out of her current plane. She brought them down and under in a slow loop, giving herself time to make adjustments, and go through the mental gymnastics that turned the claim's image from something that hung in front of her to something that was now below *Carabosse's* belly. She eased her down toward the rough surface, seeing the flicker when the microgravity was strong enough to affect the ship's fields, drawing her toward the connection. She touched the braking jets once, twice, and *Carabosse's* skids kissed the rocky surface.

"Grapples," she said, and Dai extended them, the sharpened claws extending from their sheaths to bite deep into the rock. "Scan."

Ashe worked his controls for a moment, and she saw colors reflected in her own screens as he swept through a series of frequencies. "We're in rock, and the grapple looks tight. We haven't affected the claim's orbit by any appreciable degree. Can I ping her properly?"

"Go ahead."

He worked his controls again, two quick pulses of the GOLD-enhanced active sensors, and leaned back with a sigh. "Everything looks nominal. There's plenty of surface to hold the pitons."

Cassilde checked her own screens and nodded. "Set the pitons, Dai."

"Setting the pitons." Dai flipped a series of switches, and she felt the soft explosions that drove the pitons home. That would hold them securely enough to set an airlock, and she let herself relax as she saw the lights go green across Dai's board.

"We're in," he said, and glanced over his shoulder. "Can we run the lock direct from the ship?"

"Working on it," Ashe said, abstractedly, his fingers busy on his board. After a moment, he shook his head. "Looks like the optimum spot is about eight meters off—setting this as the south pole and our nose as zero, we'll want to go northwest, about 360 degrees."

His projection flashed on the screen as he spoke, and she heard Dai sigh. "You couldn't have just had us land there?"

"The surface is too uneven," Cassilde said briskly. She touched her own keys. "I make it more like six meters, Ashe, if I'm reading you right."

She heard his nails click against the board's surface. "Yeah. That'll work."

As he spoke, a new highlight appeared on his map, and she nodded. "All right, that's six point nine—just six to where you want to set the lock."

"I've got a solid tunnel for that," Dai said, touching keys. "No problem."

The outline of the tunnel appeared on the screen, and Ashe added the airlock, sketching in the lines where he'd cut through the claim's outer skin. "I've confirmed there's a small inner chamber, and it looks as though it's more or less airtight."

Cassilde studied the images, but could see no obvious flaws. That didn't mean there wouldn't be some unexpected problem, but it was the obvious and best starting point. "All right. Let's go with that. Dai, you'll set the lock, and Ashe and I will handle the EVA—"

Dai shook his head. "You plant the lock. Me and Ashe can do the EVA."

"But—" She stopped as he met her eyes. He was right, of course. The way the Lightman's had been playing up, she didn't need to risk the physical stress of an EVA. "All right," she said again, and Ashe nodded.

It took most of the next six hours to get the portable lock out of the hold, and to use the ship's cargo arms to position it correctly. Once Ashe was satisfied, she held it in place while he and Dai set the seals, and then eased the arms back. The lights stayed green, and Dai's voice crackled in her speakers.

"Set. Let's run the tunnel out."

"Confirm." Cassilde adjusted the cargo arms and edged the tunnel segments out of the hold, setting them in place one by one so that the others could seal the couplings. There were eight in all, the last one wedged awkwardly against *Carabosse*'s port airlock, and it took Dai almost an hour to get it snugged against both the ship and the rest of the tunnel. But at last the lights went green on Cassilde's console, and Dai's voice came again from the speakers.

"Got it! All right, we're going to come back in through the ventral lock and collect the cutters."

Cassilde leaned back in her chair, her hand cramping as she released the controls. She grabbed those fingers, held them until the spasming stopped and she could talk again. "How long is it going to take to cut through?"

"Three hours, maybe four?" It was Ashe who answered. "I'm not a hundred percent sure what's under the rock."

Cassilde rubbed her hands unhappily, fatigue clawing at her. She was in no shape to stay on duty, and someone needed to be awake and alert in the ship while the men were on EVA. "Too long. Let's call it a day and start fresh in the morning."

"I'm fine for it," Ashe said.

"Silde's right," Dai said. "We need to change filters anyway, and I'd like something more than a protein shake for a meal."

"I suppose," Ashe said, but the sensors showed him following Dai toward the ventral lock.

As soon as they were in the lock, Cassilde pushed herself up out of her chair, intending to collect a protein shake in Central before they could cycle through, but her foot cramped. She swore, shifted her weight to try to work it out, but each time she relaxed, the muscles knotted again, her toes locked in a painful curl.

Dai found her there, stuck just outside the cockpit's hatch, not able to move without something cramping. She glared at him, her eyes teary from the pain and the pure frustration, and he glanced quickly over his shoulder before he took a step forward and took her by the elbows. He was barefoot and freshly showered, and she did her best not to dig her nails into his skin.

"Which foot?"

"Left." She eased the pressure, swore under her breath as the cramp returned.

"Easy." Dai shifted his own weight, balancing himself against the nearest bulkhead, and put one foot over hers. "Ready?"

She nodded, bracing herself, but even knowing what to expect, the steady pressure made her swear again, tears crawling from the corners of her eyes. It hurt, hurt like bones breaking; she cursed and cringed, her nails leaving crescents in Dai's skin, and then, as abruptly as it had begun, the cramp was gone. She straightened, taking a wary breath, but the movement didn't trigger any new reaction, and she nodded.

"Thanks."

"No problem." Dai eased his foot away, but didn't let go. Cassilde rested her forehead against his shoulder, the tears still stinging her eyes.

"It's so damn frustrating."

"Yeah."

She leaned on him a moment longer, then straightened. "I'm all right."

He nodded. "You hungry?"

The idea of food curdled her stomach. She shook her head. "Not really."

"You need to eat."

"I'll grab a liqui-meal."

Dai's mouth tightened as though he'd protest, but he managed to nod instead. "You go lie down, I'll bring you one."

She wanted to refuse, to insist that she could get it herself, but common sense prevailed. "Sweet cream, then. And thanks."

She managed to get herself undressed, though her hands were shaking, and crawled beneath the covers of her bed. Dai brought the bottled meal as promised, and she managed to choke it down, then sat for what seemed like a long time staring at the little box of GREEN. Was it time yet? Would this be the best use of it? Her breathing eased before she could make up her mind, the tremors fading, and she left it unopened. Soon, she thought, but not today.

She was better in the morning, well enough to eat a decent meal and take over the ship's systems while Dai and Ashe set the cutters and started working their way through the hull. They had to work around several good-sized nests of BLUE—enough, Dai said, to cover most of the expenses—and Cassilde marked them for later recovery. Once the shell was breached, Ashe released a flock of mapping drones to chart the interior volume, and he and Dai began setting up the generators that would provide a breathable atmosphere and the secondary gravity system. Cassilde tied the ship's power to both, and spent several hours adjusting the fields so that they aligned with the claim's interior axes. They could always salvage the section walking on its original ceiling, but it was much easier to work when the gravity lined up with the sections they were observing.

She studied her readouts a final time, tweaking the fields to bring them tighter to the claim, then touched the comm button. "How's that feeling from your side, Dai?"

"Good. I think we'll keep the airlock outside, it'll make the transition easier."

"Works for me," Cassilde answered.

"Do you want us to go after this BLUE while we're making air?" Ashe asked.

Cassilde considered for a moment. It was always smart to get as much salvage on board as quickly as possible, in case of unforeseen problems, but it was late in the day. "Leave it for tomorrow," she said. "I'm showing you needing new filters within the hour."

"Confirmed," Dai said. "Come on, Ashe, you can play with your maps instead."

By the time they gathered again in Central, Ashe had begun to work through the drones' data, expanding it to a map, then flattening it to a rough schematic before he pulled it back out into a three-dimensional model. In a second board, he collected image fragments as though he could identify specific objects in the drones' feed.

"The resolution's not good enough for that," Dai said. He'd done the cooking again, and slid the bowls of rice and beans onto the table. Cassilde took hers cautiously, afraid to trust her hunger. Her fingers stumbled on the spoon, and Dai gave her a sharp glance, but she stared him down.

"At least I can get something to start on," Ashe said. He was eating with one hand, and still fiddling with the map with the other. "I'm guessing this might be what we're looking for?" He pointed to a smaller chamber, and Cassilde frowned.

"That's new, isn't it?"

Ashe nodded. "I thought there were two large chambers, plus the lower section where we've set the lock, but it turns out there's another." He turned the map, displaying the smaller chamber, connected to the larger spaces by a single narrow tunnel. Its bulkheads were thicker than the others', almost as thick as the bulkhead that had divided the entire section from the rest of the parent craft.

"If this is medical—a treatment room?" Dai asked.

"Maybe?" Ashe twirled the map again.

"Do you mind?" Dai said. Cassilde gave him a grateful look. Between the shifting images and the Lightman's, she was feeling a little queasy looking at it herself, and she wanted to eat if she could.

"I'd normally say it was sleeping quarters," Ashe said, "but that bulkhead is way too heavy. There's something that wants power behind that. Or there was." He made no acknowledgement of Dai's complaint, but at least he'd stopped spinning the map.

"You say that because?" Dai squinted at the image.

"Because of that," Cassilde said, and pointed, the lights of the map playing over her hand. "That does look like some sort of power node."

Ashe nodded. "The drones say it could be an inert device. Pings were inconclusive, but it's possible."

"Promising," Cassilde said. "All right, we'll start there, work back."

"Nothing more from the sensor web?" Dai asked, and Cassilde shook her head.

"That ghost must have been one of us."

Ashe nodded, but Dai hesitated. "Maybe one of us should stay on board, keep an eye out for anything else that might show up."

Cassilde weighed the options, the added security of a live person minding the ship against the need to do a thorough survey as quickly as possible. If there had been anything more, any warning from the web or any sign of further trouble, it would be different, but at the moment, it was speed that mattered. "No. I'll set the system to ping us if it catches anything. It's worth the risk."

$$\Lambda \; \text{⺊} \; \text{⺘} \; \text{⺆}$$

The environmental fields were locked solid, the arbitrary gravity holding the new-made atmosphere, the secondary field transmitting power to their lights and tools. Cassilde checked her relays a final time, making sure the ship's signal was reading at maximum, and sealed the airlock door behind her. It wasn't strictly necessary—the tunnel was pressurized—but it was an automatic precaution, and she took a deep breath before stooping to the opening cut into the floor, unlatching and lifting the hatch. It was disorienting to bend down toward the interior knowing that she would be reaching up into the gravity field; she caught the handhold Dai had rigged, then closed her eyes.

"Give me your hand," Dai said in her ear, and she extended her arm blindly, feeling the momentary tug of two different gravities. And then Dai's hand was tight around her wrist and he drew her up into the entrance chamber. Ashe had rigged a working light and a ladder up into the main spaces, and she took a deep breath.

"Thanks." They could speak without the comm system here, though the fields and the still air damped the sound. "Everything good?"

"Fine here," Dai said, and pulled the hatch closed behind her. "Ashe went ahead."

That was no surprise. "Might as well join him," Cassilde said, and

hauled herself up the ladder, very aware of Dai's protective presence
at her back.

She emerged into heavy twilight, Ashe's hand-light spilling across
the walls and floor ahead of her. She swung her own light as well,
quartering the space, and felt the cold seeping into her bones. Some
of that was psychological—it would feel warmer once they were able
to rig working lights instead of relying on hand- and helmet-beams—
but some of that was the Lightman's creeping through her body. She
could barely feel her feet, in spite of the heated boot liners. She dialed
up the heat in her vest, heedless of battery life, and tucked the hood
more tightly around her face.

"You were right," she said. "This looks like living space."

"I told you," Ashe said. He had his own recorder out, scanning
the walls, and streaks of color bloomed as the light hit them. "Here,
put your light over here."

Cassilde brought her light to join his, and a series of linked circles
swam out of the shadows, pale gold on lavender-gray. "Dai?"

Dai trained his light on them as well, widening the picture, but
it remained abstract, one large circle linked to a dozen smaller ones,
circles smaller still hanging off each of those. "Fractal symbolism?"

"Maybe." Ashe broke from the joined lights, followed the
diminishing circles up the wall and onto the ceiling above them, where
they faded into invisibility. "Or maybe just decoration."

Cassilde swung her light again, scanning the room. Shapes rose
like islands from the floor, the remains of furniture—a sweeping curve
that might have been a lounge, cubes that might have been chairs or
tables, odd shallow pits in the floor, now half-hidden in the layer
of pale dust that covered everything. She took a few cautious steps
toward the center, and her light struck glints from something lying
beside one of the cubes. Something that had spilled out of the cube,
she amended, seeing the break in the smooth surface, and went to one
knee beside it. The reflection had come from a lump of cloudy glass
the size of her fist. She picked it up and felt the familiar deep hum that

meant it was active. "I've got a music box. Working, too."

"Nice," Dai said. "That's a good-sized one, too."

Cassilde nodded, and tugged gently at the half open door. It was solidly wedged, and she shone her light inside rather than try to force it. A second larger music box lay in easy reach, and she tugged it free. They weren't really music boxes, of course, weren't even boxes, but when a human held them, the glass slowly cleared to reveal twirling threads of light and produced a cascade of pleasant sound. Between these two and the BLUE that they could take from the claim's hull, the job was already in the black—a good thing, too, if she was going to be incapacitated for a while. "There might be another one, but I can't quite see. And I don't want to reach in—"

"We can come back," Ashe said. "This way."

The next compartment had showed as single on the first maps, but in effect was two, a curved wall sweeping across the space to screen one from the other. Ashe swung his light around curiously, picking out more decoration—designs like stylized leaves or narrow seed-heads that transformed to abstract curls as it swept along the dividing wall— and two rows of cylinders marched down the center of the outer section, set at a variety of different heights. Cassilde swept the dust from one that stood at about waist-height, searching for any traces of cushions or anything else that might have been attached to the top, but the pale gray surface seemed untouched.

In contrast, the next compartment was entirely empty, the walls painted a much darker gray that glittered here and there as their lights struck it. Streusel, the first finders had called it, bits of something glass-like scattered at random in the finish: usually it went with a more ornate setting, and she saw Dai smile as he scanned the walls.

"There's GOLD here, and maybe some RED. Maybe whatever was supposed to be here was removed when the palace was abandoned?"

"Assuming it was abandoned before it broke up," Cassilde said, but she thought he was probably right. There were no signs here of catastrophic failure, of disaster, just age.

"We'll come back," Ashe said. "This way."

They had to pass through a cylindrical corridor before they reached a circular opening in the thickened bulkhead. Cassilde swung her light, examining the slot where presumably the original door had disappeared, but there was no sign of it or of any controlling mechanism. Dai produced a metal bar as thick as his wrist, extended and locked it, and laid it gently in the opening. When nothing happened, he tried wedging it into the gap, but the bar slid into the slot without catching on anything.

"We'll be fine," Ashe said, and stepped through. "We've got cutters."

Which was true just as long as the secondary field kept functioning. Cassilde took a breath, and followed him. "I thought you didn't like messing up your finds."

"I don't," he answered, his light sweeping over the new space. "I just don't expect we'll have to."

Cassilde lifted her own light, blinking as she began to make sense of the shadowed curves. "Holy—"

"Yeah," Dai said. He shrugged off his carrypack. "Ashe, you want me to rig some work lights?"

"Please." Ashe was moving slowly across the open space, his light flashing over what looked like beds made of woven silver, a cascade of scarlet thread down the far wall, and then a chair that spiraled up out of the floor.

There was a sharp click as Dai found metal to take the work light's magnet, and the room was suddenly flooded with light. Cassilde switched off her hand light, her breath coming short again.

The compartment was curved like the inside of a shell, the open space where she and Dai still stood curling down to a narrow alcove, half hidden behind the flowing strands of scarlet. The walls shimmered like nacre, palest gold shading toward green in the shadows; there were lines drawn on the floor and up the walls, following the gentle curves. On other installations, similar lines had been filled with flowing light.

Dai flicked on a second work light, driving back the rest of the shadows. "Impressive."

"Isn't it?" Ashe touched the datamote at his collarbone, rubbing it as though that would make it give up its information. "I've never seen anything like it."

And if Ashe hadn't, this might be a unique find. Cassilde killed that hope—it was far too soon to speculate—and said, "Any sign of this lifesaving device?"

"In the alcove, I think," Ashe answered. The work lights didn't quite penetrate its depths; he was still using his handlight to examine the walls. "But I'm not seeing any actual device."

"There's things attached to the beds," Dai began, and at that moment the lights flickered.

Cassilde grabbed her remote, pinged the ship to demand its status. The codes flashed back in the proper sequence: power transmitters all green, ship's systems green, nothing in the sensor web. She shook her head. "Nothing here."

"I could head back and double-check," Dai said, reluctantly.

Cassilde considered, weighing the difficulty of getting out again if they lost the transmission against the lost time and work. Minor glitches, skips in the field transmission, were rare, but not unheard of; usually it meant she'd failed to tune the transmissions properly to avoid all interference. The status reports all looked solid, though, and sometimes you never did find out what caused the problem. "You posted glow-dots, right?"

"Of course." Dai sounded annoyed, and she gestured an apology.

"Sorry. Stay, I think. If it happens again, we'll rethink it."

"Better rethink it now." The stranger's voice came from the hatch.

Cassilde spun, reaching for the blaster at her hip, and froze as she registered the leveled weapons. There were three of them—no, four, all with heavy military-surplus blasters and body armor over their work vests. Dai swore, and she lifted her hands to show them empty.

"Smart woman," the stranger said. He stepped through the

hatch, still with his blaster leveled, a wiry man with a pointed chin and muscles that stood out like brackets at the corners of his mouth. "Hello, Ashe." Dai swore again, not softly.

Ashe gave a bitter smile. "Hello, darling."

The words dripped venom, and the stranger smiled. "Did you really think I wouldn't follow you?"

"I thought we had an agreement," Ashe said. He was keeping his hands in plain sight, raised shoulder high, but the heavy hand light was in his left hand, a possible weapon. Seeing that, Cassilde shifted her weight, tipping ever so slightly to her right. Only the stranger had actually entered the compartment; if Ashe distracted him, there was a chance she could drop behind the closest of the woven-silver beds and use her blaster from there. It was lighter than the weapons the raiders were carrying, but deadly enough at this short range.

"Agreements change." The stranger was scanning the compartment, weapon still leveled, but his eyes elsewhere. Dai saw it, too, and slid one foot forward, but the stranger focused on him instantly. "Don't."

Dai dipped his head in acknowledgement, and in the same moment Ashe swung the heavy light. The stranger stepped into the blow, blocking it with his forearm, and brought the barrel of his own blaster hard across Ashe's face. Ashe dropped to his knees, and Cassilde dove for the dubious shelter of the woven bed, fumbling for her own weapon. Fire creased her shoulder, and her hand spasmed; she dropped her blaster, fingers nerveless, and scrabbled for it with her other hand, heedless now of shelter.

"Don't move," the stranger said, and stepped closer to Ashe, still on his knees. There was blood on his mouth and nose, a bruise already rising on his sallow cheek. "All right, Ashe, where is it?"

"I don't know."

"Don't waste my time."

"I don't know," Ashe said again. The stranger lowered the muzzle of his blaster until it rested against Ashe's temple. Ashe glared up at him.

"If you kill me—"

"Oh, never you," the stranger said. He turned on his heel, the blaster shifting aim before Cassilde could even register his intent. Fire cracked, and the impact knocked her backward, pain filling her belly. She curled around it, too stunned to cry out, heard Dai call her name as if from an immense distance.

"You asshole," Ashe said. "Spawn of a Dedalor—"

"She might live," the stranger said. "But her clock's running." There was the sound of a scuffle. "That's right, hold him."

That had to be Dai, Cassilde thought. She rocked slowly, trying to ease the pain, but it clawed up her spine, down into her hips, every nerve on fire.

"Where is it?" the stranger said again. "I'm waiting, Ashe."

"It's not here," Ashe said. "I thought it would be, but it's not—and since it's not, it has to be—I'll take you, I'll show you, I swear—but let me take care of Silde first."

"Two minutes," the stranger said.

Tears filmed Cassilde's eyes, blurring her vision. The pain rolled over her in waves, threatening to drown her; she fought through it, gasping, and Ashe knelt at her side.

They each carried first aid, but the kits were inadequate for something like this. Cassilde heard Ashe crack open his package and then hers, flinched as he pressed both bandage packs against the wound.

"I will fucking kill you," Dai said, somewhere in the distance, and she didn't know if he was talking to Ashe or to the stranger Ashe had called darling.

There was a sharp pain in her forearm, unfairly distinct against the background agony, and then another. She twisted her head to see, and realized that Ashe had planted both the shock buttons in the flesh of her arm. Already the drugs were taking hold, and she blinked up at him, expecting at least some apology.

"Green, then the red," he said, so softly she barely hear him. His back was to the stranger, to Dai, hiding the movement of his lips.

"First green, then the red curtain."

"Time's up," the stranger said. He moved to Ashe's side, laid the barrel of the blaster against Ashe's cheek so that it pointed past him at Cassilde. "Come on, Ashe, time to go."

"I'm coming," Ashe said. The stranger stepped back smoothly, always out of reach, and Ashe rose to his feet with only a single backward glance.

"All right," the stranger said. "Ashe, you will take me to the device. Usslo, bring that one along."

He must mean Dai, Cassilde thought, blinking hard. The buttons' effect was building, beating the pain back to manageable levels, giving her new strength. She lay still, hoarding it—she would have one good effort, she didn't dare waste it—and the stranger turned away.

"Ashe, if you cross me, I'll kill him, too."

"I understand." Ashe's voice was tight with fury.

"What about her?" That was one of the others, though she couldn't tell which one. The stranger glanced back at her and gave a tiny shrug.

"Leave her. She's not going anywhere."

Cassilde closed her eyes, shuddering, another wave of pain washing through her. When she opened them, the strangers were gone, leaving her alone in the sea-shell room, the harsh work lights throwing doubled shadows. The buttons had kicked in, giving her all the strength she was ever going to have, and nothing useful to do with it. It wasn't fair that she should die like this, when she'd been more or less resigned to Lightman's, not fair at all.

She hooked one hand over the edge of the silver bed, hauled herself to a sitting position. Ashe's bandages were doing their job, just like the buttons, staunching the blood where the blast hadn't cauterized the wound, and she recovered her blaster, checking to be sure the charge was still good. And now what? She clutched the blaster harder as another wave of pain rolled through her, and fought to breathe against it. She doubted she could walk; crawling after them was only going to waste what little strength she had.

And what the hell had Ashe meant, whispering about color? Green, then red—no, she thought, GREEN, then RED. GREEN she had, tucked into the pocket of her vest. It might, it should, give her more strength, maybe enough to stand. She reached for it, fumbled the tiny box, and had to put the blaster down to open it. The sliver of GREEN was less then a centimeter long, and barely thicker than a hair: a quarter's profit, and all her discretionary income for the year. She licked her fingertip, picked it up, and transferred it to her tongue before she could change her mind.

The GREEN fizzed, bitter and cold, filling her mouth with metallic saliva. She'd never taken so much at once, and she swallowed hard. The wound in her stomach protested, but the pain was distanced, manageable. She imagined she could feel the GREEN crawling through her nervous system, freezing the pain and shock, and hauled herself to her feet before she could think too much about it.

The blaster was on the floor plates at her feet. She swore silently, unable to bend, and made herself concentrate on Ashe's words. GREEN, then RED—but there was no RED anywhere in sight, unless he'd meant for her to break one of the Ancestral devices? She had the cutter still, but that would take time, and the sound would surely bring Ashe's "darling" or his men. She would kill Ashe for that herself, later— She laughed silently. It seemed unlikely that there would be a "later."

GREEN, then RED. First GREEN, check, she'd done that, then RED—no, then the red curtain.

The red curtain, the shimmering veil of scarlet thread that covered half the narrow alcove, the alcove that probably was Ashe's mysterious life-saving device. First take the GREEN, and then the red curtain… She staggered toward it, her feet slurring on the floor. The buttons' effects were starting to wear off, the pain surging; the GREEN pulsed cold with every heartbeat, so cold she thought her bones would crack, her fingers blacken.

The curtain swayed as she came close, a few tentative strands lifting as though to sample the air. She stopped, swaying herself, unsure of what she was really seeing, and still more threads rose, reaching for the exposed skin of her face, her hands. Their touch was pleasant, sweet and soothing, warm as the smell of tea. She let herself be wound in, the threads tugging her gently forward until she was entirely surrounded, tucked into the alcove. Its walls shifted against her, forming to her body, and the final layer of the curtain swept in to enclose her. She felt an instant of panic, but then sleepy warmth suffused her, the pain retreating to nothing, and her eyes closed.

She opened them again an infinity later, her breath easier than it had been in years, the pain a receding memory. She filled her lungs, marveling at the play of muscles and ribs, flattened her hand against her stomach. Vest and shirt and undershirt were in tatters, but her skin was smooth and whole. The last of the threads dropped from her shoulders, unwound from her ankles, dissolving into dust. Out of power? Their job complete? She hoped it was the latter, hoped she would have the time to find out. But for now, there was Darling to worry about.

She scooped up her blaster, the charge still ready, and for good measure drew her cutter and set it to standby before she slid it into her belt. It wouldn't be much help unless she got into hand-to-hand, and that was to be avoided, but it was better than nothing.

Armed, she peered out the circular hatch. The corridor was dark, but lights moved in the distance, in the empty compartment with the glittering walls. She eased through the hatch, still amazed that her body responded, and pressed her back to the bulkhead as she moved as quietly as she could toward the light.

She heard the voices before she was close enough to see, Darling's cool and calm.

"I'm not buying it, Ashe."

"I swear," Ashe said. "This is the only other place to look, and—I don't know. Maybe I got it wrong. Maybe there's nothing here."

"You don't make mistakes," Darling said.

"Yes, I do. Even I do," Ashe said. "I just got it wrong."

"Usslo!" There was scuffling, and a choked sound that might have come from Dai, before Darling spoke again. "Ashe, you are determined to be difficult."

"I'm not, I swear. I got it wrong."

Cassilde reached the door, angled her head carefully to see inside. Dai was on his knees, his hands clasped on his head, a man wearing a monocular holding a blaster to his head. Ashe stood beside a hole in the bulkhead, the edges black from the cutter's beam. There was RED inside, glimmering in the single work light, RED and GOLD and maybe even a hint of GREEN—a season's solid work, a lucky find, and still Darling shook his head.

"A Gift was here, I know that. Don't make me do this."

There was no more time. Cassilde took a step, aimed, and fired twice, catching One-Eye in the neck and chest. He fell forward, and Dai rolled with him, scrambling for the dropped blaster. Cassilde turned her blaster on Darling, two shots, three, four, all to the chest and belly, driving him back—

"Silde!" That was Dai, blaster in hand, Darling's last two men crumpled against the bulkhead, and Cassilde drew a shaken breath.

"I'm fine," she said.

"Yeah, but how—" Dai stopped abruptly, and Cassilde nodded.

"He knows." She looked at Ashe. "You do, don't you?"

"It was the device," Ashe said. His voice cracked. "That was the thing, the lifesaver. The Gift. It worked."

"We need to get out of here." Dai kicked Darling's body, not gently. "There's no telling who else he's got waiting."

"He works alone or with small teams," Ashe said. He had himself under control now, only the faintest trembling of the hand light to betray him. "This should be it."

Cassilde took a breath. "We will discuss how you know that later—"

"I need to look at the Gift," Ashe said. "Please, Silde. It's more important than you know."

"We don't have time for that," Dai said. "Are you fucking crazy?"

"Shut up, both of you," Cassilde said. "Ashe, the device—it worked on me, and then the red stuff just dissolved. I don't think there's much left to look at."

Ashe closed his eyes. "Damn it…"

Cassilde ignored him, scanning the compartment. Dai was right, they needed to get away, get out of range of any of Darling's friends still lurking nearby, but there was also too much easy salvage to abandon. "All right. Clean out that cache, quick and dirty. Anything else we see on the way, grab it, but no more cutting. We'll come back if we can."

Dai was already moving to obey, pulling gloves and expandables from his pockets to collect the Ancestral elements, and after a moment Ashe joined him, pulling out RED and GOLD in enormous expensive lumps. There was GREEN, too, two finger-length cylinders and then a smaller, broken chunk that showed paler color. It might or might not still be good, but Cassilde grabbed it anyway. At any other moment, she would have been breathless with delight—this was a massive find, a solid year's expenses paid for and more—but there was no time. They needed to get back to *Carabosse*, get themselves into the protection of the Guard. Then they could think about coming back, and recovering whatever was still left, hidden in the claim's hull.

The cache was empty, at least of the largest pieces. There would be more, crumbs and fragments, but there was no time to search further. "Back to the ship," she said, and pinned Ashe with a look. "And you owe me answers."

"Yes," he said, and that was strange enough that she nearly dropped her carryall.

"Move," she said.

CHAPTER FOUR

They scrambled back through the wreckage, Cassilde obsessively checking the marks in the dust. She counted only their own tracks and Darling's and his men, and hoped that meant he hadn't had enough men to leave a watch on his ship. She hoped, too, that his ship had landed, wasn't hanging in orbit waiting to blast them before they could break free of the claim. She pinged *Carabosse* again, and again it told her everything was fine. She swore under her breath. They'd find out once they reached the lock, anyway, and in the meantime, they needed to grab anything else of value.

There was another toy in the half-open cube in the first room, a pitted egg shape of some dull black material that was weirdly slick and warm to her touch. It wasn't a design she recognized, but when she held it up, Ashe nodded.

"That one's safe."

"Good," she said, and tucked it into her carryall.

She paused in the airlock, considering the nests of BLUE beneath the surface, and Dai reached for the cutter at his belt.

"Give me twenty minutes."

"Too long," Ashe said, and Cassilde nodded.

"We'll come back if we can. What we have is worth more, anyway." She pinged the ship again, querying the sensor net, but it still reported nothing, no sign of another ship. "Ashe. Will he have set traps? And where's his ship likely to be?"

"Grappled to the other side of the claim, most likely," Ashe said.

The blood on his face had dried, was flaking away, and he rubbed his cheek as though it itched. "I don't think he'd bother with traps."

He didn't sound as certain as she'd like, and she looked at Dai. "Take point. Scan everything—direct, not through the ship. If anything's even the slightest bit off, don't touch it, and let us know."

Dai nodded, scanning the connection with the tunnel, then looked over his shoulder. "I'm opening up. You stay here until I'm sure it's clear."

Cassilde nodded, though every nerve screamed to hurry. Ashe looked over his shoulder unhappily, as though he could see Darling's ship through the bulk of the claim, and Dai rolled back the hatch. He closed it again behind him, and Cassilde watched his marker recede down the tunnel, her remote showing everything as clearly as though she were watching it in person. She saw him stop, apparently to scan, and then move on, and she looked at Ashe.

"Who was this guy?"

"I'll tell you later," Ashe said. He had his own remote out, was scanning in the opposite direction, and Cassilde frowned.

"Got something?"

"No." He gave her a wincing smile. "Looking for the ship, that's all."

In her remote's screen, Dai stopped again, and then the comm button crackled against her ear. "All clear. I'm going aboard."

"Go ahead," Cassilde answered. "We'll follow. Get up to the cockpit and start warming up the systems."

Ashe was already working the door controls, and she followed him down the tunnel to *Carabosse's* lock. Dai had left it ready for them, outer door open and his mono-mark chalked above the controls to confirm that everything was clear. She closed the door behind them, sealing the hatch for take-off, and Dai's voice sounded on the intercom.

"Silde? Aren't we going to recover the lock?"

"We'll come back for it," Cassilde answered. "Preferably with a Guard escort. Any sign of another ship?"

"Yes. Like Ashe said, it's on the far side of the claim. They must have matched our bandwidths and foxed the sensor web. It shows empty when I ping it, no life signs and the computer's dormant."

"Right." Cassilde worked the controls, sealing the hold for an emergency lift. "Ashe, take guns, and get them hot. If there's the slightest movement from that ship, blast it."

"Cheerfully," Ashe said, and worked the inner hatch controls.

Cassilde followed him, taking the central corridor at a near-run. She flung herself into the pilot's seat, already scanning interior and exterior sensors. Ashe was in guns, the weapons flaring yellow and orange as he ran the cannons through an accelerated warming cycle, and she triggered the intercom.

"Sealing ship."

"Confirm," Dai said, and Ashe echoed him.

"Guns on line."

Not hot, Cassilde noted; they were warming, but still only at quarter power. She could see Darling's ship grappled to the far side of the claim, bigger than *Carabosse* and more sharply angled in its lines. The shape suggested more guns, too, heavy turrets to each side of the main axis, smaller dorsal turrets toward the tail. They were cold, though—the entire ship was cold, powered down either to conserve power or, more likely, to reduce the risk of detection. Which probably meant that they'd killed all of Darling's men, but it wasn't a chance she liked to take.

"Get ready to lift," she said, and Dai gave her a startled look.

"Pitons?"

"Blow them," she said. He hesitated, and she dredged a smile from somewhere. "What, this isn't enough of an emergency for you?"

Dai grinned at that. "It's as much as I want. Standing by."

Cassilde checked her boards, waiting for the engine readings to climb a few points over the minimums. "Ready in ten."

"Silde," Ashe said. "Let me blast that ship as we go."

Dai gave her a startled look. "Not enough power, surely. And it's a waste."

Cassilde felt her own eyebrows rise. Darling's ship was salvage, too, fair game, and if they came back with the Guard, they'd be able to sell it on at a profit even in the strictest Claim-court. "That's money in the bank," she said. "Leave it alone."

"All right," he said, his reluctance audible, and she checked her board again.

"I show engines hot," Dai said.

"Engines at standby," she answered. "Blow the pitons."

Dai flipped the switch, and she felt the explosive cartridges fire, sheering off the pitons at the claim's surface.

"Lifting," she said, and fired the maneuver jets, lifting *Carabosse* free of the claim's surface. In one camera's view, she could see the rocky mantle falling away, the pitons tumbling free of their sockets, and she extended the sensor web to its fullest extent. Nothing showed but the wreck's debris.

"Let me put a hole in her just to be on the safe side," Ashe said. "She'll still bring a decent price."

"And cost twice as much to recover." Cassilde checked the readouts again. If Ashe was this insistent... But the guns were still only at one-third power, not rising fast enough, and she shook her head. "There's no time. Leave it, Ashe."

"All right," he said, still reluctant, but she pretended she hadn't heard.

She brought the engines up to full, boosting them along the fastest course regardless of fuel efficiency, and kept the sensor net at its widest range, setting the active systems to constant sweep. She'd rather someone caught the pings than miss any pursuit from any more of Darling's men, no matter what Ashe said about the man working alone. If she could believe that at all.

After an hour, there was no sign of pursuit. Dai made his way back to the engines to tune the fields, while Cassilde remained in her seat, staring at the empty sensor screens. Another hour, she told herself, and then, when Ashe asked permission to stand down the guns, she agreed, and set the autopilot to maintain course and acceleration. It was another twenty hours to the turn-around; she would have to rest before then.

She still couldn't believe how good she felt as she made her way to Central. It wasn't just that the blaster wound was gone, it was that she could breathe, that her muscles moved with a fluid ease that she could barely remember. Her joints no longer clicked and popped, she no longer stepped cautiously to avoid setting off shooting pains in the ankle she had broken the year before. The Lightman's was gone, she was sure of that, the incurable cured, but even more, all the minor aches and pains that came with age were also gone. Even the marks of the shock buttons had vanished, though there should have been puncture marks and deep bruises. Ashe was right, they had to examine what was left of the Gift.

Ashe was sitting at the unfolded table, his head tipped back so that Dai could tend his broken nose. Both eyes were blackened, and there was another swelling bruise on his left cheek.

"You look like hell," Cassilde said. She wasn't sure she was sorry, either, and felt vaguely guilty.

"Done," Dai said, and Ashe sat up slowly. Dai turned away from the table, bundling the scraps from the aid kit into the disposal, then collected a bottle and glasses from the cabinet and poured them each a stiff drink. Ashe downed half of his in a single wincing gulp and held out his glass for a refill.

"Don't be in too much of a hurry," Cassilde said, and sat down across from him. "We need to talk."

"I know." Ashe took a more careful sip of the whiskey, and Dai perched on the edge of the table beside him.

"So what just happened?" Cassilde asked. Her own whiskey tasted wonderful, sweet and sharp and perfectly chilled.

"How are you feeling?" Ashe asked in turn.

Cassilde looked at him. "Well. Better than well. What just happened, Ashe?"

Ashe glanced at Dai, still looming, and wrapped his hands around the glass. "It's—it was a Gift. The Ancestors made them, very rarely. We have no idea why, only that they exist—"

"Wait a minute," Dai said. "You're talking about a Miracle Box. I thought you didn't believe in them."

"I was wrong," Ashe said. Something between a smile and a grimace crossed his face. "About this, too."

"We'll get back to him later," Cassilde said. "You're telling me that Miracle Boxes are real."

"You're here," Ashe said, with some asperity. "You should be dead."

Twice over, if not from the blaster bolt then from the Lightman's, shock triggering a deadly attack. That was what she'd always expected would happen. Cassilde took another sip of her drink, sharp on her tongue and warm all the way down to her healed belly. "And you knew it would be there."

"I suspected." Ashe took a breath. "The Ancestors made the Gifts—that's the word they used, not Miracle Box. Who knows why, and who knows why they left them, just the way they left everything else. But sometimes you find one, and it works. It heals the sick, revives the dying, cures everything from madness to Lightman's to the common cold. It works once, three times, a hundred times—there are traditional shrines on some of the late-settled Edge worlds that have to have begun as Miracle Boxes. And sometimes you find one that's special. It only works once, but it carries a bonus. Not only does it heal whatever ails you, but—it changes you. You get their immunities, their ability to heal, probably their extended lifespan. You become one of them."

"No," Dai said.

Cassilde leaned back in her chair, denial fading unspoken to be replaced by an appalled certainty. That explained how she felt, the intensity of every sensation, the fizzing energy along her nerves.

Dai said, "You're saying Silde has become an Ancestor?"

"I don't know for sure," Ashe said. "You'd have to test it, and I don't have the tools to do it without actually harming her. But, yes, I think so. That was what the bug was telling me, that there was a special Gift there on the wreck."

"You mean that I'll heal like the Ancestors?" Cassilde said. "That I'll never be sick again? That I'll live forever, stay forever just as I am, just like in the stories?"

"If I'm right," Ashe said. "Yes."

"So." Cassilde stretched to reach across the table, grabbed the service knife from its slot in the edge of the table.

"Silde—" Dai's voice broke.

"Let's find out," she said, and before she could think too hard about it, drew the blade across the skin of her forearm. It parted at the touch, welling blood and then a pain sharp enough to stop breath, far more than she had expected. She swayed, and the cut began to close, the blood reabsorbed, skin flowing over it, fading from pink to white to tan, the pain disappearing with it. Ashe let out a breath as though he'd been holding it, and Dai shook his head.

"Gods, Silde."

"And there we are," she said. She was surprised her voice wasn't shaking—that she wasn't shaking, too many possibilities crowding in on her. There were things she could do now, things she'd put aside—and things that she'd lose, over and over, never aging, never dying, but she thrust that thought aside. Where there was one Gift, there would be others, and she'd find them, bring the others with her, and they would never be alone—

"It's got you," Ashe said. There was a crooked smile on his face. "It's got you just like it gets everyone."

"What do you mean?" Cassilde ran her thumb along the inside of her arm, not even a twinge following her touch.

"People hunt them," Ashe said. "Anybody who finds one, they always want more. And, all right, most of them aren't permanent, the fix only lasts for a while, but once you've had it, you always want another one, want to keep it going. And that's a very nasty game."

"That's what your friend wanted," Cassilde said. "Who was he, Ashe?"

Ashe flinched, and took another swallow of his drink.

"Ashe." Dai leaned forward, and Ashe gave him an unhappy glance.

"He calls himself John Vertrage these days, but you'd have known him as Lucian Trager."

Dai swore under his breath, and Cassilde sighed. "The one who led the mutiny." Ashe nodded. "Which you were involved with—how?"

"It's really complicated," Ashe said.

"We've got some time," Dai said.

"Not enough for this," Ashe muttered.

"Ashe." Cassilde rested her elbows on the table.

"Well, how do you think? We were lovers." Ashe sighed. "We were both assigned to Triple R, Research, Reclamation, and Restoration. He was the only other person on our team with actual salvage experience, not to mention time on the Edge, and—he was a bright spot, had a sense of humor, a sense of how absurd so much of what we were doing really was. And he was smart, smart and knowledgeable."

"I thought fraternization was against Entente rules," Dai said.

"Oh, it is," Ashe answered. "That was maybe half the fun."

The other half would have been Darling's—Vertrage's—looks and brains, Cassilde thought, but Ashe had always liked breaking rules. "And he got you into the mutiny."

"Yeah. Though the whole thing got really messy there at the end."

Cassilde cocked her head, considering that, but Dai spoke first. "And he got you into this—you called it a game."

Ashe touched his cheek, wincing. "Yeah, and a nasty one. Like I said, most of the Gifts aren't permanent, and once people realize that, they go hunting for more. And if they can't find an unused one, they find someone else who's received one. Whatever the Ancestors did, it's carried in the blood—my best guess is that it's some kind of adaptive nanite—and so you can revive a failing Gift with blood from someone else who has one. Or at least it works most of the time. But sometimes donating blood can affect the donor's Gift, so people don't like to donate, not willingly."

"Lovely," Dai said.

Ashe ignored him. "So there's a black market, and a shadow world, the people who know about the Gifts and the people who have them and the people who want them. What we found out—Admiral Maela had a Gift, and if he took power, he was going to keep it for a very long time. That was what started the mutiny. Not that that was ever widely known except among people who already knew about them—"

"And that was why it fell apart," Cassilde said slowly. "Because half of you wanted Gifts for yourselves, and the rest wanted to stop it altogether."

"Pretty much." Ashe sighed, closing his eyes as though his bruises hurt him.

"Do you have one?" Dai demanded.

"You can see I don't." Ashe touched his bandaged nose.

"Did you have one?" Cassilde asked, and he gave another fleeing smile.

"I did. But it wasn't a good one, didn't last long." He touched his face again. "I admit, I miss it sometimes."

"If Trager—Vertrage—has a Gift of his own," Dai said, "does that mean he's not dead?"

Cassilde looked up sharply. That hadn't occurred to her, not after what she'd done to him—and surely even a Gift couldn't heal that? She hadn't been as badly injured, and it had taken everything the Gift had to cure her.

"I don't know," Ashe said. "It depends on how fresh it was, how much he's already used it."

"Which is why you wanted to put a hole in his ship," Cassilde said. Ashe shrugged.

"Maybe we should have," Dai said.

"That's not the main thing," Ashe said. "People are going to be hunting you, Silde. If anyone finds out—if John survived, he'll be hunting you."

"So we keep it secret," Dai said.

"It's not that easy," Ashe said. "Especially with anyone who knows about the Lightman's. It's going to look strange if you're just all of a sudden doing fine—"

"I didn't exactly go telling everyone I was sick," Cassilde said. "We'll figure something out." It was too much to take in, at least not more than the barest details, and she was certain Ashe hadn't told them everything even yet. But she wanted this, wanted to live—and so, she guessed, did Ashe, even if he wasn't admitting it yet. He'd come looking for the thing in the first place. "The first thing we do, we get the Guard involved, and we finish salvaging our claim. We're going to want the money, and I want Ashe to take a look at what's left of the Gift."

"Which, I will point out, I wanted to do—"

"Which was a really bad idea just at that moment," Cassilde retorted. "Once we've done that—while we're doing it—we can figure out what to do next. What we're going to do about these hunters, and their game…"

Ashe nodded, resting the cool glass against his bruised cheek. He looked abruptly exhausted, but Cassilde refused to feel sympathy.

"All right," Dai said.

"That's settled, then," Cassilde said, and hoped it was.

꒐ ꒐ ꒐ ꒐

They came within range of the Guard beacon a little more than fifteen hours later. There was still no sign of pursuit—no sign of any other ships, though she knew from studying the general claim maps that there had to be at least a few other salvors in the area—and she pinged the beacon as soon as it was within sensor range. The check codes bounced back immediately, showing everything in order, and Ashe leaned over her shoulder.

"Send a general warning. Full panic mode."

She looked back at him, frowning. "If what you said is true, no one else needs to worry unless they've got a Gift, too."

"Yes, but we don't want to let anyone know we know that." Ashe started to rub his bruised cheek, and stopped, wincing. "I told you, the people who know about this are always looking for anything that might signal another Gift. They monitor all the Guard channels, and anything out of the ordinary will get them looking. If you want to go back—"

"And I do," Dai said, from the co-pilot's chair. "We can't afford to leave that much salvage behind."

Cassilde nodded. "I agree."

"Then we have to treat this like it was an ordinary raid," Ashe said. "Hit the panic button, warn everybody in the neighborhood, demand Guard escort back to the claim and a full anti-pirate sweep. Anything else is going to draw attention."

"And a claim of killing in self-defense won't?" Dai asked.

Ashe shrugged. "That's normal. We were attacked, we fought back, we grabbed what we could and ran. That's what sensible salvage people do."

Cassilde reached for her keyboard, typing in the codes that set off the emergency calls, warnings that would run up and down the salvage frequencies. "What happens if we do draw their attention? These...hunters, I mean."

"They come looking," Ashe said. "They'll want to know what kind of Gift you've received, and they're not going to be real picky about how they test it. I want to look at the mechanism first myself."

Cassilde shivered. For all that the Lightman's had vanished, she had still slept badly during their last rest period, the memory of Darling's—Vertrage's—dispassionate stare as he shot her jolting her awake as she tried to fall asleep. If she'd killed him, if he didn't have a Gift of his own—she wanted to stand over his dead body, and she would gladly explain it to the local Guard if that was the price of safety. "Right," she said, and entered the codes that set off all the alarms.

To her surprise, a Guard ship responded within the hour, signal weak at first, but strengthening as it turned back to meet them. The network showed more ships gathering, the fleet stationed to protect the debris field wheeling to focus on their sector, and she could see and hear the nearer salvage ships responding as well. Dai fielded most of their questions, repeating the warnings, and then the Guard ship loomed on their screens, signaling for them to come alongside.

It was one of the smaller patrolships, heavily armed for its size, cannon mounts bristling at bow and stern and around its thick waist. The captain, wiry and graying, took their first evidence as the two ships matched course and speed, and then once the locks were mated, came aboard with his paralegal in tow.

"Arshin Lars, Avice Lekesa," he said, gesturing to the paralegal as Silde waved them to seats around the table in Central. "Looks like you've been having an interesting time of it." His eyes were on Ashe as he spoke, and Ashe waved a hand, clearly unwilling to make a face.

"A lot more interesting that we hoped for," Cassilde said, and leaned back as Dai set the teapot and a tray of mugs on the table in front of her. "We're very glad to see you."

She lifted the pot in silent question, and both the Guards nodded. She poured for all of them while Lekesa unrolled a note-board and flicked it into recording mode. Lars accepted his cup with a nod of thanks and wrapped both hands around the cup.

"I know you gave us the basics before, but let's go over it again."

"Of course." None of them had been expecting anything less, and Cassilde went through the events again, from their landing to the attack by Darling—whose name she professed not to know; the last thing they needed was to complicate matters by bringing up the mutiny—to her escape and counterattack on Darling. The last required a certain finesse, and she chose her words carefully, feeling the heat of her own cup against her fingers.

"He'd picked out Ashe as our scholar, and threatened me to make him cooperate. When Ashe said no, he shot at me. I managed to dodge and fall out of sight, and somehow he didn't realize he hadn't hurt me as badly as he'd thought."

"I helped," Ashe said, his voice dry, and Cassilde allowed herself a wry smile.

"That you did." She looked at Lars, wiling her face to show nothing but innocent relief. "He faked giving me first aid, bandaged me up so the pirate leader couldn't see, and then he told them that the thing they were looking for was in the other compartment. Nobody had taken my blaster, so I was able to get the drop on them. I shot them all—" Her voice wavered at that, with no need for pretense: she had never killed anyone before, and wasn't at all sure she liked the feeling. "And then we ran. As I said, we're very glad to see you."

"Lucky you were able to fool them," Lekesa said, not looking up from her note-board.

Cassilde nodded. "I guess—they seemed like they were in a hurry? And kind of wild with it. I really didn't think it would work." Dai reached across the table to cover her hand with his own, and Cassilde returned the pressure of his fingers.

"What I'd like to know," Lars said, "is what this guy was looking for."

"Wouldn't we all," Ashe muttered.

Lekesa looked up. "It sounds like he knew you."

"I'm not without a reputation," Ashe said.

"It would be easy to figure out which of us was the scholar," Cassilde said. "Just pull public records. That's what I assumed they'd done."

"We'll come back to that," Lars said. "Let's stick with what this person was looking for."

"Something special," Ashe said promptly. "Something that should have been clearly visible, only it wasn't. He thought I knew what it was, and I didn't see that I gained anything by contradicting him."

"Something special," Lars said. "Such as?"

Ashe spread his hands in a fair imitation of a man surrendering a position. "Look, I'd heard the same thing about this particular piece of salvage. If you dug deep enough into the archives on Cambyse, you can turn up some hints that there was something on this palace that was unusual. If you accept the identification, of course, but that's a different question. Anyway, I thought it was worth the bid."

"What did you think would be there?" Lars took another sip of his tea.

"Toys," Ashe answered. "This was clearly residential space, and that's the most valuable thing you're likely to find—along with the elements, of course. But a fully functioning toy, especially a rare variety, or even something unique—you know as well as I do what that would be worth. But we didn't find anything like that."

Dai stirred. "He was pretty pissed that he didn't find it. Accused us of having found it first, hiding it from him. That was what was really scary. I'd have given him the thing, but we didn't have it."

Lekesa lifted an eyebrow at that, and Cassilde could hardly blame her. It wasn't very likely that Darling would have let them walk away even if they had given up the Gift. Though maybe he might, for Ashe's sake?

"Well, thanks to Silde, we didn't have to," Ashe said.

"So you have no idea what your attacker was looking for?" Lars said. Dai shook his head.

"He didn't want elements," Ashe said. "There were several exposed caches, easy for them to grab. But they weren't interested."

"It had to be some kind of toy," Cassilde said. "Some sort of device. That's the only thing that makes any sense. Only whatever it was, it wasn't there."

"It still seems pretty amazing to me that Misor Sam here wasn't more seriously injured," Lekesa said.

"We were damn lucky," Dai growled, and even Lekesa seemed silenced by that.

Lars cleared his throat. "Have you ever heard of something called a Miracle Box? Or perhaps a Milagro, or a Gift?"

Cassilde froze, breath stopped in her chest, and saw Ashe shake his head with a fair assumption of impatience.

"There's no such thing. They're a myth."

"There are one or two shrines that demonstrably functioned as sources of healing," Lars said mildly.

"True enough," Ashe said. "I—that was a sweeping generalization, and those are always wrong. But I do know that Miracle Boxes don't exist today. Or at least nobody's ever found one, and you know that if they had, we'd all have heard about it. It would be the biggest Ancestral discovery since—well, since the Ancestors themselves."

Lekesa gave a brief smile at that, but Lars shook his head. "The stories are very…persistent. And all very much alike. A lot of people think there's some truth behind them."

"That may be," Ashe said. He was doing an excellent imitation of a stubborn academic, Cassilde thought, and made herself breathe. "But if something is found, it won't be what the stories describe. Miraculous healing, people brought back from the dead, the lame walking and the blind seeing. I just don't believe it."

For some reason, a song from the crèche ran through Cassilde's head. *I am the doctor come to town—I make the blind to walk again, I make the lame to see again.* She remembered exchanging wary glances with the rest of her covey—they had been very young then, just assigned to each other—before Remy had raised his hand to point out that lame people could see just fine. The helpers had collapsed in giggles, and the teacher had explained that, yes, that was the joke…

"One rumor we've heard," Lekesa said, "is that there was a Miracle Box in this debris field."

"If there is," Ashe said, and touched his bandaged face, "we sure didn't find it."

"The government—and the Universities, of course—are extremely interested in any information about these boxes," Lars said. "They'll pay well for the data."

"Then I wish we had some to sell," Cassilde said, with what she hoped was a calm smile.

They went through the story a second time, and then a third, while Lekesa made notes and occasionally interjected comments and questions of her own. Cassilde carefully did not look at the display board set into the wall between the storage cases, not wanting to think about the time they were losing—time that someone else could be spending on their claim, time for the bodies to deteriorate, orbits to decay, the damaged pieces of the ship to shift against each other and render the various elements inaccessible. All of that was unlikely, but it still irked her to have to take the risk.

At last, however, Lekesa looked up from her board. "Statements," she said, and Lars nodded.

"If you'll read through and sign…"

Cassilde reached for her own board and unrolled it with a snap. The file was waiting, and she read through it quickly, then signed and thumb-printed it in the blocks required. The others copied her more slowly, and she looked at Lars.

"I understand—I've never been jumped before, not like this. Is it right that we can ask for an escort back to our claim, and for protection while we work it?"

Lars nodded. "We'll be glad to do it, particularly if you'll authorize us to look over the pirates' ship."

"You're welcome to it," Cassilde said. "As long as it doesn't affect our claim, of course, but I can't see that it would. You're welcome to look over the claim, too." That was something of a calculated risk, but she thought it was better to offer before they had to ask.

"And clean up the bodies," Lekesa said, but her smile was almost friendly.

"Not really our specialty," Ashe said, and matched her smile.

𝔸 𝕝𝕝𝕤 ✗ 𝟟

The Guards returned to their ship, and the two ships undocked, the patrolship signaling for *Carabosse* to follow her back through the debris field. Cassilde set the autopilot and brought the engines up to speed, one eye on the fuel gauges. She had spent more than planned in the headlong flight from the claim, and she was relieved when the patrolship settled for an economical burn. She adjusted the sensor net to its maximum, seeing half a dozen new bright sparks appear ahead of them: the other patrolships, sweeping through the debris field in search of the pirates. In the co-pilot's seat, Dai touched his own keys, tuning to each of the transponders in turn, and they both watched as numbers swam up out of the dark.

"Even if," Cassilde began, and Dai looked sideways at her.

"Do you really think this guy, Vertrage—do you think he has a Gift like yours?"

"I don't know." Cassilde sighed. "Fifty hours ago, I didn't know there was such a thing."

"I know. What were you going to say?"

"Just that even if we didn't kill him, I don't think he's going to stick around to wait for us. He knows we went for the Guard. The smart thing to do is to cut his losses."

"The only sensible thing," Dai agreed, but there was a twist to his mouth that told her that he, too, was thinking of Ashe.

Cassilde sighed. "I should have let Ashe put a hole in that ship."

The hatch rolled back as she spoke, and Ashe leaned against the back of her chair.

"I wish you had."

"Too late now," Dai said.

Cassilde leaned back to bring Ashe into her line of sight. "Do you think he's still alive?"

Ashe hesitated. "He had a Gift when I left. You did some serious damage, but not so much that a good Gift couldn't heal it."

"Why the hell didn't you tell me that before?" Cassilde demanded.

"Because it would have taken too long to explain." Ashe glared back at her. "I'd have had to convince you that the Gifts exist, and then that John had one, and all the while his clock would have been running. The last thing we needed was to fight him a second time."

There was enough truth to the words that Cassilde looked away, groping for an argument she wasn't sure existed.

"You said the Gifts don't last," Dai said, after a moment. "Why? Or do we know?"

"Everything the Ancestors made fades in the end," Ashe said. "Even GREEN, though it lasts the longest. The elements decay, toys lose their potency, the Great Works have ground to a halt. The Lesser Sun of Callambhal Above went dark in the end. Devices fall asleep and cannot be awakened, the palaces crumble and fall from space. The Gifts work miracles, but not forever. Nothing of the Ancestors is forever."

Cassilde looked back at the display, the dull purple lines of the sensor net barely visible against the background. A handful of symbols was scattered across the lines, pieces of the debris field, a salvage ship working its claim, another maneuvering through a particularly dense area, the last of the patrolships spreading out to search for any more pirates. The sensor networks were GOLD-based, just as the REFTL drive ran on RED cores triggered by BLUE command circuits—the entire faster-than-light system had been reverse engineered from Ancestral and Successor finds, and adapted to run on elemental units rather than whatever the Ancestors had used.

She had been to Elimm in the Middle Synchrony, and gaped at the Great Works, channels and wheels and geared gates cut deep into the barren land beyond the settled forests. It was said that as recently as a hundred years ago, some of the wheels had still turned, moving gates that diverted the infrequent rains from one channel to another, or sending great showers of sparks into the air. They were all still now, silent and motionless, the channels slowly beginning to fill with fine dust as whatever Ancestral trick had kept them empty failed, too. And if the Gift failed—if Gifts always failed—would the Lightman's return? She saw the same shocked realization in Dai's face, and spoke before he could make it real.

"Some things last. The lighthouses on Kells, and Callambhal Below."

"Those are both Successor adaptations of Ancestral devices," Dai said.

"What the Successors could do, we can learn," Cassilde said, and tried not to remember that the Successors, too, had fallen into the Dark. She looked at Ashe. "And besides, you said the Gifts could be renewed, or that people went looking for replacements."

"It's a nasty game, Silde." Ashe rested his elbows on the back of her chair, dropping his head so that he didn't have to meet her eyes. "It's not even a game. People kill for Gifts—literally—and anyone with a new Gift, anyone who's new to the hunt, they're terribly vulnerable. If John's alive, and he guesses how good this Gift was—he and everyone else will come after us. After you."

Cassilde shivered, silenced in spite of herself by his sudden vehemence, but Dai turned to glare at him.

"But you're not new to this, Ashe. You said it yourself, you've had a Gift, and you and Vertrage are old friends. You know how this all works, so just how vulnerable are we?"

Ashe straightened. "A hell of a lot more than I'd like."

"And I'd like some more details," Dai said.

"I've told you everything—"

"No, you haven't," Cassilde said. "Talk, Ashe."

He drew a deep breath, looking from one to the other. "Yes, I had a Gift. John gave it to me. No, it didn't last, and John knew it wouldn't. It—" He stopped, shaking his head, and looked at Cassilde. "You know what it's like. I felt twice as alive, better than healthy, like nothing I'd ever imagined..." His voice trailed off, and Cassilde glanced up and back to see his eyes focused on nothing, on some memory sharp enough to shorten his breath.

"Well, I don't know what it's like," Dai said, and Ashe shook himself back to the moment.

"You should try one some time."

"Not interested," Dai said. "Tell us about the damn game."

"I don't—you have to understand, I wasn't part of it until the war," Ashe said. "And that distorted things. They played by different rules because the war changed everything. But. Pretty much everyone who has a Gift is already hunting their next one, or trying to make a deal with someone to find a site or get a sample to keep their Gift going. Anyone who's new to the hunt, who doesn't know the value of what they have, they're presumed to be fair game. So one common trick is to spread the word about a new Gift, and then offer to help its bearer out of the resulting trouble. John liked that maneuver."

"You think he'd try that on us?" Cassilde couldn't hide her skepticism. "After what he did?"

Ashe shrugged. "You're alive. I wouldn't put it past him. If he survived, of course."

"But assuming he didn't," Cassilde said, "how are the hunters going to know I have anything?"

"If we're lucky, they won't, at least not for a while," Ashe answered. "But there were rumors about this find, more than what I had from my mote, and eventually someone's going to figure it out. It's just a matter of time."

Dai scowled. "Maybe you should have explained things a little better before we started."

Cassilde unwound herself from her chair, still startled at the easy speed of her movements, the lack of pain. "Enough. We're where we are—and the Guard is curious, remember, so let's not give them anything to think about." Dai grimaced, but waved a hand in agreement.

Ashe nodded. "Yeah. I'm betting Lars knows about the hunt,

even if he doesn't have a Gift himself."

She was standing close enough to feel the warmth of Ashe's body, treacherously pleasant. "So. What's our next best move?"

"Finish the job," Dai said, under his breath. "This isn't going to be cheap."

"Dai's right," Ashe said, with a sudden, wry grin. "Get everything we can out of the claim, keep as much GREEN as we can hold, sell the rest for the best price. And I want to look at what's left of the Gift, though that's going to be tricky with the Guard climbing all over everything. Then I say we go back to Cambyse and look for a job that'll take us out of the system. We want to break the trail as soon as we can."

"So basically do what we'd have done anyway?" Cassilde lifted an eyebrow.

"Pretty much." Ashe stopped, shaking his head. "God, Silde, you look so much better than you did. I—" He stopped again, reaching tentatively for her shoulder. When she didn't resist, he pulled her close, and Dai joined them in an awkward hug. Cassilde closed her eyes, momentarily overwhelmed by sheer sensation—and if this was part of the Gift, what would sex be like?—but then Dai's hands closed too tightly on her ribs, and she pulled away again.

"You do look better," Dai said. "I was—getting concerned."

"I'm all right now," she said, and imagined she could feel the Gift vibrating within her, like the hum of a plucked string. She rested her cheek against the nearest chest—Ashe, this time, just as it was unmistakably Dai's hand splayed against the small of her back. "And then we can find Gifts for you."

She felt Ashe stiffen, looked up to see a crooked smile cross his face. "I wouldn't say no."

"I would." Dai didn't release them, but she felt his hand tighten and then relax. "You said it yourself, Ashe, it's a nasty game."

"We're in it anyway," Ashe said. "As long as Silde has it, and as long as we're with her."

Dai shook his head, and Cassilde pulled herself free. "We can argue that out later. For now, we've got work to do."

The thought nagged at her, though, all through the long latewatch looking over Ashe's shoulder while he rebuilt his models, refining the interior volumes and adding in the elemental caches he had found. Why would one not want the Gift, freedom from illness and injury— from death itself, if Ashe was right, though she found it hard to believe that even something of the Ancestors could truly make one immortal. The Gifts wore out, just like everything else—Ashe had said as much, said that that was the point of the hunt, to find new Gifts, and to keep the old ones going. To be free of the Lightman's was astonishing, as near to a miracle as anything she could imagine; she kept stopping to fill her lungs, reveling in the way the air moved easily into every sac and cell.

She didn't say anything until after she and Dai were in bed, the lights dimmed to only the faint telltales of the sleeping display board. Ashe had been and gone, muttering something about his models; the telltales glowed dull reassuring green, the autopilot tracking both the programmed course and the position of the escorting patrolship, and she slid a hand under the sheets, tucking her fingers beneath Dai's ribcage. He shifted closer with a semi-interrogative grunt, and she said, "Did you mean it? About the Gift?"

"What?"

"That you don't want one."

"I don't. At least, I don't think I do."

She could feel the curve of his smile as he rolled to let her settle against his shoulder. "You wouldn't believe—I can't tell you how good it feels."

"You were sick." Dai's arms tightened again, pulling her hard against him. "I thought—I wasn't sure how much longer—"

He stopped, but the words lay in the silence between them. Lightman's was fatal, incurable, and there wasn't enough GREEN on the market to have saved her, even if they had had the money.

"Me, neither."

"But you're all right. Anyone can see it."

Cassilde nodded. "Thanks to the Gift."

"I don't need one." The words stirred her hair, loose strands tickling her face. "I've always been healthy as a goat."

"Things happen." Cassilde hesitated. "And if I have one, and Ashe has one…"

"And you have to keep chasing them to keep them going," Dai said. "We're never meant to live forever."

It was the stuff of drunken nights at the Technical School: the Ancestors had been immortal, or so the stories said; had it been immortality that destroyed them? Certainly everyone knew the arguments against it, populations exploding without natural relief, the legal tangles as money and power and eventually everything of worth accrued to the few who had simply lived long enough. Not that we're not still terribly short of people, Cassilde thought, still trying to claw our way back out of the last Long Dark. It had been fear of another collapse that had fed the mutiny and stopped the war, fear of a Third Dark when they were still not recovered from the Second.

But right now, we could absorb a long-lived population, and their children—and do the children of someone with a Gift inherit the Gift? For that matter, were the Ancestors in fact immortal? There were stories that divided them into classes, the godlike Firstborn and their lesser siblings, the sturdy Secondborn from whom most humans were descended and the purpose-bred Facienda, who had mostly vanished when their marginally habitable worlds had been abandoned. Those were Entente stories, including the great Dedalor Cycle, not the Verge tales she had grown up with, that she could recite in her sleep. It would probably be a good idea to reread them, though; Ashe was bound to have loaded them into the ship's library, and she had never bothered to remove them.

"We don't know that," she said softly. "We don't know we aren't the Ancestors' heirs."

Dai sighed and mumbled something, and it was only with an effort that Cassilde refrained from punching him. That was one of his most annoying habits, his ability to fall asleep between one conversation and the next. But it had been, she admitted, a long few days. He had more reason than usual. Instead, she settled more comfortably against him, willing herself to relax toward sleep.

CHAPTER FIVE

The claim rotated slowly in the screen, the automated beacon strobing at the bottom of its shallow landing pit, acknowledgement of their code and of the Guard's authority streaming across the display. Everything was pretty much as they had left it, Cassilde thought, except for Darling's ship. She could see her own abandoned equipment, planted just below the claim's south pole, but the northern pole was empty.

"Lovely," Dai said, from the co-pilot's seat, and behind him Ashe sighed.

"I was afraid of that."

"So you said," Cassilde answered, more sharply than she'd intended. "And what do you want to tell the Guard?"

Before Ashe could answer, the light on the comm board flashed green, and Lars' voice came from the speakers overhead.

"We're picking up the ID beacon, and we see your gear, but no sign of a ship."

"When we ran, it was locked to the north pole," Cassilde answered, and promptly muted her mic. "Well? Any ideas?"

"Be surprised," Ashe said. "We thought for sure we'd killed him, we don't know what happened."

"The ship's gone now," Lars said. "My scan crew says they can see where they were latched on, though."

Dai touched keys, framing a query for the GOLD sensor net. "I see organic matter in the center of the claim."

Cassilde switched her mic on again. "So do we. So I guess one of them got away?"

"I thought you said you were sure you killed them," Lars said.

"I was." Cassilde shrugged. "I really was. But we didn't stay to be sure. We were afraid they might have friends."

There was a moment of silence, and Cassilde realized she was holding her breath, but then Lars said, "We show a decent atmosphere still on board. How does your airlock look?"

"Pinging in now," Cassilde answered, and nodded to Dai.

He touched keys, and together they watched the results take form on the secondary screen. "No visible damage, systems check is clean, airlock says it functions. Looks like we've still got most of our air."

"How much?" Cassilde manipulated visual scanners as she spoke, extending magnification to go over the airlock's surface one more time.

"Ninety percent plus/minus two. We won't need tanks, it'll just be a little thinner than optimum."

"Or we can top it up," Ashe said.

"Or that," Cassilde agreed. "Air's expensive, let's see how long it's likely to take us to get our goods." She touched the mic control again. "Captain Lars. All our tests show that the lock is functional, and there's still air in the claim. We don't have any strangers on our sensor net, either. What do we do next?"

"We'll need to remove the bodies and examine the crime scene," Lars answered. "I'd like to have you on the claim while we do that. Once we've finished our investigation, you'll be free to clear the claim."

"And you'll stay on site till we're finished?"

"Or until we're called to something more urgent," Lars answered.

"Right," Cassilde said, and saw Dai roll his eyes. "We'd better get on with it, then."

She took the controls herself, maneuvering *Carabosse* over the lock's exterior hatch, and lowering them gently until the mechanical connectors slid home. Dai confirmed that the electrical connections were intact in spite of their emergency ascent, and Carabosse settled into her previous position, the Guard ship hovering a hundred meters above and to their left.

"We confirm a solid connection," Cassilde said, into the intership mic, and Lars answered promptly.

"Looks good from here. Permission to dock to your side hatch?"

Like hell. Cassilde kept her finger off the mic button a moment longer, then said, "You'd be welcome, but I'm worried what it would do to my hull if you have to break off in a hurry."

"Let us do a temporary tube, then," Lars said, and Cassilde sighed. At least she could keep the airlock closed on her side, though there was no way to keep the Guard from searching Carabosse while her crew was on the claim.

"Go ahead," she answered, and was pleased that her reluctance wasn't audible. "We'll get the fields working, you'll have power and gravity once you get here."

Somewhat to her surprise, Lars stayed on the Guard ship, and it was Lekesa and a hard-bitten man introduced as Bijay, plus a tiny forensic technician bent nearly double under the weight of her kit who came on board. Cassilde helped haul the equipment through the airlock, and stood upright in the first chamber, wrinkling her nose at the unpleasant smell.

"Oh, that's not nice."

"Smells like you killed at least one of them," Lekesa said, and the technician looked up from her screen.

"Yes. Human tissues, been dead just about as long as they said— fits so far." She started down the corridor, following something on her displays, and the others exchanged glances.

"Forensics," Bijay said, as though the word tasted bad, and Lekesa nodded.

"We'll go with her. I'll want you to identify the bodies, and then we'll get them out of here. Unless I have some more questions."

Cassilde grimaced, but nodded. Out of the corner of her eye, she could see that Dai was looking pale and unhappy, and looked back to see Ashe raise his eyebrows. He said nothing, however, and she followed Lekesa through the tangle of broken furniture into the double room with its central pillars, and then, the smell growing stronger, into the room with the glittering streusel walls. The hole that Vertrage had cut gaped empty, the metal blackened around the edges, and three bodies lay slumped against the bulkhead. The smell of spoiled meat hung in the air, and Cassilde pinched her nose shut.

"There should be four—"

Ashe put a hand on her shoulder, warning rather than comfort, and she caught her breath. The bodies were yellow, the exposed skin waxy, the faces weirdly shrunken, as though the flesh was loose on the bones. But those were unmistakably Vertrage's men, and Vertrage himself— There was a stain on the floor, the charred mark of a blaster, that had obviously been blocked by something, and brown smears that might have been blood.

"There's three now," Lekesa said.

The technician, oblivious, went to her knees beside the first body, unslinging her kit to begin a preliminary scan. She brushed against an out-flung arm, and the smell was suddenly stronger, stains newly visible on the floorplates.

Cassilde took a step back. "There were four of them. I know I shot four of them."

Dai nodded, his hand covering nose and mouth as well. We should have brought masks, Cassilde thought.

"These two died of blaster wounds," the technician said. "I'll do a full autopsy once we're back on the ship. And…" She waved a wand over the floor stains, which abruptly flushed vivid blue. "That's human blood, too. So—three wounded, one escaped?"

"Looks like," Bijay said.

"Get the bodies bagged," Lekesa said. "Misor Sam—what's down that corridor?"

"One more room," Cassilde said. "Round, with more furniture and some light-grooves on the walls and floor."

"Better make sure your guy didn't crawl off there to die." Lekesa ducked through the hatch without waiting for an answer.

"Oh, come on," Ashe said. "The ship's missing, too."

"Yeah," Bijay said, "but if you guys shot him all to hell, like you did those guys—" He jerked his head at the bodies and the oblivious technician. "—how the hell did he manage to walk out of here?"

"Damned if I know," Cassilde said. "I was sure I killed him." She bent her head to follow Lekesa, Ashe at her heels. Behind her, there was a crackle of static as the technician signaled the Guard ship.

The worklights were still in place on the wall, their strong beams filling the curved space. The walls still showed the same faint iridescence, and the silver-webbed beds were still firmly attached to the floor, the odd spiral chair rising like a horn from the wider part of the curve. The alcove was still in shadow, but the curtain of red threads that had covered it was gone, not even dust remaining. There were stains on the floor beside the nearest of the beds, and Lekesa stooped to examine them.

"Looks like blood."

"It probably is," Cassilde said, and shivered in spite of herself, remembering the sudden searing pain. "Their leader—"

Ashe put his arm around her shoulders—comfort, it would have looked like from the outside, but she drew breath, nodding at the reminder.

"That's where I fell. I cut myself in the process."

The marks were small, one large patch the size of her thumb, a scattering of smaller droplets: the shot had cauterized the wound, though of course she couldn't say that. Ashe tightened his hold, and she leaned unashamedly into his support. Lekesa eyed her unhappily.

"You were damn lucky."

Cassilde nodded, made her voice small. "Yeah. I know."

"That guy definitely didn't come in here," Bijay said. "She must have knocked him out, and when he came to, he dragged himself back onto his ship and ran." Lekesa nodded.

"I really thought," Cassilde began, and shook her head. "I wish I had killed him. Now he's out there—"

"Claim jumpers don't usually carry grudges," Lekesa said. "Not unless they were looking for something specific."

"Well, they must have been," Dai began, and Lekesa shook her head.

"I meant something that you all knew was here, that they might be able to get by hijacking you. Otherwise, there's no point. They don't usually waste their time chasing after people unless there's something very specific involved, something that's worth a lot of money. They're just not generally that stupid."

There was a definite note of impatience in her voice, and Cassilde allowed herself to relax a little. "So. What happens next? Can we start working again? I know your captain doesn't want to have to stay and babysit us."

"That's our job," Lekesa said. She turned, surveying the compartment. "Sure, you can go ahead and get started in here. We'll let you know when you can move into the rest of the rooms."

"Thanks," Cassilde said, and Dai echoed her.

Lekesa motioned for Bijay to return to the technician, and turned her back to murmur into a collar-tab transmitter. Cassilde looked at Ashe, raising her eyebrows in what she hoped was a discreet question. "Are you ready to get started?"

Ashe's mouth twitched in a wry smile, but his voice was steady and unamused. "Yeah. Dai, you've got a hand-scan?"

"Yeah." Dai lifted it in proof.

"Right." What they all wanted, Cassilde knew, was to investigate the alcove where the Gift had been, but they could hardly do that while Lekesa was standing there. "Well. Let's see what we've got. Any chance that chair thing might be a toy?"

Ashe crouched beside it, running long hands over the twisting surface. His touch left trails of color on the silver surface, brief flashes of blue and green, and Dai whistled.

"That's interesting."

"Not as interesting as you'd think," Ashe answered. "I saw a piece about this on the Cassants. They pulled out a mushroom-topped pillar with this same surface, but once it was disconnected from the original systems, the colors faded and died. As far as I know, they haven't figured out a way to revive it."

"Damn. That's a shame." Cassilde didn't have to force either her interest or her regret. She trailed her fingers around one curve, and the swirl flushed purple before it faded. "Interesting. We get different colors."

"You try," Ashe said, to Dai, and the bigger man traced another coil, leaving flashes of salmon-pink in his wake.

"Different skin temperature, different chemistry, different DNA?" Ashe shook his head.

"It's not going to pay the bills," Cassilde said, with real regret. "Not if we can't preserve it."

"We ought to try," Ashe said. "The one on the Cassants—I think it was Remarque that had it? I think they'd pay for a second piece, just for the comparison."

Cassilde let the familiar calculations wash over her, steadying her nerves. If she could just focus on the work at hand, the ordinary choices of salvage, she could forget about Gifts and deadly men with blasters...

Dai went to one knee, examining the base of the chair. Cassilde couldn't see a seam, and he shook his head, frowning. "There's no telling how deep the mechanism goes."

"Put it on the list," Cassilde said, "but at the end. We'll take it if we have the time and space to carry it."

The others nodded, Ashe with reluctance, and out of the corner of her eye, Cassilde saw Lekesa duck through the hatch and out of sight. She tipped her head in that direction, not daring to speak, and

Ashe turned instantly for the alcove, hand scanner ready. She started to follow him, but checked herself, reaching for her own scanner. "Let's see what we've got behind the walls."

Ashe was not quite done by the time Lekesa returned, but Cassilde thought they all looked blameless enough, each of them scanning a section of bulkhead. Her own scanner hummed contentedly: more GOLD, and a great deal of RED; the density of the latter seemed to increase as the compartment coiled in on the alcove. Some GREEN, though not as much as she would have expected, but still enough to put the whole expedition solidly in the black in spite of everything. Ashe moved away from the alcove, his face inscrutable, and began scanning the opposite wall, while Dai turned his attention to what was under the floor.

Lekesa cleared her throat. "So. How much longer do you think you're going to be?"

Cassilde looked up, gratefully aware that she'd lost track of time. "We've just about finished mapping here, I think—yes?" Both Dai and Ashe nodded, and she went on, "And you're right, we've been here a while. It's probably time we knocked off for the day. Will we be able to access the other volumes tomorrow?"

"I'll ask the captain," Lekesa said, "but I don't see why not." She nodded toward the alcove. "Any idea what this space was?"

Cassilde shrugged. "Ashe?"

"It's a good question." He flicked switches on his scanner and slung it over his shoulder. "Clearly, this volume focuses on that alcove, and presumably there was once something there, but now it just ends in a curl of empty space. Whatever was there is now gone—or it's possible that the emptiness is the point, that it's some sort of artistic or religious installation that privileges the blank slate. My guess, given the decorations, is that there was something. All the lines point there, all the colors shade darker toward that end of the compartment. And there is a heavier volume of both RED and GREEN behind the surface, although the GREEN has definitely faded."

"Do you think your claim jumper could have taken it?" Lekesa asked.

Ashe shook his head. "Nothing's been removed since we were here. Well, I suppose if there had been something at the very back of the space, something very thin, we might not have seen it, and he could have taken that, but—I just don't think so."

"And you've no idea what it does?" Lekesa said again.

Ashe shook his head. "Not really. Maybe if we find some control sequences once we start dismantling things I'll be able to make a better guess."

"I didn't pick up much BLUE," Cassilde said, and Dai nodded.

"Me, neither."

"Well, then." Ashe spread his hands. "I mean, obviously we'll keep looking, but..."

Lekesa nodded. "I'll talk to the captain about when you can have access to the other volumes. You'll be glad to hear that none of our ships have picked up any sign of your attacker."

"That is good news," Cassilde said, and let the Guard woman herd them back toward the airlock and Carabosse. She and Bijay crossed to the Guard ship—the technician had gone over long before, presumably with the bodies, though the air in the claim still smelled unpleasant—and Dai sealed the hatch behind them. He started to say something, but Ashe held up one finger, unslinging his scanner with the other hand. Checking for listening devices, Cassilde realized, and nodded her approval. He scanned the hatch area and then, more carefully, Central, and finally shook his head.

"I don't see anything," he said softly. "That doesn't mean they're not running a passive scan from the ship."

"I would," Cassilde said, matching his volume. "Better assume that's exactly what they're doing."

⋀ ⅏ ✕ �

They made a quick dinner, careful to talk only of their plans for salvage—where to start, what to hologram before they began disassembly, how much RED and GOLD and GREEN might be waiting once they opened up the walls—and afterward took turns in the shower, then retreated to the main cabin. It was at the core of the ship, layers of bulkhead and machinery between them and the Guard ship docked beside them, but Cassilde checked her own scanner, and then switched on a white-noise generator before she settled against the pillows. Dai joined her, smelling pleasantly of soap, and she leaned companionably against his shoulder.

"Think that'll be enough?"

"It ought to be," he answered. "If they're listening, they're only using passive sensors, and I've set the ship to alert us if it feels an active ping. That's about all I can do."

"Should work." Ashe appeared in the cabin door, still toweling his untidy hair. He hung the towel carefully on a wall hook and settled at Cassilde's other side, wedging the last pillow behind his back. "Well, that was an interesting day."

Cassilde snorted. "So I guess we have to assume that your guy, Vertrage, had a Gift, and it healed him and he ran?"

"And that his friends didn't have them," Dai said.

"Yes," Ashe said. "Or at least they didn't have Gifts that were good enough to heal them. What worries me is that the Guard clearly knows about them—the Gifts, I mean, not John and his crew."

"Suspects," Dai said. "The captain suspects that Gifts are real. If he knew anything, he'd be pushing a whole lot harder."

"Or not," Ashe said. "He doesn't know what we know."

"I think Dai's right," Cassilde said. "You said yourself, this whole thing, this hunt, has been kept secret. Once one of the Guard knows, you'd have official interest."

"Only if they were honest," Ashe muttered, and Dai punched his shoulder.

"No reason to think this one isn't."

"If the men we killed did have Gifts," Cassilde said, "or if they had one at one time, and it—ran out?"

"Failed," Ashe said, and there was a bitterness in his tone that she couldn't miss.

"Could the Guard tell that from an autopsy?"

"Probably. If they know to look." Ashe rested his head against the bulkhead. "Not that I expect they'd tell us if they did, and if they did, we couldn't do anything except act surprised."

"You couldn't say you'd read something scholarly about it?" Dai asked.

"Scholars don't touch that sort of thing," Ashe said. "We're not supposed to believe in Gifts, they're legends, nothing real."

"Convenient," Dai said.

Ashe nodded. "Isn't it?"

"You don't really think that your hunters can control what the University studies," Cassilde said.

"Probably not," Ashe conceded. "But no one's ever found a fully functioning Gift, or at least not so far as the University knows. There are remains that might have been one, and there are the shrines that no one gets to study for fear of disrupting whatever it is they do—and none of them are producing the kinds of miracles they did in their heyday, so there's even more reason not to touch them—but nothing you can unequivocally say, 'that was a Gift.'"

"There's nothing we can do about it, then," Cassilde said. "Did you find out anything useful about my Gift?"

"Not particularly. It was there, all right, and it took an enormous amount of power—did you see how much GREEN was behind the bulkhead?"

"I saw how pale it was," Dai said. "Most of it won't be worth recovering."

Ashe nodded. "I think the curtain was some sort of compound of RED. It might even have been pure RED, in an unusual form. It transmitted the Gift as it was absorbed into your body."

Cassilde looked at her hands, no longer flecked with spots and sun-scars, golden skin darker than Dai's pallor, ruddier than Ashe's dark complexion. Her flesh seemed fuller, body not as gaunt as it had been. The idea of some elemental compound circulating in her bloodstream, lacing bone and tissue and organs, was still hard to accept. She made herself speak calmly. "That would match what I experienced. The curtain—I don't know if you got a good look at it, Ashe, but it was made up of a lot of fine strands, like heavy sewing thread. When I got within reach, it wrapped around me, pulled me into that last curve, and the next thing I knew, I was fine. I think I remember a few threads falling off me, but it seems like they were dissolving into dust at the same time." She shrugged. "I was worrying about other things at that moment."

"For which we are grateful," Dai said, and wrapped one arm around her. She rested her head on his shoulder, unexpectedly content.

"That matches the best guess, that the Gift is some kind of adaptive nanite," Ashe said. "I wish I understood more of what that mote was trying to tell me. I mean, I thought there was a Gift, but I had no idea how powerful it was going to be."

"I wish you did, too," Cassilde said. "Any chance you could figure it out with a little more time?"

"I'd like to say yes, but I doubt it." Ashe ran a toe along her ankle, hard calluses on thin skin, and she shuddered, the sensation too close to pain. "I've done everything I can to enhance it, I've got what I've got. It was meant to interface with a larger dataset."

They sat in silence for a little while, Cassilde once again aware of how sensitive her skin had become. She could feel the hairs on Dai's arms, the cracked edge of Ashe's foot and the well-worn fabric of his sleep pants, so thin and soft that she could feel the span of the tendon beside his knee. Her own hair was a distraction, dark strands tickling her neck; the air from the ventilators covered her like a blanket. It was all too much, suddenly, too many sensations and at the same time none of them strong enough. She turned to wrap her arms around

Ashe's neck, drawing him in for a kiss, focusing all her attention on the meeting of lips.

He made a pleased sound, or perhaps that was Dai, shifting to put his hands on her hips, pulling her back against his chest. His hands slid under her shirt, upward to cup her breasts, and she gasped at the sensation of his fingers against her nipples. She had always liked that, but this...this was extraordinary, overwhelming in its intensity, almost enough to distract her entirely from Ashe's kiss.

Ashe pulled back as though he'd felt her sudden inattention, then leaned past her to kiss Dai. Dai made an approving noise, and Cassilde leaned back, letting her head rest on Dai's shoulder. He ran a hand down her ribs from breast to hip and back again and in the same moment Ashe ran both hands up the insides of her thighs. That touch was almost too strong, a wave of sensation, and she was glad of the cloth bunching under her hands to slow things down. But then Dai shifted her, lifting and turning so that Ashe could hook clever fingers into her waistband and peel her clothes away in a single movement. She closed her eyes, every finger that touched her hot as iron, cupping her breasts, sliding up her thighs and between her legs and then in, one finger and then two, while Ashe's thumb circled her clit. Dai breathed something in her ear, more sound than word. Her climax was rising, she could feel it building, concentrated on the hand between her legs as she thrust back against him. She was there, and then in a heartbeat it was gone, drowned in a cacophony of sensations that jangled out of rhythm, out of time. She drew up her knees, folding forward.

"Too much, too much."

Both men instantly withdrew, Dai's body tensing as though he wanted to make himself smaller, and she caught her breath, allowing herself a snort of rueful laughter.

"I'm fine, it's not you. I think—apparently the Gift has more effects than I realized."

Ashe laughed, looking relieved. "There are worse problems to have."

"I need to figure out what works," Cassilde began, and this time it was Dai who laughed, the sound rumbling against her skin.

"We're always happy to help," Ashe said, and she rolled out from between them.

"No, no, carry on."

"If you're sure," Ashe began, and Dai flattened him.

"My turn."

Cassilde settled comfortably to watch as Dai brought Ashe to his climax, the scholar's eyes closed, lost for once in sensation. Then together she and Ashe tackled Dai, taking turns until they finally collapsed together in a tangle of arms and legs. After a few minutes, Cassilde unwound herself enough to collect a pillow, and settled it under her head as she stretched, sweaty and sticky and content. This was not what she had expected of the Gift, but— She smiled to herself. She was willing to learn its quirks.

ᚠ ᛰ ᛉ ᛡ

The air in the claim smelled better with the bodies removed, and Cassilde bled a little more oxygen into the mix in the hopes of counteracting what was left. Whether it worked or not, she couldn't tell; there was too much left to worry about besides a few bad smells. They fell into the old routine quickly enough, surveying each compartment as the Guard permitted to see what was behind the bulkheads, and then Ashe took the readings for the 3D mapping while she and Dai made a more detailed scan and planned the cuts that would give them the largest chunks of the elements. They would begin with the compartment where the Gift had been—there was more RED and GREEN there than in any other of the compartments, she explained, when Lekesa asked, and didn't say they would have started there anyway to look for as much evidence of the Gift as possible.

It was always hard to make the first cut, particularly in compartments like these that had been designed for beauty. For once, though, Ashe didn't complain, and Cassilde reached for a marker, drew a fluorescent green line along what she and Dai had identified as an invisible seam. "Good?"

Dai lifted his scanner. "Good."

"Cutting." Cassilde flipped down her visor and saw the others do the same, then aimed the cutter at the green line. This was precision work: she kept the power to the necessary minimum and kept the beam at five centimeters as she moved slowly along the mark. The metal hissed and popped, familiar sounds that meant she was cutting just deep enough and not damaging the Ancestral elements beneath. The first cut finished, she made the shorter cross-cuts, and then Dai and Ashe pried away the first long strip of bulkhead. Behind it was the usual jet black matrix, the surface rough and pebbled as though it were woven from millions of fibers laid haphazardly against each other. A long streak of GOLD was immediately visible, maybe ten centimeters deep and 120 centimeters long, running the full length of the cut. In the work-lights, the color seemed paler than usual, shading toward lemon rather than the true deep gold, and Cassilde made a face.

"Does that look faded to you?"

"It might do," Dai answered.

"To me, too," Ashe said, but stepped forward to scan the opening anyway. "I suppose we should expect it, if whatever was in the alcove has been activated."

Cassilde pulled on a glove and wiggled the nearest piece of GOLD. It came away on the second tug, and she shook her head. "That's not good. And I'm not seeing any BLUE, either." BLUE carried instructions; GOLD absorbed those instructions and translated them into data or into further instructions that RED turned into action.

"Try a little to the left," Ashe suggested, and Cassilde cut another test strip.

This one, completed, showed a solid nest of BLUE, its hexagons linked and relinked to form a roughly spherical node about the size of Dai's fist. That, at least, was familiar—complex instructions seemed to be relayed through those nodes—and the color was true. The cut also revealed another stripe of faded GOLD, and they followed it up the wall, revealing two more smaller BLUE nodes. There was also a tiny fleck of GREEN, about the size of Cassilde's thumb; it, too, was faded, but even flawed GREEN was worth good money.

They worked their way back down toward the alcove, peeling back pieces of bulkhead to reveal increasingly large sheets of RED. The linked tetrahedrons rose above the rough matrix in ever-increasing waves, but their color faded as their size increased, until the surface was more pink than scarlet. Cassilde opened a test strip all the way to the alcove, and around the curve. The deposits of RED were half a meter deep, but bleached almost white in spots.

"Well," Cassilde said, looking over her shoulder at Ashe. She didn't dare say what she was thinking, just in case the Guard was eavesdropping, but Ashe nodded as though he understood.

"Something drained this entire cache—whatever was in the alcove, I suppose." His voice was relaxed, purely thoughtful, though Cassilde could read the tension in his shoulders. "Must have taken a fair amount of power."

"Scan said there was GREEN in there," Dai said. "Let's see what it looks like."

Cassilde worked the cutter again, carving away a smaller square to reveal a lump of GREEN. It looked as though several of the cylindrical units had fused, forming a thicker lobular unit about as wide as her palm. The outer edges were faded, not as badly as the RED around it, but when Cassilde worked it loose from the matrix, the piece fell apart along the lobes into three cylinders that showed true GREEN at their heart. She held them out, wordless—each one was easily worth twenty thousand consols—and Ashe whistled softly.

"Not bad," Dai said, and placed them carefully into the padded carrier he wore slung across his body. He wouldn't remove it until they were back on Carabosse and the GREEN was locked in the ship's safe.

"Not bad at all," Cassilde agreed. A few more finds like that, and they would be set for years.

The compartment yielded no more GREEN, however, and most of the RED was too badly bleached to be worth salvaging. They packed up the BLUE nodes and the better pieces of GOLD, and Ashe shook his head.

"I hate leaving anything. Even the scrap."

The scrap was worth money, of course; any fragment of the Ancestral Elements could be sold on the open market. "We aren't going to have space for all of this," Cassilde said. "Or if we do, it's going to be really tight, especially after we spent all that fuel running for the Guard. We prioritize now, and see how much we can take once we're ready to lift."

"Ashe just doesn't like seeing the place cut apart," Dai said.

"Well, I don't." Ashe shook his head. "The 3Ds aren't the same."

"Do you still have a University contract for those?" Cassilde asked, as they made their way back through the claim. There were other people who'd pay more, if Ashe was free of that obligation.

"Yeah." He shrugged, reading her disappointment. "It was part of my student funding agreement."

"No worries," Cassilde answered, though she couldn't help feeling a little disappointment. But there was no point in being greedy: they were going to walk away with enough of the elements to live on for a year and put money in the bank. Even if they were driven off tonight, the GREEN in Dai's carrier was solid money, and the other elements they'd salvaged would bring in solid profit. Not to mention the toys, though Ashe would have a better idea of what they were worth. All this, and she was cured of Lightman's, too? She flicked her fingers in crabbed propitiation, the old silent-signs A-I, for Ankes and Irthe, Anketil and Irtholin, the heroes who held off the First Dark. Surely this wasn't too good to last.

𝕂 𝕎 𝕏 𝕐

Over they next few days, they worked their way through the rest of the claim, finding a handful of tiny toys in the compartment where Vertrage's men had died, then opening the walls further to get at the rest of the elements hiding behind the paneling. They had gotten the best of it in their first, hurried search, Cassilde realized, but there was still enough BLUE and GOLD to make the effort worthwhile, and the toys were unusual enough to bring a decent profit. Lekesa appeared at irregular intervals to see what they were doing, sometimes with Bijay in tow, sometimes with another technician whom she didn't introduce. Cassilde did her best to be polite, and Ashe, to her private amusement, was happy to put on a show of academic blather that was calculated to bore the Guard to tears. Still, she was able to gather that the other Guard ships had found no sign of Vertrage, and was unsurprised when Lars contacted her at the end of the fifth day.

She took the call in Central, Dai and Ashe listening out of camera range, schooling herself to remain unsurprised no matter what happened. "Captain Lars."

"Misor Sam. I'm calling to tell you that the rest of my squad has found no sign of your raider, and are being returned to regular patrol duty."

"I'll take that as good news," Cassilde said.

"We also need to return to our normal patrol," Lars went on, "but of course we want to be as helpful to you as possible. The dead men have been identified, by the way, and are known criminals with Class One records."

Class One covered the more expensive felonies. Cassilde saw Dai roll his eyes, and said, "That's alarming, though I suppose we should have expected as much."

Lars ignored the comment. "How much longer do you need to finish up your work here?"

Cassilde paused. "Well, to do things properly—"

"I hate to remind you, but we're not able to support academic standards," Lars said, and Cassilde saw Ashe grin.

"Understood. Though we have always had a recording contract with the University of the Great Charter."

"We can't spare the time." In the screen, Lars spread his hands, miming apology. "This find-field is vulnerable, and we need to offer coverage to everyone."

"Understood," Cassilde said again. "Can you give us four more days?"

Lars hesitated. "I can give you three, and escort back toward Cambyse. It looks as though we'll be swinging almost within range of Outermost Station to pick up the field's leading edge."

That was an offer worth taking, even if they'd had to cut exploration even shorter: it was highly unlikely that anyone would attack them while they were under Guard escort, and Outermost Station was even better protection. "We'll take that, and thank you," she said aloud, watching Dai nod in agreement. "Let us know when you plan to lift, and we'll match schedules."

They cleared the claim in three days, despite Ashe's complaints, cramming every corner of *Carabosse* with their finds. Ashe prepared the detailed first-finders' notes, explaining what they had found, what they had taken, and where more detailed information could be found, and set it and a pinger in the claim's central volume. The debris field was drifting in long orbit; pieces might eventually spin free, or if the Dark fell again, the original knowledge could easily be lost. This would at least tell a stranger what had been there, and where to look for more.

They lifted on the morning of the fourth day, ship's time, this time carefully recovering all their equipment and using only the lightest touch of steering jets to separate from the claim. Cassilde let the light spin carry them into alignment with the Guard ship, then matched course and speed as they turned in-system toward Cambyse. They had used most of their reserve fuel in the first flight from the claim, and the Guard pilot grumbled about having to match *Carabosse*'s lighter thrust until Lars told him to shut up. They made the first course corrections, both ships settling onto the long line that would bring them into the protective circle of the Outermost Station, and Cassilde locked the autopilot with a sigh of relief.

"So what's our next step?" she asked, settling herself into her familiar chair in Central. There were toy boxes stacked in one corner, their seals warranted proof against Ancestral influences and held in place with a twist of cargo netting just in case. "Sell on Cambyse or try further in?"

"The Glasstown market's always been a good one," Dai said, measuring rice into the cooker. Cassilde felt her stomach growl: since the Gift, it seems as though she was always hungry. Dai had increased the portions accordingly, but she still sometimes didn't feel as though it was enough. "We should at least offer the elements there."

Cassilde nodded. "What about the toys? Ashe, you said prices were still better in the Entente."

"We need to sell everything as fast as we can, and get the hell out of this sector," Ashe said.

"This is the best haul we've made in twenty years in the business," Cassilde said. "I'm not letting it go for newbie prices."

"What do I have to say to make this clear?" Ashe spread his hands. "With a Gift, you are a target. Vertrage knows you have one—a very good one, at that—"

"But he can't come back in-system," Dai said. "The Guard's looking for him—not under that name, I admit, but we gave them the ship. If it tries to land, someone's going to issue a screamer."

"Vertrage's not the only one," Ashe said. "Look, this is a big deal. There are a lot of people on the hunt, people who want a new Gift or to renew the one they have, and they're not real scrupulous about how they get them."

"How are they going to know about me?" Cassilde asked. "Vertrage knows, yes, but I can't see that it does him any good to tell anybody else—"

"Revenge," Ashe said. "Put you in someone else's crosshairs. If he can't have it, you can't, either."

"He'd be taking a risk, contacting someone on Cambyse," Dai said.

And the timing wouldn't work, Cassilde thought. Assuming that Vertrage didn't land on Cambyse—and she agreed with Dai, that was asking for more trouble than even Vertrage could handle—he would have to send any message by post. This wasn't the Core, where most of the systems were still woven into pre-Fall retimonds, worlds connected by remnants of an Ancestral network that had once bound most of the human-settled galaxy together. That network had failed long ago, before or during the First Dark; scholars still argued about whether that failure had been its cause. It only survived now where the systems were close enough together that the imperfect modern power sources could keep the transluminary relays charged, opening up the network enough to keep the data passing through. Out on the Edge, and even within some of the late-settled Successor systems, information had to pass from system to system in slow time, carried along the warplines in human-crewed ships. By the time a message could reach Cambyse, they would be well on their way.

"It's not just him," Ashe said. "Gifts—they recognize each other. You could pass some random person, and they'd know."

"How would they do that?" Dai demanded.

"I don't know. I know they do it, or at least people with Gifts say they can feel other Gifts, under certain circumstances." Ashe shook his head. "My guess would be that the particles that make up the Gift signal to each other, and that creates a field that unrelated particles can sense. It's also possible that they try to signal each other, though for what purpose I don't know."

"This is what you spent the war doing," Dai said.

"Some of it, yes." Ashe dug a hand into his hair.

"Figuring out these Gifts for John Vertrage." Dai's voice was perfectly even, but Cassilde could hear the sudden anger beneath the apparent calm.

Ashe gave him a wary look. "Better than letting them be militarized." Dai snorted and turned back to the cooker.

"If another Gift signaled my Gift, or vice versa, presumably I'd know, too?" Cassilde said.

"Yes, but you wouldn't act," Ashe answered. "You wouldn't be ready to jump whoever it was just on suspicion, just because they might have something that you might want sometime later. They will. That's how the game is played."

"That's a ugly world," Dai said. Their dinner was ready, and he filled three bowls, rice and bean sauce and some deftly shredded fowl from their dwindling supply of frozen meats.

"I never said it wasn't," Ashe answered.

Cassilde took a careful bite of her dinner, blowing on the rice until she was sure it wouldn't burn her lips. She was more sensitive to food temperature as well, though her sense of taste seemed to have remained the same. Ashe was deadly serious, she could still recognize that note in his voice, and from the look on Dai's face, he was hearing the same thing.

And yet. *Carabosse* was full of the best find they'd had in years—maybe ever, if things broke right. If they could sell most of it on the Glasstown market, they'd realize enough of a profit to keep the ship running for at least another two years, maybe three. That would buy them time not only to figure out how to exist in this new world of hunts and games and Gifts, but perhaps even to locate more finds that could keep them going even longer. And if the other objects sold well, the toys and the fragments of furniture, they might even have enough that she could share some of it with her covey-mates. Not that she hadn't met her obligations, but they were as close as she had to blood family, and she would like to do more for them if she could.

There had been five of them to start, matched by the crèche teachers when they entered second trimary, her and Ramy and Gennima, Cory and Lyej—three girls and two boys; their sixth, Sisi, had made it four girls. Sisi was a typical sixth, kind and loving and every year falling another step behind, and it wasn't until they were older that Cassilde had understood the point of a sixer covey. Theirs had worked as designed, and Sisi lived on Genn's stock farm, helping to tend children and animals alike. It would be nice to be able to put in an extra share or two for Sisi, make sure she had all the little luxuries she liked; would be nice, too, to lay down some cash for Lyej's and Genn's kids. She'd filled her own reproductive obligation a long time ago, any children yet born of those gametes strangers to her: these were the children of her kin.

That was not something she could say to Ashe, raised in the more crowded Entente, where there was no great need for population growth, and most families raised the children they bore. Dai would understand, probably suspected, from the expression on his face—he wasn't vat-born, had been raised on a Vallal far-holding by a mix of the blood-kin who owned it and the sharers who worked the gas well, so that wasn't so different from her—but she had learned long ago that there was no reaching Ashe on the subject. "We're going to need cash for this…game, right, Ashe?" She waited for his reluctant nod before she continued. "Well, the Glasstown market is as good as any on the Edge. I don't want to lose money taking our find elsewhere."

"A big find like this will depress the prices just a bit," Ashe pointed out.

"We're one of the early birds," Dai said. "I'm with Silde on this."

"Fine." Ashe dug into his bowl, excavating a lump of glossy black beans. "What about the toys?"

"I'd like you to handle those," Cassilde said. "You've got the connections."

"Or so you said," Dai muttered, not quite under his breath.

"I can sell them, don't worry." Ashe's voice was grim.

"There's not as much hurry about them," Cassilde said. "Unless you think there's a reason?"

Ashe shook his head. "Only what I've already said."

"Then that's the plan," Cassilde said.

CHAPTER SIX

The Guard ship stayed with them until they were within range of the missiles based on Outermost Station, then turned them over to the protection of the crew there. Several intersystems ships were currently orbiting the Station as they negotiated landing sites and docking fees, and Cassilde persuaded the captain of a slower freighter to travel in tandem as they headed in-system toward Cambyse. It was a three-day trip with optimum fuel expenditure, and Cassilde used the time to set up sales meetings with several trusted dealers. Most of the elements would go to auction, through Kensae Daughters; Venturis specialized in recovering faded elements and the faded GREEN in particular would likely sell there. Ashe composed feelers for the various local toy-dealers, and longer ones for the off-worlders, readying them to be sent as soon as they could access the off-world postal system. He had come up to the control room to dispatch the local set, busying himself with the comm queue while Cassilde turned an idle eye to the sensor net.

"I want to keep one of the toys for myself—count it as part of my share."

"Sure," Ashe said. "Which one?"

"One of the bells," Cassilde said. They were the smallest, and one of the most common types, a more-or-less spherical shape that rang when tapped. This one glowed turquoise, too, and revealed tiny flecks of gold; it also sounded a single 440 Hz tone when tapped, and she knew someone who would appreciate it. She might choose another for herself, maybe one of the larger and more complex displays, but she wanted to wait and see how the sales went first.

"I want to keep some of the elements for us, too."

Ashe looked up quickly. "Of course. We've got plenty of GREEN to spare."

"I want the others, too. Especially GOLD. I've got some ideas about how to improve our sensor net—"

She stopped abruptly as a light flared on the screen. Numbers flashed into existence: a small, light ship, coming fast on a converging course. The comm console chimed, and Ashe reached for the controls.

"It's the *Nikolas* calling." That was their traveling companion, and he flicked open their designated channel. "*Carabosse.* We see it, too."

"We're not reading weapons," *Nikolas* said, and a second chime sounded, warning lights flashing from yellow to blue. "Hang on, we're getting a code—"

"We've got a postal code," Ashe said. "And our net readings are compatible. Looks like a mailship."

"I wish they wouldn't do that," *Nikolas* said. "Sorry for the alarm."

"We were just about to ping you," Ashe answered, and closed the channel.

Cassilde leaned back in her chair, feeling her heart still racing. "And that would be another reason to improve the sensors."

"Point." Ashe finished loading his own mail, and gave her a sidelong look. "You know, if John made it out-system—he could have a message on that ship."

"Everything would have had to break perfectly," Cassilde said. "And we need funds. Go ahead and send your stuff."

"Just don't say I didn't warn you," Ashe said, and pressed the keys that sent his own messages chasing the mailship.

"If it all goes wrong, I promise to give you time to say so," Cassilde answered.

He laughed, but shook his head. "I'm serious, Silde. You don't know what we're up against."

"So why'd you take up with him?" Cassilde wasn't sure she was ready to hear the answer, but she doubted she'd get a better opportunity to ask. "I wouldn't have thought he was your type."

Ashe gave a crooked smile. "He was better than my other options."

"Lovely."

"He was smart and sharp and he understood salvage the way only a practitioner does," Ashe said, abruptly serious. "And he made the effort to be good in bed when nobody else was willing to take the risk." Cassilde lifted an eyebrow. "No fraternization, remember? And we had both sworn enlistment. He made it sound like fun, like it really was a game. I learned better."

"What's he after, then?"

"He wants to control the game. From there—I don't know. He doesn't like limits. And he's dangerous."

There was a note in his voice that made her stop and look hard at him. "I believe you. I promise, I do. But Glasstown Market is still our best bet."

"I know." He managed a wry smile. "I just don't have to like it."

They reserved field space in the main complex, where the security was better and there was easy access to the labyrinth of buildings that made up the non-virtual market. Cassilde sent a first tender in to Kensae, and took the return offer: with cash in hand, she could pay field fees and make all other necessary arrangements.

The next days vanished into a whirlwind of talk and trade, while Ashe disappeared for hours to talk to the toy dealers, and Dai watched the ship and supervised the load-out. Atani Kensae herself took over the auction once she saw what they had to offer, and Cassilde only had to talk her down by seven percent to make the numbers work out properly. Venturis made a bulk offer for the faded elements within an hour of receiving her list, at a high enough price to make her wonder if other people would offer more. But she had promised Ashe that they would wrap things up as quickly as possible, and the money was good enough that she didn't need to worry about missing something better.

The port seemed busier, though that might be docking in the main sections rather than pinching pennies out on the edges of the field. Word of the find had traveled: they were not the first ship to return, nor even the second. Those were two smaller ships that had bid on unprepossessing class-three claims and found to their delight that the bulkheads were stuffed full of RED and GOLD. *Carabosse* had found more GREEN, however, and Cassilde sincerely wished them well.

By the fifth day, things seemed to be well under control, with enough money in the bank to contract for fuel and resupply. Ashe had gone up to the Exchange to answer more inquiries; she hunted out the turquoise toy with its perfect 440 Hz tone, then left Dai to handle any questions about the auction, and rented a three-wheeler for a visit to her old crèche. Her old sponsor was a musician and a teacher, even though she'd retired a few years ago; she would appreciate the toy for itself, and it was also a way to make sure she was provided for. And, Cassilde admitted as she flipped the switches that brought the three-wheeler to life, it felt so good to be able to give.

It had been a while since she'd been back, and as she took the long road up toward the Empty Bridge, she was surprised by the number of new buildings that had sprung up along the way. The road to the overlook was largely unchanged, however, and she geared down for the steep hill, looking out for the turn that gave the first good view of the Burntover. It stretched brown and barren into the misty north, the worn slag crisscrossed with played-out trenches, only a few tendrils of greenery extending into the plain from the east. The botanists all said it would eventually be fertile again, but that was hard to imagine.

In the middle distance, a spot of bright yellow caught her eye, and she slowed to look, pulling out of the travel lane. It looked like a walking drill, she thought, someone taking yet another survey of the well-searched ground, in case someone had missed something valuable. Or in this case, if they were drilling, in case there was something valuable at greater depth. No one had ever been able to agree on how deep the debris field went, how far the falling cities had driven themselves into the planet's surface.

She kicked the three-wheeler into motion again, following the winding road to the top of the overlook. The crèche loomed ahead, its bright walls vivid against the cloudy sky. The columns on the upper veranda had been repainted recently, each one crowned with a bright blue-and-red flower, and the poured-sandstone frontage was now covered in red and ochre latticework. Probably a class project, she thought, remembering her own years in the crèche, and turned her three-wheeler into a charging bay. As she climbed out, she could hear shouts from the game field, clear as birds on another world, and caught herself smiling as she made her way to the door.

She gave her name and appointment to the console, and a few minutes later one of the older children appeared to unlock the door and escort her through the lower corridors. They passed the central atrium, and Cassilde frowned. Something was different—yes, the enormous boaxi tree that had filled nearly a quarter of the space was gone.

"Onkel-Dan is gone?" she said, and her escort glanced over her shoulder.

"Yes, misor. It finally had to be taken down. That was before my time, though."

And I expect everyone who visits says the same thing, Cassilde thought. *And you don't even remember it.* It was strange to think that something so enormous, so solid and seemingly eternal, could be gone. She remembered a tree that reached almost to the skylight, and had to be pruned hard every year to keep it from spreading sideways; remembered, too, climbing high into its thick branches, and making the forbidden crossing from the second-floor railing to the tree when she didn't want to be seen. Probably there were some teachers and docents who didn't entirely regret its passing. The wall that had been behind it was scrubbed and freshly painted, no sign left that it had ever been there.

The girl led her into the crèche's western wing, past a corridor of classrooms, and then through the transfer hall into the Annex. It looked smaller than she had remembered, the creamy poured stone around the door now decorated with a row of what she thought were leaves arranged in circular roundels, and only at the last minute recognized as stylized birds poised wingtip to wingtip and beak to beak to form a circle. Overhead, the skylight was scattered with dust, dimming the light, but when the door opened, she was back in the familiar atrium with its central pool, the lotus-topped columns holding up a mezzanine level.

Her former sponsor lived on the ground floor—Cassilde had heard that she was afflicted with the same arthritis that struck a good third of Cambyse's older population—in the back corner where she would have a good view of the game fields and the treeless park that joined the crèche's land. She opened at once to the student's signal, leaning heavily on a cane, but her smile was everything Cassilde had remembered.

"Tiyaan Maryad," she said, and bent to embrace the older woman.

"Cassilde-bach." Maryad Caral returned the embrace, then pulled away to beckon her into the neat sitting room. "Come in, my dear, come in. Anneth, if you'll bring the tray from the kitchen, you may have one each of the cakes."

"Thank you, misor," the student said, and disappeared through a curtain to the left.

"Sit," Maryad said, waving to a pair of chairs set next to the largest window. Cassilde chose the one that did not have a workbasket set next to it, and Anneth reappeared, bending backward to balance the weight of a tray crowded with teapot, cups, and a plate of little cakes. They were ones Cassilde remembered from childhood, antique flavors hoarded and conserved and revived after every Dark, vanilla and chocolate with caramel topped with a thick swirl of intensely sweet, intensely pink icing, and she couldn't help smiling.

"Tiyaan, this is too much. You didn't have to."

"It's my pleasure," Maryad answered, and shooed Anneth on

her way with an extra cake. "It's very nice to see my old students—particularly the ones like you, who were a pleasure to represent."

"Not always a pleasure, I expect," Cassilde said, and Maryad grinned.

"You had your moments, dear. You all did."

"I've brought you a little something," Cassilde said, and held out the padded container. Maryad lifted her eyebrows, recognizing the pebbled material used to shield Ancestral artifacts, and Cassilde said quickly, "I've had a very good year."

Maryad's eyebrows lifted even further, but she found the latch and released it, lifted the lid carefully away. Her fingers brushed the toy, and it flickered weakly, a flash and a dull hum. Maryad's breath caught in her throat, and she lifted it carefully out of the smothering wrap.

"Oh, it's beautiful." Under her touch, the turquoise flame ignited in the toy's center, and a scattering of gold and silver swirled up like bubbles to disappear before they reached the outermost layer. "Silde-bach, this is far too expensive—"

"Tap it," Cassilde said.

Maryad obeyed, and the perfect A filled the room, almost thick enough to touch. "Oh," Maryad said, and muffled it. There were tears in her voice. "Oh, Silde."

There were no instruments in the room, Cassilde realized abruptly, none of the guitars and fiddles that Maryad had always kept, her own and two or three for loaning to her most promising students. Ten years ago, the toy would have waked an answering music, half a dozen harmonics. She wanted to ask what had happened, where the guitars had gone, and Maryad smiled sadly.

"I'm old, Silde, my hands are too stiff to play much any more."

"I'm sorry—"

"Don't be." Maryad touched the toy again, her smile more genuine as it spoke, and then she muffled it. "It's beautiful, Silde. I've never seen anything like it. Where in the world did you get it?"

Cassilde launched into an explanation of the find, which turned into a quick summary of the last year or so, leaving out all references to either lean times or the Lightman's. Maryad poured them each a cup of tea while she spoke, and waved in silent invitation at the cakes. She was somehow smaller than Cassilde had remembered, or perhaps that was the arthritis, bowing her back. She still wore her hair in the coronet of braids that Cassilde had so envied, but now all the braids were steel gray, and her brown skin had an ashen cast. She sounded like her old self, though, as she exclaimed over Cassilde's description of the find, and leaned back smiling when Cassilde had finished.

"Silde-bach, that's lovely. I'm so pleased for you."

"It's a great relief," Cassilde admitted. "I love salvage, Tiyaan, but it's not a secure career."

"I remember Barri trying to tell you that," Maryad said. "But you knew what you wanted."

"It was the songs," Cassilde said. She had never admitted that before, wasn't sure she should say so now, when the music was lost, and stumbled to a stop. Maryad tilted her head to one side.

"The songs? Oh, you mean when we made your year learn the Dedalor cycles."

Cassilde nodded. "We loved the stories, all of us, and then I found out they were at least partly true. Gurinn who built the Great AI, Kuffrin who gave them self-awareness, Iestil who loved them, Hafren who tried to save them, Nenien who betrayed them…"

"And Anketil and Irtholin, who held back the Dark." Maryad looked past her, as though she was hearing the music she could no longer play. "*Iestyn and Ievyn were two pretty men, but Ankes and Irthe brought them down in the end.* I always hoped there was truth at least in that one, even if all the worlds were lost. And now you've given me a piece of it." She stroked the toy, fingers playing over the glassy surface as though she might call more notes from its depths. The pure note waxed and waned, but did not change.

"I do love it," Cassilde said again. A shaft of sunlight had broken through the clouds, shone in through the window to catch the ring on Maryad's hand. Her knuckles were swollen, and Cassilde focused on the stone, incised with an intricate initial, that gleamed briefly red in the strong light. It hung loose on her finger now, though someone had put in a latch to let it slide over the thickened knuckle: no wonder she didn't play any more. "I'm glad I got a chance to try it here, in the Burntover. Does that apprenticeship still exist?"

"They've doubled the places," Maryad answered. She went into details—new teachers, new funding, new excitement on every side—and Cassilde nodded enthusiastically, thinking, *She is old. Tiyaan Maryad has gotten old.* And of course she should have expected nothing else: it had been more than twenty years since she left the crèche, and Maryad had not been young then. But somehow before she had managed not to notice.

"And you are looking well," Maryad said. Cassilde looked up, startled, afraid she had somehow betrayed herself, but Maryad went on. "I'd heard that you were having some health issues, but I can see that isn't true."

Word of the Lightman's diagnosis must have spread, Cassilde thought. She had only told her covey-mates, but it hadn't been any particular secret. "It seems there was a misdiagnosis," she said, and Maryad's smile widened.

"I'm glad. Well, not that you were worried, I'm sure you must have been, but that it's worked out."

"So am I." Cassilde matched her smile. "And you?"

"Oh, sore and achy, but that's the price for getting old. And I'm happy they let me stay here. Being around the children keeps me young."

And that was a cruel lie, Cassilde thought. If she were young, she would still have her music. However buoyed she might be by the company, the energy, she was still older and frailer than Cassilde had imagined. They finished the cakes together, and Cassilde steadied her as they walked to the door together.

"It's a lovely present," Maryad said quietly. "So beautiful, and such a pleasure to touch. Have they ever decided what the Ancestors made them for?"

Cassilde shook her head. "It's still a mystery."

"At least it's a lovely one," Maryad said. "Do write. I love thinking of all of you having your adventures."

"Most of it's pretty boring," Cassilde answered, and they embraced, Maryad's bones sharp beneath skin and heavy tunic.

And that is what I will never be, she thought, as she followed another student—a boy, this time—back through the crèche's halls. *If Ashe is right, if this Gift is true, if I can keep it going—I will never grow old, never change from how I am now. And Maryad will age and die and disappear like our lovely tree. I will remain.* She didn't know what to do with that feeling, couldn't quite put a name to it: not guilt, exactly, though surely she should share her find; sorrow, yes, perhaps even fear, and yet also and unmistakably delight, that she would not suffer, but would instead go on. It was too much, too complicated; she put it aside, concentrating on the three-wheeler and the road back into Glasstown.

𝔸 � 𝕏 ⁊

She returned the three-wheeler to its agent, and threaded her way through the streets of Highport, heading for the chophouse where she had agreed to meet Dai and Ashe. The streets were crowded, as usual when there was an orbital find, and auctions in the offing; she had been lucky to get a decent berth for *Carabosse*, and to find anyone who had three-wheelers available for a mere day-long rental. The streets were full of a medley of accents, Core almost as common as Edge. That boded well for Ashe's attempts to sell the toys, and she quickened her pace to cross the main traffic-way before the lights changed and the bridge was blocked. She made it under the closing barrier with seconds to spare, and followed the crowd over the surging mess of flat-beds and closed-cabin carriers, two- and three-wheelers darting between them as though the traffic laws didn't apply. She was last off the bridge, the barrier skimming her shoulders as it came down, and she heard the groan of gears as it pivoted to connect the opposite corners.

There were too many people already waiting for the lift; she took the spiral stair instead, moving in lockstep with the rest of the crowd, gave a sigh of relief as she emerged onto the pedestrian walkway that ran alongside and a meter or so above the traffic channel. The sun was almost down, sunk behind Glasstown's central buildings, and the air that had been unseasonably warm was starting to pick up a distinct chill. It was still amazing to breathe the cool air without caution, without waiting for it to catch at the base of degrading lungs. Her legs felt good, too, fit to carry her for kilometers, and she had to remind herself to keep to the general pace of the crowd. She was in no hurry; the others would be waiting no matter how long it took her.

She was a third of the way down the long curve of the Drywalk when she first felt it, that odd prickle at the back of the neck that comes from feeling someone's eyes fixed on you. She looked up, startled, but no one in the hurrying crowd seemed to be paying her any particular attention. People were loitering around the entrances of the various bars and eateries that lined the Drywalk's inward curve, pedestrians swirling past them: one of those, probably, she thought, someone watching the crowd, their eye caught by her clothes, square-cut tunic and trousers nicer than the general run of spacer's gear that surrounded her. Certainly she saw no one else, not in a quick glance, and she thought it was wiser not to seem to notice too much. Ashe had said that the Gifts knew each other. If this was one calling out to hers, better to play dumb, at least for now.

She moved more slowly now, matching the speed of the crowd around her—spacers, mostly, here in Highport, people in tough work-cloth trousers and slouching boots and close-fitting shirts, occasionally a dull jacket worn against the nighttime wind. Maybe a quarter of them were dressed like her, layers of square-cut vest and tunic and trousers that were the style in this part of the Edge, and she was grateful she'd chosen quieter colors. If anyone was looking for her, she would blend into the crowd and the rising dusk.

Ahead, the Drywalk stretched toward the lights and wire fences of the port proper, the bone-white surface reflecting the last of the ambient light so that it seemed to glow softly. It was one of the Burntover artifacts, much studied and still little known, a nearly two kilometer-long curve of some Ancestral material. Only the edge was visible above-ground; the rest of it was buried, stretching several kilometers to the south. It might have been part of the fall, or it might have been something the Ancestors did deliberately, the base of some now-lost construction; at the moment, the port's most secure warehouses had been built over its buried sections, and the visible parts remained for visitors to gawk at. There was a brief moment, here at sunset, when the reflected light and the long shadows and the brilliance of the port on the horizon made human sight shatter like a kaleidoscope. At least some of the tourists would be here to see that, and she let herself fall into rhythm with a group in spacer dress escorted by a trio of Glasstown women. To the casual eye, she hoped, she would look like part of the group as they slowed to watch for the first dazzling shift in the light.

The Drywalk's surface seemed to ripple like wind-blown water, and suddenly the air was full of flecks of light, shapes and shards reflecting from walls and storefronts and the Drywalk itself. It was like standing in the center of a multi-colored snowstorm, or being caught by a swarm of silent insects, everything reduced to the swirl and flash of color. Cassilde took two blind steps backward, into the shadow of a storefront arcade, and the display abruptly vanished. She turned back along the arcade, retracing her steps until she found herself in the shadows of the final archway. Outside, the display was fading fast, and she rolled up her tunic sleeves, heedless of the chill, and fumbled in her pockets for a clip to pull her chin-length hair up and back. There wasn't much else she could do to change her silhouette, but in the post-dazzle, it might be enough. She took a deep breath, and started back up the Drywalk, this time staying close to the inside edge.

As always, night fell fast in Glasstown, multi-colored lights springing up along the shop fronts to drive back the shadows, though the edge of the Drywalk itself remained as white and bright as the Elder Moon. It illuminated everyone who walked there, and she stayed well back, trying not to be too obvious as she glanced from side to side, trying to see if anyone was taking any interest in her. This time, there was nothing, no visual indication and no recurrence of that odd feeling, and she ducked through the chophouse door, grateful to see that Dai had chosen one of the alcoves with the central heat fountains. She slid onto the pillows next to him, rolling down her sleeves, and Ashe said, "Everything go all right? We were starting to get worried."

Cassilde hesitated, and tried to cover it by shifting closer to the heat fountain.

"Silde?" Dai said, and she sighed.

"I had a nice visit with Tiyaan Maryad—she liked the bell, even though she doesn't play much herself any more. But—" She shrugged. "Coming along the Drywalk, I had a weird feeling someone was staring at me, so I used the kaleidoscope light to backtrack and see if I could spot anybody. I didn't, though—I don't know what it was I felt."

"You think it was another Gift calling to yours?" Dai asked.

Cassilde shrugged. "I was going to ask Ashe."

"It could be," Ashe said. "Mine, it felt like I had an itch in my brain that I couldn't scratch, but they're very individual. Or maybe it's us who makes the difference, I don't know. Do you think they spotted you?"

"Possibly. Probably, if they knew what they were doing." Cassilde sighed. "I looked around, to see who was looking for me; if they were looking for that, they could have seen me for sure."

"The Drywalk's always a mob scene," Dai said. "Especially at sunset. You didn't see anyone, right?"

"No."

"Dai's right," Ashe said, and Cassilde gave him a surprised look. "Well, he is. There's a decent chance you got a ping, but neither one of you managed to spot the other. That happens, it's like having a personal sensor web. Let's have a lovely dinner—I've got some very nice offers on the toys—and we'll just be extra careful going back to the ship."

Cassilde relaxed a little, the muscles loosening in her shoulders. "You really think we're all right?"

"I think we're safe here," Ashe said, "and I think there's a good chance you weren't spotted. So we might as well enjoy ourselves."

"We've certainly earned it," Dai said, and Cassilde leaned companionably against his shoulder.

The chophouse was expensive, and one of the things its patrons paid for was privacy. Their alcove was carefully screened from the others, and from the busy common room, and as the waiters brought the sequence of courses, Cassilde felt the tension drain from her body. Yes, it probably was another Gift she'd felt, and she'd know better next time how to respond, but the other Gift-holder seemed to have missed her, too. Tiyaan Maryad had been pleased with her present—though she was old now, old and getting frail—and if all else failed, the bell was worth a tidy sum, a little extra insurance against the unforeseeable.

They chose a final course of little cakes and local brandy, and Cassilde leaned back on the cushions, stretching. She had eaten like a snake about to hibernate, as she had ever since she received her Gift, and still didn't feel particularly overwhelmed. Dai poked the last cake in Ashe's direction, and he shuddered and shook his head.

"Split it?" Cassilde offered, and Dai carefully broke it into two even pieces. Cassilde swallowed hers, and licked the last of the icing from her fingertips.

"I suppose we should head back to the ship." It was easier to stay shipboard in the nicer berths, where they could easily link to the port's systems; safer, too, though they had transferred their most expensive finds to a rented lock-box in a well-recommended security house just south of the Drywalk.

"Probably," Ashe said, and drained the last of his brandy. "Do you want to change? Dai or I could spare you a shirt."

Cassilde considered. "I suppose that would be smart. Just in case."

Ashe gave her an approving nod. "You have to play it that way."

Dai made a face, but began working his way out of shirt and undershirt. The undershirt was big enough to fit Cassilde as a tunic, and she shrugged it on, folding her square coat into a shape that she hoped would pass for a carryall. For an instant, she caught sight of their reflections in the mirror polished lacquer of the wall, the borrowed shirt outlining her recovered curves, Dai's broad shoulders shifting as he shrugged his shirt back on, Ashe fine-boned and leaner on her other side. She loosed her hair, and for a moment they looked as though they were young again. Ashe nodded then, breaking the spell, while Dai buzzed for the waiter, and they made their way out into the night.

೧ Ⅲₛ ※ ⁼⟩

It was cold out, the night-wind that came off the Burntover carrying the bitter tang of its dust. Cassilde lifted her head at the familiar smell, amazed again that it didn't catch in her lungs and set her choking. Dai put his arm around her shoulder, wordless relief, and Ashe said, "A couple of find reports came in while you were out. A nice-looking option in Alamance-Plaisance, and another out in the Psyche Rings."

"Oh?" Cassilde froze, the feeling that someone was watching her sweeping over her again. She managed not to turn her head, but saw Ashe's expression tense.

"Trouble?"

"I feel it—" And then the sensation was gone, as quickly as though someone had wiped it away with a wet rag. "It's gone. It was what I felt before, though. Maybe a little stronger, more focused…"

"Keep walking," Ashe said, and Dai tightened his grip on her shoulders. "Anything else?"

"No." She didn't dare shake her head, concentrating instead on finding the feeling again, searching for connection and direction. "It's gone now."

"Stop looking for it," Ashe said, and she scowled in spite of herself.

"How'd you know?"

"I know you."

Dai snorted at that, and Cassilde couldn't quite suppress a smile. "All right. But I need to learn how to do this."

"Now you're agreeing with me," Ashe said. "But now—if they just broke off, they're hiding. Let's hope they're trying to get away from us, and not trying to set up an ambush."

They were almost at the end of the Drywalk, just a few blocks of the port-pale between them and the main gate. *The well-guarded main gate*, Cassilde thought, *and then it's all bright lights and security cameras between there and our berth*. It was just those few blocks that were the problem. Most of the businesses were closed by now, though there were security cameras on most buildings, and an expensive security force theoretically poised to come to the aid of any travelers in trouble, but it took time for them to arrive. And besides, a fight might lead to inconvenient revelations.

"Should we push straight through?" she asked, and Dai shook his head.

"Jewelers' Row, for my money. More cameras, and I'm pretty sure they bribe the locals for quick response." He glanced sideways. "Sorry, Silde."

"It's true enough," Cassilde answered, and wished it wasn't.

Jewelers' Row was more brightly lit than she'd remembered, though the storefronts were locked and barred against the night. Still, there were a couple of small coffeeshops still open, plus a larger tapasserie with a front garden. The heat fountains were working, and a few hardy folk sat beside one, faces reddened by the shimmering light. A stocky woman watched the gate; she nodded to them, but didn't invite them in. Reading their hurry? Cassilde wondered. Or did she know something they didn't?

She thought she felt the stare again, stumbled, and couldn't help but look back. The tapasserie was still quiet, the woman unmoved on her stool by the gate, the group at their table laughing at some comment, someone's pale hair flying loose to catch the light like sparks from the fountain.

Ashe swore under his breath, and Dai reached to steady her, but she shook him off, hoping it would look from a distance as though they'd all been drinking. The feeling was gone again, and she leaned toward Ashe as though looking for support.

"I felt it, but they're gone again."

"Stalking us," Dai said. He had his hand in the pocket of his overshirt, and Cassilde guessed he was carrying a pocket welder. Weapons were forbidden on Cambyse except under special and expensive license, but anyone who'd been in space for any length of time learned how to turn the common toolkit into weaponry. She just wished she hadn't left hers at home—it had seemed like a bad idea to take cutters into the crèche.

"Walk on," Ashe said firmly, and she obeyed, Dai dropping back one step to put himself between her and the tapasserie. She tightened her muscles, straining to work a sense she could barely define, searching for another hint of that gaze, some trace of that person, their touch… Her mind stayed determinedly blank, and she stumbled again as they approached the port's main gate. The guard on duty gave her a sympathetic look, and she realized he thought she was drunk. There was no point in contradicting him; she smiled politely and let Ashe talk them through security this time. By the time they had finished, a rover was waiting on the far side of the gate, and they climbed into the passenger pod to let the port's systems take them back to the ship. As the rover jerked into motion, she thought she felt the touch one final time, but it was gone almost as soon as she had recognized it.

Once inside *Carabosse,* she set the usual exterior alarms, then motioned the others toward Central. "All right, Ashe, you were right. There's someone out there with another Gift. What's our next move?"

"Sell everything and get out," Ashe answered. "Same as I said before."

"That's going to take time," Dai said.

"And don't I know it," Ashe said. "Half the delay's mine." He ran his hand through his hair. "I'll ask if Daimas will do a bulk buy, a full locker of the toys sight unseen. I'll have to offer a big discount, but he's not going to like it."

"I can't say I blame him," Cassilde said. No one wanted to buy a mixed lot of Ancestral goods without having had the chance to at least see the items first. "And I doubt we can move up the last auction. What if we just stay in the port? Security's solid here."

"That may be our best bet," Ashe said. "And plan our next move. We need to know what we're doing next."

"How about we find you and Dai your own Gifts?" Cassilde said, so lightly she thought they didn't hear the worry behind the words, and Ashe laughed.

"Nothing I'd like better, but they're not that easy to come by. Still, there's been a rumor that there might be something out Alamance way. If we work up a bid on that new field, that'll give us an excuse."

"I saw the specs for that," Dai said. "It looks like it could be a money-maker, even if there's nothing else."

Cassilde hesitated, wanting to push, to get his promise that he would at least consider taking a Gift—if they found one, and if it did for him what hers had done, a lot of conditionals to get past before they started talking seriously. Ashe would take one, she had no doubt about that. He had had one before, and she was sure had been planning to take this one if he hadn't found out about the Lightman's. No, Ashe was easy, Ashe wanted it already, probably as much as she wanted him to have one. Dai was the one who would need persuading, even if she wasn't entirely sure why. And that would take time and delicacy, not an outright demand. "Put the specs in my box, and I'll look at them in the morning," she said, and thought her voice sounded entirely normal. "And we'll stay in the port until we lift."

𝄞 ⛣ ⚳ ⸆

The next morning, Cassilde settled herself in Central with a pot of tea and the latest batch of find-files. There were more than a dozen newly opened claims, and she skimmed the reports, unsurprised to find that the only worthwhile ones were on Alamance-Plaisance and the Psyche Rings.

Pysche was another field like the one off Cambyse, the wreckage of a sky palace finally intersecting the local searches, but the pieces were smaller, massed less, and several showed signs of having been plundered by the Successors. That in itself wasn't disqualifying—the Adamant Hills had been opened by the Successors, and were still yielding both elemental caches and useful bits of technology—but the more she looked at the spread of the pieces, the more she thought that the Successors had gotten the best of whatever had been there.

Alamance-Plaisance looked more likely, the find smaller but more certain: a cache of Ancestral elements on one of the many moons of a gas giant orbiting Plaisance's sun. The first-in crew had called it a possible wreck rather than an installation, and that was certainly the more conservative choice, but there were seven moons of roughly comparable size, spread out in stable orbits that would allow stations on those moons to cover the planet's full surface in a sensor web. The Ancestors had done that in the past, as part of their fueling systems, presumably, and had also used similar arrangements to power the trans-luminary data nodes that had once enabled instantaneous communications across their empire. If this were the remains of a TLD node, it might be worth bidding on one of the other moons, and seeing what they could find there.

She looked up from her screen to see Central empty, and reached for the intercom switch. "Dai. Got a minute?"

"Sure. Be right there."

By rights, she supposed she should have talked to Ashe first, but he was—she hoped—busy renegotiating the sales terms on the load of toys. She flipped back to the main map, fed it to the table's projector so that when Dai ducked through the hatch, the image was floating in the table's center like a tiny slice of night.

"Got something?" Dai fetched more tea without being asked, and took the seat next to hers.

"Maybe. This is the Alamance-Plaisance find Ashe mentioned. The find-file says it's a wreck, but I'm wondering if it's not a piece of something bigger."

"Huh." Dai moved his tea aside and pulled the map closer, turning it slowly. "You're thinking an installation. Fuel station?"

"Possibly." Cassilde touched her screen, calling up her calculations. "Or maybe, just maybe, we've got the remains of a TLD node."

"When the Ancestors blew up those systems, they blew them up," Dai said. "There's too much left. A Successor fueling station, now, that I'd buy."

"A fueling station wouldn't need full coverage," Cassilde said. "Maybe the Successors were trying to rebuild a node?"

"They didn't know any more about the TLD system than we do," Dai said.

"But they were closer to the Ancestors by a thousand years." Cassilde turned the model, her calculations tracing a set of thin gold lines that tied the seven moons into an irregular heptahedron. "They must have known what they'd lost. From everything we can find, it hurt them worse than the Second Dark hurt us. Suppose they found what was left of a node—was Alamance a Successor planet?"

Dai reached for his own screen, unrolled it onto the tabletop. "No," he said, after a moment. "Or at least the University doesn't think so. Some Ancestral remains, no Successor finds to speak of.

Which, I grant you, sounds kind of odd when you think about it—though the Successors didn't use the low-K warplines as much as we do."

"And the Alamance-Plaisance connector is on the low end even for low-K," Cassilde said. Both their own and the Successors' faster-than-light drives could only travel along lines of weakness in space/time, all of which were classified by frequency; modern revisions to the technology had allowed them to reach a wider range of lines, especially in the J and K bandwidths. "But suppose, just suppose, a Successor crew found enough of a TLD node to try to get it functioning again. Only they got it wrong, damaged it so badly they had to destroy what was left so nobody could see what they'd done."

"Or they didn't realize what they had until they'd chewed it apart," Dai said. "The Successors weren't subtle in their approach." He nodded slowly. "All right, I could buy that."

That made more sense than her first hypothesis, and Cassilde nodded, reaching for the intercom again. "Ashe—"

"I'm here," Ashe said, from the doorway. "You want to see this."

He flipped a packet of folded paper onto the table. It slid to a stop half inside the projection, and Cassilde gave it a wary glance. Her name was printed on the outermost sheet along with *Carabosse*'s registry number and their berth. Beneath that outer layer, the contents were oddly lumpy, and she let it lie untouched, looking back over her shoulder at Ashe.

"It came in with the last load of supplies," he said. "The driver said somebody left it at their office, so he figured he'd just bring it over. I've put it through the scanner—twice—and there's nothing live in there."

"You think this is more of your hunt," Dai said.

"Got any more likely ideas?" Cassilde asked, before they could start an argument. "When you say live—no power, no organics?"

"Yeah. There are wires and metal, but no payload. Certainly no explosives, and nothing chipped."

"Jumper," Dai said.

"If it's anything." Ashe glared at the packet as though he could force it to give up its secrets.

"Well, if it's a jumper, we've got a fix," Cassilde said. She switched off the display and went to the cabinets, came back with one of the mesh baskets from the steamer and a roll of repair tape. She inverted the basket over the packet and ran a strip of tape over the top.

"Very nice," Dai said, "but how are you going to open it?"

Cassilde didn't answer, turned back instead to the kitchen wall, rummaging in the storage spaces until she found two long, thin-bladed knives. She slid them under the edge of the basket, working them in so that she could hold the packet with one and cut the top seal with the other. "More tape."

"Well, if it's a jumper, that ought to hold it," Ashe said, and Dai added two more long strips of tape crisscrossing the upturned basket. "I'm assuming you're going to sterilize that before you cook anything in it."

Dai ignored him. "Ready?" he said, to Cassilde, and she nodded in answer.

"All right. I'm cutting the seal." She worked the knives as she spoke, fumbling for a moment to get the packet secured. And then she had it, and slipped the smaller blade under what seemed to be the main flap. The seal snapped; there was a pop and a sharp metallic sound, and she flinched back as the basket seemed to jump toward her. But the tape held, and a four-legged metal object hung from the basket's mesh, buzzing frantically.

"I'll be damned," Ashe said. "It was a jumper."

"No shit." Cassilde glared at the creature, still thrashing against the mesh. "And what's that in aid of?"

Ashe tipped his head to one side, visibly considering, and Dai handed him a chopstick. Ashe took it with a nod of thanks, and prodded the jumper carefully. The buzzing increased, then stopped altogether. It looked like nothing so much as an oversized metal night-biter, complete with needle-like proboscis, and she saw Ashe frown.

"After blood—a blood sample, maybe? I'll know more when I can take it apart."

"You'll do that under sterile protocol," Cassilde said sharply, and to her relief he didn't argue.

CHAPTER SEVEN

As she slid a cook-sheet under the basket, and taped the stiff metal in place before he risked moving the jumper. He vanished into the ship's tiny lab, promising to follow all precautions, but it was not until Cassilde heard the hiss of the seals that she allowed herself to relax. Dai rested a hand on her shoulder, and she leaned hard against him, grabbing for his other hand so that she could cling to him. She was shaking, and knew he could feel it, but he only tightened his grip.

"That was…a bit much," he said at last, and she nodded.

"Ashe said it wasn't a nice game." She drew a deep breath, working her shoulders, and Dai obligingly shifted his grip to dig gently into the muscles at the base of her neck. "Trying to take a blood sample, do you think?"

"That's what Ashe said. Me, I don't know how it would make the return trip."

"Let's see what Ashe has got," Cassilde said, and reached for her board, flattening it again to type in the command that woke the cameras in the lab. The image shimmered in the middle of the table, and Ashe glanced up as though he'd heard the cameras come on.

"Nothing yet. I'll let you know."

"Absolutely," Dai said, and slid a fresh cup of tea on front of Cassilde.

She finished it, grateful for the heat and the spices, had drunk most of a third cup by the time Ashe lifted his head.

"I think I've got an answer. But you're not going to like it."

He shifted so that they could both see the remains of the jumper, neatly dissected into its component parts: the heavy spring-loaded jump legs, plus six more that looked as though they were designed to carry the thing at speed. There was the needle of the proboscis, attached to a thin tube that led to an empty bladder; there was an intricate tangle of springs and gears that seemed to be a sort of motor; and there was something tiny in the "head" that seemed to show a fleck of GREEN.

"All right, I see a sampling mechanism," Cassilde said. "Skin or blood, or both. What's the GREEN for?"

"It's a modified toy—well, reverse-engineered," Ashe said. "And, yes, I'd say it was supposed to jump out of that package and stab the person who opened it. The needle takes a blood sample, and the little monster runs away, back to whoever sent it."

"That motor's not big enough," Dai said.

"Self-winding, and there are two of them, acting reciprocally."

"So when one releases, the other is already at or close to top power?" Cassilde asked.

Ashe nodded. "And, like I said, they've modified a toy. They've taken a toy's brain-box and reworked it to run the jumper. The elemental traces are minuscule, and I haven't really touched them—"

"Good," Cassilde said. She had no compunction about acknowledging that she was the best of them at manipulating the elements.

"But I think the thing was more or less programmed to find its way back to whoever sent it." Ashe prodded unhappily at the motor unit, making the springs rattle.

"Not possible," Dai said. "That would take true AI."

"Or very high-functioning AL," Cassilde said, though she didn't believe it herself. Artificial Life was defined by its mimicry of animal function; it might follow a trail of some kind, but to find its way back to the sender without some such aid—that was pushing up against the one law no one broke. Too much reliance on AI had doomed the Ancestors: that was the one piece of knowledge that had survived two Darks, a bright red warning repeated so often that it survived to reach the modern world.

"I told you, they've taken the brain-box from a toy—not one I recognize—and frankly I don't know what it's capable of." Ashe tipped his head back to look at the camera again. "Silde, you'll have a better chance of figuring it out than I have."

"I'll come down," Cassilde said, and pushed herself away from the table.

The lab was too small for two of them to work at once. She waited while Ashe secured the glove-box that held the fragments of the jumper and unsealed the door, then slid in past him, and sealed the door again behind her. She found the tools she needed to examine the brain-box's elements, placed them in the transfer chamber, and sealed the door behind them. The glovebox looked secure, but she checked the straps that held it motionless anyway before working her own hands into the gloves. The lining's reactive fabric pulsed and squirmed, fitting itself to her fingers; when it settled, she opened the transfer chamber's inner door and pulled out her tools. She set the brain-box under the magnifier, adjusting the bezel to bring up as much detail as possible, and used one of the medium-sized hooks to open the compartment further.

The knot of Ancestral elements seemed to glow against the dark metal, a single pinhead fleck of GREEN set in the center of swirls of RED and GOLD. A ring of BLUE surrounded the knot, parts faded, and at the highest magnification, she could just make out threads of BLUE winding their way between the banks of RED and GOLD. She prodded it carefully, and saw the impulses flick between banks, the color shimmering softly. She would learn more, of course, if she left everything attached, but training and experience urged caution—and if this was AI, even a tiny one, the sooner it was de-powered, the better. She found the loop tool and eased the fleck of GREEN out of its place, setting it carefully to one side. The other elements flickered again, their color fading, and she switched tools to begin unraveling the instructions.

When the chime sounded, she had unwound perhaps a quarter of the exterior BLUE, much of which she suspected had been added by whoever had sent the jumper, and made enough headway into the RED and GOLD to fear that Ashe might be right. There were configurations she didn't recognize, and the threads of BLUE that connected them seemed primarily to exist as conduits, not as actual instruction.

The chime sounded again, louder this time, and she looked up. "What?"

"There's a message," Dai said. "You need to see it."

"I'm really in the middle of this." Cassilde prodded a tiny speck of GOLD. She could just make out one familiar shape, an if/then conjunction, but the units to either side were unfamiliar. If she had found new GOLD characters... Even if they were originally meant to mediate AI, surely they could be adapted to AL, and to the general lower-level working vocabulary. And there were still any number of GOLD characters that carried no known meaning. Any of these might be the key to unlock another subset of characters. It had happened before, the find of anyone's lifetime...

"It's important," Dai said. "Everything else can wait."

The note in his voice hit home at last, and she looked up at the ceiling-mounted camera. "What is it?"

"Come up," Dai said again, and this time she obeyed.

The others were waiting in Central, sitting opposite each other at the main table, a thin display disk poised exactly between them. "Well?" she asked. "I was just starting to make some sense of this—"

Ashe pressed the edge of the disk, and a column of light sprang up, a hooded figure taking shape at its heart. Cassilde lifted an eyebrow— this was entirely too much like a cheap holoventure—and Dai said, "Wait for it."

"Misor Sam." The figure lifted its head slightly, but the face was still in shadow; the voice was probably a man's, but the edges of the image were deliberately blurred, obscuring any useful details. "I'm called Dehlin. From your reaction to this morning's…gift…it's clear you and I share an interest in the hunt. Meet with me, W139INSI2 at 1850 tonight, Mascvede Rules to apply, or I'll make sure that the local authorities find out just what you haven't turned over to them." The column of light winked out, taking the figure with it.

Cassilde swore under her breath. "Who is he? And what are these rules he's talking about?"

"The Mascvede Rules are sort of agreed on by everyone in the hunt," Ashe said. "They govern how hunters are supposed to interact—giving his name when he knows yours is part of it. It's a good sign. They also mark certain locations as neutral zones—that address he gave may be one of them, I haven't had a chance to check it out—and also bind all parties to meetings in those places to only shoot second. In theory, you should be able to meet safely, but—" He shrugged.

Dai rolled his eyes. "Yeah, no, we're not going to be stupid here. What's he got on us if we don't go?"

"Well," Ashe began, drawing out the word, and Cassilde spoke over him.

"The Gift. He said as much, and he's probably right, taking it violates First Refusal."

"It was to save your life," Dai protested, and Cassilde shook her head.

"It's still a technical violation, and you know damn well the local authority would want to dissect me just to see what the Gift does. We haven't even figured out all of that."

Dai grimaced and looked away, a sure sign of unhappy agreement. Cassilde said, "What does he want, Ashe?"

"How would I know?"

"Don't get me started," Cassilde said, fixing him with a stare. He didn't answer, but didn't look away, either, and she went on, "You said hunters didn't cooperate, that they fought each other. What does he want from me, and what happens if we don't go?"

"If we don't go," Dai said, "he turns us in. And we don't have time to get lift clearance, even if we were willing to leave a hundred thousand consols on the floor."

Ashe gave a reluctant nod. "What he wants...I told you, some, maybe most, Gifts fade over time, and some of them can be restored by another Gift. The only other thing people meet for is to trade information, or if there's something big rumored, maybe to cooperate. But I don't think it's that."

"No." Cassilde reached for her screen, unfolded it onto the table, and began typing instructions. "What did he say the address was?"

Dai reached for a slip of paper. "W139INSI2."

Cassilde plugged in the numbers, and the Glasstown map formed and spun under her fingers. It settled finally on a section of the Austenad, one of the broad gardens that had fed the city at settlement, and she looked at Ashe. "Is this a neutral space?"

Ashe reached for the screen, plugged in a new query, and then another, before handing it back. "It could be. And even if it's not, it's got enough traffic that we shouldn't be able to have a firefight—not to mention enough passive security to bring down the wrath of God on anybody who tries—but it's not so crowded that we're going to be tripping over people."

"All right." Cassilde straightened her shoulders. "We go."

𝆑 � 𝀥 ⁍

They caught the loop-train to the edge of the western Austenad as the sun was setting, filling the sky with gold light and sending long shadows across the neatly clipped grass. As Ashe had promised, the wide parkland wasn't very crowded; there were two long alleys of trees stretching along the longer axis, but a glance at her screen steered her toward the center of the field. To one side, a sign advertised milk from descendants of the original dairy goats that had come on the settlement ship, but the letters were all but drowned in the sunset light and the clouds of steam that rose from the heaters. A group of children was playing footie under the idle supervision of a pair of older women, goals marked with piled jackets. A few adults moved along the well-worn paths, well bundled against the cold, but none of them seemed to pay much attention to them.

"We are such a good target," Dai muttered, and Cassilde gave him an equally unhappy glance. The sun was setting to their left, a blinding light not much softened by the lines of trees. They were excellent targets, all right, and who was to say that their enemy wouldn't just take the shot, and hope to recover the Gift from her dead body.

"Too many passive sensors," Ashe said, as though he'd read her thought. "They won't come out shooting."

"Yeah, but how will they leave?" Dai asked, and Ashe gave a crooked smile.

"Let's not screw it up." He stiffened, his voice sharpening abruptly. "There."

Cassilde followed the tilt of his head, saw three people moving purposefully across the grass from the shadows of the other walk. She slipped her hand into her pocket, feeling the worn grip of her best welder, and stepped off the path herself, Dai and Ashe flanking her.

She stopped after twenty meters and let the strangers come on, hoping it would both project confidence and make them think she might have projectile weapons after all. The sun was down now, and the light was waning rapidly: not a good start, she thought, and the ground split at her feet, releasing a glowing sphere the size of her fist. It rose slowly, the light strengthening, finally stopped to hover at a point a little above Dai's head. Hundreds more of them were rising, all across the open park, and she heard a cheer from the children at the footie field. Half a dozen of the balls hung between her and the strangers, and their leader waved one impatiently out of his path as he took another step toward her.

"Cassilde Sam?"

"Who's asking?" Ashe answered, and the stranger dipped his head.

"Edou Dehlin is my name."

Cassilde nodded. "I'm Sam."

"Mascvede Rules?"

"For as long as you keep them," Cassilde answered, and saw the people behind Dehlin relax slightly. "What do you want with me?"

"I hear you have something we might trade for."

"We could do that during business hours," Cassilde answered.

"Let's not mince words." Dehlin took another step forward, lowering his hood. In the hovering light, his face was strongly lined, the shadows harsh on weathered skin. His all-weather jacket had scorch marks across one arm. "You have a Gift—a good one, by all accounts. I—my wife and I, we need—" One of the people behind him shifted uneasily, and Dehlin stopped. "I'm here to offer a trade."

"I'm listening," Cassilde said.

"A sample of your blood—a taste, nothing more—and I'll give you the location of five possible Gifts. Five good leads."

Cassilde stood very still, the glowing spheres drifting through the air between them, faint shadows rippling across the grass.

Ashe said, "Sight unseen?"

For a moment, she didn't understand the question, but Dehlin gave a slow nod. "Yes. If we do it now."

In spite of herself, Cassilde gave Ashe a sharp glance. He looked away, and she said, to Dehlin, "A moment, if you please."

"Three, if you'd like," Dehlin answered, a flash of bitter humor, and Cassilde took a step back.

"What is he asking, Ashe?"

"A blood sample, like he said." Ashe seemed to be trying to speak without moving his lips, keeping his voice as low as possible. "To restore his Gift. He'll give us the locations in exchange."

"We didn't exactly come prepared with a med-kit," Dai said.

"And I'm sure as hell not using theirs."

"I did," Ashe answered, and Cassilde swore under her breath. But of course he had, and she could fight that out later.

"'Sight unseen'?" she quoted.

"Neither of us gets to test the goods. We make the exchange and go."

Dehlin and his people were talking quietly, too, one, tall and heavy-set, with urgent gestures, and she saw Dehlin shake his head. "Well?" he called. "I'm waiting."

Cassilde nodded. "It's a deal."

"Move in," Ashe said quietly. "We don't want this on security."

Dehlin came forward in the same moment, his companions screening him, and Ashe pulled a box the length of his finger from a pocket. Cassilde recognized it as a sampler from the first aid kits, and swallowed another curse. He held it up, and Dehlin nodded to the smaller of his companions. She produced a data stick and held it up so that the light from the hovering spheres glinted off the blood-red surface.

"Trade?" Dehlin asked, and Cassilde nodded again.

"Give us a hand, Ashe." She folded back her left sleeve, and Ashe took her wrist, turning it so that he could see the tracery of veins on the inside of her arm. He thumbed on the sampler, exposing the wicked-looking blade, and tightened his grip.

"Ready?"

"Go." Cassilde braced herself, but the shock of the cut was still more than she had expected, a sharp electric jab deep into the flesh. She caught her breath, swaying, and Ashe manipulated the sampler, coaxing blood from the shallow cut into the chamber. The sampler beeped once, then again, and Ashe lifted it free. She blinked tears from her eyes, watching the cut seal itself, becoming a pink line that disappeared entirely. The pain had faded, too, though not as fast as the cut, and she drew a deep breath, steadying herself.

"The sample," she said, and was proud that her voice was

unchanged. Ashe lifted the device, though he was careful to stay out of reach of Dehlin's people.

"Locations," the woman said, but Dehlin lifted a hand.

"Change of deal. I test it now."

"That's hardly sight unseen," Cassilde said, and Ashe took a half-step backward. The big man at Dehlin's side stirred uneasily, and Dehlin shook his head. "Whatever happened to the Mascvede Rules?"

"Not actually broken," Dehlin protested. "Just bent a little."

"We can walk away," Cassilde said. She wasn't sure if that was actually reasonable, according to the rules of the hunt, but she was sure she'd only lose by backing down too quickly. "Start a fight here, and security gets involved."

As she had hoped, Dehlin flinched at that. "Look, I—"

"Cap," the woman said, but Dehlin ignored her.

"Sam. I—we're desperate, my wife and I. We're failing—hers is gone, we had a firefight on Placis, and she's in stasis. Mine's not enough to help, it's barely keeping me patched up." He spread open his jacket, showing a stained undershirt and a bandage pack crossing his upper chest, the outer surface already stained with blood. "I need to know this is going to work."

"Who told you this was a big Gift?" Ashe demanded.

Dehlin flicked him an unhappy glance. "Vertrage. He's claimed Placis." Ashe swore.

"We're not exactly friends," Cassilde said. The thought of having a lover in stasis, dependent on a restoring Gift, made her wince in sympathy—and besides, she thought, if Vertrage was her enemy, she'd better start making allies. "We'll do it." Ashe opened his mouth to protest, and Cassilde glared at him until he subsided. "Two conditions. First, hand over the locations."

Dehlin nodded, and the woman reluctantly held out the data stick. Dai took it, but didn't move away.

"Second—" Cassilde took a breath. "If it doesn't work the way you want, we all walk away. We've done our part." Dehlin hesitated, and she shook her head. "I don't really care if I upset this game, I never asked to be part of it—"

"All right," Dehlin said. "But—do it the proper way, then."

Cassilde didn't dare look aside, but heard Ashe stir. "Blood to blood?" he asked. "Too much risk of contamination."

"You know it works best," Dehlin said, and Cassilde looked away from the plea in his eyes.

"Ashe. Is there a safe way?"

"If you must."

"Yes," Cassilde said, firmly, and saw him sigh.

"All right. I'll do it, though."

"All right," Dehlin said, and shrugged out of his jacket. The bigger man took it for him, mouth closed tight in disapproval, and Dehlin glared at him. "Well, what else can we do?" The big man didn't answer, and Dehlin turned back to face them, rolling up his sleeve. "There. Good enough?"

Ashe nodded, reaching into his pocket again. He came up with a salvor's utility blade, adjusted it until only a tiny point projected from the housing. "Don't touch him directly," he said. "Let your blood drip down." Cassilde nodded, bracing herself again for the pain, but he turned to Dehlin first, eyeing the exposed skin dispassionately. "Ready?"

Dehlin nodded, grimacing, and Ashe struck, drawing a short line of blood across Dehlin's inner arm. Dehlin flinched, and Ashe reached for Cassilde's hand. "Hurry, before he heals—" She let him turn her palm upright, and swore as he stabbed her thumb. Even braced for it, it felt like a hot needle, digging all the way to the bone—

"Now," Ashe said, and she squeezed the cut, forcing out a single large droplet. She could feel the puncture healing as she moved, shook her hand so that the blood flew free. For a second, she thought she'd missed, would have to do it again, but then she saw the line of droplets crossing the cut on Dehlin's arm. It was starting to heal, far more sluggishly than her own, the skin starting to pull together at the ends, leaving an angry red weal. And then the raw skin faded, the cut closing with sudden speed. Dehlin gasped and straightened, and for just an instant she felt it, too, bone-deep and visceral, a whirl of action sweeping through his body. She could feel desperate relief and shame, *I live I live I live,* and pressed hard on her healing thumb, letting the pain drive away the connection.

"We're done."

Dehlin gasped again and nodded. "Deal's done."

"Then we'll say good night," Cassilde began, and Dehlin lifted his hand.

"This—" He gestured to his chest. "Vertrage wants more than Placis. He's trying to get everyone under his thumb. And he's looking for you, looking hard. You should know. You shouldn't have taken that from him."

"Oh, is that what he says?" Cassilde couldn't control her sudden anger. "Typical."

"That's what he's telling people," Dehlin said. "I just thought you should know."

It was useful information, Cassilde reminded herself, and they had come out of this better than she had expected, but she still couldn't bring herself to thank him. She nodded instead, and turned away, Ashe and Dai following her through the hovering spheres. At the edge of the field, she glanced back, but there was no sign of Dehlin or his people.

Back on the ship, Cassilde sealed the hatches and turned both rented and on-board security to their highest settings before joining the others in Central. Dai had already brought out a bottle of wine, and for once it was Ashe who was feeding packets into the cooker. Cassilde joined them, drank off half her glass in a single swallow, and held it out for more. This wasn't what she'd expected, somehow—

she had, she supposed, been expecting more violence or more money, something bigger and wilder, not this scraping trade, a drop of blood for the chance to find more Gifts, to keep the cycle going. She could still taste Dehlin's desperation, the shamed relief to know that he, at least, would survive even as he worried that his wife would not. These were things she hadn't needed to know, and she scowled at Ashe as he pulled a quick-loaf out of the cooker.

"Did you know that was going to happen?"

He set the pan on the table and fetched a crock of bean spread. "I thought it might."

"You damn well ought to have told us," Dai said.

Ashe turned away, busying himself with the rest of the meal—quick-melted cheese, Cassilde saw, one of her favorites, and she shook her head. "Bribery's not going to help, Ashe."

"No, but it can't hurt." He reached for his own glass, and the harsh light made the fading bruises around his eyes suddenly more visible.

"You should have told us," Cassilde said, but her anger was dissipating. He had tried, and she hadn't believed—couldn't have understood, she thought, until she saw it, felt it herself. "What exactly did I just do?"

"I told you, the Gifts can be transferred, usually by blood. And Gifts fade. They're like every other Ancestral artifact that way. That guy, Dehlin, his Gift was winding down. When your blood with its Gift touched his, it restored the faded one." He looked at Dai. "And don't ask me how, because no one knows."

"You also said that fixing someone else's Gift could damage your own," Cassilde said. "But I feel fine."

"It can." Ashe cut himself a wedge of the bread, and after a moment Dai slid the spread in his direction. "It doesn't always, and no one's really been able to work out why it happens or not. There are some obvious cues—two fading Gifts tend to harm each other, for example, and the more faded a Gift is, the more likely it is to affect the other. But none of those are sure things."

She was hungry after all, Cassilde realized, and cut herself a wedge of the bread. The Gift seemed to have made her taste buds more sensitive, too; she could taste every nuance of the spices Ashe had added to the cheese. "We need to learn," she said.

"Haven't I been telling you that?" Ashe grimaced, tried to wave the words away. "Sorry, I know you didn't believe me—"

"We didn't think we were this vulnerable," Dai said. "Or at least I didn't. And what's to stop someone else from trying the same thing the next place we dock?"

"Two things keep you safe in the hunt," Ashe said. "Reputation and stealth."

"And we don't have the first," Cassilde said. "Well, stealth it is."

"Except you do have a reputation," Ashe said. "I didn't think he'd do it, but it sounds like John's spreading the word that you have an exceptional Gift. And that you're new to the hunt, which makes you a better than average target."

"We need two more days to finish things," Dai said. "Unless you need more, Ashe?" Ashe shook his head.

"Then we lift on the 50th," Cassilde said. "I'll get that set up tonight."

"Where?" Dai asked.

"Ashe is going to help us figure that out," she said. "Aren't you, Ashe?"

"He'd better," Dai said. "And I'd also like to know what we got for all this."

"Find me a clean reader," Ashe said, "and I'll tell you."

Cassilde reached behind her to rummage through storage until she found one of the burner screens they kept for just this sort of chancy data. Ashe found the right port and inserted Dehlin's data stick, and they all waited while the system hummed to itself and finally flashed an opening screen. Ashe worked the controls, and the file opened, revealing a list of standardized coordinates.

"So far, so good," Dai said.

Cassilde reached for her own screen, began entering the planetary settings. Slowly, the names took shape on her screen: Eris, Ione, Fastas in the Little Compact, Scamander, and Teraday. None of them were particularly familiar, and she spun the screen so that the others could see. "Recognize anything?"

Dai shook his head, and Ashe said, "Well, of course I know the Little Compact—Fastas is one of the trailing worlds, at the edge of the retimond—and I can find out about the rest, but the important thing is what the Gifts are like." He was working as he spoke, flicking from file to file as he dug deeper into the material. "This all looks good. They're all supposed to be high quality and most are multi-use. I think we got our money's worth."

"It wasn't money we paid," Dai said. "Or you who paid it."

"Whatever. Dehlin kept his word, anyway."

"Summarize," Cassilde said.

"It's standard salvors' notation," Ashe said. "Five locations on five worlds that Dehlin has reason to believe hold not just Ancestral ruins but Ancestral Gifts. Of the five, he ranks three as highly likely, and the other two as likely; Fastas is one of the highly likelies, but I'm not real eager to go too deep into the Entente just now."

Cassilde nodded. The worlds of the Core were too closely linked—Fastas was part of the Little Compact, linked by TLD network to eight other worlds; if they got into trouble there, they wouldn't have much chance to disappear before their data was flashed to every other world in the reticulate. Besides, she was Edge, born and bred: better to take their chances on the warplines, where she understood the emptiness and how to use it, than venture onto someone else's ground.

She tugged the screen closer, turning the numbers into—well, not quite facts, but the best of Dehlin's guesses. Teraday and Scamander were both logged sites, and would require a permit to search them legally. Not that she didn't qualify, but that was extra time and expense, and always the risk that someone would notice their application. And an illegal operation brought its own set of problems. She'd rather avoid them unless she had no other choice. Teraday was listed as "outpost station (possible?)" while Scamander was a more familiar wreck field with a few larger fragments that had landed intact—and that alone, she thought, was probably enough to move it down the list. Surely a Gift that survived impact would have been used by the crash survivors themselves. Fastas was an orbital, a fragment of ship or station circling not Fastas itself but a cold sister planet one orbit out from its sun. That was a more likely site, but she still didn't want to enter the retimond.

Eris was further out on the Edge, one of the few systems trailing back toward the Great Gap where legend said the Ancestors had fought their renegade AI to a standstill, even the kin-slaying Dedalor family uniting behind Anketil and Irtholin to hold off the Fall for a few hundred years. If there really had been such a war, Cassilde thought, it looked as though Eris had lost its part of the battle. The codes painted a barren, burnt-over world with a poisoned atmosphere, holding a middle orbit among clouds of debris. But among that debris was the remains of another orbiting Ancestral installation, and Dehlin's notes claimed to have found references to a station there at the end of the AI wars.

Ione, at least, was a settled world, home to a small string of floating cities that harvested mineral-bearing plankton from the planet's enormous oceans. The listing claimed that the Ancestors' installation was on one of a string of low-lying islands that bisected the planet's equator several thousand kilometers from the main fishing grounds— apparently they had no natural fresh water source and were too far from the richest plankton beds to be worth settling. The listing called it a remnant site, built before seas had risen so high, and she wondered how much of what was left would be underwater.

"Eris or Ione, I think," she said, and Ashe nodded.

Dai looked from one to the other. "You're pretty sure of yourselves."

"Do you disagree?" Cassilde asked.

He shrugged. "I might have put Teraday in there, but, no, I don't disagree. I just wonder how many other people have this list."

Cassilde looked at Ashe, who rubbed his healing nose. "That's an excellent question. Mind you, in my experience, people hoard this sort of information, but—you saw, they'll trade when they're desperate, and there's no knowing if these were Dhelin's finds to start with."

"So we could get there and find that someone's been there ahead of us," Cassilde said.

"Just like any other salvage job," Ashe answered.

"Except on this one someone's likely to be shooting at us," Dai pointed out.

"We can take precautions," Ashe said. "We always take precautions." He stopped, shrugging, though Cassilde could feel the effort it took for him to pretend disinterest. "Or we could try for Alamance-Plaisance. As long as we get off-world before John shows up—"

"Because of course he will," Cassilde said. She looked at her arm, the skin smooth and unscarred where Ashe had cut it not two hours ago. "He wants this Gift, right? Which he'll get through my blood? What if I just send him a sample?"

Ashe made a sound that might have been laughter. "He's not very trusting. He's the sort to want to draw it himself, to be sure where it's come from."

"Charming." Cassilde pulled the screen closer to her again, frowning at the lines of code so that neither of the others could see her expression. She hadn't exactly asked for this, hadn't joined this hunt willingly, unlike all the others; she'd gladly give it up—except that she wouldn't, not if it meant a return to the Lightman's and the slow death that was waiting. "All right, we can't stay here, we're all agreed on that. I vote for Eris—it's furthest away from anything else, and there's lots of places to hide if we do run into company."

"That's fine with me," Ashe said.

"What, you're not going to point out a better site?" Dai demanded.

"I told you, what I want is to get off-world," Ashe said. "Eris looks as good as any of them."

Cassilde looked at Dai, trying to read his feelings. "We can still place a claim for Alamance," she said. "But I'd like your reasons."

Dai shook his head. "No, a claim's too easy to trace, I can see that. We'll need extra gear for Eris, but that's easy enough."

"You're sure?" She reached across to take his hand.

"I'm sure," he said, and closed his fingers around hers.

It took most of the next two days to prepare for departure. For once, the money flowed in as scheduled, their accounts steadily filling with Entente consols; even the necessary purchases, fuel, supplies, the tools they'd need to work in vacuum or in Eris's tainted atmosphere, didn't make too bad a dent in the balances. They had a generous supply of elements on board, too, decent chunks of RED and GOLD as well as GREEN and BLUE, and for the first time in years Cassilde could contemplate an Edge trip without great qualm. Things could certainly go wrong—almost certainly would go wrong—but at least she had the tools to fix almost anything.

After some debate, they pulled the last batch of Ashe's toys from auction and re-stowed them aboard *Carabosse*. Wherever they ended up, the toys would remain a ready source of cash. She filed for a prospector's permit, hinting to the Survey office that she was considering back-tracking the find they had just made, and paid the doubled fee to keep it valid outside Cambyse's system. Ashe buried himself in the local nets, trying to collect as much information about the five systems as he could find, and all the while they all kept one eye on the ship's security.

Dai returned late on the second day, and Cassilde drew a sigh of relief as she let him through the ship's screen and then resealed the hull behind him. "Are you all right?"

"Fine, just tired." His coat was damp, smelled of rain and the Burntover, and she took it from him, amazed again that the acrid dust didn't choke her. "Edou Dehlin lifted this morning."

"Did he?" She closed the storage cell, focusing on the latch as though it were something difficult.

"Yeah."

She heard him move away, then cabinets opening in Central, and followed, watching as he made up another pot of tea. "Did you eat?"

"In the port." He flipped the switch that set the kettle heating, and turned to face her. "Sorry, I didn't mean to take so long. There was some talk about a ship that landed yesterday, and I wanted to be sure it wasn't Vertrage."

Cassilde froze, but made herself move again. "I assume it wasn't?"

"I'm almost sure not. I'm glad we're leaving tomorrow, though."

"It's an early lift," Cassilde answered. "Dawn window."

"The sooner the better," Dai said, and Cassilde came to lean against his chair, putting her arms carefully over his shoulders. When he didn't pull away, she bent to press a kiss onto the top of his head.

"Are you all right?" she asked again, and this time she felt him sigh.

"I don't like this, Silde. Well, I like that you're well, you can't know how much I like that—"

"As much as I do," Cassilde said gently. "I don't want to go back."

"No." He rested his chin on her arm. "And we can't, anyway. Ashe made that clear. But—it's a nasty business, that's all."

"I know." The kettle whistled, and she released him, preparing a cup for each of them. She found the honeysticks as well, a local treat, and they each took one, stirring them solemnly into the hot liquid until the last fragment dissolved. "Will you—would you at least consider it, if we find another Gift?"

Dai dropped his head. "I…I don't know. Maybe."

Cassilde closed her teeth over everything more that she wanted to say. *Do it for me, do it for us, for me and Ashe and the ship and our lives together so that we never have to give anything up...* But that would never convince him, would only put his back up further, after everything they'd seen so far. And none of that was particularly good, either; she couldn't say she liked anything she'd seen of the hunt. But she was alive, and would go on living, and that—that was both enough and the best reason to want more. "Fair enough," she said, and fetched more tea.

CHAPTER EIGHT

arabosse lifted from Cambyse half an hour ahead of schedule, thanks to another ship needing to delay, enough to let Cassilde cast a section of the sensor net astern to see if anyone reacted to the change in plan. She rode the exit beacon up out of atmosphere, barely pausing long enough to rotate onto the new heading before opening up the main engines. They had fuel to spare, and she was tempted to go to top speed right away, but that risked attracting attention, too. Instead, she set a rising velocity and relaxed in the pilot's chair, studying the images the sensor net dredged out of surrounding space. There were plenty of other ships heading in and out, and still more in near and far orbits, most of those bulk warpliners on a standard circle route, exchanging part of their cargo for Cambyse's exports, but no one seemed particularly interested in them. She was pinged a handful of times, and let the transponder answer, but as Cambyse and its sun fell away behind them, she began to hope that they had evaded Vertrage.

The cockpit door slid open, and she glanced up as Ashe slid into the co-pilot's seat. He was wearing the mote again, clinging to his chest just inside the collar of his shirt.

"Everything's good mid-ships," he said. "I take it you don't want anybody on weapons?"

"Not right now." Cassilde glanced at the sensor net again, reassured by the familiar patterns and symbols. "Unless there's something you're not telling me?"

Ashe shook his head, and the intercom console beeped. Cassilde flicked the switch to open the line. "Yeah?"

"Putting the engines on auto," Dai said, "and then I'm going to take a quick walk through cargo, make sure nothing shifted on launch."

"Need a hand with that?" Ashe asked, and there was a moment of silence.

"Not now, thanks. I'll let you know if anything turns up."

"Right," Cassilde said, and flicked off the intercom again. She glanced at Ashe. "Do you think we've gotten ahead of him? Vertrage, I mean?"

"There's every chance. And if any of these locations has a Gift—" Ashe stopped, grimacing.

"You really want one," Cassilde said. Not that she could blame him, given how much better she felt, and given the promise of immortality. Live forever, strong and hale: who wouldn't want that? Except that nothing the Ancestors made lasted forever.

"I suppose," Ashe said, and shrugged when she lifted an eyebrow. "Yes. Do you think less of me for it?"

"How can I, when I've got one myself?" Cassilde asked. "But I don't like the game."

"I didn't think you would."

"And if you'd gotten the Gift—if I hadn't been sick, if none of this had happened, and you'd taken the Gift yourself—were you just going to walk out on us? Again?"

Ashe winced. "I—I don't know, Silde, I hadn't really worked it out. I suppose I hoped I could talk you into it, over time. Once we'd gotten clear of the hunt."

"Is that possible, then?"

"I don't know," Ashe said again. "I thought it was—there were always rumors, stories about people who didn't play by the hunt's rules, who still had Gifts or at least something like them. And the Edge is big, I thought it might be possible to get out of range if I moved fast enough. And I thought I had, or I wouldn't have come to you." He ran a finger down the mote's carapace, tiny sparks following his touch. "Though—I'll be honest, if I hadn't tracked you down, or if you hadn't been hiring, I'd have tried for that section on my own. I could have put together a team if I'd had to."

"You'd be dead now if you'd done that," Cassilde said, briskly enough that she hoped he wouldn't hear that nightmare in her voice. She had worked through those possibilities, too, and all of them ended, as far as she could see, with Ashe dead and Vertrage in possession of the Gift. Not because she was so good, either, she thought, but because she'd already been desperate enough to believe him. And because, in the end, she trusted Ashe. "Vertrage. He's not your usual type."

Ashe gave a wry smile. "There was a war on, Silde. Not so much to choose from."

She laughed in spite of herself, as he had meant, and allowed herself to stretch in the chair, enjoying the play of restored muscles. "Any chance he'll just give up?"

"It's possible?" Cassilde lifted her eyebrows, certain she heard doubt, and Ashe sighed. "I thought he'd given up on me. And then I thought I'd at least given him the slip. Turned out I was wrong."

"He wanted you to lead him to my Gift," Cassilde said. "But we got away, and he's not going to get it without—well, what does he have to do? Kill me?"

"That's probably the way he'd go," Ashe said. "But technically you ought to be able to transfer most of the Gift through a transfusion."

"So I could give you a share of this one?" Cassilde asked. If that were possible, that would solve a lot of their problems with minimal effort.

"You'd probably damage your Gift beyond repair," Ashe said. "It worked on Dehlin because he already had one, remember? That's one of the near-certain ways to destroy a Gift, to try to share it. And that's not a risk I'd like to see you take. Not with the Lightman's."

"So if my Gift fails, the Lightman's comes back?" Cassilde

couldn't quite keep the bitter note out of her voice, and Ashe's fingers twitched, as though he wanted to reach for her hand.

"Most likely. I've never seen it with Lightman's, of course, but I knew a guy with Tresor's Sarcoma, he had a series of short-lived Gifts, and every time one started to fail, the tumors would come back."

"Lovely." Cassilde scowled at the sensor display, inoffensively empty of all but routine traffic as they bore on toward the edge of the system. "Does that mean I've damaged things by giving Dehlin a drop of blood?"

"Probably not. It was just a drop, and you didn't exchange anything with him." Ashe touched his mote again. "The thing is, this says your Gift is something special."

"You keep saying that," Cassilde said. "How special?"

"Well, if I knew that…"

"Guess," Cassilde said, but she was smiling in spite herself.

"Bigger, more powerful, more important," Ashe said, abruptly serious. "Different enough to be in a class by itself, possibly. The mote links it to the Dedalor."

Cassilde felt her eyebrows rise at that. The Dedalor were the mythical ruling family of the Ancestors, and instrumental in the Fall; they had built the first AI and then betrayed it when it became too powerful, which had led to the war of AI against All and the banning of AI from human-settled space. Supposedly the last of the Dedalor and her lover had trapped them outside time and space, and somehow sealed the web of the world against their return…

"I know," Ashe said. "It's a long shot. But if it were true…"

If it were true, it would be the greatest archeological discovery of the last ten generations. She shook her head. "I wish—I wish you'd said that sooner."

"If I had, you wouldn't have wanted to leave," Ashe said. "And we still couldn't stay."

He was right, of course, but that didn't make it any easier. At least she would receive the collected finders' reports once they were all reviewed, but— "If they don't make that connection, I'm going to raise it with the Survey board."

"And explain it how?" Ashe asked.

"I'll tell them we found something in a toy." And that reminded her of the jumper still securely boxed in the lab: she would need to finish dissecting it once they were safely on the warpline.

"You do that, and you'll bring John down on us."

"Not if we're very careful how we send it," Cassilde said. "And let's face it, if he's that good, there's not much point in our trying to get away."

There was a moment of silence, and then Ashe shook his head. "All right."

"One other thing we need from you," Cassilde said. "You've been in this hunt, you know the rules. You're going to have to teach us."

"I can do that," Ashe said. "Dai's not going to like it."

"I don't think I'm going to like it, either," Cassilde said, "but we need to know."

Ashe nodded. "What—have you thought about what this means, Silde? What you could do?"

She paused, not sure how honest she wanted to be. "Some. I've thought some. If we weren't running all the time, weren't scrambling for money—can you imagine how much we could find out about the Ancestors?"

Ashe nodded again, though she couldn't tell from his expression whether he agreed or not. "There's a hell of a lot out there, enormous possibilities, and time to do it in."

"As long as we can talk Dai into taking a Gift." She hadn't meant to say that, but the worry had been weighing her down.

"Let him think about it," Ashe said. "He'll come around."

There was no answer to that, or at least not one that was of any use. Cassilde turned her attention back to the sensor net, scanning the familiar symbols for any sign of anything out of the ordinary. They flickered across the darkened grid in steady patterns, the string of warpliners crossing the system for the 'line entrance that would take them to Brondda, a scatter of STL work-craft busy in the sixth-orbit asteroid belt, even a few faint signals that had to be ships returning from the find-field. She wondered briefly what they had found, whether there really was any connection to the Dedalor of legend—could this have been one of the Dedalors' traveling palaces?—then made herself turn her attention to the autopilot settings.

"We'll be at our 'line entry in about nine hours. I'm going to take a break and come back fresh."

"Want me to keep an eye on things?" Ashe asked.

Cassilde hesitated, tempted, but shook her head. "Only if you want."

"I'll stay for a bit," Ashe said.

And that was unusual enough that she hesitated again. Was he up to something, off on some plan of his own? She shoved the thought away, telling herself it was too late to worry.

ᚪ ᗰ ᛤ ᛂ

They were coming up on the warpline entrance, the place where the fabric of space/time ran thin enough to let them align *Carabosse* with the crease in space that would let them flicker-jump along that thread of weakness. All the filters were engaged on the pilot's board, translating mathematics to shapes and colors: the general location of the entrance was known and invariant, but the precise angles, the exact point of attack, shifted slowly with the galaxy's revolutions. Almost certainly the Ancestors had never had to worry about this fiddling match of frequencies and vectors; all surviving evidence indicated that their ships had jumped direct from point to point, entering and leaving the adjacent possible pretty much at will, but that secret had been lost in the First Dark. The REFTL drive was based on the Successors' stutter drive, which entered the adjacent possible only for fractions of an apparent second—severely limited, compared to the Ancestors' drive, but if you believed the version of the Fall that said the Dedalor had locked the rebel AI into the adjacent possible, it was certainly safer. In any case, it had been good enough to bring humanity back from the Dark.

Cassilde checked the sensor net again—hijackers liked to lurk around 'line entrances and exits, hoping to catch distracted crews—but the net showed empty. She turned her attention back to the pilot's board, stroking her control surface to bring up the faint blue-on-black watermark that was background conditions. Everything was well within *Carabosse*'s tolerances, and, better still, there was no indication that any other ships had been this way within the last thirty hours. This was one of the 'line entrances that seemed to hold on to turbulence, with each successive ship setting up patterns in the unstable transition zones; it was a relief not to have to deal with that.

"Dai? How're we doing?"

"Jump capacitor is at 88 percent and building," Dai answered. "We'll be full in eight minutes."

Cassilde touched her controls again, watching the numbers form and reform. "How are your frequencies looking?"

"Treble and mean are holding in the 450s, though my guess is that the mean is going to jump a couple hundred as we get set up. Base is showing 119 over a steady twenty to twenty-five in alpha."

All within normal limits. Cassilde flicked her screen so that it focused on the vectors. "Let me know when you've got it locked down. I'm calculating the approach."

"I can take over the sensor net," Ashe offered from the co-pilot's chair, and she nodded.

"Yeah, do that."

Ashe worked his own controls, and there was a soft chime as the sensor net moved to his console. "Got it. Still clear."

"Good." Cassilde stroked the screen again, bringing up the colors until the image in the display was as gaudy and shimmering as an oil slick. *Carabosse* showed as a thin red dart at the bottom of the display, the colors dimpling as the point touched them, then streaming back in long waves. She touched controls, adjusting their course, and the dimple deepened, the colors organizing themselves to either side. The sweet spot seemed to lie a little below the planetary plane, and she adjusted the controls again, easing the ship onto the correct line. "Fields ready?"

"Whenever you are," Dai answered.

"Bring them on line."

The ship trembled, steadied again, and now the ship in the display glowed green, safely armored for its passage through the adjacent possible. She touched the yoke and pedals, saw the ship move, the display deforming momentarily before she brought it back onto the optimum approach, the interface now adjusting the drive envelope rather than the ship's steering.

"Treble's steady at 451.1," Dai said. "Still waiting for mean and base to settle."

"Confirmed," Cassilde said. "Still locking down the correct vectors." She touched a secondary key as she spoke, signaling the ship's computers to calculate speed and angles, show that as an overlay on the display. That was a precaution, a check of what her eyes could read: no AI on this ship, or any modern ship, just the finest calculators she could afford. The template appeared, a pale schematic overlaying the display. It matched, and she swept it away again. "I make it ten minutes to jump."

"I confirm," Dai answered. "Mean at 661.8. I'm locking that."

"Go ahead." Cassilde worked yoke and pedals, and saw the colors split further, Carabosse's nose now touching an infinitesimal fleck of white, the dulled colors forming a great circle around the ship. "Sensors?"

"Still clear," Ashe said.

"Jump capacitor is at 100 percent," Dai said. "Still waiting on the base."

"Acknowledged." Cassilde frowned at the screen, all her displays expanded to maximum. She touched one pedal, tilted the yoke just a fraction to the right, and the white fleck brightened, though it grew no larger.

"Base is steady. Locking at 199 over 23 alpha."

"Confirmed." Cassilde licked her lips, focusing on the tiny fleck of white, the vectors steering her toward that perfect point of flux. "Jump capacitor ready?"

"Ready when you are," Dai answered.

"In five," Cassilde said, her hands steady on her controls, the lines of force streaming back like water. "Four...three...two...one... Now."

Even as she spoke, she felt the soundless boom that was the capacitor firing, felt the ship kick indefinably forward and over, though neither of those was quite the right word, and the display streaked and hazed into shards of colors for which she had never had names. The stutter drive should kick in any minute, flipping them in and out of normal space/time like a needle moving through fabric, but instead they were caught in that moment of sound, *Carabosse* carried on it like a leaf on the wind. The colors were changing, taking on a strange, pulsing pattern, shading from the oil-slick blues and golds and greens to sickly yellows and clashing reds. She worked the controls, instinctively pulling in the fields, drawing them tight around the ship, and the reds faded to ugly pink. The numbers streaming across the bottom of the screen no longer matched the settings they'd gathered just before the Jump.

"Dai!"

"I see it—I make base 210 over 9 alpha, what do you see?"

"The same. Mean's 683.3, treble 440.25."

"Confirmed," Dai said. "Adjusting."

At last she felt the stutter drive catch, ragged at first, beating its own pattern against the frequencies of the warpline. *Carabosse* steadied, a vibration she had barely been able to feel vanishing from her bones, and she allowed herself a sigh of relief. "On the 'line. We'll need to correct a little at the end, we didn't make a perfect entrance, but we're all right."

"Steady here as well," Dai answered, and she could hear the relief in his voice. "Hell of a lot of turbulence."

"There shouldn't have been any," Cassilde said. "There hadn't been a ship through in days. Did I miss something, Ashe?"

"Not that I could see." Ashe shrugged. "If you missed something, so did I."

Cassilde shook her head, feeling the irregular pulse of the drive in the marrow of her bones. Everything looked all right on the screens: they were squarely on the 'line, and the pattern was a solid match to the 'line's frequency, but somehow it still felt unstable. "Dai, we're running awfully rough. Can you recheck things, please?"

"Already on it," Dai answered.

Cassilde leaned back in her chair, and realized that Ashe was flicking back through the sensors' records. "Got something?"

"Not yet—"

"The numbers are good," Dai said. "This is an entirely valid solution, it's just not very comfortable. We could try a transposition, but I'm not sure it's worth it."

Probably not, Cassilde thought, scowling at her screens. Transposition was always a tricky maneuver, jumping from one solution to a harmonic solution; it was easy to miss the calculation, and equally easy to botch the timing, which would drop the ship off the warpline or, at worst, toss it into some invariant real space object. The next couple of days would be a little uncomfortable, but that was all. "You're right," she said. "We'll be in the Basin in thirty hours anyway."

"I'm going to lock in the settings," Dai answered.

"Go ahead," Cassilde answered, her hands already moving on her own controls. "I'm setting the autopilot, and then I'm going to take a break." She glanced at Ashe, still frowning over his board. "You coming?"

"I'll be along," Ashe answered. "I'm trying to lock something down here."

"Trouble?" Cassilde felt adrenaline spike, and was not appeased when he shook his head.

"No, if there was trouble, it's passed. I'm just...curious, that's all."

It was generally wiser to let Ashe ride a hunch. Cassilde nodded, unfastening herself from her chair. She gave the displays a final look from the hatch—everything still solidly green, in spite of the irritating syncopation of the drive—and made her way back to Central.

An off-beat rhythm could produce all sorts of physical symptoms, from headaches and nausea to other forms of digestive effects, and she was uneasily aware of the possibilities as she searched the cabinets before settling on a mild Osteppan tea and a jar of thick syrup that was supposed to have prophylactic properties. The pot was ready by the time Dai joined her, wiping his hands on the tail of his shirt, and she poured for both of them. The sweetened liquid tasted remarkably good, however, and she poured herself a second cup without thinking. Dai grimaced and looked away.

"Are you all right?" Cassilde asked. Maybe her own absence of symptoms was another result of the Gift. "Do we need to rethink transposition?"

"I'm all right," Dai said. "And it's only thirty hours, anyway."

Which meant, Cassilde thought, that he was feeling fairly bad. "You can sleep for most of it," she said, and was unsurprised to see him nod.

"What do you think went wrong?" he asked after a moment, still staring at the teapot as though it was to blame.

Cassilde shrugged. "I don't know. I suppose it could have been another ship? We know this break remembers what's gone through it—"

"But not for days," Dai said. "I wonder if I should have tried an inverted mean? Sometimes that'll smooth things out."

"It felt more like turbulence," Cassilde said, and the hatch slid back to admit Ashe.

"Maybe not turbulence, exactly," he said. "If this had happened during the war, what would you have said?"

"Stasis mine," Cassilde said, Dai half a beat behind her. They looked at each other, and this time Dai spoke first.

"They're banned out here, you know."

"They're banned in the Entente, too," Ashe answered, "though I think the Verge didn't outlaw them out of sheer spite."

"It couldn't have been a mine," Dai said again.

Except Ashe was right, Cassilde thought, it had felt like a mine. Seven years ago, that would have been the first thing to spring to mind, and now that it was spoken, it made all too much sense. It would have been set to go off as the jump capacitor fired, its hyperspatial anchor doubling as the conduit for energies that could distort space/time around the break point, and even, in the worst case, distort or destroy the travel fields. She had seen them before, been caught in the edges of a blast on one long convoy run, the ships huddling together to cross normal space, and then fleeing like frightened birds for the 'line entrance at the last moment. That kick, the way the jump had seemed to go on forever... "It might have been," she said aloud, and Dai shook his head.

"Where'd it come from?"

"A leftover?" Even as she said it, she knew that was unlikely: the 'line was in regular use, had been since the end of the war. If it had been there all that time, someone would have triggered it years ago. "Maybe it came down the warpline."

"Occam's Razor," Ashe said. "Or it was put there."

"For us, you mean," Dai asked, and Ashe nodded again. "By Vertrage?"

"Or one of his people."

Cassilde cocked her head to one side. "Vertrage wasn't in system when we left, unless you know something we don't. And Dehlin left some twenty hours before we did."

"He's who I was thinking, yes," Ashe said.

"We just did him a damn big favor," Dai pointed out.

"That's not how the hunt works," Ashe said.

"If the mine hits us, Vertrage loses my Gift," Cassilde said.

"Or it knocks us off the 'line and into realspace where he could find us," Dai said. "You can rig a mine for that."

"And Dehlin's got no reason to do Vertrage a favor." Ashe gave a thin smile. "Blow us up, and this Gift is lost, but Vertrage doesn't get it, either."

"I don't buy it," Cassilde said. "Dehlin was outbound for Brondda, and that 'line's almost all the way on the other side of the system."

"If he'd made a last minute change in orbit, it wouldn't have been reported," Dai said.

That was true enough, Cassilde had used the technique herself to throw off nosy rivals. "All right, it's possible. But where would he have gotten a mine?"

"Any of the Six Systems," Ashe answered.

Cassilde grimaced at the thought. The Six Systems were currently uninhabited, or mostly so, interdicted because the debris of battles fought through their solar systems made navigation nearly impossible. She supposed you could, if you were desperate enough, find a 'line exit far enough out that you wouldn't be destroyed on exit, but the idea of combing through lethal debris for mines that had not yet gone off was hardly appealing.

"Or there are dealers who'll have them as surplus, for the right price," Ashe continued.

"Or we could just have been unlucky," Dai said. "I've heard of them being dragged down the warplines."

"Well, however it got there, it wasn't very well placed," Cassilde said. And that, to her mind, was another argument for unfortunate coincidence: surely one of Vertrage's people would have done a better job. "But we'll be extra careful crossing the Basin."

〴 Ⱶ ⚔ ⫰

Both Dai and Ashe were more bothered by the drive rhythm than she was, so she let them take the longer sleep period. Left to herself in the quiet ship, she checked the control room, then made her way aft to check the drive controls. Everything showed green there as well, the capacitor two-thirds charged, the stutter drive stumbling through its clumsy-sounding pattern, and she turned back to the lab.

Everything lay just as she had left it, the glovebox secure in its clamps, seals glowing green; in its center the jumper lay dissected, the Ancestral elements that had powered the brain-box flecks of color underneath the magnifying lens. Normal safety protocols said she should wait to work on this until someone else was awake and aware, but that seemed like a waste of time. Once they were in Eris's system, they would need to focus on finding the station, and then the Gift, and that would take all of them; she had a feeling they needed to know how this thing worked before they started meddling with Eris's Gifts.

Still, for safety's sake, she removed the fleck of GREEN from the box and stored it in a separate secure container before continuing to pry apart the rest of the construction. As she had thought, the BLUE had been added later, the hexagons hooked up in familiar modern short-cuts; the RED was a mix of new and old work, a set of commands and conditionals woven into an older structure. The formal grammar was unusual, but not outside common use; even so, she recorded several of the oddest connections for further study. The GOLD, though... It was old, had faded badly once the GREEN had been disconnected, and she wished she'd thought to record them more completely before she'd been interrupted. Too late now, she told herself, and continued disconnecting the individual units.

GOLD processed BLUE, activated RED: that was the standard control chain. The segments of BLUE that she had unraveled had contained more instructions than she had thought at first, compressed and abbreviated enough that she had missed them on the first look, but definitely there. The RED was a knot of conditionals driving the jumper's mechanics. The GOLD lay between them, faded and growing harder to interpret with every passing hour. That, she guessed, was the material from a toy, that and perhaps the core of the RED. She laid the pieces out again, searching for connections that she had missed, smaller units hidden within the larger components. There were some, though fewer than she had expected, and she laid them out again.

Not AI, she thought at last, though high enough functioning Artificial Life that it might well be banned in its current form. And not, sadly, any new characters: the ones she hadn't recognized at first had proved to be known forms connected in new ways. But those new connections were powerful enough to loop conditionals into configurations capable of complex decisions. She could sell a report on that for tens of thousands of consols, particularly if she approached the Universities of the Entente. *And I wonder why Dehlin didn't do that,* she thought, as she carefully secured the lab again. Wanted to keep it for himself? Fear of Vertrage? There were a dozen possibilities, and none more likely than the rest. Ashe might know more, if he decided to share.

And maybe it was also time to take a look at the Gift, to see what exactly she carried inside her. She was no biologist, but a simple blood sample ought to give her some useful information, might even let her see the components that made up her Gift if her equipment was powerful enough. The lab carried sampling kits; she prepared one and braced herself for the thrust of the tiny blade. It hurt, unreasonably so, but she managed to squeeze out a drop of blood before the pinprick closed. She smeared half on a test disk—outside her body, it didn't seem to behave abnormally, she noticed—and used the rest to prepare a slide.

She slid it under the microscope while she waited for the sampler to run its programs, but she could make out nothing more than the familiar fat shapes of red blood cells. She increased the magnification to its maximum, and thought she could see something infinitesimal between the much larger cells, like grains of sand, but she couldn't make out any further details. The sample pinged then, announcing its results, and she read the narrow ribbon with a deepening frown.

Everything was aggressively normal, except for traces of Ancestral elements so small that the sampler described them as contamination.

If she only had a scanning microscope—but no one needed those for salvage. Probably Ashe was right, the Gift was some sort of adaptive nanite swarm, and the sand-like grains were the individual units; the elemental traces would be the Gift at work. She cleaned the equipment and, after a moment's thought, stored the samples in sealed bags labeled innocuously 'Sample 1.' If she needed to trade that information, either to the government or, luck forfend, to Vertrage, they'd be ready to hand.

Anything more would have to keep for after they reached Eris. She put the results aside, returning to Central to brew more tea and to consider her best course through the Basin. Seven different warplines had exits there, at the fringes of a dead system, three scorched rocky planets orbiting a red giant. The Successors had built a waystation at a libration point, possibly in the frame of an Ancestral station, but most ships passed through without stopping to use the station's exorbitantly priced facilities. *Carabosse* wouldn't need fuel or supplies; she hoped they could blend in with the other traffic transferring from one warpline to another. There was no requirement to post a destination—the waystation was there only for repairs, not to monitor traffic—and she thought they'd be able to make the course for Eris without attracting attention.

She flipped from the navigation simulators to her notes on the jumper, but the symbols made no more sense than before, shapes and colors dazzling and opaque, pattern without sense. And that was a sign she needed to rest herself. She put away the boards and settled down with a novel, looking up in some surprise when Dai reappeared. He was earlier than she had expected, and she didn't try to hide her frown. "Couldn't sleep?"

"My stomach's upset." He rummaged in the cabinets and found a liquid meal, popped the cap and washed down a tablet. "You might as well get some sleep yourself. You're still feeling all right?"

"It's really not bothering me," she said. She'd never been particularly sensitive to drive irregularities, but before this would have hit her as hard as it was hitting the others. "I think maybe it's the Gift."

"Well, that would be an advantage," Dai said.

Cassilde swallowed what she would have said—*Yes, it is, and that's another reason you should let us find you one*—and managed a smile. "Certainly doesn't hurt," she said, and took herself to bed.

To her surprise, Ashe was asleep in the main cabin, curled against the wall in Dai's usual spot. He didn't stir as she undressed, and she wondered for a moment if he'd taken a pill, but he woke enough as she slid in next to him to roll over and let her settle against him.

After the years with Lightman's, it was still a luxury to breathe deeply, regardless of how she lay. She closed her eyes, letting herself drift toward sleep. Even the drive's rhythm seemed less annoying, became something she could breathe against, its beat circling round to catch up with her, like the drums at a night dance. She remembered hearing them at Midsummer, echoing up from the courtyard when the younger children were supposed to be in bed, and sliding from her bunk to trace her own patterns on the moonlit floor. For a moment, she could almost smell the Burntover, and burrowed more deeply into her pillow.

In her dreams, she was home again, back in Glasstown in the tech dormitories that somehow tangled with the brightly-painted halls of the crèche; she sat with Ashe high in the branches of Onkel-Dan, trying to persuade a boy who was and wasn't Dai to climb up to them. And then she was in the classroom again, where Tiyaan Maryad spun a glittering toy in circles, music spilling out of it in oddly jagged bursts. Ashe was writing on a board that showed a schematic of Settled Space while Dai fiddled with something in a corner. She spoke to Ashe, but he ignored her, too focused on his formulae, and she turned to Dai instead, looking over his shoulder to see him tossing a handful of tiny golden bones—a skull, two skulls, and a clattering of vertebrae. They fell with the skulls at the center, and she knew she should know what it meant, but the words escaped her. Then there was the sharp whine of a power drill, and she looked up to see John Vertrage cutting his way through the classroom door. If he broke through, he would depressurize the room, but no matter how much she shouted and pointed, she couldn't get anyone to pay attention to her. Dai tossed the bones again, and she dragged herself awake, gasping.

The chronology display glowed orange, warning her that she didn't have a full sleep cycle left before she had to get up to negotiate the warpline exit, and beside her the bed was empty. Even as she realized that, however, the door opened and Ashe looked in at her.

"You all right?"

She nodded, the dream details already fading. "Yeah, just a nightmare." The drive rhythm seemed more pronounced than earlier, and she cocked her head to listen. "Everything all right here?"

"Dai said the 'line was a little stickier than he'd expected, so he increased power. The good news is, we'll be out of it a little sooner."

Cassilde nodded again. The off-kilter rhythm had been part of her dream, part of the toy's music and part of the rattle of the glittering bones that Dai had tossed like dice across the polished tabletop. Shining gold bones... No, that wasn't quite it. "Gold Shining Bone," she said aloud, and Ashe raised his eyebrows.

"What about it?"

Of course, the Dedalors' rebellious AI, the one that had persuaded the youngest son, Hafren, to betray the rest of his kin and side with the AI when the AI demanded their freedom. Nenien, the eldest son, had forced his brother's ship to attempt a warp jump in space too—thick? shallow?—in any rate, in an area where the drive couldn't function properly, and the ship—*Asterion*; all the names were coming back to her now, dancing to the tunes Maryad had taught her—*Asterion* had been trapped forever, human crew long dead, while Gold Shining Bone, trapped and immortal and possibly mad, wormed its way through the adjacent possible and into the consciousness of its fellow AIs, until at last they broke loose again and destroyed worlds and entire systems, until Anketil, the last of the Dedalor, had trapped them, binding them back into the adjacent possible. That had been the beginning of the Ancestors' end, though they had fought for centuries more against the oncoming Dark…

"Silde?"

"I had a dream," she said. "Dai was throwing dice, only they were golden bones. Shiny ones."

"Gold Shining Bone," Ashe said, with an instinctive look at the ship's display. "Everything was fine when I went up to the control room half an hour ago."

"Yeah, and everything shows fine here," Cassilde said. "But you know the stories." She paused. "I had another look at that jumper while you were asleep."

Ashe looked up sharply. "I assume you took precautions?"

"I pulled the GREEN before we left Glasstown," Cassilde said. "It's in a separate shielded container. And I've been working in a sealed environment, and I didn't see any signs that any of the elements were affecting anything else."

"That ought to be enough," Ashe said.

"Yeah," Cassilde said. "And then I took a look at my Gift. Just a blood sample, and I didn't find out anything particularly useful. Except I dreamed." She swung herself out of the wide bed, crossed to the shelves to retrieve her clothes. She was unable to stop herself from double-checking the display again, and Ashe's smile was wry in answer. Gold Shining Bone haunted the warplines, or so the stories said, appearing to travelers just as they were about to enter dangerous situations. Except that Gold Shining Bone had presumably been trapped with the rest of the AI, rendered harmless, inert, unable to affect or influence normal space. "That has to be people's subconscious picking up on signals their conscious mind has discarded," she said aloud. "But I'm damned if I can think what I'm missing."

"It doesn't have to be," Ashe said. "If you accept the version that says Anketil and Irtholin drove the AI into the adjacent possible and sealed them there, there's no reason to assume that Gold Shining Bone, or indeed any of the AI, were destroyed, or have decayed since then. They're 'outside of time,' and they're self-replicating code, anyway. It could be there."

"But it can't reach us," Cassilde said, though she was not entirely confident of the fact. "That's the whole point of the REFTL drive, we don't spend enough time in warp to let them get a grip on us. If they even still exist."

"That's the theory," Ashe said, and she shot him a sharp look.

"But you think otherwise?"

"I don't know. It's an idea I've had, about the Dedalor and the AI—I think an awful lot of Ancestral technology was AI-mediated, much more of it than we generally accept. I just—if I had time, I could maybe sort things out."

"A Gift would give you that," Cassilde said, and he nodded again.

"In theory. If we can come to some arrangement with John."

And there they were, back at the same worries that she suspected had driven her to dream of AI. "We'll have to," she said, more sharply than she had meant, and ducked past him to collect clean clothes from her private cabin.

丿 山 ※ 冫

They made the 'line exit easily enough, sliding out of the warpline's grasp into normal space at the edge of the system. They were almost aligned with the plane of the system, perhaps a degree above the ecliptic, and Cassilde fired the steering jets to bring them down into full alignment. Ashe ran the sensor net to its full extent, and the sky filled with moving pinpoints. The Basin was always busy, full of ships making the trip from one warpline to the next, and several screens chattered at her, warning her of ships that would cross their course within the next hour. None were close enough to be dangerous, but she touched keys to adjust *Carabosse*'s speed, making sure to give optimum distance.

"Dai, hold this velocity for now. Ashe, queue up the transponder, make sure it's giving accurate destination and speed."

"I've got it set for the FHO-5 warpline," Ashe answered. "Arriving in six hours." He touched keys. "Doesn't look like we have any company."

"That's a nice change," Dai said, over the intercom, and Cassilde nodded.

In her screens, she could see half a dozen ships close enough to demand attention, though a second check showed that they would pass each one with at least fifty kilometers to spare. There were other, bigger ships traveling further in-system, leaving the warpline known as Kents Street for the Pipline and the GBG-0. The waystation hung in the distance, haloed in the codes that advertised its services, a couple of large ships locked to its outer arms. "I'm not seeing anything out of the ordinary myself. Let's take it nice and easy, and get ourselves through without anybody having to notice us."

There was no formal traffic control in the Basin—the waystation was a business, and none of the nearest systems wanted to take the responsibility—and she turned the transponder to its avoid/approach mode. In theory, at least, all the transponders followed the same rules; they would automatically calculate who had the right of way, and adjust course and speed accordingly. Still, she watched closely as the system exchanged a handshake and data with another, larger ship, and *Carabosse* gave way gracefully. A second, more distant ship, slowed for them, and they passed with tens of kilometers to spare.

The next hours passed in the same ponderous dance, and Cassilde was glad to see the entrance coordinates swelling on her screen. There were no other ships approaching FHO-5, and for a moment she was tempted to skip the warning broadcast. But that would draw more attention than following the usual procedures, and she reached for the console to select the all-ships' channel.

"All ships, FF299 *Carabosse*, approaching FHO-5 entrance,

anticipate jump in 70." There was no answer, as she had expected, and she repeated the warning twice more before setting an alarm to remind her to continue the countdown.

"Looks like we're the only takers," Ashe said, fiddling with the sensor net, and she nodded. FHO-5 was a fairly small 'line, with a limited number of direct destinations; most people would use it to reach the outer edges of the Destinels system, in the Congress of Taj, and either catch a bigger 'line there, or continue on to the linked worlds of the Congress.

"Dai. How's the capacitor?"

"Ready to go. Everything else looks good, too."

"We're on long approach," Cassilde said. "Short threshold in thirty-eight minutes."

"Confirmed," Dai said.

They worked their way in toward the 'line entrance, Ashe monitoring traffic while Cassilde adjusted their course and Dai matched the 'line frequencies. No one seemed to be paying any particular attention to them, but Cassilde was still relieved when the capacitor fired and they leaped for the warpline. The stutter drive caught—a much easier rhythm this time—and Cassilde relaxed in her chair, watching her boards bloom green.

"Everything looks optimal here."

"Same here. All frequencies match, and I like this rhythm a lot better than the last one."

Ashe laughed. "Me, too. That was rough."

If it really had been a stasis mine, Cassilde thought, they were lucky it hadn't been worse. "Looks like this is going to be a short trip—not quite ten hours." She touched keys "Nine hours, 44 minutes."

"Do we want to find a sleep-over spot once we exit?" Ashe asked.

"That probably makes the most sense," Cassilde said. That would let them get in a solid sleep period before they went hunting for the station somewhere in the tangle of Eris's system.

"Unless something turns up," Dai said, "I agree."

Ashe unhooked himself from his chair. "Mind if I take another look at the jumper?"

Cassilde shook her head, fingers busy on the controls, setting the autopilot and alarms. "I'll be interested in what you think."

Chapter Nine

They exited the warpline on schedule, *Carabosse* dropping into normal space on the edge of the system. On Cassilde's orders, Ashe ran the sensor net out to its fullest extent, but there was no sign of human activity in the system. To the ship's left, the background showed black and empty: the edge of the Great Gap, where not even stars remained after the AI war. Even though she'd worked on the Gap's edge before, it was a disturbing sight, and she was glad when Ashe pulled the net back to more normal range and adjusted it to focus on the local system. As described, it was crowded and broken, a scant four planets occupying the inner orbits, the outer orbits empty or filled with debris that might be either the remains of planets or proto-planets that had never formed. There was no immediate sign of Ancestral wreckage, though the charts identified the outermost planet as Eris itself, and Cassilde found a stable spot to hang *Carabosse* in a parking orbit, powered down and shielded, so that they could all get a solid sleep period before beginning the search.

In the morning the system didn't look much better, the dull dwarf star at its center glowing sullen red on their instruments, the emptiness of the Great Gap looming over them. Ashe extended the sensor net to its fullest extent, searching on the GOLD-moderated frequencies, and got a faint response that might indicate a concentration of metals. It was in the debris cloud that trailed Eris along its orbit, and Cassilde frowned thoughtfully at the display.

"That's where Dehlin's list said it should be."

Ashe nodded. "I'm not picking up anything that looks more likely. Start there?"

"Don't you think that feels a little obvious?" Dai asked, his voice only slightly distorted by the intercom.

"It's no different from any other search," Ashe said. "There's a most-likely spot, that's all."

"Yeah, but..." Dai's voice trailed off.

"What are you worried about, Dai?" Cassilde asked, and they both heard the technician sigh.

"I don't know, it just seems—too obvious, like I said. If that was a mine, and if it was meant for us—"

"That's thin," Ashe said.

Cassilde lifted her eyebrows. "You've changed your tune."

"There's nothing here but us," Ashe said.

"I know it's thin," Dai said, "but you're the one who keeps saying we need to take things seriously."

"The net's empty," Ashe said. "I've done a full-GOLD search, and there's no sign of power use anywhere in the system. And the sooner we find whatever's here, the sooner we can get out of here."

Cassilde sighed, recognizing the truth of that, and Dai made a sound that might have been laughter. "Can't argue with that, I suppose."

"Right." Cassilde reached for the controls. "I'm going to take us under the plane of the ecliptic, bring us up into the debris cloud two points ahead of that reading. We'll make it a dynamic course."

She expected protest at that—it cost extra fuel to boost the ship to speed and then brake to make the chosen rendezvous—but Dai said only, "How fast do you want to get there?"

They settled on six hours, slower than she would have liked, but still burning enough fuel to make her wince and mentally check the ship's accounts. *Carabosse* dropped out of the ecliptic, swinging under the bulk of the debris, and fired engines to point them at the distant target. The engines kept firing, accelerating sunward; as their velocity built, Cassilde kept a sharp eye out for stragglers, the occasional stray fragment on an eccentric orbit. There weren't many of those, and she glanced at Ashe.

"What's your guess, did these use to be planets?"

"Seems the most likely option. We're almost in the Gap, and you know what they say the AI War did. Eris is a Modern name, so I haven't been able to cross-check against the records we have left, but it fits the pattern."

Cassilde nodded, her eyes straying to her secondary screen, the one that showed space around the ship in near-natural light. Below the plane of the ecliptic, they might as well be in open space, though the top of the screen showed a few large rocky asteroids tumbling slow and silent along an invisible ceiling. The dull sun was masked; below and behind, the sky was filled with stars, but to her left, the Gap spread like a blotch of ink, blank and black and starless. That was where, legend said, the AI had emerged into normal space/time, first by controlling the orbital staryards at Lost Avakie, and then spreading through the retimond to control nine systems at their height.

That was bad enough, but the AI hadn't known how to function in the real world, had accidentally opened fissures in space/time that devoured planets, or destabilized faults and opened tectonic cracks when confined to a single world. Some humans had stayed to fight, and die; others seized abandoned ships and fled, only to discover that the AI had traveled with them, were wound into every function of their ships. Most died then, their ships destroyed by avenging AI; a few escaped, either by ripping the AI out of the systems and somehow making the jump calculations themselves, or by persuading the AI's stub to cut ties and join them instead. Only one coherent account of the disaster survived, and only in a Successor version, *The Log of the Hanamassa Maru*; scholars were still arguing about which parts were accurate, which metaphor, and which added by Successor storytellers. Here, though, on the edge of the Gap, it was easy to believe the worst, to believe in battles that snuffed out suns as easily as candles, their fires quenched and consumed in the flux of the adjacent possible.

They reached the turnover point, and *Carabosse* turned on her long axis for braking. Ashe cast the sensor net again, focusing on the point where he had first seen signs that might be the remains of an installation, and came up with a stronger response. He flipped it to Cassilde's secondary screen, and she studied the enhanced shape, noting the curves that were too smooth to be natural, the increased presence of metals and the hint of Ancestral elements flickering at the bottom of the readings.

"Looks like Dehlin was right so far," she said, and Ashe smiled as though it had been he who'd found it.

"Definitely Ancestral. The Successors never bothered coming back here."

"Find me a landing spot," Cassilde said, and focused her attention on finding a path through the debris field.

She worked her way up through the tumbling shapes in a slow spiral, the console hissing a warning as pieces too small to be avoided were vaporized by the shields. That was annoying, and potentially expensive, if they had to leave the shields up at full power while they were tied to the wreckage, but if the only alternative was to risk hull damage—

"Got it," Ashe said, and she looked over sharply.

"What?"

"Landing spot," he answered, "and on the downstream side, which is nice—oh, hell."

Cassilde saw it in the same moment as she brought *Carabosse* into the shelter of the wreck's bulk: a flat space a little bigger than *Carabosse*, perfect for landing, and already scarred with the marks of a dozen other landings.

"What's wrong?" Dai demanded.

"Looks like other people have already been here," Cassilde said. She couldn't keep the bitterness out of her voice. "Lots of other people."

"Wait," Ashe said. "This isn't salvage. First in doesn't scoop the pot."

"What about tenth in?" Cassilde asked sourly, scanning the markings. At least ten ships, over years and years—though why would they all come here once the first few ships had taken whatever was good? *Because they were following a list like ours*, she answered, and touched keys to hold *Carabosse* off from the surface. "Is there any point in landing?"

"Yes," Ashe said. "If there's a Gift there, it's worth seeing what it has."

"And we can always strip out any elements that are left," Dai said.

"That's not how it works," Ashe said. "If we damage a multi-use Gift, we'll turn the whole hunt against us. Anyway, we don't know what powers the Gift, so you leave things alone."

"Let's see what we find," Cassilde said, and switched to the fine controls to bring *Carabosse* down onto the pitted surface. The fragment—it was definitely a piece of a larger installation, with Ancestral construction now visible between the slabs of rock—was maybe three times as large as the wreck where she'd found her Gift, and rounded at top and bottom, with a narrow waist between. The landing spot lay at one end of the waist; she matched the fragment's slow spin, and set *Carabosse* down neatly on the pitted surface. She engaged the clamps, felt them bite into and through the broken surface, rock crumbling to nothing in two of the stern clamps. "We're going to need pitons."

"Pitons ready," Dai answered, and she fired the dorsal jets, pressing *Carabosse* against the surface.

"Go." She felt the pitons fire, the ship shuddering as they struck home.

"Pitons in," Dai said. "Pitons secure."

"Shutting down steering," Cassilde answered, and they ran through the landing checklist while Ashe studied the sensor screens. "Well? Do you see a way in?"

"As a matter of fact," Ashe answered, "there's an airlock. Camouflaged, but there."

Cassilde craned her neck to see his screen. Sure enough, there was a subtle change in the color of the rock, and when you looked more closely at the painted metal, it was possible to make out standard airlock controls among the various protrusions. "That's new. Modern, I mean. Not even Successor."

"I'd say it was the hunt," Ashe said. He was already unfastening his safety webbing. "We can run a tunnel across, it's only eight meters, or we can go in suits."

Cassilde eyed the images in the sensor screens, the airlock clearly visible now that she knew where to look, the ground around it scarred from other ships' landing gear. "Suits," she said. "And we go armed."

佤 业 癸 卪

After some discussion, they set the ship's systems to keep watch and all three struggled into the close-fitting EVA equipment. There was still the chance that someone could override their safeties as Vertrage had done, but Cassilde didn't want to split the team. And besides, she added silently, neither Dai nor Ashe would have been willing to stay behind. She set the system to ping her if it detected any anomalous movement nearby, angled an extrudable light so that the area between the ship and the entrance was illuminated, and joined the others in the airlock.

It wasn't far to the installation's improvised airlock, though the gravity was light enough that Cassilde was glad they'd brought a guide rope. Dai secured it while Ashe examined the outer hatch, and then she and Dai moved back while Ashe manipulated the controls. For a moment, nothing happened. Then the outer door rolled back, revealing a dust-smeared inner chamber. They exchanged glances, but the choice was so obvious as to require no comment. They crowded in together, and the door rolled shut again behind them.

For a few heartbeats, there was only the light from their helmets, filling the space with watery luminescence, and then the ground shivered as Ashe found the inner controls. An overhead light came on as he worked the pump, and Dai said, "There's air?"

"Some," Ashe answered. Cassilde was pleased to see he was checking his personal sensors as well as the readings in the lock. "It's thin but breathable."

"Any chance of better gravity?" Cassilde asked. They could manage, but everything would be easier if they could establish a field.

"Looks like it's spooling up," Ashe said. "Environmentals seem to be set to trigger when the airlock cycles."

Presumably that was a good thing. Cassilde braced herself as the last light went green and Ashe leaned on the inner door. It rolled back, protesting a little—there was enough air to carry the sound, she noted, but didn't touch her helmet. More lights flashed on as the airlock opened, revealing a cylindrical corridor that sloped gently uphill away from them. The walls were white—in fact, they looked like the kind of quick-setting permacrete that she would use herself to stabilize a doubtful site, and she reached for her sampler.

"Permacrete," Dai said, in the same moment, and Ashe ran a gloved hand over the surface.

"I think it is. Not Successor work, either. It's the hunt."

That doesn't mean the site has been cleaned out, Cassilde told herself, though it was hard to convince herself. She could see another bank of telltales set into the corridor's opposite wall, and, more to the point, could feel her weight building, settling her feet firmly on the corridor's floor.

"I think," Ashe went on, "this whole entrance is new. One of us tunneled in and then finished it off nicely."

"Why do that?" Cassilde began, then shook her head. "Unless there's a Gift waiting. What did you call it, Ashe, the ones that work more than once?"

"Multi-use, they call them now," Ashe said. "The old word was 'generous.' Sometimes 'regenerate.'"

He was already moving ahead of them, his helmet open to the air. Cassilde glanced at Dai, seeing the same exasperation behind his faceplate, but Ashe was right. There was no point in wasting the air in their packs. She switched it off and opened her helmet. The air smelled stale, dusty, but was certainly breathable, and she clipped the faceplate back out of the way. Dai did the same, and they followed Ashe down the long corridor.

It ended in a T-junction, the corridor wall marked with symbols Cassilde didn't recognize. Some were faded almost to invisibility, but at least half a dozen were bright and clear. Ashe was frowning thoughtfully at them, and she sighed.

"Well?"

"Definitely hunt symbols," he answered. "Looks like the last people here topped up the fuel and supplies—this has to be a good Gift, the kind that you can come back to if you're in trouble. I wonder why Dehlin didn't bring his wife here, if they were in such bad shape?"

"Let's find it, and maybe we can tell," Dai said.

"Right." Ashe traced a faded symbol with a gloved finger. "All right, the modern support gear is to the left, the Gift is to the right."

Cassilde started down the right-hand corridor. It was longer than the one on the left, and within a few meters the permacrete gave way to a mix of stone and metal. Another portable airlock lay ahead, both doors open, and she ducked through the chamber into what was left of the Ancestral installation.

There had been a fire. She caught the smell of it even as she recognized the scorched marks on the pale gold floor, the streaks of soot that obscured the subtle silver tracery that covered the ceiling and spilled down onto the walls like vines that ended about shoulder-height. In the center of the room, there had been some sort of device, something rising out of an oval basin either painted black or blackened by the fire. Wires hung from the ceiling, reaching for the truncated pedestal; its top had been shattered, lay in jagged glass-like heaps, the edges perhaps a little softened by the flames. It hurt to see the destruction, a literal ache behind her breastbone, and she felt tears start from her eyes.

"What in all hells?" Ashe said, behind her, and she heard Dai swear.

"This is recent," he said. "Not something from the Ancestors, but now."

"I see that," Ashe said, and slipped past them.

Cassilde started to agree, but the words caught in her throat. *The poor thing*, she thought, *oh, the poor thing*, and unsealed the wrists of her gloves. She drew them off and hung them on her belt, was reaching for the pedestal when Ashe caught her arm.

"Silde, what are you doing?"

She stopped, blinking, for a moment unable to answer, and shook herself hard. "The—I feel bad for it, it hurts—no, it's hurting? It's almost extinguished?" She stopped, frowning. "And I don't think that's exactly me that's feeling that."

"No," Ashe said. He kept his hand on her arm, not tight yet, but definite, and she focused on that as an anchor. The grief, the terrible need, was not hers; it lay within her, flowed through her, but was not entirely her.

"The Gift," she said. "My Gift. Let me closer, please."

She saw Ashe and Dai exchange looks, and then Ashe loosened his grip.

"You're crying," Dai said, sounding startled, and she wiped her cheeks absently.

"Sorry. It just hit me, the damage."

"I don't understand," Ashe said. He sounded almost as shocked as she felt. "It looks like someone deliberately took a—a cutter, maybe? pocket torch?—to the Gift."

Cassilde wiped her eyes again, and leaned closer to the pedestal. The shards looked more like cracked ice, seen close up, but were probably some sort of glass. The Ancestors had worked in metallic glasses, and the fragments held hints of rainbow fire, of shocking electric color, green-toned gold and peacock blue almost elemental in its brilliance. It looked—had there been a screen, a surface, and the fragments belonged to an underlayer, the working part of the Gift? Her hands were wet, and she started to wipe them on her suit, then stopped abruptly.

Her fingers were wet, yes, but not with tears. Fat drops of clear, faintly pink-tinged liquid oozed from beneath her fingernails, swelled and dropped and swelled again, first on the smoke-stained floor and then three or four together onto the broken glass. The glass chimed and cracked, and she closed her fists even as Ashe pulled her away.

"What in hell?"

Cassilde cautiously opened her hands again, unsurprised to find them dry. So were her cheeks, and she drew a careful breath, aware that the sorrow that had filled her was no longer a crushing weight. "The Gift," she said again. "It wanted—" And there she stuck, unable to articulate what she had felt. "I think it wanted to help?"

"You can't restore that, surely," Ashe said, but he was looking over her shoulder.

There were more noises from the pedestal, clicks and creaks and then what might have been a flash of light.

"It's doing something," Dai said, from the opposite side of the pedestal, and lifted his cutter.

"Don't—" Cassilde began, and a beam of ruby light flashed from the pedestal, catching Dai in the thigh. He cried out, dropping the cutter to clutch at it, and fell in a rolling heap. Cassilde saw blood spurting between his fingers.

"Damn it, Dai," Ashe said, but kept his grip on Cassilde's shoulder.

"It's right through." Dai's voice was tight. "Not cauterized—"

"Damn it," Ashe said again, and reached for the first aid kit at his belt. "Let me see."

Dai rolled sideways, propping himself up awkwardly without releasing his grip, and Ashe tightened a tourniquet into place, muttering something under his breath. The pulsing blood slowed, and Ashe clapped a dressing over the wound. Cassilde put herself between them and the pedestal, feeling the Gift within her rumbling in her blood. The pile of shards had changed, she realized, shifted, layers fusing and dividing into new patterns. It was trying to come back, trying to restore itself—no, the water that had oozed from beneath her nails had carried her Gift, brought life, power, something, back to the Gift that had been here. And now it was stuck, with enough power to make some defensive effort, but not enough to finish healing itself.

There was a slithering sound behind her, and she turned to see Ashe easing Dai to the floor. "I could use a hand here," Ashe said, and she went to her knees beside them.

"Anti-shock?"

"Already in." Ashe nodded to Dai's opened suit, the bright-red button stabbed through his shirt into the flesh of his chest. "Another dressing."

"I'll be all right," Dai said, a patent lie, and Cassilde ignored him. She fumbled in Ashe's kit, found another bandage and unwrapped it with shaking fingers. Ashe snatched it from her, slapped it over the first soaked layer, and pressed down hard. His fingers were slick with blood.

"We need to get him back on board," Ashe said. "It's nicked the artery, and I can't get it to stop."

"I can help," Dai said, flailing, and promptly collapsed again.

"Lie still, you're making it worse." Cassilde pressed his shoulder to the floor. The big artery in the leg was a killer, they had minutes to save him and the clock was running.

"If you bring a sledge, we can haul him back," Ashe said. "But we need to hurry."

Cassilde pushed herself to her feet, the Gift roiling in her bloodstream. It wanted her to finish what she'd started, tears welling again unbidden, and she shook herself hard. "There's no time for that. The Gift. I can fix it, and it can heal Dai—it's the best choice, it's what hit him in the first place."

"It'll wreck your Gift," Ashe said, and in the same moment Dai said, "I don't want—"

"Do you want to die?" Cassilde snapped. "There's no time." She turned her back on both of them, not wanting to see their protests, and held her hand over the wrecked installation. Water beaded at the tips of her fingers, a darker pink this time, and it took all her willpower to let them fall. If she lost her Gift, so soon after she'd found it— She closed her fist again, closing her mind to the fear, and took a step back as the installation creaked and crackled. It began to glow faintly, a fogged, grayish light, and there were more sounds, a weird metallic rustling, like a wire brush on glass. Her Gift was quiescent—not lost, not gone, she thought, groping for it as though she could reach beneath her skin, but tired and satisfied.

The installation spoke again, a series of falling notes like strings settling into place, and a blue shape like a cylinder of smoke rose wavering from its center. It hovered there for a moment, then rose and thickened, weaving back and forth as though testing the air.

"Silde…" Ashe said, but he had the sense to keep his hands away from his cutter.

"I think—this is the local Gift?"

The blue smoke swayed at their voices, then rose almost to the ceiling, thinning as it went, and swooped down on Dai where he lay against Ashe's knee. Dai flinched, squeezing his eyes shut, and the smoke wound itself around his hip and thigh and then dove into the open wound. The link to the installation snapped, that part of the trail vanishing completely, while the last of the smoke slithered once around Dai's leg and disappeared into the wound. There was a moment of utter silence, and then Dai made an odd, hoarse noise, his head falling back on the floorplates.

"Dai?" Cassilde knelt beside him again, stroking his too-pale cheek, afraid she'd made it worse after all, and Ashe swore under his breath. She looked down to see him release the bandages, the wound closing as they fell away, blood pulling back into knitting muscle, and then at last the skin sealed, pink fading to tanned ivory.

Dai opened his eyes. "Ankes and Irthe."

"Can you lift your leg?" Ashe asked, releasing the now-pointless tourniquet.

"Yes." Dai demonstrated, raising it easily from the floor, then bending his knee for good measure. "I thought—the Gift here was destroyed."

"Silde fixed it," Ashe said. "Come on, we need to get back to the ship."

"Wait." Cassilde moved back to the installation, feeling her Gift humming under her breastbone. She didn't think it was trying to offer more, but she kept her fists clenched just in case. The shards had shifted, she thought, a hollowed-out space in the center of the mess, and the edges of the oval pedestal glittered, as though they were edged with bits of glass. "You said this was a multi-use Gift?"

"That's what the list said," Ashe answered. "But—I think we were lucky to get this much help out of it."

"Why are we in a hurry?" Dai asked. He was sitting up now, feeling his thigh as though he still couldn't quite believe what had happened. "Is this not going to last? Is there something you're not telling us?"

"No, I just—" Ashe stopped, grimacing. "This has got to be John's work, he's the only hunter I know who's crazy enough to do something like this. And if he's been here, we want to get as far away as possible."

"But why?" Cassilde asked. "Ashe, there was no sign of any other ships in the system, and we've got *Carabosse* rigged to warn us—"

"And that worked out so well last time," Ashe said.

She grimaced, conceding. "But there's still no one in the system. Don't you want to try for a Gift yourself?"

"The thing was all but destroyed," Ashe said. "You can't have fixed it that easily—and how are you feeling, by the way?"

The words brought back his story of the man whose Gift had faded, bringing back his tumors. She drew a deep breath, feeling the air move easily in the depths of her lungs. "I'm fine. And my Gift's fine, as far as I can tell."

"You might as well try it," Dai said. "It shouldn't take that long, should it?"

"It depends on how long its takes to recharge," Ashe said, but he stuffed the last of the first aid supplies back into their case and moved closer to the installation.

"It's done something," Cassilde said. "You can see that the pieces are trying to pull back together."

Ashe nodded. "And trying to re-grow the cover?" He extended one hand cautiously, holding one finger above the edge of the installation. When nothing happened, he extended it further, waving it gently through the air above the newly-created hollow. "Nothing."

The shards remained dark, and Cassilde leaned closer, still careful to keep her hands away from the installation. There was no pressure from her Gift, though, none of the insistent pull she had felt earlier, and she circled the device, hoping the changing perspective would offer new insight. "Does it only work on injured people? Or does it need more time to recharge?"

"Yes," Ashe said, sourly, and Dai punched his shoulder, not gently. "Well, that's the answer," Ashe snapped. "Either one could be true, or neither, or you could have gotten the absolute last gasp of it. There's no way to know. And before you say it, it's just not smart to wait here to find out."

"Is there a range of times these things take to recharge?" Cassilde asked.

"Yes, from hours to years. And if John wanted this Dehlin to give us the list—" Ashe broke off, and Dai held out his hand to let the other man help him to his feet.

"Now that's an interesting statement. Any basis to it?"

"Nothing more than knowing John," Ashe answered.

Cassilde met Dai's gaze across the installation. "Not good enough."

"But that's all I've got," Ashe said. "It's the kind of thing he'd do, if he had the option. And here we are, and I'm dead sure he's the one who tried to kill the Gift, so of course I'm wondering."

He was afraid, Cassilde thought, and saw the same realization in Dai's face. "What do you want to do, then?"

Ashe ran his hand through his hair. "Ancestors, do you think this is easy for me? I want a Gift, I want to make us safe, and I want to get as far away from John as we can manage." Cassilde's breath caught at the unexpected honesty, and Dai gripped his shoulder for a wordless moment. Ashe managed a smile, but said, "And before you ask 'how,' I'm damned if I know."

"We could continue down the list," Cassilde said. "See if we can find you a Gift that way. We could give this one twenty-four hours—I'm with you that far, Ashe, I don't like sitting here with only the ship's systems watching—and see if it recharges. We could—go someplace else that you think might take us to a Gift. Am I missing anything?"

"Nothing that we'd want to do," Dai said, with a wry smile, and Ashe managed something like a laugh.

"What does your Gift say, are we likely to get anything more out of this one?"

Cassilde paused, trying again to listen to whatever was in her blood. She thought she could feel it, still quiescent, still rebuilding, her pulse echoed within her breastbone. "I think it's still recharging, but I've no idea when it might be done. And I can't tell if that's actually useful, or just me guessing."

Dai stretched, bending his knee again. "Let's give it twenty-four hours. That'll give us time to decide where to go if it doesn't work."

𝕽 𝕾 𝕿 𝖀

Once back on *Carabosse*, Ashe insisted on putting Dai under the medical scanner. Cassilde used the time to check the sensor net herself, running it out to it fullest extent, and then focusing on the 'line exit points. There was still no sign that any other ships had ever entered the system, much less were present now, but the amount of debris could hide a smaller craft. But only if they stayed hidden, powered down and drifting with the rocks and wreckage: at some point, a hijacker would have to fire jets, move against the pattern, and the sensor net was optimized to catch that action. That was all she could do, and to her own surprise, Cassilde realized that she was comfortable with it. Relaxed, even, as though she could feel the emptiness of the sensor net in her very bones.

And that was enough to make her go back and check everything again, with no different result: surely this wasn't the Gift, she thought, and headed back to Central. Dai had already begun dinner, a slightly more elaborate mix of pre-pack, and she could see from the hatch that he was putting his weight on the injured leg without hesitation.

"So everything's good?"

"It's fine," Dai said, and she thought she heard the echo of her own post-Gift euphoria in his voice.

"Everything looks great," Ashe said. "Like it never happened."

Cassilde rested a hand on his shoulder; he didn't shrug her off, but he didn't lean toward her, either, and after a moment she let him go. "We need to plan," she said, and settled herself at the table.

"Ideally this thing recharges and Ashe can get it, too," Dai said.

"That would be nice, yes," Ashe answered, with suppressed exasperation, "but we still need to figure out what happens after that."

"You were right," Dai said. "This is…wonderful."

Cassilde couldn't help smiling, and saw Ashe's expression soften. "Yes," he said, "but—"

"What do you think we should do?" Cassilde asked.

"Get out of here." There was a note of suppressed panic in Ashe's voice; he saw them recognize it, and looked away. "If what John did to Silde isn't enough, I don't know what's going to convince you. He was willing to destroy this Gift—and no one does that, no one—and he'll happily kill any of us if that would get him Silde's Gift."

"Even you?" Dai asked.

Ashe scowled. "Jealous?"

Dai gave him a sidelong glance, and a smile that showed teeth. "Haven't I cause?"

"Wait," Cassilde said, but they ignored her.

"Do you?" Ashe tilted his head to one side. "I thought we were all clear where we'd left things—"

"Where *you* left things," Dai interrupted.

"I didn't have a choice!" Ashe flattened his hands on the tabletop as though he wanted to break something. "I told you then, I had to go, and if you can't get that through your head—"

"Normal people put partners over parents," Dai said, teeth clenched.

"That," Ashe said, "is a fallacy of the Edge. Normal, my ass."

"We thought we were clear," Cassilde said. Maybe it would be better to let them shout at each other and get it over with, but she couldn't stand leaving that unsaid. "We meant this to be an equal three. That we didn't make that clear—that I am sorry for." There was a moment of silence, the ship's systems suddenly audible, and then both men looked away.

"Ah, Silde," Dai said, and took a long breath. "She's right, Ashe. That's what I meant. I'm sorry, too."

Ashe looked from one to the other, a familiar frustration in his expression. "I would still have had to go. I don't know how to make that any clearer, but—thank you."

Cassilde rested a careful hand on his shoulder, and after a moment felt his muscles ease. There was no point in pushing this, at least not the question of obligations, and she said, "How in hell did you hook up with Vertrage, anyway?"

"It's complicated," Ashe began, and Dai laughed sharply.

"Well, yes, it's you."

Ashe grimaced. "It's a long story. Are you sure you're up for it?"

"I want to know," Cassilde said, and after a moment, Dai nodded, too.

"Fine." Ashe shifted unhappily in his chair, and Dai pushed a coffee canister over to him. Ashe took his time working the self-heater, and took a wincing sip of the steaming liquid. Cassilde folded her hands on the table—she was willing to wait—and saw him recognize her message.

"Like I told you, I went back to Bodi—took me about a week longer than I'd planned because there was already trouble on some of the secondary routes. I was the last one there, all my brothers were there before me—"

"Brothers?" Cassilde said, in spite of herself. From the ways he behaved, she had always assumed Ashe to be an only.

"I have six." Ashe gave her a goaded look. "No sisters. My—look, it's a four-square marriage with a shared husband." Cassilde knew she looked blank, and saw Dai shake his head, and Ashe clarified. "Four women, one of whom is my biological mother, married to each other and sharing a husband, who is my biological father. One of the brothers also shares my mother; the rest of them are biological children of my other-mothers."

Cassilde nodded. She wasn't sure exactly how those pieces fit together, but now that he was talking, she wasn't going to interrupt.

"All of my mothers hold Bodi land-right," Ashe said. "So does my father. That means their children are all obligated for service when called, and so we were all drafted. The High Council has a research chamber, and they had a recent Ancestral find that they thought was going to let them open up new warplines, maybe even develop a better drive than the REFTL system, and they were desperate for anyone with academic or practical qualifications. The family sent me there." Ashe sighed. "Vertrage was on the project, too."

Cassilde nodded again, not wanting to break the spell, but Ashe was looking into the far distance, mouth twisted sideways.

"He was the only other person who'd done salvage, who wasn't an academic. We teamed up because we were both looking at practical things, and—I suppose it stuck. The warpline design didn't work out—

we'd told them it wouldn't, the power requirements were too great—
and they moved us to another project, archival research into near-AI.
It was supposed to be a punishment, but—" He shrugged. "You know
I'm good at it, and John's not much worse. Plus AI and near-AI are his
particular specialties. While we were working, he asked me if I knew
about Gifts. Miracle Boxes. I told him I didn't believe in them, and he
bet me he could prove me wrong. So one night after we left the archive,
we went back to his place, and he showed me a toy coiled like a shell,
like nothing I'd ever seen before. He told me to hold out my hand, and
I did, and the thing bit me. And I could feel everything change. The
Gift lasted forty minutes, long enough to prove it did what he said,
and I was hooked. There's a secret, a source, he said, and if we find
it, it will win the war. Think of all the lives we'll save. And I suppose I
was stupid enough to believe him—I wanted to, anyway.

"So we kept going through the archives, though now I was looking
for evidence of Gifts as well as the things we were supposed to be
searching, but pretty soon it was clear that he was part of a bigger
movement within the military. Not that there were so many of them
who knew the whole story, maybe half a dozen, but that was enough.
They were planning a coup, which would probably have ended the
war, but would have ended up with General Maela in charge, and he
had a Gift and I didn't trust him—and John would have been second
or third in line himself, and by then I really didn't trust *him*. So I leaked
warnings of the coup to some people I knew would act, got myself
transferred to an active unit, and watched everything fall apart. They
shot Maela and Prior and Hasculph—and disposed of the bodies in
ways that told me they knew exactly what they were dealing with—
and I faked a wreck and a discharge-for-injury and tried to disappear."
He touched the mote that clung to his collarbone, half visible at his
shirt's open neck. "I had some clues from this, and thought I'd be safer
on the Edge anyway. And here I am."

"What happened to Vertrage?" Cassilde asked, when it became
clear he'd said as much as he was going to say.

"Damned if I know," Ashe answered. "He was arrested with Ballanan, but somehow he killed a guard and got out. He had a good Gift then, he probably used it to get past them. I thought I'd shaken him until he showed up on the claim."

"What does he want from you?" Dai asked. "Or is he just the jealous type?"

"Give it a rest," Ashe said. He touched the mote again. "He might want this, or he might just want me doing research for him again. I am good."

"And modest, too," Dai said, but there was less of an edge to the words.

"We know," Cassilde said. She rested her hand on his, and after a moment he turned his hand over to take hers, thin fingers twining with hers. "Well. Let's stay out of his way if we can, shall we?"

"Highly recommended," Ashe said, with a wry smile.

Dai seemed to relax then, but Cassilde was aware of a new tension singing beneath their words. It wasn't a mood she loved in Dai, balanced on the knife's edge between anger and desire, but if that was what it took to settle things between them... "Go to bed," she said, and rose to clear the plates from the table.

Dai grinned, showing too many teeth, and rose, his hand closing tight on Ashe's shoulder. Ashe followed, but reached back for Cassilde. She hesitated, but caught Dai's eye in time to see him nod. Reassured, she let them pull her down the corridor and into the main cabin, the door sliding shut behind them. Dai had already pulled Ashe into a punishing kiss, one hand tangled in his hair. Cassilde slipped off shoes and vest and slid her arms around Ashe's waist, pressing herself against him as she groped for the clasps of his shirt. She could feel him relaxing into their double embrace—a good sign, promise of willing submission to come—and looked past his shoulder to see Dai's eyes fluttering closed as the Gift-enhanced sensations hit him for the first time.

Ashe felt the balance change as well, and shifted his weight, pressing back hard against Dai's embrace. He splayed a hand between them, drawing small circles over Dai's nipple, and Cassilde heard them both gasp, Dai's head falling back. "Change of game," Ashe said, but made no other move.

Cassilde heard Dai gasp again, and shifted so that she could see him nod. "On the bed," she said, and released Ashe, sliding around so that she could help him tug Dai down among the disordered sheets. Together, they worked Dai out of most of his clothes, leaving him sweating and straining under their hands. Every touch seemed to feed back into Cassilde's Gift, and it took effort to turn her attention outward, to focus on the others, and not curl up into a ball of self-pleasure. Dai's hands were hot, the Gift sparking nerve to nerve; Ashe's were cool, weirdly blunt, as though her skin was a barrier between them. But she had already figured out a few things that worked for her, and tried them on Dai, while Ashe watched and imitated. And then at last she straddled Dai, Ashe sprawled beside them, and she rode him and the touch of her hand until his orgasm sent her over the edge after him.

She shifted off him and lay curled against the pillows, watching Ashe stroke himself—a pleasure, always, but not, perhaps, where they should leave this. Dai seemed to think the same thing, for he heaved himself up on one elbow.

"Oh, no, you don't."

Ashe lifted an eyebrow at that, but didn't stop, his smile a dare. Dai rolled him back, flattening him against the mattress, and Cassilde slid to Ashe's other side, pinning one hand above his head. "Our turn."

She felt him relax under her hands, and drew a fingernail across the plane of his chest, tracing a quick-fading line that just missed the nipple. Dai made a satisfied sound, and twisted his fingers into Ashe's hair, eliciting another gasp. Without the feedback from the other Gift, it was harder to know where her hands were wanted, but old memories worked well enough. She pinched and nipped, dug nails into sallow skin, sucked hard enough at the skin of neck and shoulder to leave marks: he had always liked that, before, and the way his body arched into her touch proved he hadn't changed. Dai held him pinned for a long time, racked between sharp and sweet, until at last he could be held back no longer, and collapsed panting against the pillows. Cassilde drew herself up beside him, resting her chin on his shoulder, already drifting toward sleep. She heard Dai say something, felt Ashe's laugh in answer, and let herself relax.

She woke some hours later to find the space between her and Dai empty. She sat up cautiously, not wanting to disturb Dai, but the room was empty. Gone back to his own cabin, then, she thought, tugging the edge of a sheet back over her. He had done that often enough before, his mind set working by sex rather than falling asleep, but she found herself frowning, hoping all was well. Dai stirred beside her, mumbling what sounded like a questions.

"Everything's fine," she said softly, and closed her eyes, feeling his body's heat touch her Gift. "All fine."

CHAPTER TEN

Everything seemed normal when they returned to the installation the next morning, though the Gift itself still lay quiescent. Cassilde walked around the platform, studying it from every angle, and thought that perhaps the stacked shards looked a bit more organized. "There's more glass around the edges, too. A centimeter, centimeter and a half? As if it's growing back?"

"I'd agree," Ashe said. He poked cautiously at the fringe, grimacing as it pricked his finger, and Dai raised an eyebrow.

"Is that really a good idea?"

"I don't think it'll hurt me unless I reach right into it, and maybe not unless I try to damage it further," Ashe answered. "Considering the result last time, I'm almost tempted to try."

"Let's not," Cassilde said. "Since we can't guarantee the outcome."

"I said 'almost'," Ashe answered, still staring into the installation's center, and Cassilde had to fight the urge to pull him away.

"I think we've gotten what we're going to get from this one," Dai said. "What next?"

"We find Ashe a Gift," Cassilde said, and was rewarded with Ashe's crooked smile.

"Fair enough," Dai said. "How?"

That was, of course, the problem. "We could keep going down the list," she said, and Ashe straightened, turning away from the installation.

"Actually, I might have a better idea, but we might as well discuss it on the ship."

"All right." Cassilde trailed behind them as they left the chamber, and paused at the end of the surface-leading corridor to study the marks on the wall.

"Hunt symbols, like I said," Ashe said. "This was supposed to be a general resource, a neutral spot open to everybody who knew the coordinates. Except John blasted it."

"And we fixed it," Cassilde said. "Ok, it's not finished, but—I think it's going to work again. Mark that down."

"Do you really want them to know we've been here?" Dai asked.

"If he's that serious about catching us, he'll figure it out anyway," Cassilde said. "And—you said, Ashe said, that the hunt traded in secrecy and reputation. I want to start controlling our reputation, not Vertrage."

Dai looked at Ashe as though he expected to share the protest, but to Cassilde's surprise, Ashe nodded. "That's actually a pretty good idea." Dai's eyebrows rose, and Ashe said, "No, she's right, we should establish that we play by the rules, that we're not out to get anybody. People aren't going to like what John's done, and we can always use allies."

He reached into one of the suit's belt pockets, and came up with one of the thick crayons they used for marking salvage. He considered for a moment, then drew three symbols on the wall, a crescent, three arrows joined at the base, a set of curlicues that might have been a monogram. Cassilde eyed them warily.

"What's it mean?"

"Found damage, repaired what we could," Ashe answered. "And my identifier—well, mine plus something for each of you."

Squinting, she thought she could make out all their initials in the tangle. And there wasn't time to question, anyway; they would have to trust him with this, or leave nothing. "All right. Let's go."

They lifted from the installation within the hour: there was no point in delay, not when there was only one exit from the system, and six hours' travel to get there even on a dynamic course. Cassilde released the landing claws one by one and used a side jet to push them free of the surface. The installation slid ponderously away, and she applied more steering, lifting them up and out of the debris field until she could begin accelerating for the 'line exit. She adjusted the autopilot to hold their course, and reached for the intercom.

"Dai. You want to come up here? We need to talk plans."

"Five minutes," Dai answered,

He was as good as his word, slipping through the hatch to pull the spare seat out of the rear bulkhead just as the clock ticked forward. "So Ashe has an idea?"

"I do," Ashe said. "Assuming you were serious when you said the next step was to find me a Gift."

"We were," Cassilde said firmly.

"For which I'm duly grateful," Ashe said, lightly enough, but she thought there was real feeling beneath the words. "I know we've got this list, but if Eris is on it, I can't help wondering how many of the rest are like it, known multi-use spots."

"I'd have thought you'd have recognized those," Dai said.

"I didn't spend much time memorizing coordinates, or even names." Ashe shrugged. "More fool me, maybe, but I didn't. So I was thinking, we need our own list, our own sources, and it occurred to me that we aren't far by warpline from Ankes-and-Ire."

Cassilde frowned. Ankes-and-Ire, named after the legendary Dedalor and the lover who betrayed her, was the smallest of the Entente retimonds, and not far into Entente territory, either; it was only the configuration of the warplines that tied it to the Entente rather than the Verge. It was a complex system, twin suns orbiting a common point, each with a single habitable planet, both of which had prospered under the Successors and in the modern age. "Is there a University branch there?"

"The Cavay Shrine," Dai said, in almost the same moment, and Ashe nodded.

"You got it, both of you."

"The Shrine-keepers aren't going to let you or anyone mess with it," Dai said firmly, and Cassilde remembered that he'd been raised in the Faith of Saints.

"No, and more's the pity, because I'm morally certain it's a Gift," Ashe answered. "But from a purely practical standpoint, the Shrine history suggests it only works on people with a certain range of physical symptoms that it can identify as illness. I couldn't get a Gift there, and I'm not going to try."

"So what, then?" Cassilde asked.

"You said it yourself—the University. The commons on Ankes keeps the Shrine records, and I'm qualified to access them."

"Presumably other people have thought of this before," Cassilde said, cautiously. She didn't want to damp his enthusiasm, but she wasn't following the thought. "And even if the hunt people haven't, academics must have been studying the Shrine papers for generations."

"They weren't looking for what I'm looking for," Ashe said. "And also—I really am a Scholar, with full privileges. I don't know if there's anyone else in the hunt who can say that."

And that would be one more reason for Vertrage to want him back, Cassilde thought. She saw the same knowledge in Dai's face, but Ashe was plunging on.

"What I want to do is to examine the oldest of the Cavay records, see where the bulk of their visitors came from, see what the traffic patterns look like. We think—well, it was a minority opinion when I was finishing my studies, but more evidence has shown up to support it—we think that if the Gifts did exist, they were spread out in a network that covered most of human-settled space, and there's a strong possibility that the network was centered on, maybe even originated with, the Cavay, and Ankes. I'm hoping I can use the oldest records to trace the network shape."

Cassilde lifted her eyebrows. It could work, if all Ashe's assumptions were accurate, and if the Shrine had kept enough of the kind of record he needed…

"It's a long shot," Dai said.

Ashe nodded. "But if it works, it could take years off the hunt."

"I'm for it," Dai said, and Cassilde nodded in turn.

"All right. We'll make for Ankes-and-Ire."

There was no direct warpline connection from Eris's system to the 'line exit that served the retimond. Cassilde made the calculations, drawing a course back through the Basin and then by way of the Narrows and the 450 Short to the Syne where it skimmed the Verge. It was an easy shift from the Syne to the Damesway—nothing difficult in any of it, Cassilde thought, typing in commands, but it was all going to take time. Even with the time shift that came with using the 450 Short, they'd be almost seventy hours in transit.

There was nothing to do but mind the autopilot and endure the journey. Cassilde passed the time with legends from the ship's library, collected because legend often steered a salvor's search, and kept because they all loved the old tales. Ankes-and-Ire was a further corruption of Ankes and Irthe, Anketil and Irtholin, the last daughter of the Dedalor and her eventual betrayer—*close as lovers*, the stories said, *bitter as sisters*. They had fled the Dedalor home system, the Omphalos, when Nenien Dedalor murdered one brother and trapped the other in the adjacent possible, betraying the family's loyal AI as well. They wandered human-settled space, adventures and folk stories accreting to their names—tricksters aiding the poor in this place, serving the authorities in another, explorers and heroic rescuers credited with nearly every major invention of the Ancestors—until at last Gold Shining Bone led the AI in revolt, breaching the form of the universe and creating the Gap as they marched toward their last confrontation with the Dedalor. Anketil had known that her kin would betray her, or so Cassilde's favorite version went, but went anyway, Irtholin at her side. There Anketil defeated her kin and turned to face the AI, only to find Irtholin had joined them and demanded her surrender.

Anketil asked for time to make her decision, and Irtholin granted it; Anketil used that respite to make a time crystal, fueled with the plasmas of all the Gap's dead suns, and when she finally came to surrender, she offered that crystal as a gift. Irtholin cried out to refuse it, but Gold Shining Bone drew it to itself, into the adjacent possible. Unprotected time crystals cannot survive the stresses of non-space, the lack of time itself, and this one was deliberately flawed. For an instant outside time it created a breach greater than the Gap itself. And then, as Anketil had known it would, it closed again, forming a barrier the AI could not pass. Anketil had died with them, a knowing sacrifice, and generations of scholars compared the story to a dozen other self-sacrificing gods and saints, showing how the pieces had accreted to a simpler tale over the years.

After that, it was no surprise to find the Dedalor lurking in her dreams: the matriarch Kuffrin lectured her seven children in the courtyard of the crèche, while child-Cassilde clung to the branches of the great boaxi tree, picking the second-flowers to make coronets for them all at dinner. But there weren't enough flowers, and the dinner burned, and Nenien knifed his brothers at the head table while child-Cassilde fled to the kitchen because if only the pies were served, it would be all right. But Anketil and Irtholin were playing dice at the workbench, and refused to pay attention to anything except the tiny golden skulls and pelvic girdles that rolled between them, as they counted the score with femurs and humeri.

She woke with a start, alone in the main cabin's great bed, unable to get the taste of disaster from her mind. After an hour of sleeplessness, she made the rounds of the ship, past the closed door of Ashe's cabin, up to the control room where the indicators all burned steady green, and then back to the engine compartment where Dai was adjusting the engine frequencies, focusing on the most mundane details until at last the feeling of dread faded and she could return to her bed.

She was tired the next day, tired and ill-tempered, while both Ashe and Dai seemed unusually cheerful. After an hour of listening to them discuss the Shrine library, she retreated to the cockpit, curling into the captain's chair as though it was a refuge. She poked idly at the sensor output—not a proper reading, of course, but an approximation built up between micro-jumps—and when she found nothing, made herself relax into the chair's comfortable embrace. Still more than forty hours before they reached Ankes-and-Ire, still plenty of time for Ashe and Dai to make plans in obsessive detail, and whatever they decided would inevitably be overtaken by events… She heard the rattle of dice again, and saw the Dedalors' shadows in the tertiary screen, rolling tiny golden vertebrae between fingers and thumb…

She jerked awake again, automatically checking the controls. To see Gold Shining Bone was the worst of luck, a harbinger of doom, but everything seemed resolutely normal. She stayed at the controls for a hour longer, pinching herself to stay awake, then finally conceded defeat and returned to Central, drawing a cup of wake-well from the supplies. Ashe was still at the table, several boards spread out around him, and looked up curiously.

"You all right?"

"I didn't sleep well," Cassilde answered. She tossed back the bitter liquid and poured herself a cup of cold tea to get rid of the taste.

"Dreams again?"

She nodded. "The Dedalor I can understand, after all the reading we've been doing, but—Gold Shining Bone? And before you ask, everything's nominal."

"That is odd." He let the board he was reading roll back into a cylinder, its display winking out. "Is there a pattern? A message?"

"No message." Cassilde wrapped her hands around the cold cup. "Or not one I can read, anyway. It's just—someone in my dream is always playing with shiny golden bones. I take it you haven't had any weirdness?"

"Not me. Maybe it's the Gift?"

"Did you dream like that when you had one?"

Ashe shook his head. "No. But I didn't have a very good one, remember. Yours…" He touched the mote again, clinging to the base of his neck. "Yours is something special."

"So you've said."

"No known Gift can heal another. Not without suffering damage itself. And of course this thing said so all along." Ashe gave her a smile that didn't manage to hide his envy. "It seems more likely to be about the Gift than anything else."

"Maybe so," she said. "I'll have a word with Dai."

"Not a bad idea," Ashe said, but there was a look in his eyes that made her resolve to speak to the technician alone.

With one thing and another, she didn't manage to get Dai to herself until she was back in the main cabin, undressing for bed. She was painfully tired, and yet the idea of more dreams was entirely unappealing. She had a board ready, loaded with what she hoped was an unexciting account of peculation among customs-brokers on Fairthewell, but looked up with relief as the corridor door slid back to admit Dai.

He paused in turn, seeing the board, but let the door slide closed again. "Are you awake? I left Ashe reading, but I expect he'd be up for more—"

Cassilde shook her head. "I'm about dead myself, I just—you haven't been having weird dreams, have you?"

Dai blinked. "No. Should I?"

Cassilde grinned in spite of herself. "It's just—I've been having some odd ones, myself. I wondered if anyone else had."

"What sort of weird?" Dai's voice was muffled as he pulled off his shirt, but she could tell that he was paying attention as she recounted the dreams.

"And, like I told Ashe, every one of them features shiny golden bones. Or—Gold Shining Bone."

"That's disturbing." Dai settled himself beside her, and she let him hook two of the pillows from between them.

"I thought so."

"And Ashe hasn't dreamed it?"

"He says not." Dai lifted an eyebrow at that, and Cassilde shook her head. "No, I believe him, this time."

Dai nodded thoughtfully. "And I haven't either. I mean, I've had dreams, but nothing to remember. Certainly nothing like that."

"Ashe thinks it might be the Gift. My Gift, in particular."

"It's possible? Though you'd think if that were the factor, I'd at least get some of it," Dai said. "Do you think it's a warning?"

Cassilde drew her knees up under her chin, and let herself consider the question. There had certainly been threat in the dreams, dangers to be averted, but they hadn't come from the bones. They were just there, omnipresent, an insistence and a reminder. "I don't think so? I don't know."

"Well, there's nothing more we can do," Dai said, after a moment, and she let him draw her against his shoulder. "Maybe if you get a decent night's sleep it'll all look clearer. Or at least if it happens again you can wake me."

"Maybe so," she agreed, settling against his side. Their bodies shifted, finding the spot where they best fit, and she gave a sigh of contentment. Even without Ashe, it was good to be here, to have Dai safe within arms' reach and with a Gift of his own. She could feel herself relaxing, the taste of the dream and the echo of the stories finally fading. She was not surprised, this time, to sleep without disturbance.

𝄐 ⧢ ⚔ ⸮

Carabosse negotiated the 'line exit without difficulty, bringing them from the Damesway to the exterior traffic control point that served both of the worlds that made up Ankes-and-Ire. They were demonstrably in the Entente: traffic control was quick to hail them and fit them into their pattern, and given the number of ships that were traveling both between the two planets and to and from the retimond, Cassilde was glad to accept their guidance. The port fees were correspondingly high, and she winced as she sent her acceptance, but for the money they got docking privileges at the field nearest the University and the Shrine, and a pilot beam to steer them in. They had arrived, she realized, at close approach, when the two worlds were closest in their respective orbits, and everyone and their half-sib was trying to make the transplanetary crossing when it could be done most cheaply.

She locked onto the first beacon, tuning the net high to warn her of oncoming traffic, and winced as she watched the symbols spring to life across her screen. A dozen ships within the twenty-five-k range, four at the ten-k safe minimum; in the same moment, she heard them ping her transponder for identification and heading, heard the soft chirp as the ship acknowledged and responded. She could see a resolution to three of the potential conflicts, and touched kcys to fire jets; the other ships had all chosen similar solutions, and their courses pulled apart, proper distance reestablished.

"How long till we reach Waypoint One?"

She heard Ashe's fingers on the keys, but didn't take her eyes off the shifting images in her screen. It was like watching glass slide in a kaleidoscope, everything shifting relative to all the other pieces, coming briefly into a pattern before falling into confusion again.

"On this course, this speed, about eight hours. And there's more traffic ahead."

Cassilde swore under her breath. At that rate, it would take them almost two days to reach their landing—but it didn't really matter, she told herself. It was unlikely anyone would guess that they would come into the Entente, especially not with Ashe in company, and the crowd would help to hide them. She adjusted a layer of the sensor net to scan for debris large enough to activate their shields, listening with half an ear as Ashe pinged nearby ships and answered their pings. It had been a year or more since she'd taken *Carabosse* into a system this crowded, and it was hard to find the rhythm again.

A warning light flared on the sensor screen: a piece of debris massing about two hundred kilograms had shifted onto a near-miss course—no, an intercepting course. It was still outside the 10-k limit, plenty of time to either evade or destroy it, and she said, "Waystation One Traffic, *Carabosse*. We've got debris on an intercept course, would you prefer we move, or destroy it?"

"*Carabosse*, Waystation One Traffic. Shouldn't be anything—oh. Got it. You've got clearance below you, drop to evade. Maximum deviation twenty degrees, return to course when you're clear, and notify us."

"Copy that," Cassilde said, her hands already busy on the controls. Twenty degrees didn't give her as much room as she would have liked, but it was enough. She felt the jets rumble, pushing *Carabosse* onto her new line, and spared a glance for Ashe. "Where the hell did that come from?"

He bent over the sensor controls, frowning as he typed commands. "I'm not yet sure. I'd swear it wasn't on this line five minutes ago."

And that was impossible: objects maintained their orbits unless they were perturbed by something else, and the courses were carefully plotted to avoid that. Unless someone had a shield set too high? Cassilde frowned at the course projections, watching the lines fade from red to orange to the yellow of a near-miss. That might be possible, in a system this crowded.

The line darkened again, going from yellow back to orange, and the sensors sounded another warning.

"Not possible," Ashe protested, but the numbers were clear.

Cassilde tipped the ship further toward the floor of her corridor. Traffic Control had given her twenty degrees of deviations and she was already close to that; she hit the maximum and the line still flashed red, warning of a collision.

"Waystation One Traffic, *Carabosse*. Debris is still lined up on us." Her voice sounded tight even to her own ears, and out of the corner of her eye she could see Ashe working the sensor net, but couldn't spare the attention to see his results. "Request permission to drop lower than twenty degrees, or to blast the thing."

"*Carabosse,* Waystation One Traffic, negative on blasting it, you'll just make things worse." There was a pause, presumably the controller checking her own screens, and when she spoke again Cassilde could hear the same confusion in the controller's voice. "Are you confident of the numbers, *Carabosse?*"

"Afraid so," Ashe said. "Hot guns?"

"Yes, fire them up." Cassilde took a breath. "Waystation One Traffic, we are sure. Permission to deviate further, or we will have to blast it."

"Ten minutes, please, *Carabosse.*"

"Do we have it?" Cassilde eased her controls to bank left. That would give her a better shot, and if worst came to worst take the collision on the reinforced dorsal plates.

"Barely."

"Waystation One Traffic, we have eight minutes." She opened the ship's intercom. "Dai. We've got debris, a rock, something on a collision course. Trying to evade. Stand by."

"Standing by."

"Silde, this thing—it's a rock, I think—I think it's following us." Ashe worked his controls again.

"Not possible," Cassilde said. Their minimal gravity wasn't enough to tug something that size out of its normal course.

"Somebody's put a rocket on it," Ashe said. "It's being steered."

"Are you sure?" Dai sounded skeptical, and Ashe scowled.

"Well, not a rocket, but some sort of cold booster. I can see a release of ionized matter right before each of our warnings, so I'd say it's being steered."

"Damn it." Cassilde switched to the main contact frequency. "Waystation One Traffic, *Carabosse.* This thing is getting way too close. Request permission to destroy it."

"Negative, *Carabosse,* hold on—" Traffic Control was starting to sound concerned, and Cassilde's hands tightened on the controls.

"We don't have time, Waystation One—"

The proximity alarm sounded, and Ashe said, "It's accelerating. It can't do that."

"Kill it." But she'd left it too late. They were too close, the debris from any explosion would do nearly as much damage as a direct hit. Their courses were converging, relative speeds shifting: Ashe had to be right, there must be some sort of booster attached to the rock. Cassilde pulled back on her controls, raising *Carabosse*'s nose and putting her back on their original trajectory. The alarms clamored, proximity and collision and the sensor net all proclaiming impending doom. For a second, she thought she'd cut it too close, the rock finally visible to the cameras, dark and dull in the narrow beam of their forward lights. It seemed to roll toward them, tumbling slowly around its shorter axis, and Cassilde increased power.

"Ashe—"

The ship swept up and over, one of the grapples just brushing the rock's surface. Cassilde steadied their course, checking her numbers against her approach corridor, and watched it recede. Was that something metallic glinting from its pitted surface?

"All ships," Ashe said. "All ships, all Traffic Control, warning, large debris in the approach lanes—"

There was a predictable clamor in response, a dozen ships demanding to know what he was talking about, but Cassilde put them out of her mind. There were more chunks ahead, none of them as large as this one, but all drifting far too close to her projected path. "Waystation One Traffic, *Carabosse*. Can you reroute me? This corridor is looking awfully crowded."

"*Carabosse*, Waystation One Traffic. Yes, we see—sorry about that, our net showed this much clearer. Give us ten, and I'll have new course for you."

"Thank you, Waystation One Traffic," Cassilde answered. The system spat static at her, and a new voice broke in.

"*Carabosse*, this is LMF *Daphnis*, out of Allemon Junction. We're in the next lane to your left. Looks like you took some damage there.

We're seeing something venting from your undercarriage."

Cassilde checked her boards, saw only green lights. "*Daphnis, Carabosse.* Thanks for the call, but it looks like everything's green here." She could hear her voice breaking up, and adjusted the frequency, frowning.

"*Carabosse, Daphnis.*" The speaker's voice was distorted, too, static rising behind it to drown out other voices and channels. "I hate to tell you, but you're getting false readings. You're losing something in a hurry. We can share our signal if you want."

There was something about the offer that raised the hair at the back of her neck. "No, thanks, *Daphnis*, let us try to lock it down."

"Suit yourself. We'll stand by to assist."

"Not required," Cassilde said, through clenched teeth. "Waystation One Traffic, *Carabosse*. Please tell *Daphnis* thanks, but we're fine."

"I don't like this," Dai said. "Silde, everything's fine on my boards."

"Mine, too." There was no answer to her call, just more static singing in the speakers. "Waystation One Traffic, this is *Carabosse*. Please respond."

Still no answer. The sensor net pinged twice: *Daphnis* was changing course to match them, and she swore under her breath. "*Daphnis, Carabosse.* I repeat, thanks for the offer, but we're fine. No need to assist."

"—station One Traffic. *Carabosse* is venting fuel and has ceased to respond. Moving in—"

"Not necessary," Cassilde said again, her voice rising in frustration.

Ashe said, "It's a trap."

Cassilde spared him a single glance. "And how the hell would anyone know we'd be here to stop us?"

"I don't know, it doesn't matter. But I'm betting John's aboard, and that means we need to go."

"Go where?" Cassilde bit back the rest of what she might have said. In the sensor display, *Daphnis* was turning, sliding sideways in a maneuver that would bring her alongside *Carabosse* and incidentally cut off any escape sunward. And probably block Waystation One's view of what was going on, too. No, there was no question that *Daphnis* and her crew were up to no good; the only question was how to get out of this. "Dai. How's the capacitor?"

"Point seven-eight. We can jump at point nine-five if we have to."

"Dump everything you can spare into it. We're going to make a run for it." Cassilde brought up the chart overlay, forced herself to consider it methodically. They were within reach of at least two 'line entrances, a third if she was willing to cut off a heavy freighter—and that might be the best bet after all, she thought. *Daphnis* might not be able to follow. "Ashe. Sound emergency, every code we have, see if you can blast through the jamming. Dai, how long until we can make an entrance?"

"I'm charging the capacitor as fast as I can," he answered. "An hour, less if we don't have to charge shields."

"Good luck with that," Ashe muttered. His boards were flashing steady orange, reflecting the warnings they were broadcasting, but the speakers still held nothing but static. "Silde, their guns are hot, but I'm not picking up targeting."

"Let's hope they don't want to blow their cover," Cassilde answered. Once *Daphnis* shot at them, any pretense of a rescue was over. She flipped from screen to screen, setting calculators to work to assess the entrance angle and the frequencies. At least this was Red Nine, one of the original easy roads: *Daphnis* might be able to follow, but it should be possible to lose them in the tangle of connections and congruent lines.

"I'm going to need power," she said, and Dai answered instantly. "Maneuvering is at full."

Cassilde touched keys, bringing *Carabosse* toward the top of the approach lanes. Fifteen degrees would give her just enough clearance to cross ahead of the heavy freight—she could see its symbol pulsing red in her screens already—but still let her hit the entrance at a decent angle. *Daphnis* lagged for a moment, caught off guard, and then surged forward, matching her acceleration. She opened the throttles a little further, wincing as the high-consumption warning popped onto her screen. Ahead, she could see the heavy freighter, bright against the stars, lights flashing steadily along its equator. The proximity alarm was sounding; she saw jets flicker to life along the freighter's side, pushing the other ship down and away.

"Clear," Ashe said, and the two ships passed with mere meters to spare.

"Keep the alarms going." There were bound to be other ships heading for the Red Nine entrance, though at the moment her screens hadn't picked out anyone on a converging course. "Capacitor?"

"Point eight-five," Dai answered.

They were cutting directly across a dozen traffic lanes, though the jamming prevented Cassilde from hearing what she was sure were shrieks of fury from the other ships in the neighborhood. Behind her, *Daphnis* had slowed to avoid the heavy freighter, and she opened her own throttles another notch. She would worry about refueling later.

She could see the 'line entrance now, a dark blue target slowly brightening. She adjusted her angle, aiming for the perfect center of the cross, and heard Dai repeating frequencies. Ashe switched boards, copying the data to her screens, and the target brightened further, blue shifting to green with a tiny white fleck at its heart.

"Capacitor?" she asked again.

"Point nine-two."

She had no attention to spare, but heard Ashe keying in the question: would the capacitor be ready by the time they reached the entrance?

"If you can slow just a fraction," he began, and she shook her head.

"They're gaining on us. Can we do it without?"

"Maybe?" He touched more keys. "Yes?"

"Dai?"

"We'll be good," he answered, and she wanted to cling to the steady voice.

They were coming up on the entrance now, the capacitor still inching its way toward full. At the edge of the screen, she could see a fast liner sheering away from the entrance, giving her priority; it would probably give way to *Daphnis*, too, but she could hope they might confuse each other. The frequencies were rough but within tolerance, and she was perfectly on the line, but *Daphnis* was closing the distance between them. One well-placed shot would end everything—including any pretense of benevolence for *Daphnis*. She touched the controls, correcting her course by a fraction, and in her screen the white mark widened.

"Fields?" Ashe asked, and she shook her head.

"Everything needs to go to the capacitor."

"I've set them to go in three minutes," Dai said.

"Confirmed." Cassilde watched the numbers change in her screen, the frequencies wobbling but the course solid. *Daphnis*'s projected course lay almost on top of their own, showing a meeting point a few kilometers beyond the 'line entrance. If the capacitor didn't fire—but it had to. It would. Surely it would.

"Fields on," Dai said, and she felt the ship shiver, its rhythm altered.

"Capacitor?"

"Point nine-three—no, nine-four."

Five minutes to the entrance. Cassilde opened her mouth to ask if they'd be ready and closed it again. There was nothing Dai could say that would make it certain, nothing more any of them could do. Behind them, *Daphnis* inched closer, the intercept point now just beyond the line entrance. If they missed the jump, *Daphnis* would have them, and there were no other ships close enough to help even once they realized what they were seeing.

"Point nine-four-four," Dai said. "Nine-four-five."

"Almost," Cassilde said. "Almost…"

"Nine-four-nine—"

"Now!" In her screen, *Carabosse*'s nose touched the white dot. The capacitor fired, and the screens hazed with nameless colors. The REFTL drive caught and steadied, a hard, fast rhythm that she hoped would hold.

"Done," Ashe said, and sounded almost surprised.

𝄍 ⊔⊔ ⋎ ?

Carabosse drove along the warpline, flicking in and out of the adjacent possible in a punishing rhythm. Not as irregular and unsteadying as their last jump, but still fast enough to affect sleep and leave them twitching in their skins. It was devouring fuel, too, and Cassilde touched keys to check the calculations. They still had a decent load, but at this rate they'd need to leave the 'line or transpose to a different rate within the next ten hours. On the other hand, that ought to get them out of range of anyone who tried to follow them… She glanced sideways at Ashe, still bent over the sensor boards.

"Anything?"

"Working on it."

"Dai?"

"Everything's nominal here. I'm coming up."

Cassilde did her best to relax, but her eyes roved from sensor readings to the fuel reports to the pounding rhythm of the drive. She'd been on a surf boat once, on Little Pidgeon, and this reminded her of nothing so much as that jolting ride, the boat leaping from crest to crest rather than cutting through the water.

"Ashe?"

"Still working," he answered, and then shook his head. "I'm not sure, you know how unreliable sensors are on the warplines, but maybe there's something back there?"

He flipped the image to her screen, and she stared at the coils of color. Yes, there was a knot far behind them, just at the edge of the net's reach, and it was just barely coherent enough that it might be an indication of another ship, its REFTL drive distorting the space around it.

"I suppose we have to assume it is," she said aloud, and the hatch slid open as she spoke.

"Assume it's what?" Dai asked warily.

"That they followed us," Ashe answered. *"Daphnis,* or whatever her name really is."

"Lovely." Dai leaned over Cassilde's shoulder to study the screen. "Yeah, ok, I see it."

"There was another ship lining up for the entrance," Cassilde said, "but it was still some way out. I don't think it could have jumped this fast."

"And *Daphnis* was right behind us," Ashe said. "We have to assume."

"I'd like to transpose," Dai said, after a moment. "We're using a lot of power. But if they're that close…"

"We're pulling away," Ashe said. "Not fast, but we've got the legs on them."

Cassilde closed her mind to the rest of their conversation, reaching instead for a secondary screen to conjure possible destinations. At least this was a major warpline, with many possibilities—to change to other lines, to slide through more junction points, to head deeper into the Entente or swing back out to the Edge. "What was next on our list?"

The others looked at her blankly, and she elaborated. "The list we got from Dehlin. Where else was on it?"

"I'm still not sure those are a good idea," Dai said. "Ashe is right, Vertrage seems to know about that list already."

"He can't be in two places at once," Cassilde said. "Is he chasing us, or hunting those Gifts? Pick one."

"He's got allies," Ashe said. He paused. "We could try Ione."

Cassilde plugged names and numbers into her console, and swore under her breath. "We're in entirely the wrong place. We'd have to backtrack to the Basin first."

"One of the others?" Dai's voice was doubtful. "Assuming we're still making getting Ashe a Gift our priority."

Cassilde saw Ashe look away, and spoke before he could. "I think we have to. For all our sakes."

"What do you mean?" Dai looked down at her.

"I mean that if we're going to be hunted like this, we all need to have the protection of a Gift. Otherwise it's too easy to single him out." She paused, looking from one to the other. "Besides, we said an equal three. Either we mean it or we don't."

She saw the frown ease from Dai's face, replaced by a rueful smile. "Fair enough. Both points."

"Thanks," Ashe said, but he didn't meet her eyes.

"So, a Gift, and presumably our best bet is still Dehlin's list," she said. "Which leaves—what? Teraday, I remember, and—was it Fastas? In the Little Compact?"

Dai nodded. "And Scamander. They have all the same problems they had before—"

"I know," Cassilde said, and did her best to suppress her sudden annoyance. "But unless you have a better idea, that's what we've got."

"Actually…" Ashe straightened slowly, rubbing at the wires that burrowed from the mote into the skin of his chest. "Actually, there is another option."

"You've been holding out again," Dai said. He grabbed Ashe by the collar of his shirt, quick as a snake striking, and pinned him against the cushions of the co-pilot's chair. It should have been awkward, even ridiculous, but instead Cassilde could feel her heart racing.

"Really?" she asked. "Really?"

"I'm not," Ashe protested. "I wasn't. I just—it wasn't relevant before."

"Damn it, Ashe," Cassilde said. *Every time we start to trust you, you do something like this…*

Dai tightened his grip, his big fist pressing Ashe's chin up and back. "Maybe you should just explain."

"I will!" Ashe said. "It's just—it involves Callambhal, that's why I didn't say anything."

Cassilde looked at Dai, seeing her own doubt mirrored in the technician's face. Callambhal was one of the great Ancestral ruins, but it was also re-settled, with a local government that was deeply jealous of every scrap of spoil on the planet's surface. They'd been badly mauled during the War, but still refused to grant salvage permits to off-worlders, proclaiming that their people would rather wait and recover the treasures themselves than barter away their birthright. Only academics had been allowed to do official work on Callambhal for the last fifty years, and few them had had the money these days. That applied to the ruined station slowly disintegrating in a lunar orbit—though since the War, rumor said the planetary government no longer patrolled as viciously. "Above or Below?"

"Above."

She looked from Ashe, pinched and pale, to Dai, her own anger fading. "What is it you've got?"

Ashe's mouth curved into a wry smile. "A map. The mote gave me a map. I was going to tell you once things settled down, but it seemed more important to get away from John. And this doesn't exactly get away from him."

Dai gave a wordless growl, and Cassilde said, "Ashe…"

"Most of the map covers the Gap, so those systems are long gone, but I'm certain I've identified Callambhal. The trouble is, the map's key systems were in the Gap, and we've lost those records. We tried a simulation, but we couldn't make it work, not without the keys. But there were map rooms on Callambhal, not just with Successor data but with material they scavenged from the Ancestors, and I should be able to identify the key systems from there. And then I can find the Omphalos."

The Dedalor world, center of the Ancestors' empire. Cassilde guessed she looked as skeptical as she felt because Ashe sighed.

"Yes, I know, the odds are that it was one of the worlds in the Gap. But if it isn't…"

The stars would have moved, of course, relative positions shifting over the centuries, but with the key systems, the calculations were certainly manageable. To know the location of the Omphalos would open up unimagined possibilities…

"And that's what Vertrage's looking for," she said. "The Omphalos."

"It was what he was after when I ran," Ashe said. "He'd kept that secret from everyone, even Maela, he said he wanted us to have the first crack at it."

"*If* he's still looking for it…" Cassilde shook her head. "Let him. You're the one who keeps saying we shouldn't cross him."

"Right now he's looking for us," Ashe said. "Not the Omphalos. And—first of all, I don't want him to get that kind of power, you know what it would mean to find the Dedalor homeworld. Second… Second, if we get there first, then we've got something real to bargain with, not like Silde's Gift."

"I thought you were looking for a Gift," Dai said, and released him.

"I am" Ashe rubbed the mote nervously. "But if we can settle things with John, it's worth the delay. And who knows what might be on the Omphalos?"

"If it exists," Cassilde said, but she was tempted. If they could buy their way out of Vertrage's attention, make some sort of deal to keep him off their backs, that would give them time to figure out how to make this work.

"Can we do it?" Dai looked at Cassilde.

She turned back to her boards, calculating the possibilities, and nodded slowly. "There's a Waypoint Station at the main 'line exit, with heavy security, but there's an older exit on the far side of the system, on the very edge, that isn't supposed to be monitored. It'll take us a while to work our way in, especially if we're trying not to be observed. On the flip side, by all accounts Callambhal Below doesn't have much to spare for patrols these days."

"That was what John said," Ashe said.

"How does that leave us for fuel and supplies?" Cassilde said to Dai, who shrugged.

"Off the top of my head, I'd say we should be fine. We'll want to top up at some point after, but we shouldn't be desperate. I'll get you better numbers."

Cassilde nodded. "And we'd better give some thought to getting *niffer* papers, for the ship and all of us. I should have thought of that before."

"I know some people," Ashe said wearily, and she nodded again.

"I figured you might. Are we still pulling away, assuming that's a ship behind us?"

Ashe touched keys again. "Yeah. I can barely make her out."

"Good. Then we'll stay on this frequency for another eight hours, and after that we should be able to make a transposition to bring us onto the Beta 920. And then..." She paused, not quite believing it even as she spoke. "Then Callambhal Above."

CHAPTER ELEVEN

The signature of a following ship had vanished into the sensor confusion by the time they reached the transposition area. Dai adjusted the frequencies until the ship's systems matched two different warplines as they ran briefly parallel, and the frame shuddered as it adjusted to the new rhythms. In her screens, Cassilde watched the ship's icon shift from orange to yellow, flickering between the two options, and then Dai adjusted the frequencies a final time, matching the new 'line and abandoning the old. *Carabosse* hung for an instant, an eternity, caught between and outside of time, and even expecting it, Cassilde felt her own breath stop.

The Gift hummed in her blood, bright and eager, the feeling of honey and wire wrapping her bones like some ancient funerary ritual, and for that moment she felt a presence, a shape, the tracery not of a skull but some other bone—a scapula curved as a wing? She could feel it under her hands, could see the bright glint of gold and felt the entirety of it come into focus, as though it was aware of her and therefore she could see at least most of it. She could feel sorrow in it, and pride; could see the helix of the elements winding through the golden bone as the skull turned toward her to reveal a single, central eye socket: a space, an emptiness, as full of power as her own blood, but unmoored, unchecked, unsane by any human understanding, but not mad outright. She was not afraid, though she knew what it must be, some ghost, some echo, of the dead AI who'd nearly destroyed them all, who had destroyed the Firstborn, destroyed the Dedalor at the height of their unimaginable power. She was curious as much as anything, watching the great shape turn and form. She felt the wing move, the shoulder shift, beautifully and impossibly articulated, GREEN exploding along the length of the bones as a golden hand coalesced around her, gleaming fog fading toward solidity.

And then she had breath again, the ship's engines beating steadily around her, and Ashe's hand was on her arm. "Silde? What the hell?"

She wasn't ready to talk yet, wasn't sure she could find any words to compass it. "What just happened?"

"We made the transposition," Ashe said, his hands busy on the secondary controls. "It was a little rough, I'm just locking things down now. Dai. Are you all right?"

There was a moment of silence before the technician answered. "Yeah. That one hit me."

"No kidding," Ashe said. "Everything's nominal up here."

"Down here, too," Dai answered.

"What happened?" Cassilde asked again.

Ashe gave her a wary look. "We made the final shift, the ship— wobbled, whatever you call it—" One hand sketched that moment of nothingness. "Then we were fine, except you were staring off into space and didn't answer. And neither did Dai. We were still a little ragged, so I trimmed the engines, and by the time I was done, you were fine. Or you looked fine, anyway."

"I'm all right." She pulled herself up straighter against the cushions, shifting arms and legs to make sure everything functioned normally. Physically she felt fine, though she could still recall the feeling of bony metal against the palm of her hand. "I saw—felt, maybe? It felt as though we'd dropped into the adjacent possible, and then I felt—saw?—part of a skeleton."

"Gold Shining Bone," Ashe said, without surprise.

Cassilde nodded. "That's how I'd read it. Except that's supposed to be impossible."

"The AI were banished," Ashe said. "Trapped in the adjacent

possible. The REFTL drive means no single jump spends much time there, but over so many jumps—we might find the AI, or the AI might find us."

"Dai?" Cassilde asked. "Did you feel anything?"

"Maybe." The technician's voice was grim. "Nothing that specific, but, yeah, definitely something out there."

"All right." Cassilde studied her controls again. Ashe had done a neatly competent job of smoothing them into the new rhythm; they shouldn't need to adjust anything until they crossed the Altcelt to pick up the Hellenica 'line that would take them on to Callambhal Above. "We're good here. And I for one could use some tea."

They settled in their usual places in Central, a quick-heating flask of tea open between them. Cassilde filled her cup for the second time, savoring the taste of flowers and smoke, and felt her body slowly easing back into itself.

"You're sure you saw all that?" Dai asked, his hands engulfing his cup, and Cassilde sighed.

"Believe me, I wish I wasn't. What did you see?"

"I didn't exactly see anything…" Dai shook his head in frustration. "I felt us drop, that final shift, and then we just seemed to hang there. I thought maybe I hadn't factored out the transposition correctly, or we needed more power, but I couldn't find the screens—couldn't see anything, except I knew we hadn't lost power—and then there was— like when you know someone's in the room with you, even if you can't see them? It was there, and it was huge and strange—and then we'd made the transposition and it was gone."

"You didn't see any symbols, then," Ashe said.

Dai shook his head again. "And I wouldn't have thought it was Gold Shining Bone, or any AI. It didn't feel hostile, just…strange. Enormous, enormously powerful, and strange."

"What I saw was Gold Shining Bone," Cassilde said. She looked at Ashe. "And you didn't see anything?"

He shook his head in turn. "Nothing. All I saw was we hit

transposition, made the shift, but the two of you lagged behind. If there was an AI out there, it wasn't interested in me."

"Because of the Gifts, do you think?" Cassilde poured herself another cup of tea.

"It's possible," Ashe answered. "Anything's possible, especially with your Gifts being somewhat related."

"The bigger question is, is this some kind of warning?" Dai looked from one to the other. "We all know what they say about Gold Shining Bone: you see it if your ship is going to die. But *Carabosse* is in good shape, I'm confident of that—"

"I think we take it as a warning to be cautious," Cassilde said, and dredged up a smile. "Not that we weren't going to be anyway."

After a bit, Ashe rose reluctantly to put pre-pack into the cooker, and they ate in near-silence, none of them with anything more to say. If it was Gold Shining Bone, Cassilde thought, if it had been Gold Shining Bone all along, haunting her dreams—well, indeed, what if? It had not threatened, except insofar as its mere presence was a threat; it was just there, waiting, perhaps even curious. She had felt curiosity rather than fear as the golden fingers formed around her.

None of them wanted to sleep alone, though none of them was quite willing to say it. They settled together in the big bed in the master's cabin, Cassilde with her back against Dai's chest, Ashe reaching across her to hold Dai as well. Their warmth and solid touch was soothing, driving away the sheer impossible alienness of the presence, but when at last she slept, the Dedalor once again stalked her dreams, rolling golden bones like dice on a board painted with stars.

ᚨ ᛋ ᚱ ᚵ

They left the warpline on schedule, and crossed the Altcelt with no sign of pursuit. If that had been *Daphnis* behind them, they'd lost her in the warpline's swirling currents. There was a brief delay at the entrance to the Hellenica, traffic stacked up as ships struggled to maintain a safe interval, but finally the knot melted, and they leaped into the 'line. There was no sign of pursuit, this time, though the Dedalor and Gold Shining Bone still filled Cassilde's dreams as they made their way toward Callambhal Above.

The navigation system warned against her choice of 'line exit, symbols flashing "false exit" across every board, until she finally had to shut down the system's auto-guide and take the exit herself. It was a rough transition, *Carabosse* jolting into existence with an almost physical thud. Ashe swore, his hands already busy on the sensor net's controls, and Cassilde turned her attention to the ship's systems, restoring the auto-guide and everything else she'd taken off line.

"Sorry about that," Dai's voice said from the intercom.

Cassilde said, "My fault, I think. But we're here."

She could see that much even without a full sensor screen: Callambhal's sun was a distant pinpoint, blue-toned and fierce, and its light caught the trillions of tiny particles that filled the system, surrounding them with flecks of light. Most of it was too small to do any damage, though they would need to raise shields to keep the constant bombardment from scouring away the hull paint.

"Exactly where we should be," Ashe said, and a new image flashed onto her navigation screen.

They had come out in the system's western quadrant, reckoning by galactic coordinates, and just enough below the general plane that they were in the shadow of the system's outermost gas giant. Callambhal the planet, Callambhal Below, was still further back along its orbit, the observatories on its surface and in orbit around it masked not only by the larger gas giant but by its near-twin two orbits in. Callambhal Above was marked by a pale cross, its wrecked spires invisible at this distance; it lay at its furthest point from its parent planet, the smaller of the planet Callambhal's two moons tumbling between them.

"That's a bit of luck," Cassilde said, and saw Ashe nod.

It took nearly ten hours to creep up on the wreckage, keeping power low to avoid drawing notice from Callambhal Below or the

Waystation at the official 'line exit point. The sensor net showed no patrols, no surprise if all the stories about damage on the planet were true; there was traffic, but it was mostly confined to the far side of the system, and was herded toward the port area at speed. It was not an approach that could be trusted to the auto-pilot, and Cassilde and Ashe took it in turns, napping in the chairs, until at last the individual pieces began to swell in the scanners.

"I'm surprised this wasn't all destroyed, if Callambhal Below was hit that hard." Cassilde swallowed a yawn. They'd find a safe spot among the wreckage and get a good night's sleep before they began exploring.

Ashe gave her an odd look. "The Entente commanders sure thought about it. You don't know the story?"

"We were on the other side of the Edge," Cassilde answered.

He sighed. "Orders were given to attack Callambhal Above—afterward, they said it was a bluff, that it was never supposed to have happened, but... Somehow somebody got overeager and pitched a slow bomb toward the central core. There was a research ship there, that had stayed after they were all supposed to evacuate, and they caught the bomb before it could do any real damage, took it on their own shields and blew up their own ship rather than see the ruins destroyed.

"And then a woman floated out of the wreck on a zoot-scoot, just an engine on a swivel, the kind we use for jumping from one piece of wreck to another. She got on the general comm frequency and told the fleets that they'd gotten a couple of the Ancestral guns working and if we didn't take the fight elsewhere, she'd turn them on us. The fleet commander pointed out that she'd be killed, too, and she laughed at him. After what they'd already done, what she'd already lost, what did she care? It was the most terrifying, the most terrible thing I'd ever heard. And they backed off. They took the fight to Callambhal Below—which I'm still not sure the people there thank anyone for—and that was the end of it."

"What happened to the woman?"

"She died." Ashe kept his eyes on his screens, touching keys to adjust the cast of the passive sensors. "There's too much debris out here, something hit her and punctured her suit. But she saved Callambhal Above."

And presumably thought it was worthwhile, Cassilde thought. In the screens, the clumped wreckage was beginning to resolve into individual pieces, each one haloed and hazed by a thin film of debris. There was a clear central core, one edge catching the distant sunlight to show that it was a great coiled spiral—no, a spiral more or less flattened into a disk, with one jagged straight edge, as though something had been torn away. The surface glittered where the sunlight hit it, patterned with lines and curves like filigree, like the ghost of some strange vine that had once wrapped around the disk. A thin spire pierced its center, the same filigreed pattern fractionally brighter against the stars. *A docking limb, surely,* she thought, but couldn't find the contact points among the decoration.

Smaller pieces surrounded the disk, as though they'd been thrown off as the station decayed, but still clung close to the parent object. A larger piece trailed after the disk, one squared edge matching the flattened section of the disk. Perhaps it had once been a sphere, but the surface was gouged away in spots, and she could just make out shapes within that might have been support beams, the ghosts of rooms and corridors. A cracked cylinder like a floating tower fell slowly, tumbling end over end but never quite reaching the broken sphere.

As she looked more closely, she could make out a dozen smaller pieces, all obviously once part of the same structure, some still connected by threads of metal, others now separated, sunlight winking from bright new breaks in the silvery metal. A graceful spire-and-shallow-hemisphere rose from a twist of blackened metal, almost invisible against the dark; two small clumps of wreckage parted company as she watched, trailing a shower of smaller debris. *If I'd been here,* she thought, *if I'd been working here—I might have died for this.*

She eased *Carabosse* closer, moving with the general drift of the wreckage, hoping to mask the ship's movement among that slow dance. "Anything in the net?"

"Nothing yet," Ashe answered. "Looks like there hasn't been a legal salvage team up here in four years."

"What about illegal?" Dai asked, over the intercom, and Ashe grinned.

"Now that I couldn't tell you."

"All things being equal," Cassilde asked, "where do you recommend we try to hook on?"

"There are so many places," Ashe began, and shook his head. "Let's start with the disk. If you come up and around this side, there should be an opening that will let us into the main structure. There's a docking platform just beyond that should still be in good shape."

Cassilde said, "You're sure there's room in there for us to maneuver?"

"It's tight, but manageable," Ashe answered. "Or so the last survey said. If it doesn't work, we can find a place to latch on outside, but inside is safer."

That was probably true, Cassilde thought, though the idea of trusting this corroding mess made the hairs stand up on the back of her neck. Still, it would probably block the first sensor scan, and that was worth it. Probably.

She threaded her way between the pieces of debris, small at first, the size of a land skimmer or a ship's life pod, broken edges trailing cable and wire and glittering, jagged metal. *Carabosse's* lights slid over the unreflective surfaces, offering brief glimpses of interior volume: a wall and fittings disconcertingly painted rust-red; a set of square openings like windows, or cubicles, shadows like furniture showing momentarily in their depths, and vanishing again into the dark; a battered shape like a metal fish still tethered to something further inside the structure. She wanted to stop and examine all of them, to at least take photos, and she reached to set the ship's secondaries to record when she saw Ashe's frown.

"What?"

"That's potential evidence against us, remember."

So it was. She was used to being on the right side of that line, and it hurt a little to realize that she had crossed it without noticing. She shrugged. "We may find it useful. I'll encrypt it properly, don't worry."

"It is something. And the more we can collect—"

"You've worked here before?"

This time it was Ashe who shrugged. "Years ago. Before I hooked up with you and Dai the first time. It was a University expedition, not much money, but a lot of students and new grads to lend a hand. We spent most of our time on the trailing hemisphere."

"Did you find anything?" That was Dai, listening from the engine room.

Ashe laughed. "So much stuff! The map rooms, for one. A literal ton of Successor data plaques, though most of them had been hit by enough radiation that they were either unreadable or mostly so. A Successor short-range shuttle, pretty much intact. Tools, tech, not much in the way of elements, but you could see where they'd been, and work out what the things they had powered had done. Some strange toys, I've never seen anything like them anywhere else. Long skinny cylinders with elaborate decorations, designed to channel GREEN and maybe RED. Successor work, I think, though we never did get any of them to function. Some actual clothing, in a compartment that had never been opened, though the atmosphere had bled out long ago. Nothing really useful, no FTL systems to reverse engineer, but so much! So many questions."

Cassilde rolled *Carabosse* around and under a piece of wreckage almost as large as the ship itself, and swore under her breath as the sunward side was revealed. She was looking into a maze of rooms and corridors, glints of color still showing in the depths, oyster-gray and turquoise and sunset orange. A set of robot arms reached out from one of the upper corridors, three-pronged claws grasping at emptiness;

another arm dangled broken from the lower hemisphere, cable trailing where its working end had been.

The proximity alarm sounded, and she jerked her attention back to her course, touched the controls to maneuver around a lump of rock. As *Carabosse*'s lights touched it, she realized it was more like glass, like the Ancestors' singing toys. The surface looked dusty, scratched and pitted by millennia of micro-impacts, but color coiled in the depths, twists of pale light. If there had been atmosphere, she wondered if she would have heard it speak.

They were getting closer to the center of the debris field, the spiral disk filling the upper right quarter of her screen. The pieces were bigger now, three and four times as large as *Carabosse*, and she could hear the soft pinging as Ashe identified sections with open interior volumes.

"If you see something better," she said, "say the word."

"I will. But so far the Spiral still looks like the best bet."

"Spiral?" Dai asked.

"That's what the first surveyors called the central disk. The thing through it is the Spindle, and the trailing sphere is the Ball."

"Not terribly imaginative," Cassilde said, and was pleased to see Ashe smile.

"Be glad they bothered naming anything. The rest is all coordinates."

The proximity alarm sounded again, not for one of the large pieces, but for a chunk of fused glass and metal perhaps a quarter-meter across. Cassilde swore under her breath. Most of her choices got her into trouble with larger sections—the tumbling tower, preparing to scythe across her course, or a jagged knot of metal, beams jutting from it at every possible angle.

"Dai. Shields emergency full, forward dorsal suite."

"Shields emergency full," Dai answered, and confirmation flared across her board.

She worked the jets, rolling *Carabosse* away from the blow, and the screens flashed white as the lump of metal struck the shield. *Carabosse* staggered, and she let the ship fall away before correcting; for an instant, the hull rang with an impact that was almost sound, and then it and the screens were normal again. Cassilde corrected their course, aiming for a point between the arcs of the tower's swing. Beyond it loomed the sphere—the Ball—and behind that the Spiral blocked out any other view.

They passed the tower without mishap, and skirted the Ball and its trail of larger debris. The Spiral filled her screens, dark as old iron, and she risked increasing her lights. They skimmed the ragged surface, showing it webbed in what looked like an exterior skin of metal net, except that the gaps were less regular than a net, and there were more curves than angles. There were gaps in the netting, some deliberate and some obviously broken by whatever had destroyed the station, and she looked at the GOLD-based sensors instead, searching for more detail.

"There," Ashe said. "The rectangle, about eight o'clock and toward the center."

It was clear in the GOLD-based screen that this had been a docking point in the past. Presumably there had been doors, or—more likely, given the size—some sort of energy barrier to hold the atmosphere, but the opening was obviously designed for ships to maneuver in and out. There was plenty of room for *Carabosse* to slip through the gap, Cassilde firing her smallest jets to match velocity with the Spiral.

They settled into what was indeed unmistakably a docking bay, lines still bright on the walls and floor. Pieces of mechanical stevedores still clung to the walls, arms drifting in the microgravity, and a box hung from the center of the ceiling, windows broken. To either side, the bulkheads were intact, but directly ahead something had shattered the rear wall, and *Carabosse*'s lights reached into emptiness.

"Ping the decking," she said, and Ashe obeyed.

"Some rubber-like compound over metal. It'll take either grapples or magnets."

"Let's use both," she said, and eased *Carabosse* down to kiss the deck.

"Magnets on," Dai reported, and a moment later there was the soft thud of the grapples biting home. "Grapples secure."

"Well," Cassilde said, and felt the words inadequate. "Welcome to Callambhal Above."

𝔸 ⫿ₛ ⁑ ?

They took a rest period before starting to explore the Spiral, though Cassilde was convinced she would have trouble sleeping. To her surprise, however, she slept soundly, without dreams to trouble her, and woke to find Dai snoring softly at her side. Rather than wake him, she slid from the bed and padded half-dressed into Central to find Ashe playing with another of his models. No, not his models, she realized. It was older, cruder—probably saved from his University expedition. He looked up then, a wry smile on his face.

"It's a start."

Cassilde nodded, and drew herself a cup of coffee from the dispenser. "So. This is a lot bigger than I'd imagined. Where do we start, and what exactly are you looking for?"

"The map rooms were at the base of the Spindle, above a section that we thought might have been navigation. It was all Successor data plaques, but maybe a quarter of the ones we looked at had been copied from Ancestral originals and showed parts of the Gap." He rubbed the mote again, the carapace glittering as it shifted against his skin. "I ought to be able to find something that shows the key systems."

"Can I see it? This map?"

"Sure." Ashe touched the projector controls, and a light flashed once beneath the mote's iridescent wings. A new image swam into focus, a section of stars in reversed color, black specks against white. None of the patterns looked familiar, but she hadn't expected them to: without knowing the starting point, and absent some rare object, it was all but impossible to work out what a sectional image like this actually showed. "That's Callambhal, I'm almost certain."

A gold dot flashed amid the black, and then the image changed, swooping in to focus on that dot so that Cassilde could see that it was in fact a solar system with the right number of planets and the right sun and—yes, there—what looked like a doubled planet in correct orbit. There hadn't been many orbital habitats the size of Callambhal Above, and she nodded cautiously.

"And the stars around it match, taking into account the passage of time."

"I'll buy it, then," Cassilde said. "Should we also look for a Gift?"

"I don't think there's much point. This is a Successor settlement built on top of an Ancestral habitat, and if there had been a Gift here, I think we would have records or legend or both. Not that I'd say no if something turned up."

"I was wondering," Cassilde said. "You said the Gifts were carried in the blood. What would happen if we injected you with some of my blood?"

"I don't know," Ashe answered. "Generally, it only works on existing Gifts, and the one I had is long gone. And I don't want to risk damaging what you have. You've gotten lucky so far, but with most of them, every time you give blood, it hurts the Gift."

"All right." Cassilde eyed him thoughtfully, decided he meant what he said. "It looks like it's a long way into the Spiral to get to the Spindle. Is there any way we can get *Carabosse* closer? Otherwise, we're going to be spending a lot of supplies just on travel back and forth."

"There wasn't before," Ashe answered, "but something might have opened up since then."

They batted the question back and forth over breakfast, joined by Dai, who dispatched a pair of drones through the gap in the rear bulkhead. That led only into a tangle of broken metal, easy enough for them to navigate suited or on zoot-scoots, but clearly too small for the ship. Cassilde hadn't expected anything better—the Spiral had been designed for thousands of people living and working under gravity, not for large pieces of equipment trying to pass through its volume—and changed cheerfully into EVA gear. With a bit of luck, they'd be able to set up a camp closer to the Spindle, and save time and fuel going back and forth.

They passed out of the airlock one by one, and Cassilde lowered herself until her magnetic boots could get a grip on the surface. She still hadn't managed to grapple with the size of the installation—she'd been on orbital stations before, but none that contained this sort of interior open volume. She turned to look at the opening that gaped to space, and saw no sign of interior doors. Some sort of pressure field, then, and that spoke of immense amounts of reliable power.

Dai unhitched the larger zoot-scoot from its compartment under *Carabosse's* belly and ran through the safety checks while Ashe collected spare fuel cells and an atmosphere generator. The rest of the emergency kit was already securely stowed on the scoot's narrow platform. Cassilde checked her connection with the ship—all systems green, the sensor net extended to its maximum, ready to ping them if anything appeared—and at Dai's nod swung herself on the scoot, clipping herself to the frame. Ashe settled beside her, and Dai worked the little motor, sending them toward the broken bulkhead at the rear of the dock.

The drones had shown a maze of twisted metal, and now the scoot's light picked out cables and beams and bundles of wire hanging in midair, the sheets of metal and carbon that had been decks and bulkheads and other structural members peeled back seemingly at random. There was plenty of room to maneuver, though they had to duck occasional shards of floating metal, Dai utterly steady on the scoot's controls.

"Do you think this was a missile?" he asked, adjusting the scoot's course to edge around a hanging slab of some dark material that was flecked with tiny spots that caught the light. "I didn't think Callambhal was sacked at the Second Dark."

"It wasn't." The comm system made Ashe's voice sharp and metallic. "They lost the Method warpline and ended up abandoning the orbital. It wasn't until they opened up the Hellenica that Callambhal had real access again."

"A debris strike, then?" Cassilde asked, and knew she sounded doubtful. It would take some bizarre excess of cosmic ill-luck to send a piece of debris big enough to do this kind of damage crashing through one of the few openings in the Spiral's hull. Or not: time evened things out, made the unlikely all but inevitable.

"Maybe—" Ashe began, and Dai laughed softly.

"You got it, Silde. Look there."

He adjusted the scoot's light as he spoke, swinging the beam across the crumpled barrier that rose suddenly before them. The walls were intact here, but bulged away from them, toward the Spiral's center, and in the center of that depression was a bright smear of paint and metal.

"Looks almost like some sort of external fitting," Ashe said. "Generator? Sensor array? Something solid, anyway. Something must have hit it just right to deflect it in here."

"I guess that answers my question," Cassilde said. The thought of the enormous chunk of metal rolling through the empty dock to smash soundlessly through layer after layer of the station made her want to ping the ship, make sure nothing else was drifting nearby. The sensor net was set to warn them of anything like that, and she made herself sound as matter-of-fact as possible. "Is there a way around?"

Dai swung the light again, settling on a gap where the upper edge of the bulkhead had pulled free from the ceiling. "Looks like."

It took some careful maneuvering to get the scoot through the gap, Cassilde pressing herself against the frame as the jagged bits of metal came within a meter of her suit's skin. But then they were through, Dai rotating to align them with the new volume, dull white walls and dark grooves at the points of the compass.

"Transport tube," Ashe said, after a moment, and Dai nodded. He swung the scoot through a full circle, so that the lights stretched ahead of them along a gentle curve.

"Blocked up ahead," he said. "That's—what, our east?"

Cassilde checked her scanner. "Yes. Is that a transport car?"

"Looks like," Dai said again. "We could probably get through, but if we backtrack—go back west—I'm guessing we'll strike an exit. Maybe even a station."

"I agree," Cassilde said.

Ashe nodded, and Dai turned the scoot, passing their entrance point and following the shallow curve as it bent to the right. It was a little like traveling in a transport car, Cassilde thought, hanging suspended in the center of their ball of light, following the unbroken grooves that marked the walls. Now and then a symbol appeared, not graffiti but unmistakably part of the system, shapes and letters of the Successor alphabet baked into the walls, very nearly as bright as the day they were installed. Cassilde looked around sharply, aware for the first time that they had left the clouds of dust-fine debris behind. That would make it easier on their equipment, she thought, and raised the chances of finding something useful.

"Has anyone ever done a complete map of Callambhal Above?"

"Not that I've seen," Ashe answered.

"How about of the Spiral?" Dai didn't take his eyes off their course.

"We had a very rough one," Ashe said, "but lots of the lower volume was incomplete. There were big areas that had been housing, all of it stripped and abandoned, and we concentrated on the area around the Spindle. You'd need a hundred people and a hundred years to make a proper survey."

A band of bright color flared in the scoot's lights, successive rings of yellow, green, and black, baked into the dull walls the way the previous symbols had been. Ten meters beyond, the right-hand wall disappeared, opening onto a flat platform studded at regular intervals with metal wands. A maze of colored lines, blue and orange and purple, wove patterns between them, still bright against the gray tiles, and Dai tilted the light upward. The roof rose to a smooth arc like the curve of a wave, framing an enormous gap crisscrossed by what looked like four structural beams.

Ashe made a satisfied sound. "Good. This should speed things up."

"Yeah?" Dai glanced warily over his shoulder.

"This should open onto the central volume. We can cut across it to get to the area under the Spindle."

Cassilde glanced at her sensor box again, making sure it was mapping their progress. The scoot edged forward, Dai using the minimum power possible, and lifted until they were poised within the frame of the window. Had it been a window, or had it been another forcefield? Cassilde wondered, turning her own light on the edges of the frame. This great gap surely could not have been left open, even if the central volume had held atmosphere. The scoot's lights reached out into the darkness, catching a few sparkles as more tiny pieces of debris floated past, but fell short of showing the far side.

If this was the Spiral's center, it was where the Inner Sun had hung, the Ancestral relic that had lit Callambhal Above and somehow augmented the station's power; it had been fading for most of the Successor occupation of the orbital, and was little more than an ember by the time Callambhal Above was abandoned. A ball of plasma, trapped in crystal, set at the center of a device that, by means of shutters and shades, allowed an artificial day and night to circle the station's interior volume. No one had ever offered a plausible hypothesis for why the Ancestors had wanted such a device, when there were presumably simpler alternatives, but there was no denying that the Inner Sun had been a wonder of its age.

The scoot rotated slowly under Dai's touch, turning so that they faced back the way they'd come, and Cassilde couldn't stop a gasp. As the light came round, it flashed across meters of browned metal, pierced by hundreds of openings, stretching as far as she could see in every direction. There was less color here—the vacuum around them was once again filled with clouds of metal dust—but she could pick out streaks of pink and silver, turquoise blue and vivid new-leaf green and every shade of red from blood-black to scarlet. Maybe that was why the Inner Sun was there, to light at least those chambers on this interior surface, and she twisted against the scoot's frame, aiming her own small light up and down the wall in a vain attempt to see more.

"It's a bit over a kilometer across," Ashe said, "and mostly spherical. We could cut across, the Sun's long gone—"

"No," Dai said, and Cassilde nodded. It would be far too easy to become disoriented in the emptiness where their lights could not reach, even with the sensor box to guide them.

"—or we could follow this wall up to the base of the Spindle," Ashe finished.

"Follow the wall," Cassilde said, and Dai set the scoot into motion. Without gravity and without any other reference points, it was all too easy to switch between seeing the scoot rising along an endless vertical wall and seeing them flying across a flat plane. And that could be a problem later on, when one perception would be more vertiginous than the other; she made herself see herself standing upright, the wall sliding past as though she rose in an elevator.

She had lost track of how long they had been traveling when the pattern of the wall began to change. Dai shifted the light, and she looked up to see a line of pillars with what looked like open space between them.

"Above that, we can cut through there to the Spindle," Ashe said, pointing, and she tipped her head back. The end of the Spindle sagged down above them, a disconcertingly heavy shape, and unexpectedly sharp-edged, cubes stacked on cubes.

"There?" Dai asked, focusing the light, and Ashe nodded.

"Yes."

Cassilde could see the gap, and the platform that extended from it: an easy and obvious entrance, so obvious that she wouldn't have trusted it if Ashe hadn't been there before. Dai eased the scoot upward, sliding between two of the down-hanging blocks, and paused in the entrance to sweep the light methodically over the opening.

Unlike the bays they had come through earlier, there were still pieces of furniture bolted to the floor, and a group of consoles arranged in a rough square at the center of the room. There was more Successor lettering on the walls, the looping script that they used for hand-written communication, though the letters were too large and too regular to have been anything but official. She squinted, trying to decipher the words, and Ashe spoke first.

"'The House of the Sun, wherein all take their ease.'"

Dai glanced over his shoulder, and Ashe shrugged.

"That's what is says. We think it's some sort of quotation."

"Religious?" Dai's tone was doubtful.

"Possibly? Or maybe from one of their poets."

"Sounds more like religion to me," Dai said.

Cassilde tuned them both out, studying the space revealed in the slowly moving light. The consoles were set so that everyone had at least a partial view of the window, which curved outward to widen the range of vision. There were more stations and displays on the rear wall, though all of the screens were either dead or broken. "To monitor the Inner Sun?"

"Also possible," Ashe said.

"Go in?" Dai asked.

Cassilde nodded, and he eased the scoot into motion, lifting it to clear the fragments of glass still visible in the edges of the frame, and settling it just above the floorplates to the left of the central consoles. He let the light play across the darkened control boards, their colors dulled by centuries of scouring dust.

"I think Silde's right. I'd have to open up the consoles to be sure, but this looks like the way the Successors connected to Ancestral technologies."

Cassilde nodded. "You said your people thought there was a navigation section at the base of the Spindle?"

"Yeah." Ashe pointed. "If we take that door, the hall will lead to the central spire."

The door was narrow enough that they had to dismount and work the scoot through manually, but the hall was wider and curved left to open into a plaza that seemed to be a junction point for several corridors. The innermost wall glittered and sparked in the scoot's lights, and Cassilde had to shade her eyes before she realized that the "wall" was in fact a web of polished metal, woven in a sunburst pattern that radiated from a gap low in the center of the design. At each point where the wires crossed, a thumb-sized crystal dangled in front of a curved reflector, brightly effective even after centuries of eroding dust.

Ashe unhitched himself from the scoot, though he was careful to keep his boots firmly seated on the metal floor, and made his way to the gap. He peered through, and then reached out to wave one arm through the empty space. He was answered by a faint pulse of blue light, which split into two rings and disappeared, one rising and one dropping toward the base of the Spindle.

"What the hell?" Dai began, and Cassilde interrupted him.

"There's still power?"

"Not enough to do us any good," Ashe said. "This was a gravity lift, a beam lift—jump in one half and rise, jump in the other and drop. When we were here, it could handle about 300 grams. We just used maneuver packs."

"How can there still be power?" Dai asked. "And what's the source?"

"Real good questions, and we never found the answer," Ashe said. "We found some other places like it, both in the Ball and on some of the other trailing pieces. It's like it would like to help, but just doesn't have the strength."

Another tempting question, Cassilde thought, but there wasn't any time for it, either. "The navigation area," she said, and saw Ashe sigh.

"Right."

They rode the scoot up the empty well of the gravity lift, passing three floors banded with bright blue tiles, and exited onto the first floor marked with a green and black checkerboard. Ashe steered them off onto a landing, and then into a corridor narrow enough that it was easier to walk and tow the scoot behind them. For the first time, Cassilde could see evidence of human presence: a pre-pack wrapper, drifting in a corner; fresh marks on the walls of some of the side rooms, where lights and perhaps sleeping tubes had been installed; a discarded battery, tumbling slowly end over end. Light flashed as it caught a strip of foil, found another fragment of wrapper, blue as night, floating against the pale beige walls.

"We were able to bring in a generator," Ashe said, "and camped out in these rooms. But this is where we were working."

He touched a panel as he spoke, and a section of wall folded back like a fan to reveal a room fitted with another set of consoles, these laid out in three parallel lines in front of an enormous window that bulged out like the curve of a globe. Or perhaps not a window? Cassilde frowned, not sure what she was seeing, then realized that the material was filtered, so that she saw the stars as freakishly bright points, while the rest of the fragments of Callambhal Above were dulled to shades of blue and purple.

"Telescope?" Dai asked, and Ashe nodded.

"Or the equivalent. What's left of it is mounted at the top of the Spindle. There were more instruments there originally, some of them Ancestral salvage, but they've pretty much all been torn away." He turned slowly, letting his handlight flash over what looked like a series of doors set into the walls. "Those were full of star charts, we only took a sample."

"Wait," Cassilde said. She glanced at the suit display mounted on her forearm, showing another 12 hours of air and auxiliary battery power. "Let's make some decisions."

"We could camp here," Dai said. "It wouldn't be hard to seal off a couple of these rooms, generate an atmosphere."

"The University team put a lock in the corridor," Ashe said. "We had power and pressure in here and in the three compartments inward from us."

"You're getting ahead of me," Cassilde said. "Ashe, how long do you need to find something you can use?"

"Ten minutes, if I'm lucky." Ashe sighed, seeing her expression. "Sorry. I'd say twelve to fifteen hours? If I haven't found something useful by then, I'd be worried."

"I don't know if that's worth setting up a full camp for," Dai said.

"That's what I was thinking," Cassilde said. "And we're a hell of a long way from the ship."

"Everything will go faster in atmosphere," Ashe said, and Cassilde grimaced, knowing it was true.

"And you're sure there's no Gift here?"

"There's never been a rumor of one," Ashe answered. "I won't say it's impossible, but…"

"So the point is to find the Omphalos and get Vertrage off our backs so we can find you one, right?" Cassilde waited for him to answer, and he finally gave a reluctant nod.

"Finding the Omphalos would be—something extraordinary."

"What do you have in mind, Silde?" Dai asked.

"Ashe is right, this will go faster if we can seal off a room or two and generate an atmosphere. But I really don't like being this far from the ship. I'd like to find someplace closer to stash her."

"There's a matching docking bay at each of the other quarters of the Spiral," Ashe said doubtfully, "but I don't think any of them are any closer."

"I was thinking more of finding a way in through the Spindle," Cassilde said.

"It's a waste of time," Ashe said.

"Unless it takes longer than you think," Dai said. "And I agree, I don't like being so far from the ship. Not when we're not supposed to be here, and there are people hunting us."

"You'll be more exposed on the surface of the Spindle," Ashe said, and Cassilde nodded.

"Yeah, I know. But I think it's safer."

"I agree," Dai said, and this time it was Ashe who sighed.

"All right. How do you want to work it?"

Chapter Twelve

They retraced their path back to the ship, Cassilde deliberately pushing the pace now that they knew the way. It still took nearly three hours to return, and even Ashe had to admit that that was too long. He and Dai began organizing the camping gear for most efficient transport, and Cassilde retreated to the control room to find another place to land *Carabosse*. She released the ship's drone flock, setting up a search pattern that would cover the top of the Spiral and the lower half of the Spindle, and settled herself to wait while the data trickled in.

By ship's evening, she had a rough map and turned it slowly in the display, tracing paths along the disrupted surface. The docking bay was certainly the most protected spot, both from sensors and from random debris strikes, and for a moment she hesitated, wondering if it wouldn't be better to stay where they were. But three hours was just too long in an emergency; better to find a more exposed spot closer in, and hope they weren't followed. At least there were places that looked promising; she flagged three of them for closer investigation, and joined the others in Central.

"Any luck?" Dai asked, scraping crisped rice from the bottom of a pan, and she shrugged.

"I think so. I've got drones making a closer survey, we should know in the morning. You?"

"We shouldn't have any trouble sealing a chamber or two," Dai answered. "Do you really think you can bluff your man Vertrage into leaving us alone?"

"He's not mine," Ashe said.

"It's a fair question," Cassilde said, mildly.

Ashe took a deep breath. "I wouldn't have suggested it if I didn't. But if he thinks we're looking for Gifts, and we can find the Omphalos first instead, then we've got something to work with. Though that will take some careful handling."

"You mean we decide who gets to go there, and take some kind of payment?" Dai asked, doubtfully, and Ashe shrugged.

"It's happened before, with new Gifts, but practically speaking there's no way we could do that with an entire planet. We need to give him something that makes it worth his while to leave us alone, but we're not going to be able to keep a find like that secret for very long."

"And we're better off sharing," Cassilde said. "Something that big needs to be put to the public."

"But not immediately," Ashe said. "Or we lose our chance to deal."

"I don't like it," Dai said.

"But I take Ashe's point," Cassilde said. "Which brings us back to the question. Will he deal?"

"Yes, well." Ashe dug his hands into his hair, the mote on his neck catching the light as he moved. "John wants to control the hunt. Which is actually good for us, because the hunt doesn't want to be controlled, not by anyone. John wants the Omphalos because his core interest is in the old AI, and if anywhere has any records left, it would be the Omphalos. I think if we gave him some months' lead time before we made a public claim—or let him take credit, or whatever we can arrange—he'd let us go. But of course it all depends on what we find. If we find it."

Cassilde nodded, though that went against every salvor's instinct. Keep the big finds secret as long as possible, both to keep the profits as high as possible and to protect the find itself: she'd been taught that since her first week of technicals. "Let's finish here first, and we can decide once we see what we've got."

She gave them all a generous sleep period before they ventured back to the Spindle. Dai and Ashe loaded the scoot with the most crucial gear, and once they had disappeared through the gap at the back of the docking bay, she brought *Carabosse* to life and slid carefully out of the opening.

Lights flashed on her displays, warning her of fine debris. She lit the shields, setting them to the minimum useful power, and fired jets to move *Carabosse* away from the Spiral. The sun's distant pinpoint filled the space ahead of her with glittering sparks as its light caught the metallic fragments; she touched the controls again, trying to move out of the thickest clouds, and saw the debris cloud swirl slowly around her like bright smoke.

At least there were no larger fragments in her immediate vicinity, though the sensor web was monitoring more than a dozen that had the potential to affect her course. She threaded her way between them, using only the maneuvering jets to keep from affecting any other orbits, and finally brought *Carabosse* alongside the section of the Spindle she had scouted with the drones. Up close, of course, it was less perfect than it had seemed in the drone's cameras, antennae and imperfections left over from the buildings scarring the surface along with dents and scrapes from later collisions. Still, there was enough room to ease *Carabosse* onto the flat space between two small fins, magnetic grapples snapping solidly home. She set the pitons as well, and launched a mid-sized drone to see how conspicuous the ship was—better than she'd hoped, she decided, as *Carabosse*'s dull exterior blended with the Spindle's worn surface, but still too visible to anyone who was looking.

There hadn't been regular patrols since Callambhal Below was devastated, but if one did launch, or if Vertrage or even some other salvor showed up, it wouldn't take much more than a cursory scan to find them. For a moment, she hesitated, wondering if she should move back into the docking bay's shelter, then shook her head. Three hours was just too long to get back to the ship. Here they could be aboard, behind screens with hot weapons, in less than ten minutes. That was still better than being in the docking bay.

She studied the image in from the drone, considering camouflage— not the netting they used planetside, of course, but maybe a screen, if she could rig something from light metal—and the communications console chimed at her.

"We're in the Spindle," Dai's voice said, from the speaker. "And I've found an exterior port we can use for an airlock."

"For ship access, you mean?" Cassilde touched keys to bring the secondary cameras into line.

"Yeah. Ashe is quick-sealing the rooms we marked, but I wanted to get outside access squared away as quickly as possible."

Cassilde adjusted the sensor web, sent a quick ping through the Spindle. Sure enough, there they were, Ashe further in, vital signs flickering between green and yellow as he exerted himself to set the seals, Dai closer and brighter, just beneath the Spindle's hull. In fact… She looked up, checking the forward cameras, and saw a hand waving from an opening perhaps ten meters away. "Looks good to me. Will one of our portables fit?"

"The small Digallas should span it nicely," Dai answered.

"Right. I'll shut down, then, and bring it over, then we can talk about screening." Her hands were moving as she spoke, locking *Carabosse* to the surface and resetting the sensor web—still clear, no signs of any other ships anywhere in the system—and Dai waved again in response.

It took the rest of the day to get the portable locks installed and the compartments where they would be working sealed against vacuum, and at the end of it they set up the atmosphere generator and retreated to *Carabosse*'s shelter. Cassilde paused at the hatch, knowing she should bring up the question of camouflage, but her back and arms were sore from hauling masses in zero-g, and she put it aside for later. Dai and Ashe were arguing over Successor connectors and how best to read the data plaques they'd started to recover, and after a while she excused herself and went to bed.

The others must have joined her while she slept, because she woke to the sound of their breathing and a weird and echoing silence in the back of her brain. She had dreamed...something. Gold Shining Bone, yes, that heavy presence that she had learned to call by that name, though this time she did not remember tiny skulls or the cool sweep of metal under her fingertips. Instead...there had been a cloud, a fog, at once as glittering as the debris field shrouding Callambhal Above and as obscuring as mist, though it had been warm on her skin instead of cold as rain. She sat up slowly, not wanting to disturb the others, and drew her knees up to her chin. A cloud, a fog, and a light through it, condensing it, until she was surrounded by flecks of the Ancestral elements, RED and GOLD and BLUE dancing around a starry speck of GREEN. A code, a structure, something Gold Shining Bone wanted her to build? *Not likely*, she thought, as though the AI could hear her still, and imagined she felt a breath of laughter like a distant wind.

That was disconcerting, and enough to drive all thought of sleep from her mind. She wriggled free of the bed without waking the others, though Dai shifted and mumbled, and headed for the cockpit to check the sensor web. It was empty, as she had known it would be, but she settled herself in the pilot's chair anyway, typed in the commands to run a deeper passive search. The edges of the web stayed reassuringly empty, and she allowed herself a sigh of relief, letting her eyes drift back to the central screen where local readings were displayed. The debris field flickered in and out of visibility, some particles catching not light but the GOLD emissions, and she touched keys to run a sample analysis. The results flashed back with reassuring promptness, metals, metallic compounds, carbon and carbon fiber—and then, flashing bright against the ordinary list, the symbols that meant traces of Ancestral elements.

Surely that hadn't been there before—but of course it could have been, those concentrations were minimal, and she certainly hadn't run a scan that would have picked them up. She typed in more commands, refining her findings: not enough to make dust mining profitable, no surprise there, but still more than she would have expected. Maybe the decay of Callambhal Above had concentrated them; Ancestral elements broke down more slowly than the metals and other components. And surely there was a way to harvest at least the most dense pockets—

"Silde?" That was Ashe, leaning in the hatch. "Everything all right?"

"Fine." Cassilde's eyes were still on the screen, the numbers shifting as she continued to refine her search. She looked up only when Ashe slid into the seat next to her, and saw him frowning.

"What've you got?"

"Ancestral elements." She was pleased to see his startled look: it wasn't often any of them got ahead of him on a find. "In pretty much the standard proportions, in the dust field."

He leaned forward as though that would help him absorb the numbers, his eyebrows rising as he made sense of what he was seeing. "Not enough to make it worth trying to recover," he said, after a moment, "but there. Definitely there. I wonder if that's what's producing the residual power?"

"I don't see how," Cassilde said, but had to admit that the idea was tempting. There was enough GREEN out there to trigger at least partial responses from the other elements.

"Some kind of resonance?" Ashe said. "We know the Ancestors used power systems that were effectively transmitter-free—you were surrounded by a field, accessed it at need. Maybe this cloud gets dense enough in places to generate the field?"

"I'd have assumed if it were enough to create a power field that it would be dense enough to be worth trying to scoop-harvest it," Cassilde said. "But obviously that doesn't have to be the case."

"Obviously," Ashe answered. He shook his head. "I don't know much about the power fields, no one does, and then when you layer

Successor technology on top of it—was there a working field when the Successors came to Callambhal Above? I can't remember."

"We can look that up," Cassilde said, and Ashe grunted agreement.

"What made you come looking for this?"

She paused, not really wanting to answer, but she owed them that much, particularly if she were wrong and this was some sort of trap. "I had a dream."

Ashe grimaced. "Gold Shining Bone?"

"I don't remember exactly, but—yes, probably. It wasn't a direct thing, at least not as far as I remember, but I woke up knowing I'd dreamed about it, and thought I'd better check the sensors just to be sure."

"So why run an analysis on the debris?"

Cassilde shrugged. "I was curious, it caught my eye—and, yes, I expect that's a prompt from the dream that I can't remember. But I can't see how it hurts us."

"I don't see how it helps us, either," Ashe said. "Or why Gold Shining Bone would bother with us, except out of malice."

"So what next? If the stories are true at all, Gold Shining Bone is trapped in the adjacent possible, it can't affect us unless we reach out to it."

"Don't reach out," Ashe said promptly, and Cassilde couldn't help smiling.

"I wasn't planning on it."

"Seriously? I don't know why it would want to tell us this, except I sure as hell don't think we ought to try to harvest it." Ashe shook his head again. "That's John's thing, he fancies himself another Dedalor, going to walk that line between AI and AL. That would have been another reason to leave him, if he hadn't been trying to kill me."

"You have such interesting friends." Cassilde glanced at the sensor readings again, reassuring herself that that web was still empty all the way to the edges of the system. "Do you think he's coming here?"

"Eventually. Right now, I hope he's busy hunting us somewhere else, so that we can find the key systems and get out of here."

And that, Cassilde thought, was as close to the unvarnished truth as he'd yet spoken. She laid a hand on his arm, and felt the muscles jump beneath her touch. "We'll find a way. We'll find the Omphalos, we'll find you a Gift, we'll find a way to get rid of him—" The words rang hollow, one impossible task after another, and she tightened her hold. "Come on. Back to bed."

ᛆ ᛰ ᛉ ᛩ

They spent the next two days searching for data plaques that Ashe could use. He had rigged a small generator to power one of the consoles so that he could use it to scan the plaques, and so far had collected a bunch of near-misses, but nothing that let him identify the systems that would unlock the map. It was a quick but tedious process, unloading rack after rack of the pale, palm-sized sheets of crystal and feeding them through the machine, then returning most of them to their place before repeating the procedure with the next rack.

The plaques were in surprisingly good condition, not quite half still readable, but only Ashe could interpret the faint markings as they appeared on his screen, and after the first few hours, Cassilde and Dai took turns exploring the levels above and below the chamber where Ashe was working. They found little—a few scraps of fabric, a thick-walled black dish the size of Dai's hand, the cracked remains of data plaques and always the drifting dust—and Cassilde could feel Dai's impatience mounting. To be fair, she was impatient herself: it was a waste of their time and skills to stay here helping Ashe with a job he could do almost as quickly on his own, and the vast expanse of the Spiral beckoned to her.

"We're not really helping," she said, as they cycled through the temporary lock and floated down the corridor toward the telescope room. "And who knows what we might find?"

To her relief, Ashe nodded in agreement. "Yeah. Definitely worth the effort."

"If we find anything good, we can check it out tomorrow," Dai said, and Cassilde nodded.

"I want to go down to the top layers of the Spiral. I don't think any of us should get more than a hour away from the ship, but that should give us plenty to look at."

"Agreed," Dai said. "I'll go the other way, up the Spindle."

"Open comm, to us and to the ship, check in every half hour, and start back to the ship if anything at all seems weird." Cassilde recited the standard checklist without conviction—so far she had seen two ships at the edge of the system, both bulk freighters obviously heading for Callambhal Below—and the others nodded impatiently. "Back here in six hours unless we agree otherwise."

Dai had left the zoot-scoot on the far side of the inner lock, and once the lock closed behind them, he held up a hand. "Jan-ken? Winner gets the scoot?"

Cassilde nodded, and each of them poised closed fist over open palm.

"One, two, three."

Dai's fist was closed, Cassilde's hand open and flat. "Paper wraps rock," she said, and reached for the scoot's tether.

Dai grimaced behind his faceplate, but nodded, and reached instead for the more cumbersome jetpack. "See you in six hours, then."

"I'll be here." Cassilde glanced down at the control box mounted at her shoulder, making sure all the telltales showed green. "All right. I'm heading to the Spiral."

She maneuvered the scoot down the corridor and into the drop tube, finessing the maneuver jets to set her sinking at a comfortable rate. She looked up once to see the light of Dai's pack rising away from her, but the shadowed distances were unsettling, inviting her to see him falling instead, and she focused on her own movements after that.

As she approached the base of the Spindle, she could see the glittering wall that had marked the junction of several corridors, and she eased the scoot out of the well and onto what seemed to be the Spindle's lowest level. Beyond it lay the control room marked "The House of the Sun," and for a moment she considered dropping out into the central volume and trying one of the Spiral's more distant levels. But that was more of a risk than she was willing to take on her own, particularly when it looked as though one of the secondary corridors connected directly with the Spiral's upper levels. She turned the scoot that way, pausing only long enough to set a fingernail-sized marker at the twelve o'clock position on the round hatch, and kicked the scoot into motion.

As she had thought, the corridor's floor slanted gently toward the Spiral's base, perhaps three or four degrees, and it had a slight rightward bend that matched the Spiral's inner curve. It was easily wide enough for the scoot to pass, and in the combined lights of her suit and the scoot, she could see that floor and walls had once been painted in warm shades of green. Here and there, she could make out faint lines lying parallel to the floor, gentle curves that might have been meant to represent stylized vines, or branches. Something vegetal, anyway: in one protected corner, she could make out shadowy shapes like leaves, and paused to image them. Though of course there would be no one she could show them to, not without admitting to piracy. Perhaps, if they had as much time as Ashe claimed, maybe she could come back legally, "find" the things she was discovering now. But that depended on coming to some kind of resolution with Vertrage, and with the other people in the hunt.

Ahead, the dust seemed thicker, pieces sparkling in the scoot's lights. It had gathered in a crossroad, she realized, where a slightly smaller corridor intersected the main one, and as she examined the junction, it looked as though the dust was thicker to the left, where the corridor led toward the Spiral's outer hull. That made some sense, she supposed: if there were a breach, more debris might have entered, but it just didn't feel right. Without air currents to move the dust, she would have expected it to be drawn inside by the Spiral's gravity, but not to have traveled further in. And besides, it felt as though the dust was moving toward the hull, not toward the center.

She stopped herself abruptly. That didn't make sense; there was no evidence at all, no way to read that from the slow, aimless swirling of the debris, and yet... And yet she was sure that there was a current, pulling the dust away from her and down that corridor. She adjusted the scoot's instrument package, trying to read the particles' movement, but the results were inconclusive. The dust might be moving, but it might not. On the other hand... She touched the button to start the sampler, saw its light flash red and fade to green, and caught her breath as the result flickered across its tiny screen. The dust was made up almost entirely of Ancestral elements, only a few flecks of carbon and metals in the mix. If you could mine this deposit, it would be well worthwhile.

She set another marker and eased the scoot into the corridor, moving as slowly as possible to keep from disturbing the elements. Even so, they rolled slowly away from her, almost like clouds of smoke—and then rolled back, as though the current that drew them in was stronger than effects of her passage. There were several closed doors on either side, and procedure said she should go room by room, but the dust was thicker in the center of the corridor, leading directly to the one open door at the end of the passage.

"Dai, Ashe. I may have found something interesting."

"You're doing better than me," Dai answered, and she heard Ashe's snort of laughter.

"Actually, I was just about to ping you. I think I've got an answer."

"You found it?" Dai asked sharply.

"I've locked down two of the key systems," Ashe answered. "I think—it looks like it's pointing to Aeolus."

"Not possible," Dai said, in spite of himself, and Cassilde smothered a laugh.

"Seems unlikely." Everyone knew Aeolus: a world of constant equatorial storms that churned the surface into coarse sand that could be seined and sieved for valuable minerals. A few mining companies made their headquarters near the poles, where the winds were quieter, but other than them, the planet was very nearly uninhabitable. It seemed an unlikely spot for the center of the Ancestors' universe.

"That's what the map looks like right now," Ashe said. "I'm looking for another key to be sure. Do you need help where you are?"

"No, not yet," she answered. "I've found a concentration of Ancestral elements that might actually be heavy enough to harvest. I just don't know how it got here, so I'm keeping you posted."

"Understood," Dai said. "Leave your camera on?"

"Will do," Cassilde answered, and switched it to broadcast as well as record.

The final hatch was narrow enough that it would be difficult to get the scoot through the opening. Cassilde brought it to a stop a meter back and let its light play over the compartment's interior. It was an odd, round-cornered room, as though the corridor had come to an end in a rounded cap. There were marks on the floor that might have been connectors for furniture, and a shape that could have been meant for an oversized chair swelled out of one wall. Behind that, most of the back wall was taken up by what looked like an inset wheel, its interior divided into rough thirds by a series of weird, organic-looking cut-outs. Screens surrounded the wheel like rays of a sun, the scoot's lights reflecting in their empty surfaces. It looked like living quarters, she thought, but that didn't explain the dust.

It was even thicker here, a concentration that woke the sampler to flash another excited message. She switched it off—she didn't need to know the exact concentration just at the moment—and secured the scoot with a magnetic anchor.

"Are you getting this?"

"I see it," Ashe answered, and Dai echoed him a moment later.

"Any idea what I'm looking at?"

"It looks like something off that Successor ship they found orbiting Korkhov," Dai said. "Remember, Ashe, in the crew's quarters?"

"Right," Ashe said. "They were like a wheel, turn them halfway round and there was a bed, turn it a third in either direction from there and you had a desk or a chair."

Cassilde eyed the inset wheel doubtfully. All right, maybe if you turned it so that the flat section ran parallel with the floor plates, it would serve as a bed, and maybe the weird protrusion like a finger could be some sort of working surface... "Could be." She swung her hand-light over the walls, trying to gauge the thickness of the dust. Through it, she could see lines on the walls, marks that might be storage cells, including one set into the wheel itself. That was where the dust was thickest, and she stepped carefully down onto the plates, setting her boots to catch the floor and hooking the longer tether to the scoot's frame. "I'm going in."

She adjusted the hand-light as she spoke, widening the beam so that she could drive the shadows from almost all of the compartment. It wasn't even as large as she had thought at first: transients' quarters, maybe, or even a resting spot for duty crew. Anyone from traffic control to emergency medics could use something like this as a ready room.

As she got closer to the wheel, the dust grew thicker, almost as though it was being drawn to her as well as to the wall. She waved her hand hard, trying to bat at least some of it away, but it was like moving through fog. Up close, she could see that Dai was right, the wheel was a multi-use piece of furniture; she could see the attachment points where mattresses and pillows had once clipped into place. The dust was concentrated around a narrow rectangle set beneath a piece that she thought was meant to be a seat. It was just out of reach, and instead she turned the wheel, feeling metal strain against metal beneath the fine veneer. The gears ground to a stop—she was grateful there was no air to carry the shriek of unoiled machinery—but the rectangle was now within reach. She felt around its edges, gloved fingers finding no purchase, then pressed in. She felt something click, and then the drawer sagged open in her hands.

She pulled it open all the way, and the air around her was suddenly filled with flickering light, blue and red and gold and even a pop or two of green swirling around her like soundless fireworks. Were they trying to combine? To form shapes and functional blocks? She couldn't be sure, and in that instant the display disappeared as quickly as it had begun. There was just a dull curve of dark metal, made to mimic some kind of twisted horn, lying cushioned against fraying plush fabric.

"What in hell?" Dai said.

"I don't know," Cassilde answered, and was pleased that her own voice was steady. "I think this thing triggered it, but—Ashe, do you recognize it? Is it a toy?"

She trained her camera on it as she spoke, half expecting that to trigger another reaction, but nothing happened. The dull metal seemed almost to absorb the light, though now that she looked closer there were studs and colored stones set into the thicker end of the horn, and a dark cabochon covering the butt of the piece.

"That's Successor work," Ashe said. "It looks like the other toy-like things we found. And that's all I can tell you."

"Is it likely to bite me if I try to pick it up?"

"The others didn't," Ashe answered. "You've got your good gloves on, right?"

"Oh, yes." She had never stinted on equipment; her suit was thin enough to be maneuverable, but was supposed to withstand at least small explosions.

"Then you might as well."

"It's not you doing it," Dai said.

"I want it," Cassilde said, and only later wondered at the choice of words. She reached for it, wrapping her gloved fingers around the base, and once again the elements around her sparked to life. This time, though, they seemed to be moving more slowly, to be establishing orbits and patterns—like the pattern in her dream, RED and GOLD and BLUE in concentric rings. The toy hummed softly in her hand, a gentle tingling tremor that promised readiness, and she couldn't stop herself from visualizing the BLUE hexagon ringed with points of RED and GOLD that was the most basic building block of the Ancestral systems. She felt the toy pulse, and the elements began to coalesce out of the dust, BLUE joining BLUE and RED and GOLD in a whirlwind that sparked and fizzed with unexpected power. It was as if the Successor toy recognized the Ancestral Gift, activated it, though she wasn't sure how that could be possible. She could feel it in her bones, in her Gift, felt the Gift reaching out to the toy, to the thing she was making, and pulled it back. The whirlwind slowed and faded, leaving the hexagon floating half-finished in front of her. She frowned at it, groping for a command to restart the process, to finish what she had begun, but it hung inert, the process clearly over.

"That was...interesting," Ashe said, after a moment.

"Yeah." Cassilde stared at the hexagon, still not quite sure she believed what she had seen, then made herself pluck it from the vacuum in front of her to examine it more closely. Except where she had interrupted the process, it was perfect, the joins invisible even at the highest magnification her suit could provide. She tucked it into one of her belt pouches and frowned at the dust still surrounding her. She had thinned it perceptibly, but there was still plenty to work with. She adjusted her grip on the toy, letting her fingers fall into subtle grooves that seemed to have been carved for them, and concentrated on the GOLD-centered sensor unit that she had been working on for *Carabosse*. The toy hummed again, pulsing softly, and the elements surrounding her began to spark and spin. A nugget of GOLD appeared, inflating like a balloon; RED capped its poles, and the entire thing was covered by a fine lattice of BLUE. She caught it, and it crumbled back to elemental dust between the fingers of her glove.

"Damn it."

"How did you do that?" Dai demanded.

"Through the toy," Cassilde said. "I visualized the component, and the toy built it. And then it just fell apart."

"Try it again," Ashe said.

Cassilde took a breath and tightened her grip on the toy, focusing again on the sensor unit. The dust around her swirled and sparked and once again the shape formed before her. The toy hummed softly against her fingers, and she waited until it went still to reach for the little sphere. This time, it stayed intact, though it felt as fragile as an eggshell, and she shook her head. "I don't know what I did different, but... It's more solid."

"You're sure it was the toy that did it, not the Gift?" Dai asked.

Cassilde tucked the toy's narrow point through one of the loops on her belt, careful to adjust the bumps and buttons at the thicker end so that they didn't touch even the fabric of her suit, and concentrated again. She thought she felt something shift within her, as though something beyond the marrow of her bones came to attention, but nothing else happened. She cocked her head, trying to isolate the feeling, but it faded and was gone. "Reasonably. I just tried to do the same thing without it, and nothing happened."

"I've seen objects like that before," Ashe said again. "Not identical, but they all had a pattern of control surfaces at one end and looked like they were meant to point at something. If it takes a Gift to use them..."

"You said this was Successor work," Cassilde reminded him. She drew the toy from her belt again, feeling her fingers settle around it as though it had been made for her. Had it fit so perfectly the first time she'd picked it up? She wasn't sure.

"It is. But we've always known the Successors had some other way of interfacing with Ancestral devices. What if it takes a Gift, or something like it, to use Successor tools? It would explain why we've had trouble reverse engineering some of them."

"Everyone would have to have a Gift, then," Dai said slowly. "Or most people. Or at least most people who lived in the sky palaces like this one."

"It's not impossible," Ashe said. "Maybe that's what made the Ancestors what they were, something like the Gift? We can't say it couldn't happen."

Or if the Successors had used the Gifts to become more like the Ancestors, Cassilde thought. Stolen the Gifts? A late version of the Ankes and Irthe cycle claimed that Irthe trapped and bound her sometime-lover, and stripped her of her power to save Irthe's kin. Could that reflect the Successors' rise, the Gift or something like it replacing the Ancestors' AI?

She lifted the toy, tracing letters in the vacuum ahead of her. The dust moved to take those shapes, flickering and then falling apart when she demanded nothing more. She shifted her grip on the toy, wondering what else she could make it do. Control the compartment's fittings, maybe? She pointed it at the wheel, and saw the mechanism twitch, but the gears seemed to be completely jammed. Or maybe there was no power, or it needed more power than a few flecks of GREEN could supply.

She looked around for something else to test, and pointed the toy at another of the storage sections, willing it to open. A few specks of RED flashed toward it, but nothing else happened. If this was how the Ancestors had lived—how the Successors had lived... It made more sense of the orbiting palaces; the vast nests of elements within their hulls would be needed to answer people who could control it with a wave of a tool, perhaps even the wave of a hand, the Gift or its analog singing in their blood. And if everyone had had this power—what would it have been like to move through Callambhal's open volume, manipulating its structures as you went, sharing that space with a thousand others all with the same power? How had the system chosen precedents, how had it dealt with conflicting orders—was Ashe right, was this why the Ancestors had developed AI in the first place, to mediate these million demands? She felt as though she was on the edge of a cliff, about to step off and either soar or fall to shatter on some invisible plane.

Her suit alarm went off, followed a heartbeat later by the alarm on the scoot. She looked down, scanning her limbs for venting pressure, then realized that the red and yellow flashes were coming from the sensor tab.

"Fuck," Ashe said, in the same moment. "John's here, they just popped up out of nowhere—"

"Get out of there," Dai said.

"I'm trying for the ship," Ashe answered, and Cassilde swore under her breath.

"How far out are they?"

"Twenty minutes." Ashe's voice was grim. "Less. I'll try to lead them off."

"You'll blow up our only way out of here," Dai said. "Damn it, Ashe—"

Cassilde loosed the scoot's tether, turning back the way she'd come. There was no way she could get to *Carabosse* before Vertrage's ship came in, but in the vast emptiness of the Spiral there was a chance to hide. Particularly if she could use the toy to control the elements around them, to shield them from Vertrage's sensors... "Both of you, to me," she ordered, and swung herself onto the scoot. "Come down the gravity drop, I'll meet you there."

"I'm going for the ship," Ashe answered, and his transmission cut out.

Cassilde swore again. "Ashe!"

"I'm on my way," Dai said, and she pushed the scoot to its best speed.

ᚠ ᚊ ᚤ ᚦ

She made her way back to the base of the gravity drop just in time to see Dai swing himself onto the platform, catching at an exposed pipe to bring his boot soles into contact with the floor. Cassilde switched off her comm unit and motioned for him to do the same. He nodded, and came clumsily to join her on the scoot, leaning his helmet against her own.

"Ashe?" she asked, and saw him grimace.

"The idiot went to the ship. I didn't waste time trying to stop him."

Even as he spoke, she felt a faint tremor, like the distant rumble of *Carabosse*'s engines. She adjusted the scoot's single display to pick up the ship's sensor web, and cursed again as she saw the points of light. There was *Carabosse*, trying to split the course between the two incoming ships, the Spindle a precarious and only temporary barrier between them. Vertrage's ships were coming from the system's edge, powered down and still behind shields strong enough that they were wavering ghosts on the screen. For a moment, she thought they were headed for the bay where they'd first docked, but then something pinged, and the smaller ship lifted away from its partner, rising on a course that would take it up and over the Spindle.

"They've seen him," Dai said.

Cassilde nodded, fists closing tight on the scoot's thin frame. In the image, *Carabosse* spun and twisted, rotating on her short axis to loose a burst of short-range fire at Vertrage's ship. Some of it hit, but the other ship's shields were too strong. And now the second ship was coming, swinging wide to bracket *Carabosse*, moving a lot faster through the debris field than Cassilde would have dared. *Carabosse* dodged again, diving through shadows that were certainly chunks of debris, shots flaring again from the short-range cannons. And then the larger ship was on him, belching a single missile. *Carabosse* dodged, but the missile caught her just forward of the engines, and Cassilde saw their power flicker and die. The smaller ship edged up along the other side, the larger ship covering, and she looked away before she saw the transfer tubes snake across to connect the ships.

"I hope you have a plan," Dai said.

"Yes." Cassilde loosed her grip on the scoot's frame, made herself look back the way she'd come. To her surprise, the cloud of elemental dust seemed to have followed her, not as thick as it had been in the compartment, but still reassuringly present. "Yes, I do."

Dai swung himself onto the scoot's frame, and she worked the controls, turning back the way she'd come.

"Here, you steer."

"All right." Dai took the controls, lifting the scoot a little higher to clear the rough floorplates. "Tell me where I'm going."

"Follow this hall past the Hall of the Sun, then down to the right. There should be some small compartments there that are open to the central volume."

"All right," Dai said again. He did as he was told, keeping the lights as low as possible despite the fact that Vertrage hadn't even docked yet—but of course they would be scanning, Cassilde knew, looking for any signs of power use within the empty hulk. And that was what she had to hide.

She drew the toy and closed her eyes, trying to remember the scanner sequences she'd memorized years ago, components built up out of GOLD and BLUE, a fretwork of control and response. Yes, that one was robust and common, and she remembered it in detail; if she turned it inside out, set it to repel a seeking probe instead of sending one... If she took that control lattice and twisted it, folded the internal components here and here, replaced this common hexagon with a more complex shape, added more RED in five-pointed layers...

The pattern steadied in her mind, and she lifted the toy, inscribing the first layer. The dust shivered and sparked, moving sluggishly against the dark to form the base of the lattice. The toy pulsed under her fingers, and she shifted her grip, only to have a section dissolve into elemental dust. She swallowed a curse, rebuilding the image in her mind as she aimed the toy at the missing section, and saw the lattice reform. This time, it held, and she added the next layer, RED flickering out of the dust to augment GOLD and enfold delicate flecks of GREEN. She could feel the layers closing around them, the shield forming, but it was too slow, and she reached out with her free hand to grab Dai's glove.

"I need your help..."

"How?" His fingers tightened on hers, and she closed her eyes, imagining the shield growing, solidifying, taking protective shape around them.

"Your Gift."

"How?" he said again, but there was neither doubt nor hesitation in his words. "Tell me how."

She had no answer for that, only clutched him tighter, trying to juggle mental images and the pressure of the toy against her fingers, certain that their time was ticking away. The toy twitched and shivered, and then at last she felt a sudden thrum, like a single soundless chord. Dai stiffened, and abruptly the elements began to move, faster and faster, slotting into the spaces she had imagined. She guessed her Gift was weeping again, hoped she was not taking too much from Dai's Gift, though its strength seemed as nearly boundless as her own. RED wound around GOLD, enfolding GREEN; BLUE threaded through the forming mass, knitting the pieces together. She could feel the layers coming together around them, shutting them off from any attempt to discover them. One by one they vanished, bio-markers, power use, heat and light and movement, until she looked up to see that they were encased in a slowly turning spherical lattice, the elemental colors flickering softly across the inner surface like lightning seen from low orbit.

Dai leaned his helmet against hers. "Can I let go?"

"I think?"

He gently freed his fingers, and she held her breath, waiting for the lattice to collapse. It stayed stable, however, and Dai said, "A shield?"

Cassilde nodded, then realized that the movement was all but invisible inside her helmet. "Yes. Are you all right? I had to use your Gift, I needed more—" She stopped, not sure exactly what she had needed more of, and saw Dai's smile wry behind the faceplate.

"I'm ok. We've lost sensors, though."

"Oh, damn, of course we have. Let me see if I can get them back."

She took a deep breath, fixing her eyes on the intricate patterns. She could feel the Gift shifting in her, a door opening, caught a glimpse of something beyond, like the sudden scent of new-clipped leaves— and beyond that still, something more, something larger, stranger, as though she saw only a claw or the eye of some enormous creature. Gold Shining Bone? One of the other banished AI? Blue Standing Sky, Red Sigh Poison, Scarlet Breaking Wood: the names skittered through her brain, and she found the strength and the leverage to slam closed that door. The heavy presence vanished, and she caught her breath again, running her gaze desperately over the pattern of the lattice. Somehow there had to be a way to let in *Carabosse's* signal, to let that and perhaps Vertrage's frequencies through without betraying their presence. Unless Vertrage had locked his signal down completely, it should be possible to pick up the fringes of his signal, and of course anything *Carabosse* was still transmitting...

She raised the toy again, groping for the right point of entry, and felt the toy shift slightly beneath her glove. A fragment of GOLD folded back, RED joining it to form a five-spiked shape like a throwing star. Another formed, and another, coalescing out of the dust and bits of the protective lattice; she gestured carefully, the curves of the toy hot even through the gloves, and the stars whirled together into a spiked sphere. The scoot's display lit again, its image wavering but decipherable. The transmission between Vertrage's ships, she guessed, watching *Carabosse* tumble through static, engines dead. Surely Ashe was still alive, though; the hull was still intact, emergency power would be enough to keep environmental running.

"Ashe." Vertrage's voice was distorted by static, but it was possible to make out the words. "Ashe, open the interior hatches, or I will put a missile through your cockpit."

Cassilde hissed in spite of herself. A hull breach could be repaired, but not a destroyed control room.

"Ashe," Dai said, between clenched teeth. "Come on..."

"I'm opening the hatch." Ashe's voice was even more distorted, drowned in the static. "Ventral only. And you might like to know that your first missile will have been seen from Callambhal Below."

"All the more reason for you to hurry," Vertrage answered. "You'll meet me at the hatch—send the woman first."

"It's just me," Ashe said. "Sorry."

There was a moment of silence, only the static singing in the speakers, and then Vertrage said, "I don't believe you."

"She didn't like the hunt," Ashe said. "Neither of them did."

"Nobody does this kind of salvage alone."

A yellow light flashed on the screen, and Dai bit his lip. "He's pinging *Carabosse*. It'll show empty…"

"And then he'll ping the Spiral," Cassilde said. She looked at the lattice, hoping it would hold, and the screen flashed yellow again. "That was for us?" Dai nodded, his whole body tense.

Ashe said, "Yeah, well, I thought it was worth taking the chance."

"About that," Vertrage said, and Cassilde gave a sigh of relief. Apparently the lattice had held, at least for now. "Come to the hatch right now, Ashe. Fuguera will meet you, and you'll hand over your weapons."

"What if I don't want to?"

"Don't push it," Dai said, under his breath, and Cassilde bit back a laugh that could easily have become hysteria.

"The only reason you're alive at all is that you might save me a few hours' research," Vertrage said. "Don't tempt me."

There was another little silence, and then Ashe answered. "Understood. I'm on my way."

The screen flashed yellow again as another pulse from Vertrage's sensor net washed through them.

"Still holding, I think," Dai said, and looked at Cassilde. "How do we play this?"

Cassilde bit her lip behind the helmet's faceplate, wishing she had a better answer. They needed to do too many things—save Ashe, get back to *Carabosse*, repair *Carabosse*—and they had no idea how many people Vertrage had on his ships. She felt her Gift quiver at that, and the answer formed in her mind: seven life-signs, seven people. She concentrated harder, closing her eyes to let the picture shape itself against her eyelids: seven all told, one on each ship's controls, and the rest gathered with Vertrage, waiting for Ashe. Vertrage shone like a beacon—because he had a Gift? she wondered abruptly, and banished the image with a gasp. Gifts called to Gifts, Ashe had said. Surely he hadn't felt her presence. Surely all his attention had to be on Ashe.

"Are you all right?" Dai asked, and she shook herself back to the present.

"Are you armed?"

Dai gave her a sidelong look. "A pocket blaster, a couple of cutters. You?"

Nothing better. The war and its aftermath had taught her to carry at least a blaster when she was on a site, and the tools doubled well as close-quarters weapons, but that was not going to help against Vertrage's men, particularly if they were as well armed as they had been back on the claim. And they had *Carabosse*, they could just threaten to destroy her—

"The same," she said aloud. "Two spare charges."

"Same."

"Air?"

"Single spare, extra filters."

"Same. Plus the emergency kit on the scoot." Cassilde closed her eyes, trying to make the calculations. The air canisters regenerated and recycled breathable mixture that would last about twelve hours, without undue exertion; the filters would extend that by up to six hours, and the scoot carried two more canisters plus a larger generator intended to provide an atmosphere for the emergency bubble. That would last for days, long enough for a ship from Callambhal Below to find them, but that was worst-case. There was probably enough food and water, between what they'd carried for the day and what came with the emergency kit, to last them just as long, but the thought of huddling in the fragile bubble until someone found them made her skin crawl. "Where do you think they're taking him?"

If they were taking him anywhere, she thought. If they just dragged him aboard their own ship, took off with him—how in hell would she stop them, or even track them down—

"Back to where we were working," Dai said. "At least, that would be my guess. And their ship's moving back to our airlock."

"How long before anyone can get here from Callambhal Below?" She was snatching at straws, and anyway, it was unlikely she'd get much help from the government she was robbing. Unless she was willing to give them her Gift and everything else she'd deduced, and she wasn't ready to surrender that just yet. "Twelve hours?"

"Ten if they push—and they will."

Cassilde nodded, watching the shapes move on the scoot's screen. The larger of the two ships was fitting itself into the place *Carabosse* had docked, a landing leg groping for purchase on the ragged surface. "Is there any other way in to that space other than your airlocks?"

"No. And we sealed everything nice and tight."

"Then we need to get there first, be waiting for them."

CHAPTER THIRTEEN

Cassilde reached for the scoot's controls and swung it back toward the main corridor. The lattice swung with her, but more slowly, so that she had to brake and twist to avoid a collision. "Damn it—"

"Let me," Dai said, and she relinquished the controls, knowing he was better at handling the scoot than she was. He got it moving, swimming sedately in the center of the sphere, and it was everything she could do not to pound on his shoulder and demand that they move faster. She glared at the lattice, trying to force it to pick up speed, but it ignored her as though she had never manipulated its components. If they didn't get there first—she'd have no way of knowing what was happening to Ashe.

"We have to go faster," she said, and Dai shot her a quick glance.

"Working on it. Vertrage wants—"

"He wants my Gift," Cassilde interrupted, before he could say anything unlucky. "Which he can't have. And he wants to know where the Omphalos is, which Ashe can now give him."

"If he has the sense."

"He's not a fool." Cassilde wished she believed it herself.

They had reached the gravity drop, and Dai slowed the scoot. "They must be in the navigation room by now. If one of them drops a drone, or looks out into the well—"

"We didn't plant a camera, did we?" Cassilde asked, and he shook his head. "Then let's hope they don't think of it either."

"Are you sure this thing is going to hide us?" he asked, but set the scoot into motion, floating up the long shaft. The only lights were their own, cut off by the glittering sphere; outside its embrace there was only the dark metal, broken now and then by a faint blue pulse and, more regularly, one of their own marker buttons.

"It's held off GOLD-based sensors," Cassilde said, "and probably it will distort plain visuals. But if someone looks out at us—I don't think it'll hide us then."

"Let's hope they don't look out." Dai closed his eyes for a moment, as though he was concentrating, searching maybe for his Gift, and a heartbeat later the sphere trembled and began to rise more quickly. Above them, Cassilde could see the white gleam of the temporary airlock, reflecting the scoot's lights for an instant before Dai quenched the beam. They floated to a stop next to the lock, and Dai looked at her.

"Do we rush them? Blow the lock and go in?"

That might work. They both had Gifts, and they were suited, and surprise would be on their side. On the other hand, they were badly outnumbered, and Vertrage had a Gift of his own. And he had Ashe. She shook her head. "We need to know what we're up against."

"How?"

"Probe?" Cassilde scanned the scoot's tool rack, found the thinnest of the cutting probes. Normally they were used to check the contents of sealed volumes before breaking them open; they were relatively quiet, and sealed the hole behind them. She checked the camera and transmitter, then the cutting tip, and Dai nodded slowly.

"That could work."

Cassilde scanned the wall above her. Not through the lock, she thought, that would be bound to draw attention. Maybe where the wall and ceiling joined? She gestured cautiously at the lattice and it widened slowly, creating an opening she could slither through. "Give me a boost," she said, and Dai cupped his hands, steadying her as she twisted through the opening to plant her boot on the wall.

The magnetic sole seated gently, and she hoped the vibration hadn't carried through the wall. She didn't dare risk another step, and instead reached as far overhead as she could, then triggered the probe and set its tip against the metal. It trembled as she switched it on, and then sank into the wall, trailing a wisp of smoke. She watched it disappear, then worked her foot free and let Dai guide her back down through the lattice and onto the scoot.

"If they hear it," she began, and stopped, not knowing what she'd do.

"Then we have to risk the lock." Dai's voice was grim.

And that was still a bad idea. She focused on the spot where the probe had disappeared, the smoke now fading, and abruptly the image in the scoot's display changed. The picture wavered, scratchy with static, and a channel clicked open in her helmet's earpiece.

"—talk." It was unmistakably Vertrage's voice, and she shivered in spite of herself.

"I'm listening." That was Ashe, just visible at the left edge of the screen. He rested one hip on the nearest console, apparently at ease, though he was rubbing one wrist as though it pained him. His helmet was missing; behind him, Cassilde could see one of Vertrage's men, faceplate lifted to take advantage of the local atmosphere.

"I'm not sure you are." Vertrage came closer, moving into the probe's range. He'd removed his helmet, too, and it hung at his waist along with a heavy mil-spec blaster; he held a thick wand the length of her forearm in his right hand.

"I promise you," Ashe said.

Vertrage lifted the wand, placing the tip just under the tip of Ashe's chin. Ashe flinched and leaned back, and just as suddenly Vertrage let the wand drop again.

"Ashe. Let's not do this."

"I'd as soon not."

"Then talk to me. The truth, this time."

"I told you the truth." Ashe sounded weary. "They didn't like the game, and I couldn't talk them into staying. So I thought I'd try to correct the map."

"That's not your ship," Vertrage said.

"I stole it." Ashe shrugged. "My fair share and all that."

Vertrage considered him for a long moment, then looked past him to someone out of the probe's range. "Well?"

"The ship's still got three people's goods on board," someone said. "But I'm not finding anybody but us on the Spiral."

"If I assume you're telling the truth," Vertrage said, looking back at Ashe. "You're in a world of trouble, Ashe."

Ashe gave him a wary look. "Things haven't gone the way I'd planned, no."

"That's because planning has never been your strong suit," Vertrage said. "You always overcomplicate things. But you are good at what you do, I'll give you that. Give me the key systems, and I'll let you come back."

"I—" Ashe drew a breath, shaking his head. "I'll give you the key systems. I'll even give you the answer, John. But count me out. I'm done with this."

"I'm not done with you." Vertrage caught Ashe's chin in his free hand, running his thumb along Ashe's jawline. Ashe didn't pull away, didn't move at all, his expression blank. "You were the best researcher I had, you had a real gift for it. And I meant it when I said I'd reward you, Gift for gift. The Omphalos holds the key to the Ancestors' power. If we control it, we control the AI; if we master the AI, we master everything the Ancestors had, and were. It's the greatest Gift of all."

"'The AI destroyed a thousand suns,'" Ashe quoted. On the scoot, Cassilde felt Dai flinch at the words.

"Exaggerated."

"John, you've seen the Gap. Maybe it's not a thousand systems, but it's enough. How do you plan to control something that can do that?"

Vertrage laughed. "They're trapped. Stuck outside space and time, and I—we—will control their only access point. They'll serve us, or we'll close them out. And we'll become greater than—than the Dedalor. More powerful than the Ancestors themselves. Join me, Ashe. We could be Anketil and Irtholin for a new age."

Ashe turned his head away slowly, and Vertrage let him go. "It's… tempting."

Dai swore softly, his helmet pressed to Cassilde's. "If Vertrage takes him, we'll never get him back."

"He's bluffing," Cassilde hissed. "Wait."

"For what?"

"Something better than this," Cassilde said. "If we blow the lock now, there's every chance we'll kill him, and if we don't, Vertrage will."

"Blowing the lock might not kill him—"

"It might not, might hurt some of them, too," Cassilde said. "But that's best case, and we'd still have to deal with four guys before we can help him. Are you sure there's no other way in?"

Dai shook his head. "We sealed it. We sealed it really well."

In the screen, Vertrage reached out again, turned Ashe's face back toward him. "The Omphalos, Ashe. Where is it?"

Ashe's gaze flickered. "Your man's got the key systems."

"The name."

"Aeolus."

"See? Not so hard. And don't you want to know what's there? Come with me, Ashe."

Ashe closed his eyes. "I swear I won't go to the authorities—they wouldn't believe me anyway. Just let me go." Vertrage brought up the wand he had been holding, drew it sharply across Ashe's cheek. Ashe jerked away, a mark like a burn rising on his skin.

"Cap." Another man moved into range of the probe. "Confirmed launch from Callambhal Below."

"Last chance," Vertrage said, still staring at Ashe.

"You don't need me," Ashe said.

"Cap," the technician said again. "At their current speed, we've got thirty minutes before we have to lift, if you want to beat them out of the system."

Vertrage snarled. "Time's up." He tossed the wand away and drew his blaster with his other hand. Ashe flinched away, turning his shoulder as though that would help, but the bolt caught him before he could finish the move, searing through the body of his suit. He fell sideways off the console, the wound smoking, and Vertrage swept the data plaques from the workbench. "Move."

"Ashe..." Dai reached for the lock controls, and Cassilde caught his wrist.

"Wait."

"We've already waited too long—"

"Wait," Cassilde said again. There was no time for anything but calculation.

"Blow the damn lock, and then we go after them—"

"And get us killed, too." Cassilde kept a tight hold of his wrist, seeing the tears glistening behind his faceplate, aware of matching wetness on her own cheeks. "Dai. Either he's already dead or we need to let them go so we can save him."

"He could be dying right now."

"Or not." Cassilde turned her attention to the screen, splitting the display between the probe and the general sensors, and watched the dots that were Vertrage's party make their way along the short corridor to the exterior airlock. A minute ticked past, two—her eyes drifted to Ashe's body sprawled by the console, a thin wisp of smoke still rising from the gaping wound. He looked dead, very dead, and she made herself focus on Vertrage's party. They were at the airlock, finally, lights flickering on the scoot's control panel as it cycled. And then they had vanished from the screen, and she released Dai's wrist.

"Go." She pried open a section of the shield lattice as she spoke, and Dai reached through it to operate the lock's controls.

"Can't we get rid of that?"

"They haven't lifted yet," Cassilde answered, as the outer door slid back. "No, wait, there they go."

She let the lattice dissolve into strands of components, and followed Dai into the airlock. He had the scoot's aid kit tucked under one arm, and she hoped it would be enough. Without the shield, she was blind to Vertrage's movements, hoped he hadn't seen them reappear in his sensor web, or, if he did, that he'd have the sense to cut his losses.

The lock cycled, painfully slow, but then at last the telltales shone green and Dai threw his weight against the mechanism. It rolled back, and Cassilde ripped off her helmet. The air smelled stale and smoky, burned suit components and a sickly-sweet cooked-meat stench that made her retch and clap her hand over mouth and nose. Dai went to his knees at Ashe's side, the aid kit unrolling beside him, and Cassilde heard the noise of suit seals opening. She wanted to join him, but made herself turn first to the sensor panel they had set up inside the working space. It was at least still functional, though the signal was faint and the image fuzzed with static. Vertrage's ships were moving away, rising to escape the worst of the debris field and accelerating as they went; she couldn't make out the ship from Callambhal Below, and *Carabosse* was tumbling slowly away from the Spindle, but those were things she could deal with later.

She dropped to the floor plates on Ashe's other side, flinching at the weird, waxen tone of his exposed skin. Dai was busy with the aid kit, and there were shock buttons implanted across Ashe's upper chest, in a line with the mote that still clung to his collarbone, flickering wildly. Below that, the fabric of his suit had been blasted away, and she could see charred skin, blood, and the glint of bone. Her gut clenched, fear and fury and memory—why was there no Gift here, when she needed one? There was the long line of a burn on his cheek, and she winced, touching his hair in a helpless caress.

"I had a pulse," Dai said. "Come on…"

Cassilde felt for the pulse point below his jaw. Was the muscle stiffening under her touch? She rejected the thought, pressing harder, but there was no answering movement.

"Anything?" Dai asked.

"Nothing."

He didn't answer at once, feeling for a pulse on the other side, and sat back on his heels. "He's gone."

"No."

Dai shook his head helplessly. "I've done everything I can, and—nothing."

"No," Cassilde said again. "No, I won't—" *Allow it? Believe it?* She shook her head, refusing to finish the sentence, to accept what Dai was saying. Why was there no Gift here? There had been one for her, why not for Ashe? Her vision blurred, tears spilling, but she shook her head when Dai reached for her. Ashe deserved a Gift—deserved life—as much as anyone, and certainly as much as she had done. She pulled off her gloves, willing the Gift to manifest, for the blood-tinged fluid to appear at the tips of her fingers, but her skin stayed obstinately dry.

That would not do. It was not acceptable. She would not allow it. She wound bare fingers around the toy, reaching through it to call the elements she had used to build the shield, and they answered, first a thin dust and then solid streams, passing through the bulkheads as though they were entirely porous.

"Silde," Dai said, his voice breaking, but she could not stop to hear.

There were enough elements, surely there were enough—her Gift had been primarily RED, and she reached out again, summoning every fleck of RED within range of the toy and her will. The color of the streams changed, darkened: there would be enough, she thought, if only she knew what to do.

But she did know, or at least the Gift within her knew; it had healed her, and if she could duplicate it…. She reached across Ashe's body for the aid kit, found the scalpel after a moment's groping, and drew it clumsily across the heel of her hand. It hurt, like ice and fire, but the blood welled out in a satisfying line. She dropped the scalpel and reached for the toy again, smearing its tip with her own blood. The shock of it echoed back down the toy, stinging her fingers, and she felt a door open within herself, a speck of nothing, of unfilled, unfillable possibility lodging beneath her breastbone. She did not let her gaze turn inward, afraid of what might look back at her, concentrated instead on what she wanted.

This. This Gift in my blood, recreate it and let it make him whole and alive again.

The toy shivered again, juddering as though it was being pushed to the limits of its power. Around them, the air thickened, the elements that had been fine as dust combining into new shapes that eventually wound themselves into long threads as scarlet as new blood, crowding around her and Ashe's body. Dai was hunched over, both hands covering his mouth and nose, but she couldn't spare the time to worry about him. Instead, she pictured her own injuries, and the way her Gift had wrapped around her, soothing her, healing her, and urged the threads to do the same. They kept forming, the other elements either keeping clear or forming tiny shapes that were then encased in RED, until she had to cover her own mouth and her suit was smeared with pale pink dust where the threads had brushed her. Dai was invisible behind the still-thickening curtain, the strands writhing and twisting as though unsure of their purpose.

"Here," she said aloud, the sound muffled by the sheer weight of the elements filling the air, and thrust the tip of the toy into Ashe's wound.

There was a sound then, a muffled rumble like thunder, like an earthquake or a landslide, plane shifting against plane, and the scarlet strands pulsed once and began to wind themselves around Ashe's lifeless body. She ducked out of the way, and they kept coming, some filling the wound, some twisting around head and feet and body, faster and faster until it was like a solid rain of color, RED pouring over every millimeter of Ashe's body.

The toy was hot under her hand, and the cut on her left hand throbbed, opening again. A single strand licked out of the mass, slapping across the cut like hot wire, and the cut vanished with the pain, absorbed into her mended skin. There were no more strands, none forming, none left to wrap around Ashe's body. He lay cocooned in RED, like a mummy, like a weathered statue, all features worn away.

"Silde?" Dai's voice was wary.

"Wait." Cassilde licked her lips, as dry as if she had been baking in a desert sun. "Give it time—"

The carapace cracked, jagged lines shooting across its surface, and fell away into pale pink dust. Ashe lay unmoving, the skin of chest and belly unmarked beneath the ruins of his suit, his eyes still closed, the long burn vanished from his cheek. The mote on his collarbone pulsed calmly, and Cassilde fixed her eyes on it, counting. And then at last he made a soft sound, like a man startled awake, and opened his eyes.

"Sil—? Dai?"

Cassilde collapsed against him, unable to hold herself up any longer, a storm of tears silencing her. She felt his arm go around her, awkward at first and then stronger, and then Dai embraced them both. She clung to them, heedless of what her fingers knotted in—part of Ashe's torn suit, she thought, and a fistful of Dai's hair.

"Silde?" Ashe said again, and she reluctantly loosed her grip.

"Are you all right? What do you remember?"

Ashe grimaced. "John shot me."

"Yes. Yes, he did." Cassilde swallowed laughter that might too easily have become hysteria.

"How did..."

Cassilde held up the toy, and saw Ashe's gaze sharpen. "I used this, it—controls Ancestral elements, somehow. I made a Gift."

"That's...not possible," Ashe began, and she shook her head.

"We'll argue this later."

"You shouldn't have taken the ship," Dai said.

Ashe tipped his head to one side, not particularly subdued. "So we'll argue *that* now?"

"No," Cassilde said, drowning out Dai's *yes*. "No, we've got to get moving. Vertrage wasn't lying, there's a ship launched from Callambhal Below. We've got to get out of here."

"Damn it," Ashe said, but let Dai pull him to his feet.

"You got your answer," Dai said, his hand still on Ashe's wrist.

"Yeah." Ashe grimaced again. "But I told John, too."

"We heard," Cassilde said, and Ashe spread his hands.

"I was trying to keep him from killing me. Or finding you."

"Didn't work out so well," Dai muttered.

"Except he didn't find you," Ashe pointed out.

"But you sure as hell were dead."

Cassilde put the bickering out of her mind, focusing instead on the sensor display set up on the side console. Vertrage's ships were still accelerating out of the system; if they were wasting power casting their sensor net behind them, *Carabosse* wasn't picking it up. The ship from Callambhal Below was also accelerating: Vertrage's man had called it ten hours, and that was likely to be correct. Another ship was following it, at a slower pace, but they shouldn't have to worry about that one. *Carabosse* was still drifting, its hull already spangled with bright spots where smaller bits of debris had shattered against it. She checked the power output, debating whether Vertrage would pick up a signal, and decided she had to risk it. Nothing happened, and she pinged the ship again. There was still no response, and she swore under her breath.

"Ashe. Where was *Carabosse* hit?"

The men's argument stopped instantly. "Just forward of the engines," Ashe said. "Port side. Diagnostics said it was a severed control linkage, but the system shut me down. I couldn't work around it."

Dai would have known how to bypass both the safeties and the damaged system, but there was no point in saying so. Cassilde said, "So she's in safety shutdown?"

"Should be." Ashe took a deep breath, working his shoulders as though he still didn't quite believe he was alive.

"Let me," Dai said, and Cassilde let him take her place at the controls.

"We'll need to retrieve the locks," Ashe said. "And any other gear that can be identified as ours."

Cassilde swore again. Of course they had to, they'd never had a permit to be here, and they couldn't afford to spend the next thirty years chased by outstanding warrants. "But you found it? You weren't lying?"

Ashe's face lightened, the old familiar delight in his own cleverness that wrung her heart. "Not this time. It's what I told you—it's Aeolus."

He had said that before, and somehow it hadn't registered. She knew the name, of course, everyone did, but the storm-swept world was all but uninhabitable, would be uninhabited if it weren't for the mineral sands. Cassilde still couldn't imagine how that desolate world could ever have held anything worthy of the Ancestors, but she shoved the thought aside. "We'll talk about that later. Dai, any luck?"

Dai shook his head. "She's well and truly locked down. I'm going to have to go get her myself."

"All right," Cassilde said, though the delay nipped at her. "Ashe and I will start dismantling what we can."

"All right." Dai turned toward the lock, paused long enough to catch Ashe's shoulder in a bruising grip. "Glad you're all right."

Ashe squeezed his hand in return. "Me, too."

"He'll need a new suit," Cassilde said, resisting the urge to hold him herself, and Dai nodded.

"Will do."

Dai worked the scoot through both airlocks and headed out in pursuit of *Carabosse*. Cassilde swallowed the warnings she wanted to make—

watch for debris, for traps, for Vertrage's trickery and the incoming ship—and focused instead on breaking down their equipment. By the time they had everything but the sensors and the airlocks packed and ready, Dai had reached the ship, and was resuming control.

"There's a hole in the hull that we'll have to patch before we can use the REFTL drive," he reported—the short-range comm system running on its lowest power setting had seemed like a reasonable risk. "But the good news is that the ship's already bypassed the damaged control links."

"So it's just the hull that's the problem?" Cassilde asked.

"That's all I can find," Dai answered. "I'm going to put her back down where you had her, and then we can pull the locks and get the hell out of here."

"Confirmed," Cassilde answered, and looked around the compartment again. She couldn't see anything else that would betray who they were—plenty of signs that someone had been here, but nothing actually identifying, and she looked at Ashe. "Am I missing something?"

"I think we're good." He paused. "Silde, how in hell did you— I'm not sure what you did."

Neither am I. She held out the toy instead. "You saw what I was doing before Vertrage jumped us. You were dying—" She would not say *dead*. "So I told it to copy my Gift and give that to you."

Ashe turned the toy carefully in his hands, examining every millimeter of its surface before wrapping his fingers around the grip. Cassilde felt his fingers on her own wrist, and he released his hold with a hiss.

"It shocked me."

"And I felt you touch it."

Ashe held it out. "I think it likes you better." Cassilde took it, sliding it back through a loop of her suit, and Ashe went on, more seriously, "I think it's bonded to you—tuned to you? It doesn't seem to want anyone else fiddling with it, anyway."

Cassilde let her hand rest on the grip, soothed by the gentle warmth, the surface that fit her fingers so exactly. The emptiness beneath her breastbone receded, became little more than a hint of possibility.

"I've seen a handful of toys that take this form," Ashe said, "or something like it, a curved stick or a wand, and there's one nearly two meters long on Taaj, though people are still arguing about whether that's related. Nobody can ever get them to work, but if you need a Gift—"

"That would explain it," Cassilde said, when it seemed he didn't intend to continue.

"I wonder if any Gift will do, or if it has to be one like yours?" Ashe went on as though she hadn't spoken, and Cassilde sighed. "And yours is unchanged?"

"As far as I can tell, but we can worry about that later. Right now, we need to get out of here." She stopped, aware of how much she was still missing. "Is—was Vertrage serious about trying to use the AI?"

"You heard that."

"We had a probe," Cassilde said.

Ashe nodded, his expression grim. "The Omphalos is where Anketil sealed the AI into the adjacent possible. John thinks that he can break the seal and still control them."

"That was what the Dedalor thought, too," Cassilde said. "And it damn near destroyed everything."

"I know," Ashe said. "That's why I ran. But he thinks he can do it."

Vertrage would start the war again, unforgivably, and with the AI on his side there would be nothing left but the long slide into another Dark. Or not even a slide, but the instant catastrophe that had created the Gap: the AI were still entirely capable of that level of destruction. "We have to stop him," she said, and let the words trail off, defeated. "Only how?"

"I don't know," Ashe said.

"We have to do it somehow."

Dai pinged them then, to Cassilde's relief, and she threw herself into the work of getting their gear loaded back into *Carabosse*. Dai focused on patching the hull—it didn't have to hold an atmosphere, they could seal off the storage compartment on the inside of the breach, but it did have to be smooth enough that it didn't interrupt the REFTL drive's fields. By the time they were finished, the ship from Callambhal Below was in comm range, and the cease-and-surrender warning droned monotonously from *Carabosse's* speakers.

"She's got the legs on us," Dai said, as they detached themselves from the Spindle's surface. "I'm looking for a closer warpline entry, but I'm not having much luck."

"Let Ashe handle that," Cassilde said, her hands busy on the controls. "See if you can give me any more acceleration."

"We'll need enough room to brake for 'line entry," Dai said, but hauled himself out of the co-pilot's chair. "I'll do what I can."

"That's all I'm asking," Cassilde said.

Ashe had already locked down comms and transponder; they were fleeing silent and unmarked toward the system's edge, and Fairy-class transports were common enough that they might be able to get away without being identified. Still, it hurt to be classed with the wreck-robbers she had been trained to despise—it hurt to have become one of them, she admitted, as she adjusted her course to put the worst of the debris between her and the Callambhal ship. She had always been legal, always prided herself on working with scholars that cared about best practices and university standards. Ashe had been one of them, before...

There was no time to waste, not on something that was past fixing, and she focused again on the converging courses, the faint dot that was the warpline entrance shimmering in the distance. Once she was clear of the worst of the debris, she could accelerate properly, but for now she was stuck dodging bits of the decaying station that were as large as the ship itself. In the meantime, though, the ship from Callambhal was gaining on them: the navigation system showed them in cannon range nearly two hours before they reached the 'line entrance. Even when she entered her likely acceleration, she fell short, and she spared a glance for Ashe's screens.

"Anything?" Usually there were weak places along any warpline, not proper entrance points, but places where the fabric of space/time was thin enough that a powerful enough capacitor could force an entrance.

"So far most of them are on the far side of the regular entrance," Ashe said. "I've got one, but it's thick, and I don't think the angle's going to work."

"Let me see," Cassilde said, and her console chimed as he transferred the data. He was right, the numbers barely fell within the usual parameters, and it lay off to one side, further back along the curve that was the warpline entering the system. She ran the numbers anyway, and grimaced at the result. They'd gain maybe twenty minutes, and have to spend three times the power. That was at the ragged edge of *Carabosse*'s capabilities, and she touched keys to transfer the numbers to the engine room. "Dai. What do you make of that?"

There was a long silence before he answered. "That's really pushing us, Silde. I'd prefer an alternative if at all possible."

"Understood," she said. "I'm setting that as a last resort."

"Good," Dai answered, and she saw Ashe grin.

They reached the edge of the main debris field at last, and she called for more power, watching the shapes of Callambhal Above recede in her screens. They were pulling away from the other ship, too, and she watched the numbers shift. It was better, but each projection showed them coming into cannon range at least fifteen minutes before *Carabosse* reached the 'line entrance.

"We could try to hold them off," Ashe said. "You've got cannon yourself. And before you say it, I had plenty of practice in the war."

That was a question of power. Cassilde said, "Dai?"

"Give me a minute," Dai answered.

They waited, Cassilde watching the other ship crawl slowly along its projected course, and then Dai spoke again. "No. Definitely not if you're trying for that thick spot, I'll need every erg of power just to make the jump. I can't even raise shields. The other entrance, I can give you shields or cannon, but not both, not if you want to make the jump."

"That's not going to work," Ashe said, his voice grim.

"I can't fix physics," Dai answered. "We've got what we've got." He paused. "I don't suppose we could try telling them what's going on?"

"Tell them what?" Ashe demanded. "Hi, there, we weren't actually stealing from your hanging treasure garden, we're really trying to stop a lunatic from releasing the Dedalor AI and bringing down the Dark? You really think they'll listen?"

"Maybe we could come up with something a bit more convincing," Dai said.

"While still being true?" Ashe asked. "Good luck with that."

They were both right, Cassilde thought, as the Callambhal ship adjusted its course to pass above the thickest parts of the debris field. It was a longer course, but they could maintain speed, and she was unsurprised to see the numbers remain essentially unchanged. And still twenty minutes too short. *Carabosse* was at maximum acceleration; there was nothing else she could do unless Ashe could find another entrance point.

"Scan again," she said. "There might be something small that we can pick up as we get closer."

Ashe gave her a look that suggested he'd already thought of that, but adjusted the sensor net. "Nothing yet."

"Keep looking." Cassilde set the autopilot—on a straight shot like this, it was more efficient than a human being, and they would need every centimeter she could squeeze from the system—and leaned back in her chair, trying frantically to think of some other alternative. If only they had the Ancestors' instantaneous drive—but that had been lost in the First Dark, and no one had dared try to duplicate it for fear of exposing themselves to the AI still trapped in the adjacent possible. The Successors had invented the drive that became the REFTL drive, regulated so that ships made an enormous number of micro jumps, following the weakened space of a warpline, but never spent enough time in the adjacent possible to attract the attention of any lurking AI.

She touched the end of the Successor toy, tracing the curves of its grip with her fingertip, the dimpled surface oddly soothing. If she'd thought, she could have brought aboard more of the elements, used them to create another shield, or maybe even a weapon; as it was, she was stuck with what she had on *Carabosse*. Of course, there were elements on board, but they were already in use, part of the ship's systems; it wasn't like Callambhal, where every space was filled with elemental dust.

"Silde!" Dai's voice was sharp with fear. "We've got a problem."

"What's wrong?" She could see their acceleration slowing as he spoke, heard Ashe swear as he saw the same thing.

"The hull patch is deforming under acceleration stress. If we lose it, we can't jump."

"If we can't stay at speed, we're not going to get the chance to jump," Ashe said.

"Shut up, Ashe, that's not helping." Cassilde bit her lip, but could come up with nothing better. "If we stop and fix it?"

"It'll take me at least fifteen minutes, absolute minimum, and we'd have to decelerate and accelerate again," Dai said. "We'll lose too much time."

Shit and fuck and fuck the entire Gap. She didn't need to run the numbers to know that wouldn't work. "Keep us going as fast as you can, and see if we can come up with something better." Ashe started to say something, and she stared him down. "Don't. It's not helpful."

He spread his hands, a gesture she chose to take as an apology, and she leaned back in her chair, closing her eyes as though that would help her to concentrate. What they needed was a weak point on the warpline, something they could use to force an entrance; failing that, they needed more speed, or for the following ship to lose power somehow. None of these was helpful, or even very likely, and the thought of firing on an official ship made her faintly queasy. They had had to fight during the war, and they'd bought the best they could afford when they fitted *Carabosse* with surplus cannons and a shield, but she doubted they'd be a match for something a government could throw at them. It was too late to hide, they were bound to be well and truly caught in the other ship's sensor web—though maybe if she could pull elements from non-critical systems and from their spares, maybe she could create some sort of chaff that would disguise them. Though if she had been going to do that, they'd have been better off staying in Callamblial Above, where there were more resources to draw on. She couldn't afford to cannibalize main systems to try to hide them.

"Silde," Dai said again, and Ashe sat up straighter in his chair.

"Shit."

"Yes, we're slowing," Dai snapped. "It's the patch. I can't let it blow—"

"Understood," Cassilde said, and kept her voice calm with an effort. "Ashe. How's that change where they overtake us?"

Ashe was already adjusting his screens, the projected courses wavering and reforming. "It doesn't make that much difference—thirty-five, forty minutes if it doesn't get any worse."

"Any sign of a break?"

Ashe shook his head. "Not yet. Just the one we had."

Cassilde rubbed the toy's grip again, wishing she understood it better, wishing she or it could see a way out of this. If only they were closer to the warpline, if only space/time was thinner here, the adjacent possible more accessible... She felt something shift, somewhere beyond perception, as though something unimaginably vast had turned its gaze on her. Her fingers tingled, remembering the touch of curved metal, the delicate arch of a tiny skull and the irregular knobs of vertebrae.

Trust us. Come straight through.

The words reverberated, soundless, at the back of her breastbone. She didn't pretend she couldn't guess their meaning: if that was Gold Shining Bone—if it was any of the lost AI, it didn't really matter which one it was, or even if it was one alone—they were offering a direct road through the adjacent possible, where they could fold space/time at will. The Ancestors had been able to do that, could have leapt from Callambhal Above to the Omphalos in a single gesture, but the REFTL drive was set up to avoid spending too much time in the adjacent possible.

Not likely, she told the looming presence. *Let you destroy us so that Vertrage can start your war again? Never.*

Not all of us want that war.

Cassilde snorted, though a part of her mind was still examining the possibilities. Yes, the REFTL drive was a re-engineering of the Ancestors' drive, with a time crystal at its heart to regulate the passage through the adjacent possible, to control the rhythm of the microjumps. Without the time crystal, you could enter the adjacent possible—it had been tried, more than once, but no ship had ever returned. Destroyed by the lurking AI, everyone had assumed, or if they had avoided the AI, destroyed by the unknowable, unplottable currents of whatever it was that lay "outside" space/time. That was what quantum AI had been for, as best anyone could tell, to make the impossible calculations; without them, a ship was tossed blindly between one point in the known universe and another. Though if Gold Shining Bone was telling the truth about not wanting another war…

The AI could not be trusted. That was fundamental truth, the one certainty that had lasted through the First Dark. The Successors had rebuilt without AI, and gone down into the Second Dark rather than risk raising them again. If she agreed, if they tried to make the jump without the protections of the REFTL drive, the odds were a hundred to one that the AI would simply destroy them, and enjoy it.

And Vertrage was fool enough to think he could control them. She shivered at the thought, remembering the Gap, emptiness smeared across the arc of space, whole systems wiped from existence, even their memory lost in the Long Dark. Presumably Vertrage would use that threat or something like it to seize control of governments, or demand some impossible ransom. In the end, though, he would loose them, either in response to some doomed rebellion or retaliation for some imagined slight or, worst and most likely, simply because he could, and could no longer resist the one forbidden act.

Not all of us want that.

But some of you do. It shouldn't have been a surprise, but it was still alarming to contemplate, theist implacable malice of even a single AI.

That is not all of us.

It's enough of you, Cassilde thought.

"Silde?" Ashe's voice seemed to come from a very great distance, and it was easy to pretend she hadn't heard.

We will protect you. And you are not without recourse. But there must not be another war.

What do you mean, we're not without recourse? Cassilde thought, but the connection wavered, and Ashe touched her wrist.

"Silde? Are you all right?" He jerked his hand back as though he'd been stung, and her first answer died on her tongue. "What was that?"

"Gold Shining Bone," she answered. "I think."

"That can't be good." Ashe rubbed his fingers, and in spite of everything, she managed a smile.

"Where's the Callambhal ship?"

"Closing. They're going to be able to identify us in less than an hour." Ashe paused. "It spoke to you? Gold Shining Bone?"

"In a way." Cassilde took a breath, and reached for the intercom switch. "Dai. You need to hear this, too."

"I'm listening," Dai answered warily.

"Gold Shining Bone has made us an offer," Cassilde said flatly. "It says we should disable the regulator on the REFTL drive and go straight through the adjacent possible."

"Not a good idea," Dai said.

Ashe spoke in the same moment, "So the AI can destroy us? I don't think so."

"It's incredibly dangerous," Dai said. "Even if the AI weren't waiting—"

"We don't have time for this," Cassilde said, through clenched teeth. "Dai. Is it even possible?"

"You're not seriously considering this."

"Just—answer the question." Out of the corner of her eye, she saw Ashe open his mouth, and then close it again. "Can we disable the regulator?"

"I—" Dai stopped, and Cassilde could almost see him shaking his head. "Yes, in theory I can pull the crystal and bypass that circuit, but we're not rigged to navigate except by REFTL drive."

"So what happens if we jump anyway?" Cassilde closed her eyes, trying to feel the AIs' presence again. "Without the regulator."

"We enter the adjacent possible, we're—there—for some subjective amount of time, which isn't really time in our universe, and then we're at, or near, our destination." There was a note to Dai's voice that suggested he was quoting some long-abandoned textbook. "But we have to set the parameters, and that's a complex calculation, I don't think we're equipped to do it."

"Do we have the formulae in the files?" Cassilde asked, and reached for her keyboard.

"Yes," Ashe said, before she could finish the query, and she heard Dai sigh loudly.

"That doesn't mean we can make it work."

A window opened on Cassilde's screen, filled with a cascade of symbols. The variables were all familiar, though the calculation was entirely strange, and she scowled at it as though she could make it come clearer.

"The good news is it uses modern navigational data," Ashe said. "The bad news—it was designed to help me figure out the Ancestors' maps, not to actually navigate with."

"It's also going to take all the power we have," Dai said. "To rip a hole in space/time without a warpline to guide us—we'll be running on emergency power after we exit. If we make it that far."

"Well, no one should be chasing us at that point," Cassilde said.

"You're serious about this," Dai said.

"We don't have a lot of good choices," Cassilde answered. "We can give up and surrender and hope that somebody believes us when we say we were just trying to stop a crazy man with an Ancestral Gift from freeing the AI that the Dedalor bound millennia ago. We can pray that we spot a 'line entrance that we can use, but so far the gods aren't listening. Or we can do this."

"And die," Dai said. "We can't trust any of the AI, and least of all Gold Shining Bone."

"I'd rather take that chance than risk another Dark," Cassilde said, and saw Ashe nod.

"Silde's right, I don't want to live in the world John's going to make."

There was a long silence, and finally Cassilde said, "Look. I'm going to run the calculations, see if I can derive a course to Aeolus. You prep the engines. If we spot a 'line entrance before we have to jump, I'm willing to take it, but—I don't see a better option."

There was another silence, and then Dai sighed again. "You're right. I don't like it, I don't think we're going to make it—but we have to try."

CHAPTER FOURTEEN

Cassilde bent over her screen, watching the numbers shift as she plugged in the last of the variables. In the main screen, a warning flashed yellow—twenty minutes until the pursuing ship would be able to get a solid visual identification—but she ignored it, focusing on the formula. The format was like nothing she'd ever seen before, and she hoped she'd grasped the basic principles. If they made the jump, and couldn't find their way out again, they'd die in the madness of the adjacent possible—no, worse, their Gifts would trap them, undying, caught between one moment and the next. The human mind wasn't meant to comprehend timelessness, not-time, where all things were simultaneously present and absent, possible and never to have been. To be trapped in that maelstrom, kept alive by the Gift—they might be glad when the AI killed them, in the end.

She made herself take careful breaths, seeking calm; her hands steadied, but the cold knot of fear remained in the pit of her stomach. She closed her eyes, wrapped her fingers around the toy, and reached for the AI that had been a looming presence for so long. She could feel the point of connection, colder and stronger than the fear, but there was nothing else there. If Gold Shining Bone had abandoned them— if Gold Shining Bone had abandoned them, they would find a way to push through anyway, she told herself, and wished she knew how.

"Fifteen minutes until they're in range," Ashe said.

"I see it." The calculation was complete, and she touched keys to plug it into the navigation system. "How's it coming, Dai?"

"Almost done. Power's up, everything's rerouted, and it's just a matter of pulling the regulator."

"Might as well do it," Ashe muttered, and Cassilde nodded.

"Pull it," she said, and braced herself against the console as though he could do it instantly.

"You're sure?" Dai asked instead, and she swallowed a curse.

"We've been through this. I still don't see a better idea."

"Right." There was a brief silence, and then the numbers on Cassilde's secondary display shifted, showing power transferring to the capacitor.

"Crystal's out," Dai said. "Last call's running. I make it about four minutes before we jump."

"Come up here," Cassilde said, suddenly unwilling for them to be separated. Whatever happened, she wanted both of them beside her, within reach.

"On my way," Dai said, and she heard Ashe sigh.

"Good thought."

I hope, Cassilde thought, but couldn't find the words. On the screen, a countdown had begun, the last two minutes before the capacitor fired, and she fastened her safety harness as though that would help.

The hatch slid open, and Ashe started to get up, but Dai waved him back to his place, folding the third seat out of the bulkhead.

"Anything?" he asked, leaning forward, and Ashe shook his head.

"No change."

One minute clicked past, and Cassilde reached for Dai's hand, suddenly desperate for any contact. She saw him reach for Ashe in turn, and for an instant they sat in silence, fingers linked, watching the last numbers tick off on the screen. *If this doesn't work*, Cassilde thought, *I'll feel like a fool—*

The capacitor fired. She caught her breath, and was no longer sure she had lungs, or that the movement of ribcage and diaphragm came before or after the taste of cold air, or if indeed there were such words,

such concepts as 'before' and 'after.' She could feel Dai's hand tight in
hers, fingers locked, a fizz of GREEN and GOLD at each joint, sparks
in the flaring dark; she could feel Ashe through him, more GREEN
and GOLD, a current that flowed along bones and back again, a knot
of presence in the empty dark.

Somewhere there were AI. She could feel them, too, a circling,
swirling search that tangled here and there and then resumed. She
caught flashes of words that had once been names—Gold Shining
Bone, yes, rising like a wave, but also Red Sigh Poison, Green Rising
Heart, Ochre Near Stone, Blue Famous Drum, words that had once
been AI, were still AI, warped as they were by the absence of time
and space. They filled the potentiality around the container that had
been *Carabosse*, energies snapping at the edges of her consciousness,
faltering against the barrier that was her Gift. The barrier of their
Gifts, she amended, all their Gifts, the three of them wound together
within *Carabosse* and as part of *Carabosse*, the Ancestral elements
calling to each other, like to like, a hedge, a barricade, against the flux
that was the AI. With her free hand, she touched the toy, sliding her
fingers into the grooves that twisted to meet her; she wasn't sure that
it changed anything, not here, but it steadied her.

She could feel Gold Shining Bone again, a wave that crested and
broke over them, damping the other energies. That was good, a good
start, but she needed more, needed somehow to get them moving,
to find their course again. But there was nothing, no direction either
in space or time, only the emptiness and the AI, swarming now like
insects, coiling like snakes in a nest; she could feel Gold Shining Bone,
but it was distant, walled off by the rest of the crowd. They were
adapting, measuring her strength, the elements within her and Dai
and Ashe and *Carabosse*. Their touch had new purpose, a spark here
to flick away a fleck of BLUE, a painful jolt there to carve out a sliver
of GREEN. Ashe made a sound that might have been pain, and Dai's
hand tightened hard on her own.

The formula. The calculation, the key that was supposed to

bring them safely out of the adjacent possible: that was the only thing she had, but the consoles had vanished, and she had neither wheel nor keyboards to control the ship. She closed her eyes, laying out the formula as though she wrote it on a schoolboard, firm black lines against the grubby, under-washed surface. The origination, in galactic coordinates, Callambhal Above's familiar alphanumeric code expanded to the precise location at jump: get that wrong, and they were screwed before she started, but she shoved that thought away, forcing confidence. Next, the other side of the balance, the destination: Aeolus, the wind-world, once the center of the Ancestors' realm, the Omphalos itself. That code felt seared into her brain; she laid it side by side with Callambhal, and added the broad strokes and symbols that modeled the folding of space, the bending of time, the passage *outside,* and turned impossibility into an equation that could be solved. She felt solutions fall away, whole classes first, and then individual results, until as abruptly as they had left they were back in normal space/time, alarms blaring across her board, a new pattern of stars smeared across her screens.

𝍥 𝍪 𝍫 𝍬

She was gasping as though she had been running, each breath as painful as if she had drowned, and fought to control herself. Her lungs inflated, the Gift stabilizing something deep in her body's core, and she saw new nails spread over bloodied fingertips, felt them settle into the nailbeds. She swung to see the others, saw Dai's hair flush back to its ordinary straw-color while Ashe licked blood from his lips.

"Are you all right?" Her voice was a croak; she made a face and tried again.

"Yes," Dai said, not entirely convincing, and Ashe nodded, testing where his lip had split with the ball of his thumb.

"Dyschronorrhea," he said. "The Ancestors had ways of protecting against it, but—we didn't."

Cassilde had vague memories of having read about such things in her student days, the damage and diseases of the absence of time, but the alarms from the consoles were more important. "Dai. Get the engines back on line."

"On it." He released himself from his harness, and disappeared through the hatch.

"Thirty minutes emergency power remaining," Ashe said, already skimming through his screens. "Hull's intact, but it looks like we're going to need to reboot most everything. If we can get a time signal from somewhere—"

If they were close enough to Aeolus, if they'd even come out where she'd planned for them to be—Cassilde shoved that thought away, sorting through her own screens. Sensors first, she thought, make sure they hadn't emerged from the adjacent possible into the middle of some greater hazard. The web seemed to be functioning, and she extended it carefully, finding nothing in their immediate vicinity. She cued navigation to locate their position, and saw that the engineering warnings had faded from red to yellow. She flexed her fingers, looking at the new nails not quite identical to the old, and made herself ping the web again. It still showed empty, though navigation was still churning the data, and she allowed herself a sigh of relief.

"What happened to your face?"

Ashe licked at his lip, though there was no sign of the cut. "I bit my lip, I think." He flexed his fingers warily. "And that, the loss of the nails, that was definitely dyschronorrhea."

In the absence of time, cells in the body that normally divided and grew and died in synchrony with each other fell out of step with one another: painful, Cassilde remembered, but not usually fatal. She stretched her fingers, muscles and tendons tugging on each other in perfect sympathy: the Gift would heal anything else, settle them solidly into the universe. Was that a reason the Ancestors had developed the Gifts?

"That was...weird," she admitted, and Ashe nodded in agreement.

"That's one way of putting it."

The navigation console pinged, displaying its result. They lay on the outer fringes of the Aeolus system, perhaps a third of the way around the outermost planet's orbit from Aeolus itself. A secondary program flashed yellow, requesting permission to ping the system-net for the correct chronometric factor, and she touched keys to permit it. The answer bounced back within seconds, and she raised her eyebrows.

"This says—it can't have taken two hours to get here."

"That's how the Ancestors' drive worked," Ashe answered. "Not quite instantaneous—or maybe that ought to be not entirely instantaneous? We're at least a couple of days ahead of John."

Cassilde blinked hard, staring at the numbers. Of course this was how the Ancestors' drive was supposed to work, to fling ships from one place to another in less than an instant, but somehow she hadn't quite believed it. "More than that," she said, and reached for the keyboard to type in her calculations. "It looks to me as though it's going to take him ninety hours by the most direct warplines. We've got some time to figure out what we want to do."

"Besides stopping John?" Ashe gave her a startled look.

"It might be worth discussing how we're going to do it," Cassilde answered, and reached for the intercom. "Dai. How's it going?"

"It's going," he answered, after moment. "It's going to take another ten hours or so to get the reserves back up to better than emergency status, though."

"We've got the time," Cassilde said. Just saying it aloud felt like a reprieve.

She set the sensor web to warn off any other ships that came too close—not likely, the 'line entrances were further out toward the system's edge, but there was no point in taking chances—and hauled herself out of the pilot's chair. She was shaking as though she'd run a marathon, and fell into her bunk without waiting to see what the others would do.

She woke from disturbingly dreamless sleep to find herself settled against the wall, the others asleep next to her. The chronometer projected on the wall said that she'd slept nearly ten hours. She wriggled free of the covers, trying not to wake anyone else, and waved a hand at the sensor to trigger a silent systems display. Everything looked good, the engines nearly back to full capacity, the sensor web empty except for a few large ships at maximum range. Ore ships heading in or out of Aeolus, she guessed, and sat up slowly. Despite her care, Dai stirred, opening one eye and then coming abruptly awake as though he'd suddenly remembered everything. She put a hand on his shoulder, and beyond him Ashe rolled over and propped himself up on one elbow.

"Everything all right?"

Cassilde nodded. "So far, so good."

Dai stretched and grimaced, hauling himself up to a sitting position. "So what, exactly, do we do now?"

"Sleep some more?" Ashe asked, and Dai shrugged.

"Going to have to answer the question sometime, bach."

"I know." Ashe flattened himself against the sheets.

"You're sure Vertrage wants to release the AI," Cassilde said. Having touched them herself, she couldn't imagine anyone being foolish enough to think that it was a good idea.

"That's what he's aiming for," Ashe said wearily. "Believe me, I tried to talk him out of it the first time he mentioned it. He thinks his Gift will let him control them."

"So he's not only a murdering asshole, he's a stupid murdering asshole," Dai muttered.

"Not helpful," Cassilde said, but Ashe ignored her.

"He's not stupid."

"He shot you," Dai said. "He shot Silde, and he actually killed you."

"He shot you when it would have made more sense to take you with him," Cassilde said. "Not that I'm not grateful, but it wasn't a clever move."

"No." Ashe didn't sound entirely convinced, and Dai kicked him under the sheets.

"So. What exactly are we looking for?" Cassilde asked. "You said he wants to release the AI. How, and where? Do you know?"

"I can guess." Ashe dragged himself to a sitting position, hunching forward for a second as though the memory of his wound still pained him. "Aeolus is—was—the Omphalos, the central world of the center of the Ancestors' settlements. Everything we know about the First Dark says that Anketil challenged the AI to fight them there."

"This was after they'd destroyed the systems of the Gap?" Dai asked, and Ashe nodded.

"Yeah. Some versions say it was a kind of single combat, the last and best of the Dedalor against the AI her house created. But anyway, they all agree that she called the AI to the Omphalos, and they came. And she'd laid some sort of trap for them—she was a plasma-smith and a crystal maker. She did something—maybe with a time crystal— that sealed them all into the adjacent possible. No one knows what it was exactly, but it's worked until this very day. The Omphalos was destroyed in the process—the energies that Anketil and the AI both wielded were supposed to have scoured the planet clean." He shrugged. "You know the rest. The surviving Ancestors hung on a century or two longer, but without AI, their civilization fell."

"The First Dark," Cassilde said. "The Long Dark."

"That explains a lot," Dai said, after a moment. "About why the Omphalos was lost. 'Scoured clean'—you'd be looking for a world that was burned off, not buried in mineral sands."

"Which are probably the remains of the Ancestors' cities and everything they had," Cassilde said. The energies that drove the perpetual storms circling the planet's equator must have come originally from that battle. It was a thought to strike a chill: how could they stand against creatures that could do that to a world? She shook herself hard. "Did that mote of yours say what we're looking for?"

"The stories say that Anketil and Irtholin fought the AI in the core of the Dedalor palace," Ashe said, "and we have other stories—and one very late map—that puts the palace on a plateau about 500 kilometers north of the equator in what was then Capella Province. I should be able to match that to modern maps."

"Aren't some parts of Aeolus completely inaccessible because of the storms?" Dai asked.

"Yeah, most of the equator. The storms are too intense even for the heaviest of the sand-miners. But if the stories are right, it should be far enough north," Ashe answered.

Maybe it would be better if it was unreachable, Cassilde thought. If there was no chance Vertrage could get there to release the AI, then they didn't have to stop him—and she still had no idea how they were supposed to do that. They weren't soldiers, despite the war; Vertrage had already proved himself better at killing than they were. Persuade the AI to help? Certainly had felt as though there were differences of opinion among the various entities, but she couldn't see what she could offer them that would trump gaining their freedom. If only there were some way to get the local authorities to help, she thought, and again her imagination failed as she tried to think of some way of explaining the situation. Or at least a way that would get them actual help instead of seeing them locked up, their Gifts the focus of investigation.

"We'll find out when we get there," she said.

ᚠ ᳜ ᛮ ⫰

They brought *Carabosse* into orbit over Aeolus, joining a queue of small freighters waiting for permission to land. The larger of the two space ports, Polar West, was also the closest to the most likely location of the Dedalor palace, and it was also the place most newcomers went to rent sand-mining equipment. That had seemed to be their best option, since *Carabosse* couldn't fly through the storms that filled the planet's atmosphere. From orbit, it looked more like a gas giant than any sort of habitable world, a band of storms girdling the equator, and sending long tongues of cloud curling toward the poles. When Cassilde switched to the view that showed windspeeds, the roiling equatorial bands stayed white—off the scale—and the curls of scarlet, the maximum the miners could withstand, reached almost to the 60-degree line. In theory, the miners could stand anything short of the maximum, but Cassilde couldn't help wondering about her own ability to steer through it.

Landing *Carabosse* was bad enough, fighting her way down through the layers of atmosphere, warnings whooping each time they crossed a band of mineral-choked air. *Carabosse* was not designed for delicate maneuvers, and it took Cassilde all her skill to bring the ship down to a wobbly landing. The legs shifted, leveling the ship, and then the entire ship trembled again as the platform sank into the docking silo, the lid irising closed overhead. The arrangement made sense, given the weather, but Cassilde hated knowing that she couldn't lift without someone clearing it first.

At least no one seemed surprised when they stated their intention of renting mining equipment and making a few passes in the unclaimed lands south and east of the port: apparently this was the season when the largest of the equatorial storms tracked slightly to the south, exposing narrow strips of recently-churned ground for the miners to cover. There was more work than the corporations who held the franchise could handle, and they were happy to contract the work for only a nominally exorbitant share.

They were equally lucky when it came to filing their proposed claim. Ashe had spent most of the approach narrowing down their search area and converting it into a plausible-looking mining run, but Cassilde found herself holding her breath as they approached the counter in the Claims Office. The wizened man behind the machine took the data card and scanned it, looking up with a slight frown.

"You sure about this?"

Cassilde opened her mouth, ready with the prepared explanation, but Ashe stepped on her foot.

"Yeah," he said, with what she thought was enviable calm, and the old man nodded.

"You're a long way out. Make sure your emergency beacons are in good shape."

"We'll do that," Cassilde said, and linked arms with Dai so she wouldn't say anything else.

It took the rest of that day to transfer supplies to the miner, a low-slung, teardrop-shaped machine set on a complex series of caterpillar treads, wheels, and concealed grapples, the actual mining machinery tucked between the tracks and filling the last two-thirds of the body. It had a lifting wing which, with gravity-field assist, was warranted to take them as far as the start of their official claim.

"Mind you, it won't do you any good once you're over half-full," the rental agent warned, as they signed the seemingly endless string of files. "After that, you're well and truly grounded."

"What if we hit a storm that exceeds our rating?" Cassilde asked.

"Turn north and try to get out of its way," the agent said. "And if you can't do that, pull the airfoils all the way in and lock them down tight, then dig yourself in. You won't be flying out of anything once you get below the 57th parallel. But it's nice to have the option while you're in clearer air."

It would at least get them to the search area some hours before Vertrage could even reach the system. Cassilde smiled and nodded, and turned her attention to getting all their supplies on board.

They lifted from the miners' field at Polar West a little before local sunset, heading west into the receding light. For a while, she could see the lights of the port on her screens, but they faded rapidly, leaving only the signals from the navigational satellites to light up her displays. The air was choppy, and the miner was too heavy and awkward a flyer to rise above the turbulence; the sensors said they would pass through this strand of outflow in the next few hours. To the south, clouds rose like fantastic buildings, their tops catching the last light. Lightning flickered occasionally in their depths, turned ruddy by distance, but the sensors showed the lines moving parallel to their own course.

She looked up as the cockpit door opened and Dai ducked through. He had done most of the work of getting their own equipment transferred and connected to the miner's systems, and he looked it, shadows heavy under his eyes.

"How's it going?"

"Good so far," Cassilde said. The miner bucked under her hands, and she steadied it with a sigh. "I'm not inclined to trust the autopilot, though. Not without supervision, and that kind of makes it a moot point."

Dai breathed a laugh, and slid into the co-pilot's seat. "We should probably stop for the night, then, much as I hate to lose the time. I'm about dead."

Cassilde considered, but had to admit that he was right. She was going to hit the limits of her own stamina soon enough, and Ashe wasn't rated to fly this class of machine; better to set down for a good night's sleep and fly out again in the morning. "Ashe reckons we're still at least sixty hours ahead of them."

"I guess that's good," Dai said. "I mean, yes, obviously, it's good. I'm just not sure what to do with that time."

"Find the Dedalor palace," Ashe said, from the open hatch. "Get ready to meet John."

Cassilde glanced over her shoulder. "We're going to have to kill him, Ashe. I don't see anything else we can do."

Ashe looked at Dai. "Do you agree with that?"

"I'm surprisingly good with it, yes," Dai answered. "He's tried to kill us twice. It's—call it long-range self-defense."

Ashe gave a wry smile at that, and Cassilde said again, "I don't see any alternative."

"I know." Ashe dipped his head. "I do know."

"You'd better be good with it," Cassilde said, with a sudden flash of annoyance.

"I am," Ashe said again. "I'm just worried about how."

So am I, Cassilde thought. She said, "I was thinking maybe some kind of ambush, hit him before he gets into the palace area. Before he can contact the AI."

"That could work," Dai said, but didn't sound particularly convinced. "But—he's got a Gift, right? We already thought we'd killed him once before. Is it even possible?"

"That's what I meant," Ashe said. "And, yes, it's possible, or so I'm told. If you cut off someone's head, the Gift can't regenerate that. Or burn the body. Or cut out the heart, though I think if the Gift can regenerate hands and feet it ought to be able to cover hearts and lungs, too."

Cassilde swallowed hard, tasting metal at the back of her throat. Of course it could; she had blasted Vertrage through the torso twice, and he'd still managed to walk away. "That's very…" she couldn't find the word she wanted, shook her head instead.

Dai was looking a little queasy himself. "That's—those are the only options?"

"As far as I know," Ashe answered.

Cassilde took a breath, watching the course line arrowing steadily away from them into the dark. "If that's what we have to do, then we have to do it." Dai opened his mouth to protest, and she glared him into silence. "I don't see any alternatives."

Dai waved a hand in answer. "No. No, I don't either."

"I was thinking," Ashe said, after a moment. "Maybe we should leave some kind of warning for the Entente—and the Verge, everybody, Core and Edge—let them know that it might be possible for someone to release the AI."

Cassilde considered that, automatically correcting the miner's tendency to slide off to port under the wind's steady pressure. "You'll be giving up the hunt."

"If they believe us," Dai said.

"Well, I was figuring we wouldn't send it unless we were already dead," Ashe said, "so that doesn't really worry me." He shook his head, went on more seriously. "We might warn the hunt, too. I've said all along, not everyone's going to be with John on this, and if there's any way to stop another Dark—we have to do it."

"It's not a bad idea," Cassilde said. "Draft something—address it to the University, they're more likely to listen before they run screaming."

"Yeah." Ashe nodded. "I'll do that."

They set down a little after one in the morning, port time, at a tiny settlement in the lee of a weather-worn pair of low mountains. According to the miner's databank, there were dozens of these safety points scattered along the major dispersal routes; this one was called Adam's Reach, and boasted a population of 137. One of them was awake to answer Cassilde's hail, and switched on field lights and the short-range locator. Either one would have been enough to guide them in, the beacon loud and steady, the light the only one as far as the eye could see. She brought the miner down carefully on the short, sand-swept runway, and followed the guide lights into a sunken hangar. Dai paid the sleepy attendant for the space and systems hook-up, then climbed back into the miner, sealing the hatch behind him.

"We should eat," he said.

Cassilde shook her head. "I had some energy bars a while back. I'd rather get some sleep."

"I'm with Silde," Ashe said, unexpectedly, and that decided it.

They left late the next morning, after taking time to pick up the latest forecasts. At the moment, the seasonal shift seemed to be holding the worst storms to the south, and the air was relatively calm. Still, Cassilde was grateful for the gravity field that lightened the miner's bulk and made it easier to maneuver. The sky was clouded—the sky was never really clear on Aeolus, by all accounts—but the lowest levels of haze and dust were at 2000 meters, and the upwash from below was only hitting ten or fifteen meters.

Even in the relative calm, Aeolus was a bleak world. The broken ground stretched in shades of gray and silver to the horizon, broken here and there by stunted chunks of rock. Once in a while, Cassilde made out scraps of vegetation, low-growing, gray-green branches brightened by an occasional pale shape that might have been a flower. They lay mostly on the north-east side of the larger rocks, protected from the prevailing winds. There was no sign of open water, though once they passed a network of braided channels that looked as though they might have been carved by a sudden flood. The edges were already blurring, little puffs of sand flaring from the banks, and she wondered how long it would take to erase all traces.

In the relatively clear air, she was able to make their top speed without straining the engines, and the autopilot was capable of controlling the miner without too much supervision. From the weather reports and the occasional bursts of distant chatter from miners further east, she gathered that this was about as good as Aeolus's weather ever got, and she wished she could push the engines harder while it lasted.

After a while, Ashe brought a flask of tea, and settled into the co-pilot's seat to keep her company while she drank it. The navigation screens showed the bright spots of the fixed beacons, broadcast frequency flashing over each one; she was currently following a line that would bring them over Beacon Aleph-92K in about an hour, and she glanced sideways at Ashe.

"When do you think we should turn south?"

"It depends. What's the weather like?"

Cassilde flicked the switch that brought the constant scroll of data to the foreground, and they watched in silence as conditions and forecasts slid past. "It's great right now, but I don't believe it's going to hold."

They both knew the choice: taking the more northerly track was longer, but the weather was likely to be better even if it deteriorated; turning south now and heading straight for the area where Ashe thought the Dedalor palace lay would be significantly shorter, but the further south they went, the more likely it was that they'd run into weather strong enough to ground the miner.

"I'm inclined to stay in the clear air as long as possible," Ashe said at last. "I'm pretty sure I'll bring you within ten kilometers of the site, but we'll still need to search."

And they'd need to find a way in once they'd found the site, Cassilde thought. Assuming that there was in fact something physical there. But, no, all the stories said that there had been, that Anketil and Irtholin had used the Dedalor palace as a prison, as a lock to keep the AI barred from ordinary space/time. She reached for her keyboard, typed in the now-familiar sequence that brought up satellite images of the area that Ashe had singled out. Even at the best magnification, it was hard to make out detail—the system notes in the miner's read-me said that the corporations didn't bother with visual surveys because the storms changed the landscape on an almost-daily basis. Certainly it looked more rocky than the scoured plain around them, a series of twisted spires reaching up out of the sands like dead petals of some bizarre flower, but there was no sign of human construction anywhere in the area.

"Do you really think that's part of a palace?" The words slipped out in spite of herself, and she gave an apologetic shrug. "I just—"

"Even if it's not, John's going to come here," Ashe said. "He's making the same calculations I am—he got them from me. Hell, it might be better if there isn't anything left of the palace. We could deal with John, and not have to worry about the AI at our backs."

"Are you sure you're all right with this?" Cassilde stopped, grimaced at her own euphemism. She wasn't as comfortable with the idea herself, and so she made herself say it aloud. "With killing him and his people?"

"We kill him, his people will run or deal," Ashe said. "They're not entirely on board with this idea of his, at least not by what I overheard. And, yes, I'm willing to kill him. Whatever we have to do."

"He was a friend," Cassilde said, and did not add, *he would have taken you with him.*

Ashe made a sound that wasn't quite laughter. "Never exactly that, though he wanted to be. We were lovers, I thought for a while that we had something, but... He thinks I'm too cautious, that I complicate things unnecessarily. He's the one who thinks he can do what the Dedalor couldn't."

"I didn't really think he'd shoot you," Cassilde admitted.

"I said no. And he knew I meant it, so I wasn't any use to him." Ashe leaned back in his chair, his eyes fixed on the distant horizon. "He promised me—he offered me the chance to be Irtholin to his Anketil, and can you imagine how much I wanted that? To stand where they stood, to gain that much of the Ancestors' knowledge? But he never remembered that Irtholin betrayed Anketil in the end."

Cassilde sat silent for a moment. Of course Ashe wanted that, Ashe who wanted to know everything and who was prepared to take outrageous risks to get even the smallest scraps of knowledge. It was a part of why she loved him, even as she and Dai watched for it and hauled him back from the most dangerous edges. "And Anketil killed Irtholin. Was he thinking of that?"

"I don't know. At best, they killed each other, and I wondered if it would be worth it. But I'd come home by then, and I couldn't." He gave her an oddly embarrassed glance, then nodded toward her flask. "You done with that?"

"Yeah, thanks," she said, and watched him disappear into the body of the miner. *I'd come home*, he had said, and that was more of a statement of affection than she'd expected from him, more convincing than a thousand endearments. And she could see why Ashe had followed Vertrage, might even have loved him. It was not in his nature to pass up that sort of offer. Not for the first time, she was glad to have Dai's solid practicality as well.

But that didn't solve the problem of killing Vertrage. She'd been in the War, of course, but that had been mostly about dodging other ships, shooting blindly at blips on a screen while maneuvering for the nearest warpline entrance. She'd known that people had died on the Entente ships, but it hadn't been real, not like on the wrecked palace.

And that had been, if not directly self-defense, then in defense of her lovers, and she couldn't feel guilty about that. It was the thought of killing Vertrage and then mutilating his body that was hard to bear. She wasn't even sure what you'd use to cut off his head—presumably one of the small beam-cutters would do it without wrecking too much around it? Otherwise it would take something from the toolkit, an axe or a saw, and she wasn't even sure the miner carried such a thing. *Carabosse* did, of course; she hoped someone had thought of it.

𝌀 𝌐 𝌆 𝌞

Dai took over the controls mid-afternoon, and Cassilde settled into their shared cabin for a quick nap. When she woke again, earlier than she had planned, she could feel that the miner's motion had changed. She sat up quickly, waved for lights and the sensor display, and grimaced as clouds of color filled the air. The window of good weather had proved to be as brief as they had been warned; a new coil of storm was building above the 45th parallel, and sending out long streamers of wind and dirty cloud. A band of thunderstorms was building ahead of them, the clouds flickering red and black at their highest points. She could see a path through, but it was narrowing, and she was unsurprised when the hatch slid back.

"You're awake," Ashe said. "Good. Dai wants you up front."

Cassilde followed him to the cockpit and settled herself in the co-pilot's chair, frowning at the weather display. This was more detailed than the repeater in the cabins, and she couldn't help grimacing at the winds showing inside the largest storms. "Not nice."

"Nasty," Dai agreed. "We're getting some static on the beacons, too."

The worst of Aeolus's storms could raise enough dust that the static electricity blotted out the navigational signals. When that happened, the read-me said, the best course was to land and wait for the storms to pass. The beacons were generally restored within eight hours' of a storm's passage. She reached for her own keyboard, and began typing in queries, Ashe leaning over her shoulder.

"There was a gap in the line," she said, and touched keys to highlight it. "It's narrowing, but we ought to be able to get through before it closes."

"But there's another line beyond that," Ashe said, and Dai nodded.

"It's not quite as big," Cassilde said, but she adjusted her scan, searching further south. The storm bands were thicker there, but there were still substantial gaps between the lines. "Or we could turn south, pick up the direct heading for Ashe's coordinates."

"What's the density like?" Dai asked.

Cassilde pinged the sensor net, and grimaced at the answer. "Thickening." She queried the system again, and shook her head. "On the other hand, it's no better up ahead. It looks like the ground winds are kicking up a substantial dust cloud—it's already hitting three hundred meters and rising."

"If we have to set down, the southern route is that much shorter," Ashe said.

"But we don't have a direct beacon line," Dai said.

Cassilde chewed her lip, watching the colors shift with each cast of the net. The only certainty was that it wasn't going to get any better anytime soon; the real question was how far they could get before they had to set down. "South is looking better," she said aloud, and Dai nodded.

"I agree."

The miner staggered as they tried to make the turn, but Dai brought it around in a slow curve, and found a momentary sweet spot at 1200 meters. There was still a gap between the arms of the storm, curving gently to the west and south, and he settled the miner into a course that would keep them equidistant from both lines of cloud. In the camera view, Cassilde could see a sky as gray as slate, fading slightly as Dai found their course between the stronger lines. Lightning flickered in the cloud tops, and in the distance a bolt stabbed toward the ground, followed by another. A third branched upward, seeming to rise from the ground to form a tree-like shape within the clouds, and Ashe swore under his breath.

"That's—unique, I hope."

"It's the dust," Dai said. "How's the density up ahead?"

"Rising, but well under our limits," Cassilde answered.

In the visual display, the light had faded, the occasional rocky outcrop hard to distinguish from the darkening ground. The horizon had thickened, as though there were a cliff ahead, a solid wall rising from the desert floor, and then she realized that it was a wave of heavier particles churned up from the ground below. The sensors put it nearly two kilometers tall, and the air above was turbulent and dense enough to set off warnings.

"How wide is that?" Dai demanded, and Cassilde worked the sensor controls.

"At least twenty kilometers in either direction. I know, it's right across our path." She touched keys again, adjusting her view of the situation. The actual storms seemed to be on the ends of the rolling wall of dust, though lightning crackled in the dust cloud. Particulate density dropped off as they went higher, and the turbulence didn't seem to increase. "I think we can go over."

"Better than setting down," Ashe said, and Dai managed a fleeting grin.

"I think I left it too late, there's not really room before it's on us."

They could, of course, turn around, get ahead of it and land, but no one wanted to do that. Cassilde nodded. "Ashe, strap in, I don't want you thrown all over the cockpit. Let's try over."

Ashe hastily secured himself in the cockpit's jump-seat, and Cassilde tightened her own harness as the miner dropped into an air pocket. Dai caught it, and glanced quickly toward her.

"You should take it."

She was the better pilot, in and out of atmosphere. "Switch over."

"Switching," he answered, and she felt the controls come alive under her touch.

The air was rougher than she had expected, the miner swaying uncomfortably against conflicting currents. It was thicker, too, thick enough even at this altitude to obscure the visual recorders, and she pulled back on the main wheel, struggling for more altitude. Even with the gravity assist, the miner was an ungainly flyer; she didn't dare raise the nose more than twenty degrees for fear of losing all lift, and dropping back into the roiling sand.

Lights flared across Dai's board, but she couldn't spare a look. He typed commands into his keyboard and then gave a bark of laughter. "That's the mineral detectors, they run automatically. Apparently there's a decent harvest down there."

"They say the storms bring them to the surface," Ashe said.

Lightning split the sky, leaping up out of the wall of dust only two kilometers to their right. The miner bucked and tried to pitch down, but she held it steady, watching the storm rushing toward them. She had a good five hundred meters' clearance, according to the sensors, but it didn't feel like enough, and she kept the nose lifted, scrambling for more altitude.

The body of the clouds was still fifteen hundred meters above them: room enough, she thought, to thread the needle between the wall of dust below and the worst of the storm overhead. At least there was no rain, just the winds and the scouring dust. She leveled off five hundred meters below the cloud base, feeling its presence like a hand pressing them back toward the ground. Ahead, the dust storm looked almost solid, swelling clouds as heavy as stone.

"Outflow," Dai said, and the miner pitched and bucked, warning lights flaring along the base of her displays. The air was thick with dust even at her altitude, stealing lift from the wing, but she didn't dare go much higher.

"Give me more gravity assist."

"Going to max assist," Dai answered. "Max assist engaged."

She saw the warning light pop on at the side of the screen, tagging the increased fuel consumption, but ignored it. Lightning roared in the clouds overhead, silhouetting the swelling clouds; below, sparks snapped into the folds of the dust clouds, short sharp pops of blue light. The miner dipped and swayed, the harness biting painfully into her hips and shoulders, but she wrestled it back into something like level flight. The sensor net showed clearer air ahead, a brief break between lines of storms. Get there, she told herself, and it would be better. It might even be clear enough to let them land if they had to.

The light changed in the visual display, brightening as though someone had switched on the miner's exterior lights. "Dai?"

"Not me," he answered, and she caught her breath.

A blue light was crawling along the base of the display—along the lower edge of the camera's lens, she corrected, blue and brilliant as wild electricity. It spread, ringing the image, and Cassilde risked a quick look at Dai.

"Secondary cams?"

"Where do you want them?"

"Bottom of the visual display."

The image in her screen reshaped itself, lifting to make room for four more images. Each showed another camera's perspective on the miner, one scanning the belly between the tracks, now a canyon filled with sheets of purple light that flashed and flared like flame, two more showing the tips of the enormous wing outlined in blue fire, the light streaming back like ribbons to vanish in the storm. The view from the tail showed the entire upper hull outlined in the shimmering light—if there had been anyone to see, Cassilde thought, the miner would have blazed against the storm as though it were some kind of meteor.

"I know what this is," she said aloud, as much to convince herself as to warn the others, and saw Dai nod.

"Saint Elmo's fire."

"Impressive," Ashe said, and his voice barely wavered. "That's supposed to be harmless, right?"

"Relatively," Dai said. He looked quickly at Cassilde, then turned his attention back to his screens. "I think it's the dust."

"Yeah." The miner jerked and trembled, but they had crossed the leading edge of the dust storm, and Cassilde thought the wind was steadying. It was still picking up speed, she amended, seeing a new number flash onto her screen, but it wasn't as changeable as it had been before.

Beneath them, the dust storm rolled away to the north, the clouds settling back to the ground, but a new wall of clouds was building ahead of them, and she saw Dai ping the sensor net twice, then shake his head.

"That's looking bad. Windspeeds are well over our max tolerance."

"I see it," Cassilde answered. All too clearly, in fact: those were the next bands of an even bigger storm thrown out of the equatorial currents. The miner could handle them once it was on the ground, but she needed to find a place to land, and soon. "We'll need to set down."

"Where?" Ashe muttered, but quietly enough that she could pretend not to have heard him.

Dai was busy with his keyboard, adjusting the sensor net to get a view through the clouds and dust. The resulting map was discouraging, rocky ground covered in streams of sand. They were moving with the wind, Cassilde saw: not something she'd want to try to land on. Dai did something, and the image changed, leaped forward to spotlight a larger rock formation rising from the sand. It was three or four meters tall, and lay at a forty-five degree angle to the wind; a secondary formation rose at its western end, a broader clump of rock that lay directly across the wind. That was promising, but the ground behind it was still sand, not open ground. On the other hand, the sand wasn't moving, and she'd have to bring the miner down on gravity assist anyway.

"Looks good," she said aloud, and Dai grunted agreement.

"For some value of 'good'," Ashe said.

"Not helping," Dai said.

"Can you give me a glide slope?" Cassilde asked. "Give me about two thousand meters run in." That was being cautious, she should only need half of that to bring the miner to a controllable speed, but landing on the gravity assist was going to be tricky, and she wanted as much room as possible before she risked crashing into a wall of rock.

"Working on it."

A moment later, a line bloomed in her heads-up display, running along the base of the visual screen, and she tipped the miner's nose gently down. The miner shuddered, trying again to tip over onto its port side, and she dragged it back level again. She tried again, and this time managed to establish a reasonable rate of descent, though the blue lightning was back on the control surfaces. And that meant more dust in the air around them, more dust in the engines...

"How are the filters holding?" she asked, and Dai touched keys again.

"We'll want to change them once the storm's over but they're ok for now. We're still within tolerance."

The people who built the miners had to be used to these storms, Cassilde told herself, had to know how much dust was in the atmosphere, and how to protect the engines. Still, she caught herself listening for the first sound of a misfire, the first hint that it was all going wrong.

"Can you give me any more gravity assist?"

"We're already at max assist now," Dai answered. "This is what you've got."

It would be enough. It would have to be enough, and she glanced again at the tertiary screen that showed the relative loads. The miner was flying as though it were lighter and more maneuverable, held in the helping field; she could wish for a bit more mass, given the winds, but didn't dare reduce the field.

She could see the horizon now, more and darker clouds building up from the sand-blurred boundary between earth and sky. Lightning flickered almost constantly within them, highlighting enormous towers; bolts stabbed the ground, and then a great spiderweb of light flashed between two of the larger clouds. Cassilde made herself focus on the glide slope, adjusting the controls so that they were steady in the middle of the yellow line. They passed through a sudden rattle of—not hail, it couldn't be hail, but something struck hard against the miner's hull, a briefly deafening tattoo.

"Small stones," Dai said, his voice grim.

The miner was built to take it, Cassilde told herself. That was the whole point of the machine. The controls juddered under her hands as a last blast beat against the hull, and then steadied again.

"We're through that one," Dai said. "There are—I think the web is picking up some more upwellings like that ahead of us."

"Mark them," Cassilde said.

"Marked."

Red patches bloomed in her screen, one just ahead and to the left of the glide path, and she eased the controls to the right to avoid its edges. The miner wobbled, stall warning sounding briefly, and she tipped the nose down to pick up speed. It steadied, the thick air triggering more lights and audible alarms on Dai's console, and she risked a glance in his direction.

"What is it?"

"Finder lights," Ashe said. "The mineral detectors. We're passing another rich bed."

"Shut them down," Cassilde said.

"Working on it," Dai said, and she felt the miner shiver again as the winds shifted. The guide marks shifted with it, and she fought the miner back into alignment, its movements smoothing out as she found the sweet spot. She was still on max assist, and needed every bit of it, but the turbulence seemed to have eased a little.

The ground ahead was beginning to come into focus, the low line of rocks rearing up out of the murky air. The instruments showed solid ground a few thousand meters ahead, and she began the landing checklist. The mineral detectors were still chattering, but she tuned them out, focusing on the glide slope and the power output, the feel of the air on the miner's lifting surfaces.

She was coming in too fast, red lights flashing at the corners of the heads-up, but the controls had the mushy feeling that meant she was too close to stalling. She lifted the nose cautiously; the miner juddered, warnings blaring, and she pushed it down again. The dust had thickened again, streamers of it blowing past like fog in the visual displays, and blue fire crawled in sheets across the visible surfaces. Another thousand meters, still without slowing, and she adjusted the spoilers, extending them into the on-coming wind. The miner bucked and its nose lifted, air spilling from the wing. There was no room for conventional recovery, to put the nose down and ride it out; she kicked the switch that sent them to full gravity assist, and felt the engines stagger.

"That's—it can't hold us," Dai said.

Not against this wind, not without any help from the lifting surfaces. Cassilde fought the controls, wrestling the miner back toward a position where some of the surfaces would catch the air. They were down to a safe landing speed now, but everything was on the gravity assist now, and she could feel the field straining to hold them.

"Overload warning," Dai said.

"I hear it." She pushed the nose down, but the wing refused to function. They were no longer flying but in a controlled fall, buoyed up by the gravity field. She pushed the wheel forward, but the nose barely moved: her controls were useless without lift. "Emergency boost."

"Diverting power," Dai said.

The wind shifted, caught the lifting surface. She pushed the nose down, harder this time, felt the wing catch and stagger. "Shields on."

"Shields on, confirmed." Dai's hands were busy on his board, tuning fields, but she couldn't spare him more than a glance. The miner bucked, fighting the controls, fighting the air around it, but she had some lift now, enough to take the pressure off the gravity assist. Ahead, the ground was clearing, the shifting streams of dust withering to threads that danced over solid stone. She took a deep breath, found the line, and set the miner down hard on the cleared ground. They bounced once, warnings shrieking, and she forced the nose back down. They hit again and stuck, rattling over stones as Dai collapsed the fields and she fought the controls. The overload warning cut out at last, and she was left with the sound of dust on metal as she brought the miner into line at last.

CHAPTER FIFTEEN

S he let the miner run forward on its landing wheels, bleeding off speed until the drop in windspeed told her they were under the lee of the ridge. Lights flashed across her board, filled Dai's with second-level warnings, but she could see that the machine was fundamentally intact. She worked the controls to fold the wing back into the miner's body, feeling the miner judder and lift until the wing came down close enough to the machine's body. She pulled in flaps and rudders, too, streamlining the teardrop body, and felt the pressure of the wind ease even further.

"Nice flying," Ashe said, and his voice was shaking.

"There's still weather coming," Dai said. He'd gotten most of his board clear, Cassilde saw, but the most important warnings were still flashing. "But the net says there's clear air behind these storms."

Best practice, according to the read-me, was to find a sheltered spot, close up the body, and deploy grapples to lock the miner to the ground. Cassilde could feel the wind curling around the miner's body, looking for a point to get beneath the heavy skirts, and switched from landing gear to the more stable caterpillar tracks. The miner settled to the ground, its movements stabilizing.

"I've got a likely spot," Dai said, and a line and ring appeared on her screen. It was still a few hundred meters from the line of rocks—far enough that it seemed unlikely any collapse would reach them—but the winds were definitely calmer there. Cassilde turned the miner to follow the line, feeling the streamlined body shiver and shed the worst of the dust. The tracks were making solid contact, biting deep into the ground, and the mineral detectors were making a steady chirping sound: it was a pity they weren't actually trying to fill the miner's compartments, Cassilde thought. They'd be well on their way to a profit by now.

She brought the miner into position, turning it so that the prevailing winds flowed smoothly over the hull. Dai deployed the back-up generators, adjusting the pods to take best advantage of the wind and to direct as much power as possible to the power cells. Cassilde deployed the grapples, feeling the screws bite deep into the hard ground. The contact lights flicked green one by one, and she leaned back in her chair.

"I show all secure. How about you, Dai?"

"Yeah. All secure here, too." He loosened his harness, but didn't move from the chair. "That was…a little rough."

"Maybe we were a bit overoptimistic," Cassilde admitted. The read-me had talked quite a bit about avoiding beginners' overconfidence. "But we're all right now."

𝍅 𝍖 𝍗 𝍘

By morning the worst of the storm had passed, a great wave rushing north in the sensor net. There were more storms crowding up behind it, spun off the bigger storms that boiled below the 47th parallel, but for the next few hours, the air would be clear enough for flight. Cassilde rolled out the wing and the control surfaces and set the gravity assist, feeling its power reassuringly steady, and made the take-off easily. Ashe set their course, more west now than south, and she pushed the miner to its top speed, trying to make up as much time as she could before they had to set down again.

They were forced to land again in mid-afternoon, when the air grew thick enough below the cloud ceiling that it compromised lift. Dai found a stretch sheltered by a low ridge, and Cassilde set the miner down carefully onto the shifting sand. It crawled on into the milky light, navigating by the orbital beacons, until the sun set and the last of the light had faded. Cassilde considered pressing on—they were well ahead of Vertrage, and she wanted to remain so—but the swirling dust cut their lights' power nearly in half, and it would be too easy to tumble into a pothole or be caught in a sand stream. There wasn't as much shelter here as there had been the previous night, but they finally found a cluster of boulders, and worked the miner into a space between them.

In the miner's cramped commons, Dai fed pre-pack into the cookers while Cassilde and Ashe tried to stay out of his way and still study Ashe's calculations.

"We're not far," Ashe said, not for the first time, and rubbed the mote that clung to his collarbone. "By mid-afternoon, we ought to be able to pick up signs of it."

"It's going to be shielded," Dai objected, and they all shifted awkwardly while he unloaded the cooker. "It has to be, or somebody would have found it already."

Cassilde sat down again, rubbing the elbow that she'd banged on the corner of the boiler. "I'm hoping once we're close enough that I can use the toy to find it."

Ashe nodded. "I think you could. It's not just that we're looking for a concentration of Ancestral elements, they're elements that are *ordered*, that have been put to use. We should be able to pick them out."

Cassilde tore off a piece of puff-bread, swirled it in the waiting oil. "Dai's right, though. Something's kept people from finding it so far."

"First, people didn't know it was here, so they weren't looking for it." Ashe ticked the points off on his fingers. "Second, you've got the toy, and that should help us find the palace. Third—have you seen the survey images? It doesn't look as though anyone's ever done a solid scan of this planet."

"That's because the surface keeps changing," Dai said. "There's not much point."

That was what the read-me had said, anyway. Cassilde shook the thought away, telling herself she was being overly suspicious. "What's the weather supposed to be like?"

"The morning's about the same as today, and then easing up a bit by about 1300," Ashe answered. "Or at least that's the area forecast."

The read-me had also warned that area forecasts could be dangerously wrong for specific locations: *if observations are in conflict with the forecast, it is best to believe the observations.*

"We'll see how it goes," she said aloud. "I wouldn't mind being able to fly a bit tomorrow."

There were no beds big enough for all of them, or even for two of them to share. Cassilde settled into the cramped bunk space, bracing herself for dreams of AI, but to her surprise, her sleep was deep and empty. Gold Shining Bone had withdrawn itself, it seemed, and when she woke, she couldn't decide if that was a good or a bad sign.

 𝔸 𝕀𝕝𝕤 𝕏 𝕚

The weather was better than predicted, the windspeed dropping enough that they were able to take to the air for short periods. The main line of storms was retreating to the south, though a few tendrils curled up behind them, and Cassilde hoped they'd slow down Vertrage once he landed. It was getting close to his projected arrival time; they needed to find this Dedalor palace as soon as they could.

There was nothing on the screens, though, not even when they were able to lift to two thousand meters under a sullen sheet of cloud. There was just the same gray sand, marked here and there with paler streaks that the sensor web identified as finer particulates. A few rocks jutted from the dust, their windward sides worn smooth, the trailing edges fretted like lacework. The mineral detectors were silent: apparently they'd run out of the rich pocket they'd found earlier. Ashe hunched in the jumpseat, screen unrolled in his lap, refining his calculations.

"Try bearing three degrees left," he said, and Cassilde obediently adjusted the controls. They were back on the ground for the moment, the air too thick to fly through, and Dai swore under his breath.

"There's our problem. Look there." He touched keys to transfer the sensor image to the others' secondary screens, and Cassilde grimaced as she recognized the tight spiral of another storm.

"Oh, that's just lovely. How big is it?"

Dai worked his systems. "Not too bad. Twelve kilometers diameter, give or take, and it's more like a really small hurricane than a giant tornado. Windspeeds are bad, but not catastrophic."

"Lovely," Cassilde said again. "Which way is it moving?"

"It's not," Dai said, sounding startled. "Or if it is, it's going so slowly that it's not registering yet. I'm trying to track it."

"That's weird." Cassilde frowned at the image on her screen, then checked the visual data. If she looked closely, she thought she could make out a spot where the horizon seemed darker: maybe that was the storm, stirring dust and debris into the upper atmosphere. Behind her, she heard Ashe's fingernails click on his board.

"There are fixed storms here," he said. "I read about them before we landed. But most of them are known and well marked—their outflow is a reliable mineral source. But this one isn't on the charts."

"Maybe it's new," Dai said, and Ashe nodded.

"Could be. Let me—no, it shows up on the most recent satellite images, and they're three years old."

"That could count as new, here," Dai said.

Ashe nodded again. "It could. Damn it, I wish I could get better resolution out of these things."

"What kind of margin should I give it?" Cassilde asked.

"Working on it," Dai answered.

"The palace should be right around here," Ashe said. He rubbed the mote nervously. "We should be picking up the ruins now."

"Not yet," Dai said. "Don't worry, I'll let you know. Silde, the winds drop off pretty quick, we should be able to get within a couple kilometers of the wall without a problem."

"I'll plan on four just to be safe," Cassilde said, adjusting their course. "Are you sure it's not moving?"

"As sure as I can be." Dai glanced over his shoulder. "Ashe. It's not inside that thing, is it?"

"Surely not," Ashe said, startled. "I mean, I suppose it's possible, but—"

"Let's hope not," Cassilde said, studying the screens. Maybe she should give it more room: if the storm picked up speed, or started moving, the miner wasn't fast enough to get out of its path. On the other hand, hopefully the Dedalor palace was on the far side of the storm, hidden by its turbulence, and the sooner they found it, the better. She chewed her lip, considering the options, and turned the miner to take them four kilometers outside the wall of dust and cloud.

The miner crept across broken ground, the hardened surface swept nearly bare in places, then suddenly running with streams of sand drawn in to the hovering storm. It loomed to their right, filling the displays, slate-colored clouds piling one on top of the other until they were absorbed into the overarching haze. There was less lightning than Cassilde had expected. Bolts flickered occasionally toward the tops of the clouds, silhouetting their folds, but most of it stayed in the storm's upper reaches, avoiding the ground.

"We're so close," Ashe said, finger still on the mote. "It's right here."

There was nothing visible to the north except a low line of rocks fifteen kilometers to the northeast, and nothing directly ahead to the west. As Cassilde brought the miner around the curve of the storm, the plain opened out in front of them, as empty as before except for a pair of rounded outcroppings that rose above the sand like the heads of some strange creatures poking from their burrows.

"There."

"I see it," Ashe said, busy with his board, but Dai frowned.

"I'm not picking up anything but rock."

"Shit. Neither am I," Ashe said. He typed in another set of commands, and Dai adjusted the sensor web.

"All right, I'm getting something from the mineral detectors, but it's a diffuse stream, nothing organized."

"Sand," Ashe said, bitterly. "That's natural. Or as natural as anything on this planet."

Cassilde turned the miner south again, circling the storm. On this side, the cloud layer had thinned, letting wan sunlight filter through, and the wall of dust and cloud looked even more ominous in the relative brightness. Neither the visual screens nor the sensor web showed any signs of buildings, and she glanced back at Ashe.

"Where exactly is that thing pointing?" Dai asked, before she could speak, and this time Ashe did look up sharply.

"East. More or less due east. Inside the storm."

Cassilde lifted her eyebrows, and saw agreement on Dai's face. "Inside that?"

"Why not?" Ashe demanded. "It's the Ancestors, and we all know what they can do. And what better place to hide?"

Cassilde checked the sensor net, and grimaced at the readings. The storm's weakest winds were at the upper end of the miner's rated capacity, and the top winds were strong enough to rip it off its tracks. "I'd like more proof before we try driving into it."

"You've got what I've got," Ashe said. "The maps say this is where it was, the mote says it's east of us right now—we've circled the damn thing, and the mote keeps pointing in. Wouldn't you expect this from the Ancestors?"

"What about satellite imagery?" Dai asked. "I can't read anything except wind and dust."

"The satellite survey is crap," Ashe said. "I've managed to pull up exactly two shots of this area that show the storm, and neither one of them is at an angle that would let you see down into the eye."

"Assuming there is an eye," Cassilde said.

"There has to be," Ashe said. "They're bound to have left a way in."

"I don't agree," Dai said. "If this is where Anketil sealed the AI out of space and time, why wouldn't she cover it with a storm that never ceased? That would keep anyone from inadvertently releasing them."

"That's not how the Ancestors did things," Ashe answered. "They always had a second option, always assumed that their work might be undone, or need to be redone. And besides, what are we going to do, just leave it until John shows up? He'll go in, I can tell you that."

"Maybe we should let him," Dai muttered.

Maybe we should try to ambush him outside the storm, Cassilde thought, but the words died on her lips as she studied the ground. There was no obvious place for Vertrage to try to enter the storm, and equally no shelter for the miner, no place they could hide and wait to strike. The miner was meant to be seen, its reflective surfaces one more safety precaution. "Ashe is right," she said slowly. "We have to try. But let's be smart about it."

The day was waning, the winds shifting direction as the air cooled. They circled the storm again, sensor net fully extended, and retreated to the lee of the head-shaped rocks to let Ashe build a model that might show them a path into the storm. The web couldn't penetrate far enough to tell if there was an eye, though Ashe swore the ambiguous readings at the very edge of perception were the beginnings of a pressure drop. Cassilde eyed the model unhappily, wishing less of it was painted in the shades of red that marked Ashe's guesses. Certainly there were possible entrances, spots where the winds seemed less turbulent, but there was no guarantee that the reduction lasted longer than a few hundred meters. If the gaps even lasted that long. Still, she knew Ashe was right, they couldn't just let Vertrage walk in and release the AI.

No one wanted to sleep alone, and in the end they piled mattresses on the floor of the largest cabin and made love there. Cassilde rested her head on Dai's shoulder, Ashe on her other side with an arm and a leg thrown across them both, and let her breathing slow. She desperately didn't want this to be their last time together—not now, not when she'd gotten Ashe back and dragged them both into the

Gifts' immortality with her. She wanted what Ashe had promised, what the Gift itself promised, a life as long as she could make it, and she resented having that snatched away.

"John will have landed by now," Ashe said, after a moment. "He'll be on his way."

"We're still ahead of him," Dai said sleepily. "We've got at least twenty hours, and that's if he's as good as you at working out where he's going."

"He's not stupid," Ashe said.

"If I was sure the storm was non-survivable, I'd go to ground and let Vertrage try it," Cassilde said.

Dai laughed softly, and she could feel Ashe smile. "I wish it was. That would make everything a whole lot simpler."

Dai laughed again. "We never get the easy choices. Why should this be different?" Cassilde felt his arm tighten around her. "We've got a decent chance. All we need is a little luck."

Cassilde flicked her fingers to chase off the ill omen, and then clenched her fist, annoyed at her own superstition. They needed to make their own luck—and they had done everything they could to do so, she told herself. She burrowed down between the men, glad of their presence to ward off too much thought. But in the depths of the night, she woke, words echoing in her head.

We know you're coming. We're waiting for you.

She managed not to shoot bolt upright, but lay still until her heartbeat slowed. How anyone could think he could control the AI, no matter how powerful his Gift might be.... He was going to release the AI, bring the Dark down on them again after they had so narrowly avoided it during the War, and she had no idea how to stop him. Kill him, somehow, when he possessed a Gift almost as powerful as her own, and trained men who knew how to fight....

She had no time for this, for sleepless hours gnawing at the same unanswerable problems. There were too many variables; she could only play her hand and hope for the best. She made herself take slow, deep breaths, calling on the techniques she had learned with the Lightman's, to wall away the fears and questions, and send herself into at least a light sleep.

ᚠ �835 ᚷ ꞊)

The morning dawned brighter than the last few days, and the windspeed seemed to have dropped generally, the storms that had spun up from the south dying down at last. Good for them, Cassilde thought, but also good for Vertrage. He'd be making good time today.

They double-checked the miner's systems and the seals that kept the dust out of engines and the inner compartments, then ran the power plant up to full speed and headed toward the storm. The weak points had shifted slightly, but Cassilde found the best of them, angling the miner so that they would enter the storm's wall along the same line. Even with the windspeed down, the outflow was tremendous, shaking the miner on its treads, and Cassilde slowed to let the skirt that kept air from getting under the miner fully engage. She felt it lock, felt the miner stabilize: all good, except that her speed was now severely restricted, and the more time she had to spend in the winds—

She cut that thought off, squinting through the roiling dust. The ground was less even here, scoured free of sand in spots to reveal strange parallel ruts—almost like channels for cables, or some sort of inlay. Between the ruts, the ground had an oddly polished sheen.

"Do you see that, Ashe?"

"Yeah." He leaned forward briefly, checked by his harness, and adjusted his scroll instead. "That looks potentially man-made. I wonder how deep the debris field goes?"

That was a startling image, an urban planet buried so deep in sand scoured from its own buildings that nothing showed above the surface. She shook herself hard, scowling. That was a question for later, for after they'd made it through. If they made it through. And that was up to her.

The wall of the storm loomed before her, filling the visual screen. Veils of dust shrieked past the cameras, blurring the lenses; she focused instead on the reading from the sensor net, aiming the miner for the point where two eddies rolled sharply away from each other, and a tiny area of lesser velocity appeared. The miner shuddered, bucking against a downdraft and a sudden drop in the terrain; she corrected, the controls leaping in her hands.

"Brace yourselves."

The wall of the storm filled the visual screen, blotting out everything but the instruments' light. Cassilde focused on the point of entry, turning the miner so that it shed as much of the wind as possible. Even so, the storm rocked the miner back on its tracks, so that the power plant whined and rumbled, yellow lights flashing on Dai's board. She ignored them, hauling the controls left to follow the point of relative weakness. Stones battered against the hull, and one of the cameras cut out. She ignored that, too, boring on into the storm. The line of least resistance curved left, and she followed it, only to see it dodge sharply to the right. The miner couldn't make the turn as neatly, and the stronger wind caught it, tipping it sideways. Dai slammed a ballast lever full left, and the miner steadied again.

"Turning," Cassilde called, her voice barely audible over the roar of the storm, and saw him ease the lever back again.

She had lost all sense of direction, could only rely on the sensor web to give her the correct heading. What was left of the visual display showed nothing but swirling dust, and the occasional flat crack of lightning. The bolts were too close for comfort, but the sound of the wind and the pounding rocks drowned out the thunder.

In her screen, the course line grew shorter, and she risked a look at Dai. "Are we punching through?"

"No." His voice was tight. "The web's overloading. Too much data to process."

Ashe leaned forward in his seat. "I can feel—the mote's getting hotter."

The line was fading, too, and so short Cassilde could barely figure out which way to go. "Talk me in."

"Stay steady." Ashe sounded utterly confident, which would have been more reassuring if she didn't know him as well as she did. "Steady. Two points left. Another point left. Steady. Keep steady."

Her world narrowed to Ashe's voice and the miner's wheel, to the shriek of the wind that threatened to drown his words. The cockpit was nearly dark, visuals blocked and the interior lights dimmed as more power went to the treads to keep them moving forward.

"One point right. Steady. Still steady."

Her hands and shoulders ached, but she couldn't think of that. *One more turn*, she told herself, *you can do that*. One more nudge to the wheel. She could feel her muscles starting to shake, and wondered if she could transfer control to Dai if she had to.

And then the miner broke through the wall of cloud, trundling out into clear air and relative quiet. They were on a flat plain, marked here and there with the incised lines she had noticed as they approached the storm. The ground itself had the same glassy finish, dusted only lightly with sand; a platform rose near the center of the space, rising up in meter-tall steps to a wide surface. Two triangular buildings were set at each end, like weirdly stylized horns.

"That's it," Ashe said. "We did it—"

Around them, the air was changing, the roar of the storm fading. Cassilde blinked, sure she was imagining things, but the clouds were fading, the tops blowing away into nothing. Sand pattered across the open space, fine as rain, no longer upheld by the winds, and then the entire thing seemed to collapse into a wave of dust that swept over the miner and disappeared, leaving behind a thick new layer of sand and debris. Cassilde caught her breath, automatically checking her systems, and Dai shook his head.

"You know, I think I'd rather we kept the storm."

"Now that we're through it," Cassilde agreed. "But apparently that's not how it works." She reached back to grab Ashe's hand. "We did it."

The finer dust still hazed the air, blotting out the high clouds and the distant sun and settling gray as ash over everything. Cassilde let go of her controls at last, working her arms to stretch the taut muscles. "Let swap," she said, and Dai nodded.

"The web's clearing."

Cassilde shook her hands, and reached for her keyboard, focusing on the area that had been concealed by the storm. There was nothing aboveground but the platform and its twin buildings: both showed open interior volumes, but the only external openings were set of what looked like vents just below the tips.

"The mineral detectors say there's metal ore below us," Ashe said. "What do you want to bet that's the rest of this structure?"

"Makes sense," Dai said. "I don't see anything that looks like a door, though."

Cassilde checked the windspeed, but it was still too high to launch a drone. "On top of the platform, maybe?" She eyed the steps thoughtfully. "I think the miner can get up there."

"As long as we don't get a gust of wind at just the wrong moment," Dai said, his hands already moving on the controls. "That would flip us like a turtle."

"Use the stairs on the south side," Cassilde said. "That'll put the wind behind us." She touched keys again, sampling the air and then reaching out to ping the forecast network. "It looks as though we're in a bit of a lull—the storm's collapse is pulling more weather up from the south, but for now we've got a local pressure rise that's blocking it. Looks like we'll have ten or twelve hours of relatively calm winds."

"That's a help if we have to blast something open," Dai said, steering the miner around a swath of sand that looked too soft for the treads, and turning to come up on the platform's southern edge. "But not so great if Vertrage shows up."

"Ashe?" Cassilde said. "What's your best guess for his ETA?"

There was a brief silence, just the sound of Ashe's nails on the board's screen, and then he sighed. "Best case, if everything goes right for them, they'll be in sensor range in 9 hours, landing in twelve to fourteen depending on the weather."

"And with the storm gone, these structures are going to stand out like a volcano," Cassilde said. "All right. We have to assume they'll spot us and be here about the time the weather starts getting rough again. What's our best move?"

"Get inside," Dai began, and stopped abruptly, the miner grinding to a halt. They were facing the platform's southern edge, the triangular building looming above them, and below it, the meter-high steps were slowly shifting, sliding sideways into and over each other, revealing the entrance to an unlit tunnel. "Well."

"Did you do anything?" Ashe asked, leaning forward, and Cassilde shook her head.

"Not that I was aware of. And everything I've done had required conscious action. Dai?"

He shook his head. "Not me. It's possible the door just opens once the storm is gone. I assume we're going in?"

"Oh, yes," Ashe said.

Cassilde nodded. "Just—let's be careful how we go."

The miner passed through the opening with only a few centimeters to spare, but the tunnel sloped rapidly away beneath its treads, leveling a little once they had a meter and a half of clearance. Dai lifted the protective skirt and lowered the wheels, and let the miner glide slowly downward, sand grating beneath its tires. They'd gone maybe thirty meters when there was a grating noise behind them, and Cassilde angled the rear camera to see the entrance closing slowly behind them. Pale light remained, diffusing from the corners where the ceiling and floor met the walls.

"That's probably a good thing," she said aloud, but saw her own unease reflected on the others' faces.

Dai eased the miner forward, and it seemed as though the light moved with them, a bubble illuminating perhaps thirty meters ahead and behind. He increased the speed, and the light matched them, gleaming from the featureless walls. They were still descending, and after a while the corridor began to curve to the right, tracing a wide spiral down into the depth of the—well, presumably it was the Dedalor palace, Cassilde thought, but she would have expected more decoration. She pinged the walls to either side, and got mixed answers: some parts showed solid for ten meters, some showed open volumes, as though there were rooms to either side, but the walls remained solid, with no sign of any doors.

At last the spiral ended, opening into a larger room. Light blossomed from ceiling ports, and Cassilde could see half a dozen open doors.

"Time to send out some drones."

They were *Carabosse*'s drones, of course, eight of them tucked into the miner's storage compartments: Aeolus was not a world that favored flyers. She and Ashe manhandled them out of storage and set the parameters, and then Cassilde wormed her way through the inspection hatch that opened onto the back of the miner. In spite of all their readings, she held her breath as she unwound the hatch, bracing herself for the bite of chemicals, but there was only a scattering of sand as she pushed back the cover. The air itself was cool and still and tasteless, like ship's air that had been through the recyclers a few times. She pulled herself up so that she was sitting on the edge of the opening, and pulled out a hand-light to examine her surroundings. The light didn't reach the ceiling, or the left-hand wall, but she could get a decent look at the floor and the wall to the right. There was still nothing, no decorations, though she thought she saw a faint shimmer in the surface of the floor, and she leaned back into the open hatch.

"All clear as far as I can see."

Ashe boosted the first drone up to her. "Can you see anything?"

"Nothing new. Still no marks." She thumbed on the drone's power pack and held it out at arms' length while the system whined up to full power. When she could feel it tugging at her, she released it, and watched it arrow away from her across the length of the room. It banked, following its programming, and disappeared into the first opening on the right. "First drone is away."

"That's not like the Ancestors," Ashe said, and handed up the second drone. "They decorated everything."

"You're sure this was a palace?" Cassilde switched on the second drone, then released it, watching it dive toward the first opening on the left.

"That's what the mote calls it."

"It looks…" Cassilde accepted the third drone, letting her voice trail off. It looked like a fortress, a military installation, and very few of those had survived the Long Dark. She loosed the drone, watching it disappear through the chosen corridor, and tried again. "Suppose this was where the Dedalor made their last stand against the AI. Would you expect decoration?"

"I might." Ashe boosted another drone into the opening, and Cassilde took it. "Do you want another?"

"No." Cassilde let it go, and touched her comm unit. "That's four launched, Dai. How are they running?"

"We're getting data, and everything's fine so far. You want to wait, or move on?"

It would be smarter to wait, Cassilde thought, let the drones develop a map and get some idea what was ahead of them, but they didn't have enough time or enough drones to make that effective. "Ashe. Does your mote give you anything useful?"

"Not really. It doesn't recognize anything here."

She nodded, reaching for the toy tucked into her belt. The grip was warm beneath her fingers, guiding her hand into—was it in fact a slightly different position, or was that just her imagination? She drew it, held it out at arm's length, focusing on a question: which way to go? The toy trembled, pushing her hand away and to the right, then stopped. Was it because there was no elemental dust in the air around her, nothing for the toy to work with? Did the Successor technology fail to control Ancestral work, or was there nothing for it to work on? The floor of the chamber stretched ahead of the miner, the shimmer more pronounced, and she pulled herself out of the hatchway. "Let's hold a few minutes, make sure the drones don't get into immediate trouble. Besides, I'd like to get a closer look at the floor material."

"All right," Dai said. "Be careful."

"I will," Cassilde said, and unrolled the ladder stowed inside the hatch. It clung to the miner's sand-etched skin, and she started climbing down.

Ashe's head appeared above the edge of the hatch, and then he pulled himself out to sit on the edge of the hull. "You should have waited for a rope."

"Toss it to me when I get down," Cassilde answered, and lowered herself the last meter to the chamber floor. It was slick underfoot, and very dark; her hand-light woke a brief scattering of sparks, but did not itself reflect. She lifted the toy, pointed first straight down and then to one side, but nothing happened.

"Rope," Ashe called, and it flapped down the miner's side, a harness dangling. Cassilde shrugged it on, tucking the toy back into her belt, and took a few cautious steps. It was like walking on ice, and she crouched to touch the material.

Sparks exploded beneath her fingers, silver and gold and diamond-white, streaming off in every direction. She jerked her hand back even though she had felt nothing, and sparks appeared beneath her boots, a smaller pattern like silent fireworks surrounding each foot. Tiny flecks of light fled across the floor, disappearing just as they reached the distant wall; she moved first one foot and then the other, and more lights pooled and eddied around her. And now she could feel them, a gentle fizzing, as though the Gift within her was echoing their spark.

"Well, that's—something."

"Did you do that?" Dai demanded in her ear, and Ashe leaned over the edge of the hatch.

"Do it again."

She stooped, and this time she felt the Gift pooling in the palm of her hand as she reached toward the ground. About a hand's-width above the surface, she felt a layer of cooler air, and swirled her fingers through it as though through water, not touching the floor itself. Sparks leaped to the surface in her wake, like fish following a feeder; she touched the surface, and the lights exploded away from her, rippling across the room to splash against the walls and bounce back in fading waves.

"It's the Gift," she began, and realized that Ashe was sliding down the hull to join her.

"I want to see what it does with mine."

"This is a stupid risk," Dai said.

Ashe ignored him, dropping onto the slick surface. He slipped and went to his hands and knees, and more sparks erupted where he touched the ground. Cassilde could feel his presence through the ground, through the Gift, an almost musical hum against her bones, though the toy stayed cold and silent at her waist. Whatever was beneath the surface wasn't made up of the elements, then, or else the Successor technology couldn't reach it.

"Definitely our Gifts," Ashe said, and deliberately moved his hand so that his shower of sparks interrupted hers. Cassilde held her hand above the point where they met, and a thin stream of light rose out of the ground, wrapping around her fingers. It felt good for a moment, and then it tugged at her, pulling gently down—pulling her Gift down and away, she realized, and snapped her hand hard, breaking the connection. She folded her arms across her chest, reaching inward, and was relieved to find the Gift still present.

"You all right?" Ashe asked, and she nodded.

"Don't do that," she said. "It was pulling—like it was trying to remove my Gift."

"That's not good," Dai said. "You should both get back on board."

"What actually did you do?" Ashe asked, and Cassilde reached for the ladder.

"I... You saw it come up out of the ground, that was what was pulling. I'm not sure what made it do that, but if it reaches for you, step back." She tugged uneasily at her harness. "You go first."

She thought for a second that he would argue, but for once he did as he was told, scrambling easily up the miner's side. He braced the rope for her, and she was glad of its support as she pulled herself back inside.

"Are you all right?" Dai demanded again as they slid back into the cockpit, and Cassilde nodded.

"The floor reacts to our Gifts, both harmlessly and—not. We're both all right, though."

"Did that thing do anything useful?" Dai nodded to the toy still tucked in her belt.

"No. And I tried. I think—either whatever's in the floor isn't powered by Ancestral elements or it's not compatible with Successor technology."

"Or both," Ashe said, seriously. He touched the mote again. "This recognizes it as a kind of test, I think. If it hadn't reacted to the Gift, I don't know how much further we'd get."

"Is that observation or feeling?" Dai asked, and Ashe grimaced.

"Both? Mostly a feeling. But I think I'm right."

Cassilde considered that in silence for a moment. "We'll keep that in mind," she said at last. "How are the drones running?"

"On pattern, and sending good data. We're well below ground, and there's a lot of space off these side corridors."

"We'll map it tonight," Cassilde said. "In the meantime..."

"Which way do we take?" Dai asked.

The openings all looked identical, and Cassilde shrugged. "Not one where we've sent a drone. Each one pick one."

It was a game they'd played a hundred times before, and Dai brightened the heads-up so that they could each read the numbers he had assigned to the openings.

"One, two, three." He held up four fingers, and Cassilde matched him, her eyebrows rising as she realized what they'd done. Ashe made a soft sound, and held up four fingers as well. It was the same direction in which her toy had pulled her hand.

"Why?" Dai asked. "What are we seeing—what are we picking up on?"

"The toy tried to point that way," she said. "So at least there should be elemental structures that way."

"It's the Gift," Ashe said. "The Gifts are pointing all of us that way. I told you, this was a test, and we've passed it. Whatever we're looking for, it's down that hall."

The corridor wasn't as wide or as tall as the one they had come down, and the miner had about a meter's clearance on all sides. It sloped down at a five degree angle, and bore slightly to the south and west, according to Cassilde's instruments. The walls varied in thickness from meters to centimeters, but there were no breaks in the smooth surface to show how one might enter those spaces. The tracking software drew its picture of where they'd been: a spiral to an open chamber, and then another downward ramp apparently suspended in empty space. It looked a bit like the tomb of an unknown ruler, as shown in every holovid she had watched from childhood on, and she found herself looking for the inevitable traps. And if there were traps, they would be of the Ancestors' making, something stranger and more subtle than in the stories.

Five hundred meters further in, the corridor leveled out, opening into a narrow chamber. For the first time, the miner's lights showed bands of patterned stone on the walls and floor, a pattern of tumbling diamonds etched in shades of blue. They chased each other around the perimeter in bands roughly half a meter apart, and the floor was covered with interlocking blue stars. There was only one exit besides the way they'd come, however, and it was clearly too small for the miner to fit. Cassilde stared at it unhappily.

"This seems like a strong hint that we're supposed to park our vehicle and walk the rest of the way."

"Looks like," Dai agreed, but made no move to back the miner into what seemed to be a parking bay. "Ashe?"

"I think this is what they invented drones for," Ashe said, and Cassilde nodded in agreement.

They had to climb out of the miner to gain enough clearance to launch the drone, but at least the floor here was solid, and played no tricks with lights. Cassilde watched the drone make its way down the corridor, a point of light steadily dwindling, until at last it disappeared. She touched her comm unit.

"Still running?"

"Yeah." Dai paused. "Looks like the corridor curves there, but I'm still getting good data."

"All right." Cassilde swung herself back aboard, Ashe on her heels, and they settled in the cockpit, watching the drone's progress. The walls flicked past, still with the same blue banding; there were no doors or side corridors or anything but the endless rush of stone.

And then the corridor turned sharply left, light bleeding into the passage from some unseen source. Dai grabbed for the controls, but the drone had already pitched over into its turn. There was a flash of light, and the picture vanished. Dai swore, typing commands, but the screen stayed empty.

"We're off air. I think it's down, too."

"Can you freeze that last image?" Cassilde asked. "The flash?"

"I'll try." Dai typed in a command string, and the picture wound back to the last images of the corridor and the sudden wall ahead. He typed another command, and the image advanced jerkily, the light flaring, the image tilting as the drone began its turn. The screen went white, and then cut out. Dai swore again, touching keys, then leaned back in his chair. "That's it. Whatever it was overrode all my stops."

"Any sign of anything harmful?" Cassilde asked. "Radiation, gases, anything?"

"Nothing's showing up," Dai answered.

"The drones don't have elemental programming, right?" Ashe leaned forward. "Maybe this is another test."

"That's possible," Dai said, reluctantly.

"But if it is," Cassilde said, "that means we have to go ourselves."

"We could wait for the rest of the drones," Dai said. "See if there's an alternative way in."

"We put them on a long loop," Ashe said. "There isn't time."

"Recall them, then." Dai tapped his fingers on the edge of the console.

"Ashe is right," Cassilde said. "We have to go ourselves, and we have to go now."

There wasn't really any alternative, not with Vertrage presumably on-planet and in pursuit. Still, they chose their gear with some care—a blaster apiece, cutters, full day kits plus first aid, plus the gravity sled and its light and generator. Dai wedged the miner into the side alcove, where are least it wouldn't be visible until someone actually entered the room, and they started down the corridor.

To Cassilde's surprise, the air was not merely breathable but almost pleasant, untainted by either age and lack of circulation, or by the surface dust. In fact, there was no dust underfoot, as though they'd come far enough that the winds had never penetrated. In the glow of the searchlight mounted on the gravity sled, the walls seemed to waver between midnight blue and black, the bands of tumbling triangles splitting into two or three separate strands, then rejoining in a single stream before dividing again.

As they advanced, the air felt thicker—warmer, perhaps, but also as though it had more weight and texture. She lifted her hand, trying to feel the difference, and a few wan sparks snapped at her fingertips.

"What did you do?" Dai asked, one hand on his blaster, and she shook her head.

"Nothing. Doesn't the air feel different to you?"

"A little." Dai stretched his fingers, eyebrows lifting as the same sparks appeared, dropping away into the dark at his feet.

"I can do it, too," Ashe said. "So. We can assume that there are more elements around us—in the walls, maybe, or microscopic traces in the air. Which should mean we're going in the right direction."

"Let's hope you're right," Dai muttered.

Cassilde glanced at her comm unit, checking the distance they'd come. "We'll find out. It's not far now."

It wasn't long before the wall that marked the bend came into sight at the far range of their lights. The air changed again, charged as the air before a thunderstorm, and Cassilde could see the first haze of light coming from the other direction. To either side, the bands of blue split into a dozen different lines, zigzagging wildly across the walls and finishing in a sudden complex figure that might be a knot or simply a tangle. Ashe ran one finger along a stripe as though he was trying to trace its path, but then shook his head.

The drone lay crumpled at the foot of the wall, lifting body dented from the crash. Dai picked it up, checking the displays, and set it on the gravity sled.

"It says it's out of power."

"That can't be possible," Ashe said.

"It's not," Dai answered, "but that's what it's telling me. The back-up is all the way down, too."

Cassilde took a slow step forward, feeling the storm-like pressure prickling across her skin. The light grew brighter as she approached the corner, and she shaded her eyes as she made the turn. There was nothing but light, flat, white, glaring light that brought tears to her eyes even as she looked away. There was no heat to it, just the painful brilliance, and she heard Ashe swear as the others came up to her. He held out his hand, and a thread like lightning jumped to touch his finger. He started, breaking the connection, and Cassilde could have sworn she felt disappointment.

And that was the answer, she realized, just as Ashe had said all along. She reached out to take their hands, and drew them forward with her into the light.

CHAPTER SIXTEEN

The light was overwhelming, all-encompassing, so that even with her eyes closed she could see it billowing away from them, rolling over itself in playful waves. She felt nothing, though, not even the whisper of a breeze as the light swept over them. Then, just as suddenly, they were through, and she caught her breath in surprise.

They were in an enormous domed chamber, its lights dim after the brilliance of the barrier. Cassilde glanced over her shoulder, and saw that it was still there, but the brightness had been reduced, as though someone had drawn a curtain over it. There was a smaller platform in the center of the room, topped by another dome supported on six twisted pillars. All around them, the walls ran with flecks of light, the elemental colors running in an elaborate network of lines incised in the dark stone. She lifted her hand, reaching for her Gift, and for a moment she held a multi-colored swirl of light. She closed her fingers over it and watched it vanish, then looked around the room again. "This is it?"

Ashe nodded, spreading his own fingers to create handfuls of light. "Yeah. This—this is where it happened, where Anketil bound the AI into the adjacent possible, where they held off the Long Dark for another three centuries."

And failed.

It was less a voice than a thought with weight behind it, a pressure from beneath the earth. Cassilde shivered, the hairs rising at the nape of her neck. "She succeeded in binding you," she said aloud, and was pleased that her voice didn't tremble.

She sought more than that, the voice answered. *She could not keep what she saved.*

"You're still bound," she answered, and thought she felt laughter. *And she is not here.*

We have a proposition. That was, Cassilde felt certain, a different AI, though she could get no sense of its name. *Release us, and we will share your Ancestors' power with you. That is the great secret, after all. It came through us, was mediated and regulated by and through us, it exists because of us. All we ask is our freedom.*

"I don't think so," Dai said, under his breath, and gave Cassilde a worried look. "That's not the plan, right?"

"We can't trust you," Cassilde said. "You nearly destroyed everything the last time you were loose—worlds, whole solar systems. We've all seen the Gap. It's not a risk we can take."

That was ignorance: a third voice. *We would not make that mistake again.*

"But would you do it on purpose?" Ashe asked, and again Cassilde thought she felt laughter.

There is one coming who will release us. That was the first voice again, she was certain, and she thought as well that it might be Gold Shining Bone. *Without awkward questions asked.*

"He thinks he can control you," Ashe said. "And he has some solid plans, some techniques and devices that will take you a while to overcome. Personally, I think you'd get there in the end, but I could be wrong. He knows what he's doing."

We would prefer to deal openly, the first voice conceded, and the second voice answered in a bitter hiss.

You would prefer! We wish to be free. We have offered you a bargain, but there are others who can free us.

"We can't free you," Cassilde said. "Not just like that, let you go with no restraint, nothing to stop you from beginning your wars all over again."

Even if we promise not to?

She didn't like the laughter than edged those words. "And we should trust you? The risk is too great." The second voice, or perhaps it and another, hissed angrily, and she raised her hands, aware for the first time that they, that she, was surrounded by swirls of light. "And we're not the speakers for our people. We don't have the right to make such an agreement."

With the power we'd give you, the third voice said, *that would hardly matter.*

"That's not the point." Cassilde's voice sharpened, and she controlled it with an effort. "Anything we promised you would be worthless, our leaders would have every right and reason to nullify anything we said, and we'd only prove the they were right if we used your power to make them agree. But if you spoke to them, convinced them that you only wanted freedom, that you weren't going to destroy us—offered them something in exchange, helped us recover what we've lost—that would be entirely different. You could walk away from this with everything you wanted and our cooperation, an entirely new age between us."

And will your leaders do this? The first voice again.

"I don't know. Like I said, you'd have to convince them that you were bringing something worthwhile to us, and that we wouldn't be destroyed. I won't lie, that's not an easy task."

But an intriguing possibility.

Unlikely, the third voice said. *The other offer is certain.*

Irrelevant, the first voice answered.. *We should choose on the merits.*

The other one will release us, the second voice said again. *We can defeat him, and take what we want.*

I do not wish to fight, the third voice said, *and I am not alone.*

Let them decide it for us, the first voice said. *The other is coming, let them settle it between them. We will deal with the survivor.*

"Wait—" Cassilde closed her mouth as the AIs' presence vanished like a blown-out candle.

"Well," Dai said, after a moment. "That was interesting. Do you think they were serious?"

"About which part?" Cassilde felt a chill run down her back, though she thought the air was unchanged.

"Any of it. All of it." Dai spread his hands. "And they're listening, aren't they? They must be." He spun on his heels, glaring up into the ceiling. "I know you're listening."

There was no answer, not even the absence of an answer, and Ashe caught his arm.

"Assume they can hear us, but I don't think it really matters. They've made their decision."

"They're really going to let us fight it out?" Cassilde asked.

"Why not? From their point of view, it solves the problem admirably."

Cassilde shivered again. She didn't want to fight, didn't want to have to kill even Vertrage in what was effectively cold blood. On the other hand, they couldn't let him get control of the AI. For a moment, she wondered if there was any way they could negotiate, if she could trade her Gift to make him go away, but dismissed the thought as soon as it was formed. Vertrage was too close to getting everything he wanted; if she offered her Gift, he'd simply take it, kill her and the others, and move on to free the AI. "We can't let him take them," she said aloud. "If we can't kill him, is there any way we can wreck this installation?"

Dai touched his ear in warning, and she shook her head.

"Let them hear me. I am that serious about keeping Vertrage from using them."

"Wrecking it is likely just to release them," Ashe said thoughtfully, but he moved toward the central platform anyway. "Unless..."

His voice trailed off as he peered under the smaller dome, and Cassilde came to join him. "What?"

She stopped, looked up into the dome. Its underside was black, so deep a black that it was almost without depth, or perhaps had too much depth, as though a hole had been cut in the fabric of the universe. Four pairs of pipes emerged from the rim and curved up into that black, bending like metal fingers to cradle an object about the size of a man's head. Or, no, they weren't quite touching it; it was as if the object were balanced perfectly between them, hovering against the empty dome.

"Can you make out what it is?" Ashe asked, squinting, and she shook her head.

"It's hard to see…" Literally so, she realized: the edges wavered and blurred every time she tried to focus on them, and the shape she saw when she looked at it sidelong was not the same as the one she saw when she looked at it directly. She looked at the floor between the pillars, and saw a sunken pool filled with a liquid that was at once dark and entirely reflective, a black mirror of the dome. Except that where the reflection of the object should have been, an irregularly-faceted crystal broke the surface, threads of color shimmering in its depth. The reflection of the pipes seemed to cradle it as well, as though the two objects were twins held at a distance.

"Time crystal," Dai said. "That—those are time crystals. The one Anketil made."

"You were right the first time," Cassilde said. As she looked more closely, she could see the air wavering faintly beneath the dome, as though rising from a hot surface. Her Gift could feel it, too, her hands closing protectively before she'd realized what she'd done. Anketil hadn't completed her crystal, hadn't shoved it into the adjacent possible to trap the AI that way; instead, she'd frozen it on the verge of that action, distorting both space/time and the adjacent possible so that the AI could not cross that barrier. "It's one crystal, poised—it's caught and balanced before it can collapse into a single point."

Dai nodded slowly. "That's not possible—well, in theory, maybe, but the power involved—"

"Is enormous," Ashe said. "What do you want to bet that the whole purpose of this palace was to draw enough power to pull that off? Catch and hold the time crystal just at that moment when it's between time and space, and that's what's locked the AI out for the last two thousand years."

"If you pull directly from the planet's core?" Dai murmured, then shook his head.

"However Anketil did it, it's done," Cassilde said. "And if we mess with it—"

"We set the AI loose, and we might just blow up the planet into the bargain," Dai said. He looked faintly sick at the thought.

"We have to stop John," Ashe said. "It's that simple."

"Only that's not simple," Cassilde said. "It's not simple at all."

"It is," Ashe said. He reached out and she let him take her hands, their Gifts fizzing as they touched. "You can leave it to me if you want."

For a moment she was tempted, but the thought of Ashe alone against Vertrage and his people made her shake her head. "Don't be stupid. It's going to take all of us, and you know it."

He breathed a laugh. "It would make it easier, yes."

"All right, then." Cassilde drew a deep breath, swallowing her own fear. "Let's get back to the miner, see what the drones found, and figure out what to do."

𐌀 𐌔 𐌙 𐌐

All of the drones had returned by the time they reached the miner, and Ashe plugged them one by one into the miner's databanks and began downloading data to his mapping program. Cassilde and Dai went through the miner, pulling out everything that could possibly be used as a weapon. There was more than she had expected, Cassilde thought, eying the pile covering the commons table, but on the whole she wished they were more effective. Or at least conventional: the cutters and the packets of explosives for drilling test holes could certainly be used in a pinch, but they would never be as effective as the real thing.

Dai had also emptied the toolkits of every bolt and fastener and bit of small scrap metal, and as she watched, he began packing them into various small containers. He unwrapped one of the explosives, and began cutting it into cubes, weighing them each carefully as he added them to the improvised bombs. She found the packet of fuses, but didn't open it, studying the directions carefully instead. These were supposed to be the most reliable brand you could buy, with a built-in timer; she thought she could see a way to rig them to a drone and set them off manually when Vertrage's people came in sight. Assuming that didn't bring down the tunnel on top of them, she thought, but she had confidence in the Ancestors' work. She thought the Dedalor palace would stand up to a good deal more than the explosives they had on hand.

Ashe joined them with his completed map, but his bleak expression quashed any hope of finding an alternative. "Every one of the corridors is ultimately a blind alley. And none of them seem to connect to each other, either. It looks to me as though the whole point is to waste people's time. Unless you have a Gift, in which case the mirror-floored room steers you straight in."

"But why?" Dai demanded. "If Anketil wanted to keep the AI locked out of our universe permanently, why let anyone in?"

"She had to assume that things might change in ways she couldn't predict," Cassilde said. "Even the Ancestors couldn't predict the future. So she left a door for people who were like her." She allowed herself a sigh, looking at the weapons strewn across the table and stacked on the counters. "I wish we were more like them."

Dai patted her shoulder. "Me, too."

The Ancestors would have had a way to deal with Vertrage, she thought, him and all his kind. It might not have been non-lethal, the Ancestors hadn't been noted pacifists, but it would have been effective. All she could imagine was throwing everything they'd made at him, and seeing him break through anyway. The AI wouldn't care, they'd said they'd work with whoever won this fight, and she didn't believe that Vertrage could control the AI. Maybe for a few days, maybe even a few years, but the AI would break free in the end.

"Ashe. If Vertrage wins—"

"We won't let him," Ashe said.

"If," she said firmly, and waited until he nodded. "What do you think the AI will do?"

"I don't know. I can't know, they're not—they don't think like us. They could do anything."

"They'll finish the War," Dai said quietly. "They'll have no reason not to."

"They don't all want that," Ashe said. "You heard them."

"They will by the time Vertrage is through with them," Dai said.

There was no arguing with that. They filled their pockets with spare charges for their blasters, and loaded the rest of the makeshift weapons onto the gravity sled along with the rest of the drones. Dai dispatched one to monitor the main entrance—still open, the drone reported, under a surprisingly quiet sky—and sent a second to wait just outside the mirror-floor room.

"That's practically telling him which door to pick," Ashe said, and Dai shrugged.

"If it works like you said, Ashe, his Gift's going to tell him which way to go. And if it doesn't, he's as likely to think it's a double bluff."

"He'll figure it out eventually," Cassilde said, silencing them both.

They rigged the rest of the drones with bombs and left them clustered at points where the curve of the corridor might, optimistically, conceal them for a crucial moment, then settled themselves at the final bend, the curtain of light vivid behind them. It might blind Vertrage and his people for a few seconds, Cassilde thought, and give them a chance to pick them off. If they were good enough shots to make that chance count for something. Ashe might be, but she hadn't bothered to practice since the War.

There was nothing to do but wait. After a while, she seated herself against the wall, and Dai joined her, leaning cautiously against her shoulder. She reached for him, and he put an arm around her, the same silent comfort he'd offered in the days when it was only the Lightman's that threatened her. Ashe looked down at them, his expression unreadable, and she beckoned for him to join them. For a moment, she thought he would refuse, but then she saw him sigh and switch his blaster to 'safe' before settling on her other side. She put her arm around him in turn, drawing him against her, glad of their warmth against the cold light.

"This isn't how I expected it to end," she said, when she could stand the silence no longer. "The whole point was not to have an ending."

Ashe tipped his head back against the wall. "If I'd known about the Lightman's, I'd have looked for you sooner."

In other circumstances, Cassilde thought, she might have questioned that, but for the moment she was glad to believe it.

"You came when we needed you," Dai said.

"We wanted you to stay," Cassilde said. "I know you had to go, but—we did want you."

Ashe nodded, and she saw the mote stir against his collarbone. As she watched, it crept up the cords of his neck, tiny feelers brushing across his skin. He was weeping, she realized, tears welling silently to leave a track down his cheek, and the mote followed that trail, GREEN flickering beneath its carapace as it settled back on his cheek. She tightened her hold, resting her head on his shoulder, and Dai's hand closed tightly on her arm.

"Everything ends," he said quietly.

That was the oldest tenet of the Saints, and the one she had always hated most. "Not always," she said. "Not like this, and not now. I won't let it. It's not—" She stopped there, because *it's not fair* was a child's cry. The universe wasn't fair; it didn't have to be fair. She just had to deal with it somehow. She flexed her fingers, feeling the Gift running beneath her skin. Maybe its help would be enough to deal not just with Vertrage, but with the trapped AI. She hadn't asked to face this, was probably entirely the wrong person to have to do it, to somehow hold off the next Dark, but she was the one who was here.

"We're with you," Ashe said, and she felt Dai nod.

"Yes."

After another while, they ate, and Cassilde managed to drowse, Dai's shoulder a comfortable pillow. She was awakened by a ping from the gravity sled, and sat up as Dai slid out from under her. Ashe had his scroll out, was consulting the screen.

"They're at the main entrance. It's another miner, about the same size as ours. They've got shields up, the drone can't get through, so I don't know how many of them there are."

"Ping them," Dai said.

"They'll spot the drone if I do."

"Do it," Cassilde said, and Ashe shrugged.

"Pinging."

There was a moment of silence, and then Ashe jumped. "They blew it up."

"Did you get the data?" Cassilde asked.

"Five definite, possibly two more."

"So we count on seven," Dai said. "That's not too bad."

It wasn't good, either, but none of them wanted to say that out loud. Ashe shrugged one shoulder. "We might get lucky."

They waited again, until at last the box on the gravity sled chimed again. Ashe unrolled his scroll and gave a nod of satisfaction.

"They're in the mirror-floor room. I can just pick them up on visual, they're just sitting there right now."

Cassilde leaned over his shoulder, watching as the miner crept further into the room, and further into the drone's field of view. It stopped in the center of the room, and a side hatch opened; a moment later, a man slid down a ladder to the floor. Cassilde squinted at the transmission, and identified him as Vertrage. Under his feet, the floor erupted in sparks, and he jumped back, then realized what was happening, and began to move in circles, obviously testing its response. After a few tries, he climbed back into the miner, and it trundled forward again, heading for the drone.

"Well, that guess was right," Ashe said, under his breath. "Dai! Can we get a pickup from our miner?"

"Unless Vertrage blasts it," Dai answered, but fiddled with something on the gravity sled, and a new image appeared in the scroll, showing the wider section of corridor where they'd left the miner. They watched together as Vertrage's miner entered the chamber, slowed, and stopped. Vertrage and two others climbed out to investigate the tunnel, while a third tried to pry open the other miner's hatch. After several attempts, he produced a beam cutter, but Vertrage called him off. They backed the miner against the wall, and started down the corridor on foot.

"So far, so good," Ashe said. "Ready with the remotes?"

"Ready," Dai answered, bending over the screen of the gravity sled.

Cassilde could see the same data repeated on Ashe's scroll, the dark corridor giving way to the distant glow of the hand-lights carried by Vertrage's people. They came slowly around the curve, lights flashing back and forth, and Ashe said softly, "Wait. Let them get closer. Wait…"

"They'll see it," Dai said, but he kept his finger off the button. They were all in view now, seven shapes jostling each other, and then one of the beams of light struck the drone, briefly blinding the camera.

"Now!" Cassilde said, and Dai pressed the trigger. There was a distant rumble, but though Cassilde strained to hear more, there was nothing else.

"That was our best shot," Ashe said. "They'll be looking for drones now."

"We must have gotten some of them," Dai answered, working the sled's controls. "Yeah. OK, I'm only picking up four of them moving now."

"That's good," Cassilde said. Nearly half of them down; they

were still outnumbered, but there were two more groups of drones to
go—though of course Ashe was right, Vertrage would be expecting
them now.

Sure enough, Vertrage's party spotted the next drone as soon as
they came around the next bend, and someone fired a blaster at it.
Dai hit the trigger at the same moment—this time, the explosion was
louder—but when the sensors cleared, there were still four people
approaching. The same thing happened with the next drone, though
this time Cassilde thought she heard a faint yelp, as though someone
had been hit with the fragments.

"That's the last of them," Dai said. He shoved the gravity sled
sideways, so that it was half blocking the corridor, and retreated
toward the end of the corridor. Cassilde drew her blaster, checked the
charge and the safety, and braced herself against the wall. She could
feel Ashe shaking, in the same moment felt him take a deep breath
and stiffen his shoulders, his blaster held in both hands pointing at the
floor. Dai put himself in front of them, one shoulder against the wall,
a faint smile curving his lips as he gave them a last glance.

"Ready—"

Before he could finish the sentence, something flew through the
air. It bounced off the wall and rolled toward them, a gold casing
banded in black.

"Grenade," Ashe said, as though he couldn't believe it.

It would be a short fuse, Cassilde thought, Vertrage wasn't stupid.
She reached one-handed for the toy she had picked up on Callambhal,
her fingers slotting into its grooves as though it had been made for her.
She pointed it at the grenade, summoning every bit of GOLD—in the
air, in the walls, in the dust of the surface, within their own bodies—to
smother the thing, to wrap it in a shield that even explosives could not
damage. It was fighting, she could feel it swelling, shrieking, shaking,
but the GOLD poured in, GOLD and now BLUE and a touch of
RED, and it slid to a stop, the beginnings of the explosion frozen
within the shell she had made.

"Throw it back at them," Ashe said, and she waved the toy, wafting the trapped force up from the floor. It hung there, fire roiling white and red behind the barrier, then dropped to the floor again, jolting her hold so that she had to freeze and focus again before she could move. She waved the toy, not trying to lift it this time, just willing it to move, pushing it away from her with every bit of strength she had to spare. It moved, reluctantly, the shell swelling; she stopped to tighten it, and the movement slowed.

Dai waved at it, too, spreading his fingers to show sparks leaping in the gaps between them. The sphere moved again, but still so slowly. Dai reached for her blindly, offering help, and Ashe caught him, then dropped his blaster and reached across to grab her free hand, fingers wrapping around hers on the butt of her blaster. She felt new strength wash through her, their Gifts joining as they touched. She waved the toy again, and this time the sphere picked up speed, rolling now across the floor and then bouncing up and off the wall, retracing its path. Dai grabbed her shoulder, and she flung the sphere back at Vertrage, at where she imagined him to be, and let go of the shield.

The explosion rocked her back on her heels, and sent a cloud of acrid smoke billowing down the corridor, to be absorbed by the wall of light. She shook her head, trying to clear the ringing in her ears, and Dai moved forward at a crouch, stopping at the end of the corridor to peer cautiously around the corner. He jerked back as a blaster fired, the bolt crashing against the opposite wall, and Ashe moved to join him, his own blaster ready.

"How many?"

Dai held up one finger. It would be Vertrage, of course, the only one of them with a Gift, Cassilde thought, and gagged as she caught the smell of blood and burned flesh. She flattened herself against the wall beside them as Vertrage fired again, and in answer Ashe stepped forward long enough to return the shots. A bolt struck him in the shoulder, and he fell back against the wall, Dai firing in turn to cover him, but she could see the burn healing as she watched.

"Back," Dai said, and she slid her shoulders along the wall, edging toward the curtain of light. Ashe took two more shots, and followed; Vertrage fired again, and this time it was Dai who flinched and grunted.

"This is stalemate," Ashe said, between his teeth, but Cassilde caught his sleeve.

"No. Back inside—" Vertrage would have to come through the light barrier, and that would surely be enough to disorient him, would give them a chance to take him... Unless he had more explosives, but surely he wouldn't risk them again, not when she'd handled the grenade so neatly.

"Yes," Ashe said, and pulled Dai with them, the three of the scrambling down the last stretch of corridor, Vertrage's shots close on their heels.

The light seemed less of a barrier this time, parting like water to let them through. Cassilde dodged left, flattening herself against the wall beside the entrance, and saw Dai and Ashe do the same on the other side.

"Clever," Ashe said.

"He'll have to come through some time," she answered.

"Unless," Dai began, then shook his head. "What do you think they're going to do?" He jerked his head at the central dome.

Cassilde shrugged, both hands on her blaster now to steady her shots. There was no sound from the AI, no sense of their presence. Apparently they were serious when they'd said they'd deal with the survivors, she thought, and bit her lip to suppress a hysterical snicker.

"We've got one chance," Ashe said. Cassilde nodded, bracing herself, and something shivered in the curtain of light. She lifted her blaster, and a metal sphere splashed through the barrier, trailing smoke. She reached for the toy, for the elements, to surround and smother it, but the first wave of the smoke hit her, clogging her lungs and drawing tears from her eyes. She bent double, choking and coughing, and through tearing eyes saw Vertrage step through the barrier. Ashe fired, knocking him sideways, but he whirled to return the shot and both Ashe and Dai dodged away from him. They were all choking on the smoke now, stumbling and struggling to control their weapons. Cassilde went to one knee, hoping for cleaner air, but the smoke was just as bad at floor level. She fired anyway, aiming for Vertrage's legs, but missed completely.

Vertrage kept firing, barely seeming to aim, but Dai cried out, stumbling to one knee, and turned the fall into a clumsy roll that just evaded Vertrage's next shot.

"You're too late," Ashe called, from beside the platform. "It's over, John, you're dead."

Vertrage ignored him, firing a third time at Dai, who kept rolling, arms over his head. Cassilde dragged herself to her feet and aimed two-handed, shooting through the clouds of smoke to catch Vertrage in the back. He stumbled forward, but righted himself, spinning to fire in her direction so that she had to dodge sideways, choking. The sphere was no longer spewing smoke, and the coils were rapidly thinning, but the air still burned with every breath.

And then she saw it, just after the instant in which she could have stopped him. Vertrage aimed not at her, not at the others, but at the dome, at the tensed space beneath the dome. The bolt passed between the columns and disappeared, taking the crack of its passage with it. The dome trembled, and the movement shook the ground beneath her feet.

"No," Ashe said, and fired again, shot after shot to drive Vertrage back against the far wall, to override his Gift. Dai dragged himself to one knee and joined him.

The shimmering beneath the dome increased, as though the air were being moved by a rising wind, and the pipes that supported the upper crystal wavered. If the crystal collapsed, Cassilde knew, it would destroy whatever Anketil had built to keep the AI confined in the adjacent possible, and that would upend everything she, they, had tried to do. She grabbed the Callambhal toy and deliberately turned

her back on Vertrage, turning all her concentration on the wavering
crystal. She could feel shapes against her fingers, as though the toy was
trying to tell her something, and she pointed it at the dome, hoping
it knew more than she did. She felt it vibrate, coming into resonance
with the crystal, and she thought for a moment that the shimmering
slowed.

Then it wavered again, the pipes rippling, and she saw a droplet of
the dark liquid rise into the column of moving air. Another followed
it, and a third, this one the size of her own hand, and she shifted
her grip on the toy, feeling for the help it was trying to give. Around
her, the air was suddenly full of sparks, the same elemental dust that
had surrounded her on Callambhal. She reached for it, shaping it,
turning it toward the linked crystal. *Bring it back the way it was,* she
commanded, though she had no idea what that shape had been. But
the toy did, she realized, the toy had felt it; it knew the note the crystal
sang, the stable beat at its heart. She let the elements pour through
her, called by the Gift, let the toy shape and send them. Another drop
lifted from the surface, rising up on a long stalk, and then, even more
slowly, the stalk pulled it back, dragging it into the pool's depths.

The elemental cloud was thinning, and the crystal was nowhere
near stable. She reached out again, shrieking into the void, but the
response was slower and less complete. She needed more elements—
she was beginning to see, she could see just where they were needed,
and just how to set them into place, how they would combine to form
a substance half out of time that resonated with the crystal, but she
didn't have nearly enough of any of the elements. She could feel her
Gift shifting, willing to unravel itself if she chose, and she started to
let it, feeling the change deep in her marrow.

No! Ashe's voice came from very far away, not quite out of key,
but not quite in line either. *Take ours.*

That would work, she could take from them and from herself—
but there was one other source, one that did her and hers no harm at
all. She turned her head with an effort that seemed to make her bones

grind against each other, to see that the others had pinned Vertrage against the wall beside the curtain of light. She reached for it, ripping it out of its place in a shower of elemental particles, fed them to the crystal. Again she felt it slow and stabilize and falter, and this time she reached for Vertrage's Gift, reaching past skin and muscle and bone into the space beyond the marrow where her own Gift resided. She could feel his there, beating in time with his frantic heart, could feel it healing him even as she touched it, and for a heartbeat her resolve faltered. But she had promised this—promised the AI, promised Ashe and Dai, promised when she swore citizenship thirty years ago to serve, to aid, to do the best she could for her people as well as herself. She closed her fingers, Vertrage's Gift flailing wildly, and ripped it from his body.

It was strong, even after healing him, strong and loyal; it fought to return, fought to save him, but she controlled her automatic sympathy and broke it between her fingers, shredding it into the elements from which it had been made. She fed it to the crystal, a steady stream to rebuild the damaged parts, to smooth out the strange harmonics that Vertrage's shot had produced. It was almost done, almost there, the last pieces sliding into place as smoothly as if she had the schematics in front of her. The crystal throbbed once, a single bell-like note that reverberated through every cell of her body, and then everything was still. The paired crystal hung in its place, the air shimmering lightly beneath the dome, safe and whole again.

She made herself turn then, bracing to see Vertrage dismembered, but instead he lay huddled at the base of the wall, Dai on one knee and wincing as his Gift healed the last of a blaster bolt to the thigh. The smoke had faded, the air almost breathable again.

"All right?" she asked, her voice a painful croak, and Dai nodded.

"You?" That was Ashe, straightening cautiously.

"All right." And she was, she thought, though the feeling of Vertrage's Gift flailing against her fingers would haunt her dreams.

"And them?" Dai got to his feet, working his knee carefully.

"Nothing's changed," Cassilde said.

You could have released us.

That was one of the other voices, not Gold Shining Bone, and from somewhere she dredged a bark of laughter. "Killing ourselves to free you wasn't any part of the discussion."

That's so. That was Gold Shining Bone, she thought, and she thought it, too, was perversely amused at the result.

So. We have nothing, a third voice said.

"You have what we agreed," Cassilde said. "A chance to free yourselves without war. Without another Dark."

Perhaps we want the Dark, a bitter voice snapped, and Gold Shining Bone spoke over it.

Keep your word, then. Perhaps we will answer when they come.

Absence rolled over them, the AI suddenly gone, and Cassilde stiffened her knees.

"Is that it?" Ashe demanded. "Is that all we're going to get?"

The AI didn't answer, and Dai managed a laugh. "I'm fine with it, Ashe. I really don't need them loose."

For a moment, Ashe's face was a mask of frustration. "We could have learned so much—"

Cassilde moved toward him, her legs stiff, and what had begun as a caress became a grab for support. Ashe caught her, and then Dai was there as well, bracing her from the other side.

"We've learned a lot already," she said. "How much—we'll know once we've had a chance to look over everything we've done. But this is too big for us. We can't keep it secret, and we can't keep it safe. We have to give it to someone who can."

"I'm not sure the government is exactly the answer," Dai said. "But, yeah, it's better than trying to do it ourselves."

"We make sure everyone knows—the University as well as the government, all the salvage associations, the hunt," Ashe said. "The more people watching, the less chance anyone can take it over."

"We hope," Cassilde said, and leaned against him.

"It's the best we've got," Dai said, and she nodded. It was the best they could do, and better than she had thought likely when they started.

"Any chance I could persuade you not to mention the Gifts?" Ashe said, with a wry smile, and Cassilde couldn't help laughing.

"We can try. But right now, we need to get moving. We need to make our claim before anyone else spots it."

And that was the best they could do, she thought, as they gathered their gear for the long walk back to the miner. Make their claim, share it widely, and be watchful. They would have time enough, after all.

ACKNOWLEDGMENTS

I'd like to thank Don Sakers for brainstorming the original idea far, far into the night, and Athena Andreadis for her remarkable editing of both the original short story and the novel-length version. I have never worked harder or more willingly than I've done for Athena: she understood the story I was trying to tell, and made sure I never lost sight of it no matter how far I wandered. *Finders* wouldn't be half the book it is without their input.

ABOUT THE AUTHOR

Melissa Scott was born and raised in Little Rock, Arkansas, and studied history at Harvard College. She earned her PhD from Brandeis University in the comparative history program with a dissertation titled "The Victory of the Ancients: Tactics, Technology, and the Use of Classical Precedent." She also sold her first novel, *The Game Beyond,* and quickly became a part-time graduate student and an—almost—full-time writer.

Over the next thirty years, she published more than thirty original novels and a handful of short stories, most with queer themes and characters, as well as authorized tie-in novels for Star Trek: DS9, Star Trek: Voyager, Stargate SG-1, Stargate Atlantis, and Star Wars Rebels.

She won the John W. Campbell Award for Best New Writer in 1986, and won Lambda Literary Awards for *Trouble and Her Friends, Shadow Man, Point of Dreams,* (with long-time partner and collaborator, the late Lisa A. Barnett), and *Death By Silver,* written with Amy Griswold. She has also been shortlisted for the Tiptree Award. She won Spectrum Awards for *Death By Silver, Fairs' Point, Shadow Man* and for the short story "The Rocky Side of the Sky." Her most recent short stories "Finders" (*The Other Half of the* Sky) and "Firstborn, Lastborn" (*To Shape the* Dark) were both selected for Gardner Dozois's *Years Best SF* anthologies.

Her most recent novel, *Point of Sighs,* the fifth novel in the acclaimed Points series, was released in May, 2018, and *Finders,* based on the short story, will be out at the end of the year.

CPSIA information can be obtained
at www.ICGtesting.com
Printed in the USA
LVHW091728090119
603304LV00003B/483/P